DEATH AT
WINDWARD HILL

—

MURDER IN THE
FRENCH ROOM

DEATH AT WINDWARD HILL

—

MURDER IN THE FRENCH ROOM

Helen Joan Hultman

COACHWHIP PUBLICATIONS

Greenville, Ohio

Death at Windward Hill / Murder in the French Room,
by Helen Joan Hultman
© 2021 Coachwhip Publications

Cover elements: Hawthorne Hill mansion, Oakwood, Ohio, from the Carol M. Highsmith Archive, Library of Congress, Prints and Photographs Division; Higbee Department Store, Crystal Room, Cleveland, Ohio, from the Gottscho-Schleisner Collection, Library of Congress, Prints and Photographs Division

Death at Windward Hill first published 1931
Murder in the French Room first published 1931
Helen Joan Hultman, 1891-1985
CoachwhipBooks.com

ISBN 1-61646-511-7
ISBN-13 978-1-61646-511-5

DEATH AT
WINDWARD HILL

1

DEATH COMES

The night that Miss Eugenia Marrender died was cold and stormy. Windward Hill, the house wherein she lay, caught the full fury of the weather. The old brick house stood starkly upon its hilltop, half hidden by a row of ragged sycamores and a few pines which emphasized its bleakness rather than suggested a sheltering windbreak.

The soughing of the wind through the pines and the monotonous creaking of a loose shutter had got upon the nerves of Doris Randall, R.N., until she could no longer sleep as soundly as she ought to. She was on a hard case, a case which could only grow worse as time went on. Doris wondered why she had let herself in for anything as disagreeable and uninteresting as looking after Miss Eugenia Marrender. That is, she pretended to wonder about the matter at those times when she forced herself not to think about Dr. Perry Stuart. Most of the time she frankly admitted to herself that she had come to Windward Hill just because Dr. Stuart had asked her to . . . to nurse a crabbed old woman, who would undoubtedly die of an incurable disease within the next six months.

Shortly after ten Doris had settled her patient for the night, and had gone across the hall to the room which Miss Marrender had directed her to occupy when she first came on the case. Doris knew that this arrangement could not last much longer. She dreaded the time when she must sleep on a cot in her patient's room. She must ask Dr. Stuart about a night nurse. The Marrenders were not the people to make an item of added expense.

Doris shivered as she undressed and crawled into bed. Windward Hill . . . cold, creepy place on a night like this. She could hear Cubbage disturbing the furnace, but Doris knew that meant a diminution of heat. Cubbage and his cautious spoonful of coal. . . . The next time Miss Marrender's nephew came home she'd try complaining to him. Much good it would probably do, though. Gene Tracy was queer. . . .

Doris Randall so labelled all men who failed to make the proper response to her dimples and long-lashed brown eyes. All men except Perry Stuart. . . . As long as Dr. Stuart considered her his favorite nurse the daily round brought her something worth working for. She snuggled deeper in the blankets. That devilish wind. . . . She drifted off to sleep.

Perhaps two hours later Doris roused a bit and lay tense for a minute or two. It wasn't the wind, though it still howled persistently. Yet she knew she had heard something besides the single stroke of the clock in the lower hall—something like the closing of a door somewhere down within the old house. Probably it was that shuffling Cubbage. He was always prowling around, day and night. Yet Dr. Stuart himself had said something to her about the servant's being the only one who appeared genuinely concerned about Miss Marrender's failing health. The nieces and nephews who occasionally called or telephoned a punctilious inquiry would be very fond indeed of dear Aunt Eugenia about the time her estate was settled. Doris's thoughts drifted cynically. Even Gene, who lived at Windward Hill, acted as if he despised his aunt. Much Miss Marrender seemed to care, though. She rarely mentioned her relatives and when she did there would be a hard smile on her thin, blood-less lips and an inscrutable expression in her cold eyes.

Doris pulled her attention back to the noise that had wakened her. At any rate, she had not heard it again. She stirred reluctantly, slipped into bathrobe and slippers, and crossed the hall to her patient's open door. She was supposed to do this several times during the course of every night. She did it every time she woke up. Most nights she was not particularly restless. It was the wind in the pines tonight, Doris assured herself . . . not the biting memory of the gorgeous woman she had seen with Dr. Stuart that afternoon while she was doing her errands in town.

All was quiet in the square, high-ceilinged room where the mistress of Windward Hill was spending the last days of her life. The little light on the bedside table burned steadily. By its dim light Doris could see plainly enough from the doorway that everything was as it should be. Dr. Stuart had said not to rouse Miss Marrender for medicine during the night hours if she was resting quietly. In spite of the wind and the banging shutter she was certainly having a good sleep. . . . That noise must have been Cubbage. If he had been down at the furnace, she'd forgive him his everlasting pussy-footing around. Ugh-h! How cold it was in this drafty upper hall. The wind was stronger than ever.

Doris Randall crept shivering back to her blankets. She buried her head deep in the pillows and allowed herself to think long delicious thoughts about Perry Stuart. Once more she fell into heavy sleep.

It was a little after four o'clock when the little nurse next awoke. As far as she could tell, nothing in particular had aroused her. The howling wind had fallen. A cold, dark silence gripped the house on Windward Hill. Once more she dragged herself from the warmth of her bed across the icy hall to Miss Marrender's room. Again she stood at the door and looked at the still figure under the mound of bed clothing.

After an irresolute moment Doris approached the bed. She bent and looked sharply at the thin face sunk in the pillow and touched the inert eyelids. With stiff fingers she groped for the pulse in the shriveled neck. She had not been mistaken in her first impression. Miss Eugenia Marrender was dead.

"She died in her sleep. Lucky, at that. . . ." Doris pulled her professional self together. She might be Dr. Stuart's favorite nurse, but experience had not yet calloused her. So, stifling a desire to run from the room, she made methodical note of the time according to her watch and then felt for the electric switch by the door. Hard light flooded the room from a pendant center fixture, an incongruous note in the otherwise perfect 1880 furnishings of the chamber.

Not until the brilliant light illumined every corner of the room did the nurse see anything significant about the little table upon which the medicines were arrayed. There were the carafe and glass, both quite as she remembered leaving them at ten o'clock. There was the bottle containing the special prescription that was administered before the sick woman's meals. That, too, was just as she had left it at six the evening before. It was the bottle of white pills that looked different.

Doris knew the technical name of the drug that the tablets contained; she knew, too, why one or at most two of them were all she dared give a patient, no matter how bad the pain was. . . . Miss Marrender had been having the pills regularly. Only yesterday afternoon during her two hours off Doris had gone into town to renew the prescription in accordance with Dr. Stuart's instructions. It was while she was waiting that she had seen the doctor with a woman, a blonde too beautiful to add much confidence to long-lashed brown eyes.

With a jerk Doris brought her attention back to the immediate problem. After she had returned from the druggist's and replenished the bottle, it was more than half full. But now. . . . With curious distaste she picked it up. The bottom of the small phial was barely covered by the powerful little globules. Three, four, five, six . . . and last night there had been surely three times that number.

Once again Doris Randall looked searchingly at the peaceful dead face of Eugenia Marrender. "I don't blame her . . . the game old sport!" she half whispered to herself.

For a moment longer she stood staring at the rigid mound, the bottle clutched in her hand, A momentous decision faced her. What difference would it make? Such a little thing for her to do for Perry Stuart. He'd never know that she had done it, though. It would have to be her own secret happiness. Something to remember. . . . An instant of clairvoyant insight told Doris Randall that Perry Stuart's life had no place for her adoring love.

Her decision was made. She'd say nothing about the pills. No one needed to know how strangely their number had lessened. She must wake Cubbage, and then she must report the death of the patient to the doctor. He would not be surprised to hear what had happened. He had told her about the patient's heart condition when she came on the case. That was the reason that the white pills need not be mentioned. There would be no question of suicide . . . no need for coroners. A doctor whose reputation was on the up-grade as was Perry Stuart's avoided that kind of publicity whenever he could.

Gathering the folds of her blanket robe tightly about her slender figure, Doris sped down the dark, cold hall. Cubbage's room was downstairs at the end of the back hall, across from the kitchen and pantries. Stabbing lights on ahead of her, she made her way down the steep front flight. As she turned toward the back hall she saw almost immediately that Cubbage's door was open. She hesitated a moment, and then stepped across his threshold as far as was necessary to reach the swung-back door panel. Her rat-tat-tat was brisk. There was no answer. Once more she beat her tattoo. No sound answered from within, but a stealthy shuffle behind her brought her heart into her mouth.

With a strangled scream she whirled about. There stood Cubbage, a shapeless blur against the light.

"What is it, Miss Randall?" His voice, as always, sounded incongruous to Doris's ears. There was a faint echo of culture about it that was not in keeping with the menial position the man filled.

"It's Miss Marrender . . . she's dead. I have just discovered it and I wanted you to know at once. When I looked in at about one everything was all right. She was sleeping quietly. Just now when I went in I found—that she was gone."

"Are you sure that she was—all right at one o'clock, nurse?"

There was something about the accent of the words that sent a new chill down Doris's spine. Probably that was the reason she lied, promptly and convincingly.

"Quite sure, Cubbage. I was right over her, you see. Her respiration was better than it had been all week." Doris wondered afterwards how she could have been so glib.

"Ah-h. . . ." It was more like an expelled breath than a spoken syllable. "Would you like some coffee, Miss Randall?"

"Please! I must put in a call for Dr. Stuart. Maybe you'd better notify the relatives."

"I doubt if you can reach the doctor at—at this hour, though of course I can understand why you want to try. . . ."

Doris Randall gripped herself hard to keep from hysterics. There was something vaguely menacing about Cubbage. If only he would not talk in that curiously precise way. ". . . Mr. Tracy is expected today, quite fortunately. I should prefer to wait for his orders."

Doris fled to the front hall to the telephone. There was no need for her to waste time searching the directory for a number. She knew the whole series that could bring to her the sound of Perry Stuart's voice—his offices, the hospital, his club, his apartment. At this early hour it was only logical to begin with his apartment. She could hear a bell give a distant, vigorous peal. A sleepy voice answered. It belonged to Scotty, a derelict veteran that the doctor had salvaged from a rehabilitation hospital. Scotty's burr informed her that Dr. Stuart had been out all night on an emergency call and had just tumbled into bed within the hour. "I'll no be calling him," he declared.

"You don't have to, silly. Just tell him at your very first opportunity that Miss Marrender died during the night, and that the nurse is waiting for further instructions."

Shaking with cold Doris turned toward the stairs. She'd rather go back to that gaunt, old-fashioned room with its silent occupant than stay down here within sound of Cubbage's muted voice. As she reached the head of the steep flight she plunged her stiff hands into the pockets of her bathrobe. Her fingers closed upon the smooth coldness of the bottle of powerful medicine which she had dropped into one of the pockets when she left in search of Cubbage. At this reminder of the narcotic the pretty arch of her eyebrows met in a troubled frown.

"I might as well," she concluded. "It's as good a way as any. . . ." With that she slipped into a bathroom and emptied the remaining tablets into the drain of the toilet. With a decisive hand she flushed the deadly pellets into nothingness. Then she reentered the dead woman's room and replaced the empty bottle beside its companion on the bedside table. "There's no reason to hide it," she argued with the insistent question that welled within her.

She must go to her room and dress. As she turned away from the little table she saw what was lying just under the edge of Miss Marrender's bed. Strange that she had not noticed it before. . . . She stooped and picked it up. What she held in her hand was a fountain pen, a stalwart, masculine pen, a pen that she had seen racing across prescription pads many times—Perry Stuart's pen. The gold band about its dull green cap was initialed, but it did not take the inscribed P. S. to assure Doris Randall of its owner. She would have known that pen out of a thousand. Anything that was Dr. Stuart's spoke with tongues to her.

He must have dropped it when he made his last call on Miss Marrender. That had been yesterday morning. Already death had placed a singular remoteness upon preceding events. Yet how strange that she had not seen it before. . . . It must have been caught in a fold of the bed clothing. Of course that was it, she thought, and dropped the pen into the bathrobe pocket. Her hand lingered to caress it. She refused to let herself recall that she had arranged the bedding thoroughly when she settled her patient for the night. Surely she should have noticed the pen then. . . . Drains and plumbing were not the oubliettes for heavy, masculine fountain pens. After all, it was his pen—*his* pen. Having it to keep for her very own would add a little to that scant store of secret happy memories that she feared would be all she would ever have of Perry Stuart.

Rapidly the little nurse dressed for daytime appearance. Winter daylight was still more than two hours away, but the circumstances made her dishabille inappropriate. In uniform she felt equal to Cubbage. As she stepped about her room she was vaguely conscious of sounds of dim confusion from the rooms below. Just like the man to turn the house upside down in an orgy of cleaning.

The fragrance of his coffee called her down. The warmth of the kitchen was comforting. She was finishing her second generous cup when the telephone bell rang imperiously. Cubbage tiptoed away to answer it. It was several minutes before he returned. "It's for you, Miss Randall," he reported.

"That you, Doris?" It was the doctor's hearty voice. "Scotty found that I had come to long enough to give me your message. Heart, was it? I'm not surprised. . . . . She's escaped a lot of hideous suffering. I'll be out later on. I'm operating this morning. . . . But what I really called you about is this: could you hustle into town and make the 8:47 train? It's a case down at Paloma. I'd like mighty well to turn it over to you and now that you're free. . . . It won't be hard—the chap's convalescent. Who are you to turn snooty about Florida in February. . . . Good for you, little girl. I may get down myself for a couple of weeks next month. . . . Thanks a lot, Doris. You're a little peach. Taxi in to my office and Jeannette will give you all the dope. . . . Bye!"

Doris replaced the receiver, scarcely knowing what she had said. To go to Paloma on a case. . . . What a wonderful opportunity for her to forget the nightmare of the last few hours. But she mustn't think he meant anything by the way he talked. He always talked that way . . . to all the girls he liked . . . and he liked so many. No doubt there was the same intimate caressing quality in his voice when he talked to gorgeous ladies like the one she had seen him with yesterday. . . .

An outer door banged, recalling Doris from her impossible dream world. Heavy steps creaked into the kitchen. Mrs. Banney had arrived. This was one of her regular days and she always came early. Before Cubbage could have had a chance to tell her what had occurred at Windward Hill during the night, Doris could hear the woman's brisk comment.

"Well, it sure looks to me like you folks think it's the good old summer-time with your side windows standing wide open and the curtains blowing in and out. I had to laugh as I come round the house just now. Knowing you, Cubbage, I figured it couldn't be because the house had got so warm you had to cool it off, and knowing Windward Hill I couldn't hope for anything as exciting as somebody trying to break in and steal—"

There was a muted murmur from Cubbage and a sudden silence from Mrs. Banney, a silence from which the woman soon recovered. Doris scurried upwards to her own room. There was packing to do. Just like Cubbage to send Mrs. Banney into hysterics. . . . Listen to the poor creature. . . . Doris slapped open a suitcase. Thank goodness, she'd soon be on her way.

2
THE NURSE GOES

The nurse's thoughts raced on as she slid into street clothes and tossed her belongings into her bag. She must allow time to stop at the doctor's office before making the 8:47 train. Jeannette would help her out. She'd have to ask her to see about the uniforms that were at the laundry and the check that would be coming from the Marrenders.

Suitcase in hand she left her room. Unconsciously she tiptoed by the closed door behind which lay the stark body of Eugenia Marrender. She must call a taxi. . . . But just before she reached the bottom of the long dark stairs, she heard Cubbage at the telephone.

". . . the circumstances demand investigation, Inspector."

Those were the only words that Doris Randall heard, for the man who spoke them slipped the receiver into place the instant he realized that she could hear what he was saying.

She set her suitcase down, and the man gave the pretty nurse a long questioning look. "You are leaving? So soon?" The words were plainly intended to have the insinuating sound that Doris flamed under.

"I am only following Dr. Stuart's orders, Cubbage. He asked me to come into town at once. He has another urgent case for me." Why must she explain? she asked herself hotly. He was only the serving man. However, she added, "My charts and reports will of course be turned in to him."

Abruptly she seized the telephone and called the number of the taxicab company. That done, she again turned toward the stairs but stopped once more in spite of herself to address the stiff figure indistinct in the gloom of the hall. "If there is anything you'd like to have me do. . . . But I advise leaving Miss Marrender just as I found her till the doctor comes."

"By all means—just as you found her." Cubbage's reply echoed curiously. "I was just about to call the residence of Mr. William Marrender. I waited this long so as not to disturb him too early."

Doris sought the kitchen to wait until the taxi came. It was warm there and Mrs. Banney was better company than Cubbage. She found the room unoccupied. Mrs. Banney's spotted brown serge in which she made her daily trips from Canal Corner to Windward Hill was hanging on its usual hook, but her limp-brimmed hat and old plush coat were not there. "She must have gone back to the Corner to get extra help," she murmured half aloud. . . .

A raucous signal from the front announced the arrival of her cab. As she sped for the last time through the hall, it lay dim and silent. Cubbage was not in sight, but she heard vague sounds of occupancy behind a closed door to her left. Snatching a pair of gloves from the table under a gilt-framed mirror she was for an instant conscious of an odor reminiscent of cigarettes. It couldn't be Cubbage; he never smoked cigarettes. Besides, this was definitely a stale odor. . . . Then she pulled open the heavy front door and gestured impatiently to the driver of the taxi.

It was a relief to be leaving Windward Hill. Miss Marrender had been a difficult patient. For all her money the house was a gloomy, drafty horror. Gene Tracy, little as she had seen of him in the weeks that she had been at

Windward Hill, impressed her as a restless, unhappy man, and Cubbage—Cubbage was a nightmare. The mere thought of Florida was bracing. Very likely Dr. Stuart would be running down too, for golf or polo. . . . Rather awful to grow old and die, as Miss Marrender had, and no one in the family really sorry. They'd be thinking only of her money. That niece would, at any rate, the one who had stormed so, only yesterday morning. . . .

The taxi lurched into the highway that would soon bring her to the suite of offices occupied by Dr. Stuart. Mechanically Doris began to draw on her gloves and, as she did so, she came to alert attention. The soft tan suede glove into which she was thrusting her capable fingers was not hers. Her own gloves were in her bag—of course they were. She distinctly recalled looking at them up in her room and thinking, that after one more wearing, she must clean them.

These gloves that she had picked up from the old walnut table in the hall at Windward Hill were not hers. They were easily a size too small, for one thing. They were quite new, too, and faintly redolent of an exotic sachet. Doris opened her bag. There were her gloves, just where she had thrust them. The two pairs were the same sort of suede and nearly the same shade. A quick examination of the strange pair showed no distinguishing marks upon them other than the maker's stamp and size number.

A memory flashed distinctly to the surface. When she returned from town the afternoon before, she knew there had been nothing on the old table—she could still see the late sun falling across the bare polished wood as Cubbage opened the door to admit her. Whose gloves were they? There had been no other women in the house after that— except herself, and the gloves were too small for her, and Mrs. Banney, who never wore gloves of any sort, and old Miss Marrender, lying helpless in her bed.

Thoughtfully Doris folded the bits of soft leather and tucked them down into her bag. She drew out her own familiar pair just as the cab stopped before the building that housed Dr. Stuart's offices.

She found Jeannette just taking off her street clothes. "In one minute, Miss Randall. Yes, the doctor called me about you. That's why I'm down here so bright and early. I've got the notes on the case all ready for you and the doctor 'phoned that he'd meet you at the station to see about tickets and so on. It's a rush case, I'd say, but take it from me, old dear, it sounds gr-rand. A young man, not married, lots of money—all that at the swankest hotel in Paloma. . . . I'll say you're Dr. Stuart's pet nurse."

Fifteen minutes later Doris Randall found herself at the station, and there, just stepping out of his smart coupé, was Dr. Perry Stuart. He was tall and handsome; women patients thought his slightly supercilious manner attractive. As he swung toward Doris, he gave her the quick, individual smile that always made her blood race.

"That's the girl," he said, giving her arm a friendly squeeze. "Heaven fend me from the kind of female that has to have yards of explanations about everything that isn't exactly routine. This is rushing you dreadfully, I know, but I also know that I can always count on you."

She smiled up at him happily, forgetful of everything except that she was with him. "Never apologize for sending anyone to Florida in February. I'm chortling with joy."

"Not Florida, Doris—California. Did I say Florida? It's California, little sport. A gorgeous place close to San Diego. Your news about Miss Marrender must have twisted my tongue. Right-o, that's your train being called this minute. You'll get the Forty-niner out of Chicago tonight. I'll keep in touch with you by wire. It's not a hard case, but I had special orders to supply a good-looking nurse— and you're it with me, but you know that."

The lazy, beguiling voice dropped a note and for an instant Doris Randall thought she was going to be kissed. "Here, Red Cap—" The high moment was over.

Expertly he turned her over to the porter. "I must dash out to Windward Hill now and then back to the hospital. The old girl was damn lucky to have that heart condition, considering what was ahead of her."

A surge of travelers pushed Doris through the gates and separated her from Dr. Stuart. She stood in the vestibule of the Pullman, trying to catch a last glimpse of him, but he had disappeared.

3

MRS. BANNEY SCREAMS

No sooner had Doris Randall stepped into the taxi that had borne her away from Windward Hill than the door to the left at the foot of the stairs opened and Cubbage emerged. One gloved hand was closed about a small box. With the other, likewise gloved, he shot home a heavy bolt on the door through which he had just appeared. Tiptoeing softly down the hall he assured himself that Mrs. Banney was not about. Indeed he had himself suggested that under the circumstances it might be well for her to go after her daughter-in-law as extra help for the next few days. Returning from the kitchen he ascended the stairs and entered the room that had so lately been vacated by the pretty little nurse. He closed the door behind him. It was twenty minutes later when he reappeared.

Shortly after, when Mrs. Banney and Mabel, her comatose daughter-in-law, had creaked into the kitchen, their superior officer was in the silver closet, decorously considering the necessity of rubbing up an extra set of forks. The voice of authority issued orders about curtains in the long drawing-room, slip-covers for the damask chairs, extra boards in the dining table. . . . "It is rather difficult to say just how many will be here for luncheon, but we must be ready—the relatives, you know."

Mrs. Banney and Mabel yearned to talk it all over with someone, but there was nothing encouraging about Cubbage. However, the older woman could not restrain one question. "Did them burglars take anything?"

"As to that I am not in a position to say, Mrs. Banney. The police are sending out a man—I judged it my duty to notify them. In the light of Miss Marrender's death, let us hope that we are not plunged into any unnecessary publicity."

The two women nodded in timid respect. In spite of his diction he had made them feel that gossip about Windward Hill affairs would be ill-advised.

At that moment a bell pealed shrilly. "The police, I anticipate," murmured Cubbage and left the kitchen to answer the summons.

It was Tim Asher from Headquarters who was waiting for admittance. He had been sent, and he knew it, because the call concerned a Marrender. Otherwise one of the cubs could have handled a sneak thief case and Tim could have been spared a bleak trip.

The door swung open and a butler, who looked like a stage clergyman, permitted the deputy inspector to enter. Asher identified himself briskly and asked, "What's the trouble here?"

"The house appears to have been broken into, officer. I can tell you scarcely more than that because"—Cubbage paused and cleared his throat deprecatingly—"because my attention has been otherwise claimed. I must inform you before you proceed further that Miss Marrender, whose residence this is, died this morning about four o'clock. She had been lying mortally ill for some time."

"That so? Too bad. . . ." Asher's voice fell in appropriate regret. Then he snapped back officially, "Who are you?"

"Cubbage, sir. In charge of domestic arrangements. If there were a larger staff I should call myself butler."

Asher's eyes surveyed the man. A servant, and yet not quite the type. At least, he was not interviewing a relative. He let himself out a notch. "So the old lady's gone, is she? Let's see, she must be the old maid sister that had got kind of queer—only when you have a million you're called eccentric, huh? Her brothers are all dead, long ago, but there's a lot of the younger generation in town yet, if I'm not mistaken. They'll come in for a bunch of money, all right. You worked for her long?"

"Not so long that I can expect a legacy." The answer came through tightly clamped teeth. "I mentioned Miss Marrender's demise to indicate that the family will regret any unnecessary investigation of this apparent burglary."

"Sure, I get you, big boy . . . though why you rushed in a call about it I don't quite see," he added to himself.

"If you will follow me, officer, I will show you what aroused my suspicions this morning, and you can judge for yourself. I am expecting the attending physician and Mr. William Marrender at any moment. You, of course, will confer with the latter."

"Lord, what a line," muttered Asher and followed him to the door at the foot of the dark staircase.

"Since it is at hand I shall indicate this to you first. You will observe that this door is fastened by a bolt. You see it exactly as I closed it last night. It was Miss Marrender's wish that the door be so fastened every night. Her reason I do not know. The room is spoken of as the little gallery, though it appears much like the usual library. Since Miss Marrender's illness the room has not been used, scarcely opened in fact, but I always tested the bolt every night even if it had not been disturbed during the day."

It was a good thing for Asher's reputation that none of the cubs was there to witness his exhibition of inefficiency. He stood dumbly, listening to Cubbage.

"When the charwoman came in this morning, she mentioned the fact that the windows of a side room were standing wide open. I was naturally so perturbed over what had just occurred—Miss Marrender's passing, sir—that I paid little attention to Mrs. Banney's comment. It might have been an hour later—it was then quite light—that I had my first opportunity to investigate what the woman had reported. Observing that this door was still properly bolted, I did not disturb it. Instead I stepped outside and around the house to the windows in question."

"Holy gosh!" Asher murmured. "Of all the nuts—"

"I found the windows quite as Mrs. Banney had described, both open to the limit of their lower sashes. I did nothing but push the hangings back a bit—the wind was twisting them—and look in. The room appeared—not quite in its usual order, sir. Suspecting burglars, I put in the call which you have answered in person. Now, will you examine the open windows and the room from the outside, or do you prefer to enter here?"

"Go ahead and open the door. Is there just the bolt? No lock, huh?"

Cubbage demonstrated his answer. Without a sound he drew back the substantial bolt. He turned the knob and the heavy door swung inward.

Thin winter sunshine fell across the little gallery. It came from two windows opposite the door. Their draperies flapped in the chill outer air. The room was "not quite in its usual order." Cubbage had made the statement with unnecessary restraint, for order had become disorder. The drawers in two clumsy old cabinets had either been jerked out altogether or crookedly closed. The pigeon-holes of a tall desk had been untidily examined. The doors of a glassed-in bookcase stood ajar. Some of the books looked as if they had been carelessly replaced and a toppling stack remained on the floor. One corner of the rug was rolled back; chairs were huddled together.

In the midst of this confusion stood the two men. The butler clucked in faint, well-bred distress. The detective was obviously recording a mental image of the disorder.

"Well, what's missing?" Asher demanded.

"I could scarcely say, sir. The marauders must have been searching for something, sir."

"That's a hell of a bright idea, Cubbage. Go ahead and have another one. You help a lot."

In a voice as wooden as his face Cubbage replied, "I was not aware that Miss Marrender kept anything of intrinsic value in this apartment, sir."

"Who beside yourself and the old lady were in the house last night?"

"Miss Marrender's nurse, sir. A young person called Randall, I believe. The doctor can give you further details."

"How about talking to her myself?"

"She's no longer here, sir. She left before eight this morning. Her story was that the doctor had called her on another case." Cubbage's tone altered ever so slightly, but Asher did not miss the trick.

The deputy-inspector's next question had not reached his lips when a shrill scream—two shrill screams came down the, stairway just behind them.

"The voice sounds like Mrs. Banney's." Cubbage was quietly judicial. "And, I dare say, the other is the daughter-in-law. They should be hanging curtains in the drawing-room."

Asher was not interested in theoretical identification. Grasping the butler by the arm he marched out of the rifled apartment. Together they gazed up the steep flight.

"Oh, Mr. Cubbage, do come," wailed Mrs. Banney. "The corp's been murdered."

4

According to Cubbage

Tim Asher reached the top of the stairs first. The two women, white-faced and pop-eyed, moaned incoherently. Thrusting them aside, Asher strode into the room where Eugenia Marrender's body lay. Stark on the wide bed he saw the thin figure, its eyes decently closed. The sheet that had been drawn over the still face had been twitched aside and the bed coverings tossed back far enough to reveal the body to the waist.

Asher bent over, but minute examination was not necessary. A stain spreading from the left breast told its own story. Eugenia Marrender had been shot.

Swiftly Asher looked at the bed clothing. The path of the bullet was plain. For an instant his eyes darted alertly about the room. There was no sign of a weapon. Doors, windows, furniture, nothing escaped Asher's quick preliminary survey. Yet he saw nothing out of keeping with the bed chamber of an elderly invalid.

Then he turned to the group wavering about the doorway. "You said Miss Marrender died this morning. Just how did you mean—died?" The question was directed at Cubbage.

"Miss Marrender's malady was an incurable one, sir. Lately I have heard the nurse and doctor speak of an unfavorable heart condition. This morning very early, about

29

four, the nurse came down and told me that she had just discovered that Miss Marrender was dead. She gave me no particular details. She called the doctor and some time later he called her—about this new case, she said. Before she left she told me to leave everything in here just as it was until Dr. Stuart came out. How she herself left the body I do not know, as this is the first I have entered the room since yesterday. Nor had Mrs. Banney and her assistant any occasion to intrude, if I may say as much." Cubbage's glance rebuked the women coldly.

"How about it, you?" Asher thrust a blunt forefinger at Mrs. Banney, upon whose face fright, curiosity, and apology were equally plain.

"Well, mister, it was this way. I never meant to do nothing I shouldn't, but me and Mabel, we thought we'd like a look at the poor old lady, cranky and hard to suit as she was, and anyways I had to come up to the back hall to get the stepladder to put up them drapes like Cubbage said, and so the two of us—never under heaven could you of got me nor Mabel neither to even walk past the door alone—we just stepped inside and tiptoed easy-like over to the bed, but we couldn't see nothing because the sheet was drawed up over her face, and I says all right Mabel you go ahead and do it, and I guess come to think of it we both of us took a hold of it and throwed it and the covers back, and I hope to die if what I seen didn't fairly turn me, and me and Mabel, we got out a whole lot faster'n we went in, and—"

An impatient peal from below dammed Mrs. Banney's monologue.

"That will doubtless be Dr. Stuart, officer," murmured Cubbage, as if asking permission to withdraw from the group long enough to answer the call. The two women and the detective watched the man's stately descent, but none of them could see the significant look with which he greeted the young physician nor hear the toneless words, "We are in the hands of the law, doctor."

Without revealing the discovery that had just been made, Asher put the necessary preliminary inquiries, and then demanded a statement about the nurse's report of the patient's death.

Again the incurable ailment and the compensating, more merciful heart weakness were explained. The doctor's terms were deliberately technical, for there was something about Asher's manner that appeared to ruffle him.

"When did you last see your patient, doctor?" asked Asher.

"Yesterday morning, about ten o'clock." Stuart answered the detective directly, but his glance rested for a split second upon Cubbage's blank face.

"What was her condition at that time?"

"She was apparently resting in comfort, though it had already become necessary to prescribe narcotics. However, I detected an unfavorable change in the heart action and I advised against any visitors for a day or so."

"And you heard nothing more until the nurse reported that the patient had died in her sleep?"

"Nothing more."

"Then how do you account for this?" Dramatic gestures were not common with Tim Asher, but there was something theatric in the way his outflung arm commanded the doctor to take a look at the dead woman.

Perry Stuart strode forward across the room but came to an automatic stop the instant his eyes rested upon the bloodstained breast.

"God!" His voice was sharp with unexpected shock.

"And now if you'll tell me where you sent the nurse, I'll round her in right away. She's the dame that will have to do some explaining." Asher fished elaborately for notebook and pencil as he spoke.

Dr. Stuart pulled a still-folded handkerchief from a pocket, flipped it wide, and nervously mopped his temples. His lips twitched and his voice was husky. "She—she's been murdered, hasn't she?"

"Look at that wound, doctor. Elementary physiology will tell you that the bullet entered a living body." Asher's dry comment gave no sign that he was alertly interested in Stuart's bland dismissal of the question about the nurse's present address. "And you might give me your opinion about how long ago death occurred."

Expertly Dr. Stuart made the usual tests. "From six to nine hours, I should say, but I should prefer to have the coroner establish that."

Asher nodded in friendly agreement. "Yes, I must be calling in about this—and some other items. Now, how about that nurse?"

"Ah, yes," Stuart permitted himself to be reminded. "Her name is Randall—Doris Randall. She's an excellent nurse—I keep her busy. One of my patients convalescing in the South was demanding a more compatible nurse and so when Miss Randall reported Miss Marrender's death, I sent her right on to him. She's on her way by this time, but I'm not at all sure whether she was going by way of Washington or Cincinnati. My patient's name is Stevens and he's down at Paloma. I can't be sure of the exact address, but call my office and the girl there will tell you. But, I say, Inspector—"

Asher knew that the physician knew that he had no right to that title, but obligingly he stepped away from the others in response to Stuart's imperious gesture. In a carefully lowered voice the doctor went on. "I realize that you must question Miss Randall, but I must tell you that the girl is just as straight as they make them. She's young and not exactly hardened by experience, but you can believe anything she tells you. What I mean to say is—it would be ghastly for her if there was to be any slimy insinuation—"

"I get you, doctor, but she'll have to tell her story, no matter what it is. Now, you tell me one little thing. Wouldn't she—wouldn't any professional nurse have pulled down the bedclothes and listened for heartbeats, if she had an idea that a patient had passed out? Wouldn't she, huh?"

"If Miss Randall had so done, she would have seen the cause of death and so reported it. I'd take my oath to that, Inspector."

"She didn't—so you say. That means—"

"Two things, Inspector. Either she did not pull down the bed coverings or—"

"Or else she shot the woman herself."

The doctor winced but finished his statement calmly, "—or the wound might not yet have been inflicted."

"Nonsense, that woman was living when the shot was fired."

"Certainly, Inspector, but the nurse might have thought death had occurred before it actually had. After she left the room the murderer might have done his work, though why anyone should trouble to kill an obviously dying woman I do not understand. But that's your problem, Inspector."

"Haven't you forgotten that you have just told me that death took place as long as nine hours ago? No, doctor, I'd say it looks bad for the nurse."

Stuart shrugged impatiently and looked at his watch. "I'm operating at the hospital, Inspector. Call me there or at my office if I can be of any further help."

Asher let the doctor go without demur. There was a key on the inside of the bedroom door. He took it out and stepping into the hall he locked the door behind him. "Where's your telephone?" he demanded gruffly of Cubbage. "Stick around, brother. I'm going to talk to you some more after I've put in a couple of calls. You can tell those women to go on about their business."

When Asher had informed Headquarters that there was not only a case of burglary at Windward Hill but also an unexplained death to be investigated, he turned to the hovering Cubbage.

"Snap into it. What have you got to tell me about what was pulled off here last night?"

"Am I to understand that I am already being accused of complicity in these acts of violence, officer?" There was a note of rebuking hauteur in the butler's voice . . . the voice with its incongruously cultured accent.

"Lord, man, don't waste your breath trying to high-hat me. I'm only a hard-boiled cop. Just go ahead and tell me the sad story of your life as it was lived last night. A room downstairs ransacked and an old lady getting her everlasting upstairs—surely you heard a faint echo of something. Come on, spill papa the dope."

"It was a quiet evening, sir. All the evenings are that, since Miss Marrender's illness. I took her dinner tray up at half-past six. At seven the nurse came down for her own meal. It was served in the small dining-room."

"Who was with the sick woman while the nurse was downstairs?"

"No one, sir. Constant attendance had not yet been necessary. By eight Miss Randall was back on duty, and Mrs. Banney had left for the night. I gave the furnace its usual inspection and then read quietly in my room until ten o'clock, when I again made the rounds and closed the house for the night. My room is off the lower hall, you see, and I have no difficulty hearing telephone or doorbells."

"Any such calls last night?"

"No, sir, none." Asher noticed that Cubbage paused before replying.

"All right. You put yourself to bed? Then what? Did the nurse stay up all night with her patient?"

"No, she did not even sleep on a couch in the same room, though there had been some plan about that, I believe. In fact, I had been told to get down a cot from the attic storeroom. Miss Randall slept just across the hall. No doubt you would like to inspect the room for yourself under the circumstances."

Asher tucked this palpable hint away for later consideration and again suggested that Cubbage stick to the topic assigned him.

"I can't say that I heard any particular noise during the night, sir. It was a very stormy night and we get the full force of the west winds here at Windward Hill. I confess that I was somewhat disturbed—an old house like this creaks and rattles very annoyingly. I was awake from time to time during the night, not at all unusual with me, sir, but I heard nothing that the wind could not have accounted for. At one such time I arose and went down to the furnace. The fire never holds well when the wind comes from the west. I had just returned when I was informed by the nurse of Miss Marrender's death. I then made coffee and—well, after that event the night seemed over at Windward Hill."

"Surely you couldn't have thought a pistol shot sounded like the wind howling. Let me have it straight. When did you hear the gun?"

"Let me assure you, officer. I heard nothing that even remotely suggested the discharge of a revolver. However, I rather doubt that even on a still and windless night I could hear a sound of that sort while in the furnace room."

"Hear any sound from the room that was entered?"

Cubbage shook his head in grave disclaimer. Nothing more was said for a minute or two as Mrs. Banney and

Mabel trailed by, bearing mops and dusters, bound for the long drawing-room. Then Cubbage gave a sharp cough of determination.

"Perhaps I should have mentioned this before. It was quite against both the doctor's and nurse's orders, but I was overridden. While Miss Randall was dining last evening, one of the relatives called and in spite of my instructions went up to see Miss Marrender."

Cubbage's precise voice dropped as if he had said all there was to say. Asher snorted with impatience. "Just as a matter of record, who was it?" he snapped.

"A lady whom I had never seen before. All she said was, 'I must see my aunt at once.' She started immediately up the stairs and then she said, over her shoulder, 'I'll let myself out. Don't wait.' Later when I went out for Miss Randall's dessert, I thought for a moment I had heard the front door close and assumed that the caller had gone, but I could not swear to that. I did not see her go.

"Hm-m, just another reason why a little talk with the nurse would come in right," Asher said dryly, and was about to ask for a description of the caller when a startled look in Cubbage's eyes made him swing on his heel.

A man had entered the front door unheard. He had advanced along the gloomy hall as far as the door of the little gallery, still standing wide open. Asher recognized the man at once. It was William Marrender.

Marrender was taller from the waist down than he appeared when seated, or perhaps it was his thick graceless shoulders that accentuated his long legs so awkwardly. His lustreless brown eyes were inclined to squint, and there were lines on his heavy face indicating that being a senior executive before he was forty had produced attendant nerve strain. As he advanced toward middle age those who knew frequently remarked on the increasing resemblance he bore in figure to his grandfather, Robert Rufus

Marrender, a pioneer industrialist whose money had already been freely spent by his descendants.

Marrender's resonant voice boomed into sudden comment. "I see Gene lost no time. The damned bounder!" He turned away from the wrecked room as if in disgust, in which Asher could detect no trace of surprise of curiosity, and then Cubbage stepped forward to tell the eldest Marrender nephew how death had come to Windward Hill.

5

AN ALLY FOR ASHER

It was mid-afternoon before Tim Asher got back to Head-quarters. Lord, this was a tough break . . . the Inspector called out of town to testify in the Haxon trial and the Chief announcing that it was up to him—Asher—to get the goods on somebody in this Windward Hill mess.

Asher slumped wearily into the Inspector's own chair before he was aware that there was a man behind the spread-out newspaper in the window recess that looked down upon Market Square. His grunt of welcome was not as in-hospitable as it sounded, for the young man who emerged from the huskings of the afternoon editions was one for whom the more experienced men in the department had a secret and growing respect.

"Hello, Stowe. Who let you in? Smelled trouble, I'll bet."

"A call from your boss just before he left town this noon, Timmy. He sort of hinted that you ought to let yourself talk to me."

"About what, huh?"

"He didn't say, but I hope . . . whatever it was broke out at Windward Hill."

"So Peyton told you to drop around." Asher relapsed again into silence, but this time he was conscious of a se-cret relief. If the responsibility of handling the Marrender case was to be turned over to him in Inspector Peyton's enforced absence, the Inspector had left him an ally. By jiminy, he'd use the youngster.

"Here's the dope, Stowe." Briefly Asher gave the lazily attentive young man a report of the summons to Windward Hill to investigate an apparent burglary, and the discovery that Miss Eugenia Marrender had not died naturally.

"Now here's my first idea—I don't mind trying it out on you. The nurse has beat it already, and the butler—oh boy, that butler! My bet is that bird and the nurse cooked up this thing together. They had the place to themselves last night and could have staged most anything. And yet, Cubbage acts like he was going to squeal on the nurse. He certainly is throwing dirt on her every chance he gets. Then there's something phony about the room that was entered and searched—that looks like it was entered and searched. Cubbage gave me a dirty look when I picked up two or three burnt matches off the floor. There wasn't a trace of anything interesting on the ground underneath the open windows. The ground's bare and frozen and has been for the last two weeks."

"How did Marrender explain his reference to Gene?"

"You mean when he lamped the wrecked room? He didn't want to, Stowe, but at last I got him to say that Eugene Tracy, a cousin who lives at Windward Hill when he's in town, had been seen yesterday morning coming away from the station, and that their aunt had always said that Gene could have anything he wanted from the little gallery. And then, Cubbage produced a message that he had received from Tracy. It stated that he expected to return to Windward Hill Wednesday night—that's tonight."

"Where did the message come from?"

"New York. Grand Central post mark. Just a common one-cent government post card, addressed to Cubbage and signed E. T. Both Cubbage and Marrender identified the writing as Gene Tracy's. It was dated Monday and came in the morning mail."

"Did Marrender see Tracy yesterday?"

"No, it was some girl in his office. We can check up on her all right. But, say, if Tracy did tear up the room. I'll bet whatever made him do it will turn out to have nothing to do with croaking the old lady. And if Tracy didn't do it, then the butler and the nurse are in it up to their necks."

"Why theorize so soon, Timmy?" There was nothing condescending in Dick Stowe's quiet question, but Asher bristled hotly.

"Theorizing, am I? Listen to this: I took a look around the nurse's room—Cubbage was awfully-afraid I wasn't going to—and here's what I found."

He tossed across to Stowe a small box which held loads for a .38 revolver. Stowe opened it carefully.

"That's all right," said Asher. "It's already been gone over for prints. Just one of 'em missing, see? What'll you bet the autopsy will show a .38 bullet?"

"Rather like a woman, I suppose, to put only a single charge in her weapon . . . or is it?" Stowe was so apparently talking to himself that Astor made no answering comment. He had one more broadside for a climax.

"That's all I found in the nurse's room, but when I came out I noticed that the last door on the same side of the hall was standing partly open. Now, Stowe, I can't be sure, but for the life of me I can't remember seeing that door open when I first came up. Anyway, I said to Cubbage, who'd stuck right at my heels all along, 'What room's that?' and he says 'It's Tracy's.' I stepped inside. It was dark and cold as a barn—plainly hadn't been in use for some time. I pulled up the curtains and then I could see that while everything else in the room was as neat as wax one drawer in a chiffonier was jerked partly open—a lower drawer. In one corner there was folded a dressing gown of some soft flannel stuff and on it I could see the impression of a heavy object that had been lying there—an object the size and shape, say, of a .38.”

“Whew! That’s hot stuff, Timmy. What are you going to do about it?” Stowe stretched his long legs, and thrust his hands deep into his coat pockets after deciding that he did not want another of Asher’s smokes.

“I got pictures of the impression, of course, and I’m going to watch how long it takes it to fade out and maybe I can get some idea how long the gun had been lying there.”

“Good man, Timmy. But the nurse—”

“Sure, we’re after her this minute. She’s headed for Paloma, and if we don’t catch her at Atlanta we’ll get her down there. The reports from the post-mortem and from Radge about finger prints will likely be ready before I call it a day. . . .” Asher shifted his position and the Inspector’s chair squawked in protest.

“I suppose till we hear from Radge and the p.m. we ought to go a little easy, huh?” There was an edge of diffidence in Asher’s words. “Marrender tried to lay down the law about what could and could not be done about interfering with the sacred grief of the bereft family, but you know how much ice that cracks in our racket. Though the Marrenders aren’t Tom, Dick, and Harry—”

“Which also cracks a little ice, as even yours truly has observed from time to time,” drawled Stowe.

“We’ll be watching tonight to see whether Tracy comes back, if we don’t run him down anywhere in the meantime. And Downer’s out at the house now keeping an eye on the butler. There’s something damn fishy about that guy, Dick. When I finally pinned him down to a description of the woman who ran upstairs last night, it was the world’s worst—just a bunch of words. I could arrest him right now as a material witness—”

"Just what did he witness, Timmy?"

Asher overlooked this, patiently. "I talked to the woman who comes in every day to work, a plain old hen named Banney. She says she saw the doctor's car standing in the drive yesterday afternoon and heard a woman talking in the sick room—a woman whose voice reminded her of one of the nieces, a Mrs. Harris Latimer. It was during the nurse's time off. That's got to be checked up because Dr. Stuart said he hadn't been in since yesterday morning. I couldn't get much out of the Banney woman on the subject of Cubbage, but I'm not done yet."

Stowe nodded approvingly. "The nurse, the butler, and the wandering nephew are all good leads, Tim, but I'd say that all the relatives ought to be looked up. Eugenia Marrender was rich—scads of money, from the space she's getting in the papers. She had been stricken with a deadly disease, and yet someone could not wait for her to die. Someone wanted something that only her death could procure. Her will must be looked up . . . and then we may know which way to jump."

"I know what the boss meant—sending you around, and I don't mind telling you that I'll be mighty glad to turn that end of it over to you, especially the relatives." Asher tried to be offhand.

"Consider it signed on the dotted line. I'm glad to be kept out of mischief just now. My wife had to go out to the Coast to see her mother through an operation, and we had cleaned up every job we had before she left."

This was as direct a reference as Tim Asher had ever heard from Stowe himself about the partnership that existed between Richard and Laura Stowe. "Private Investigations" their professional cards read and they must have meant the word "private," for their names were never featured in connection with the sensational cases that from time to time titillated the Middle West. Yet Asher knew that Inspector Peyton's brilliant work in the affair of Burr Sanderson had been founded entirely upon the activity of the young Stowes. There was more than a rumor about the Templeby sapphires, too, and an apocryphal legend concerning the solution of the McVey murder. . . .

Thinking of all this, Asher played safe enough to add, "At that, don't hesitate to horn in anywhere you want. I mean, when you talk to the Marrenders, if you get hold of anything else—"

"Sure thing, Timmy. It's a fifty-fifty job." Dick Stowe rose and gave himself a mighty stretch. "I crave to chat with Mr. William Marrender right now. Where do you suppose I can wing him?"

"Try his house on the Levee Drive first. If he's not there, he's probably gone back to Windward Hill."

At the door Stowe turned. "I say, Tim, there's one part of your yarn you haven't finished. Just what was stolen from that messed up room?"

Asher looked heavily mysterious as one who wished to imply that the crux of a problem had at last been pointed out. "Boy, nobody'll say. They either act like they don't believe anything's gone, or else like they had never paid enough attention to the junk that was in the little gallery to be sure what was or wasn't missing, but I'm telling you,"—Asher's light voice rose to a new high of earnestness—"the family would just as soon soft-pedal the wrecked room."

Dick Stowe opened the door, and then turned and grinned at Asher before he stepped out. "Ah, Timmy, don't get my hopes up like that. You make the case sound like a magazine serial."

Instead of making his way directly to the correct establishment on the Levee Drive where the William Rufus Marrenders lived, Stowe presented himself at the United

Utilities Building and consulted "Information" about his desire to see the third vice-president.

"Information," crisply efficient and hostess-like, hoped that the caller had an appointment and suggested that Miss Wilcox, Mr. Marrender's secretary, might arrange one. Stowe was subsequently permitted to enter the outer room of the third vice-president's suite, where he was again stopped by an even more smoothly efficient young woman.

"Mr. Marrender is not in. He will not be in for several days. There has been a death in the family. . . ."

"I see. . . . Well, that's my bad luck, too, unless—" To the secretary, the diffident young salesman who confronted her was experiencing the dawn of an idea.

"Is there any way in which I can help you?" she asked mechanically. The younger they were the more necessary they thought it that they should speak directly to Big Business itself.

"It was really a kind of personal matter—not United Utilities business, I mean. Not life insurance or a new car, either. . . ." Dick stammered delightfully, and Janet Wilcox hoped she looked fresher than she felt. "I'll tell you what, if you could tell me the name of Marrender's family lawyer, it would help a lot," he blurted out in convincing youthful embarrassment.

"I can do that, surely." The girl's smile was genuine now. "Bartholomew Dexter and Son is the firm in charge of all of Mr. Marrender's private affairs. He often mentions that it is a family habit, that the first Dexter was his grandfather's lawyer."

Stowe thanked the secretary and began to back out. "You've been so kind—maybe you could tell me something else. There's another member of the family that I want to see, too, a man named Tracy." Dick consulted a notebook with ostentation. "Eugene Tracy's the name. Maybe you know where I could find him at this time of day."

A cold, non-committal mask immediately slipped down over the secretary's friendly eyes and her smile turned professional again. "I do not know, sorry . . . in fact, I do not recall the name."

"Now what the hell should she lie about that for?" Dick asked himself as the descending elevator obeyed his signal. "She may not have been the one who told Marrender about seeing Tracy, but she knows the lad and knows him well, or I'm not clicking today."

6

THE MARRENDER HEIRS

Stowe's next stop was at the old-fashioned offices occupied by Bartholomew Dexter and Son in an outmoded business block. Mr. Dexter was in, but just on the point of leaving for the day. Could the gentleman not call in the morning—at ten, inquired a pale, serious youth who doubtless attended law classes at the Y. M. C. A at night. The gentleman could not, and when he had further announced that his business concerned the police the clerk produced his superior. His excitement indicated that criminal law was not featured in the offices of Bartholomew Dexter and Son.

The lawyer was a small, cushiony man, and Dick promptly bet himself that he was the "Son" of the firm name. He introduced himself as a special agent sent out from Inspector Peyton's office. "Your probable surmise is quite correct," he went on. "I am investigating the matter of the death of Miss Eugenia Marrender, and I have come to you because you may have been in charge of her affairs."

The lawyer nodded his bald head in rapid assent. "Yes, yes, but, my dear young sir, it must be immediately understood that publicity in the matter must be held to the irreducible minimum. The Marrenders, you know, the Marrenders—in short, the Marrenders are not to be gossiped about publicly."

"But you, as a lawyer, know that the circumstances of her death cannot be left uninvestigated."

"Yes, yes, quite so," twittered Dexter. "In fact, I said as much to William this noon. Police inspection there would have to be—no power under heaven could avert it, but the publicity of the unprincipled press we could and would divert. He quite caught my idea."

So William Marrender had entertained the notion that a murder in the family need not go through the hands of the police, thought Dick. Maybe the man had his own reasons for being nervous. . . . Blandly he assured the lawyer. "That is exactly how I hope to serve your clients now. Not every activity of the local department is carried on by the men in uniform, nor by the police reporters either. Just now I'm after information about Miss Marrender's will. To whom is her money to go? Under the circumstances, I believe my question is an ethical one."

Dexter blinked his eyes and twirled a heavy dark cameo ring which he wore upon his left hand. He was no fool; he knew well enough what the Marrenders were about to be plunged into. Yet he might have hedged had he not carelessly allowed his eye to wander to the dispatch case, ready for his announced departure. The annoyed jerk he gave his glance away from the case completed his betrayal.

"If I may suggest," said Dick politely, "you have a copy of the document at hand. Perhaps you were about to check its terms before reading it to the family. All I need is a bare statement of provisions and beneficiaries."

Bartholomew Dexter capitulated. After all, this suave young man was much to be preferred to a callous reporter or a peremptory summons to Headquarters. He rumbled into speech. "As a matter of fact, I had just been looking over the instrument. I believe I can satisfy you without reading it verbatim. The will was executed some six months ago just after the physicians had become certain about Miss Marrender's physical condition. It set aside a will made a number of years ago, following the death of her father, Robert Rufus Marrender, my father's friend and client."

Thus was Dick assured that he had won his wager.

Dexter went rapidly on, as if desiring to have done with a distasteful necessity. "In brief, Miss Marrender distributed the bulk of her estate among four of her nieces and nephews, a sum approximating two hundred thousand to each. The remainder, amounting to almost another two hundred thousand, goes to various charities."

"The names of the legatees?" Dick's hint was gentle.

"William Marrender, his sister Sara, Mrs. Harris Latimer, and Miss Francesca Penrose. The two last named are sisters."

"Eugene Tracy is a nephew also, isn't he? Isn't he named?"

"No." Dexter's answer wanted to be final, but duty or something equally unpleasant committed him to further explanation. "Miss Marrender informed me at the time that she and her nephew had an agreement about his omission from her will, and that in event of her death a document would come to light that would make the matter perfectly clear. However, she took me no further into her confidence."

Dick purred at this bit of information, but he did not allow his gravity to be outmatched by Dexter's.

"Were these bequests conditioned in any way?" he asked.

The lawyer shook his head. "Not at all, and as far as I am aware, her affairs are in excellent condition. There will be no delay about probate. I might add, also, that William Marrender is named as executor." He cleared his throat abruptly, "And now, may I ask, what use do you expect to make of this information?"

The change in Bartholomew Dexter was amazing. His fussiness and air of decayed ineptitude were for the moment sloughed off and Dick Stowe caught a glimpse of the old war-eagle that his reputation echoed of.

"No use at all unless it helps to betray the murderer of your client. Why should anyone have desired the death of that helpless, dying old woman? I beg of you, if you know anything that might point to a motive, be frank with me, sir. Surely none of these four who inherit so generously—"

Dexter waved Stowe to silence. "Unbelievable, young man, unbelievable. They are persons of established position, living in comfort. They could gain nothing by forcing the time of their inheritance."

"True, of course." As one who was but mentally reminding himself, Stowe murmured the names just mentioned. "William Marrender has been remarkably successful with United Utilities, hasn't he? Mrs. Latimer is one of the younger social leaders, I believe, and her sister— why, I have it now! I knew there was something familiar about that name. Francesca Penrose is the actress that the Theater League discovered so overwhelmingly last season. Sara Marrender—Marrender's sister, did you say? Possibly a girl so young as not yet to have achieved a personality for herself."

"It's plain you don't know Sally," and Dexter laughed so humanly that Stowe looked at him in some curiosity. The old boy liked Sally, he concluded. There was something positively grandfatherly about his "She's a mere child, of course, but quite her own captain."

"I have just one more favor to ask, sir, at least for this time." Again Dick's famous smile was soothing. "I should like your word that you will say nothing to the people whose names we have mentioned. I must work in my own way, you understand, but I hope to convince you that I can work with finesse and discretion."

The cameo ring was twirled violently, but the promise was given, and Dick Stowe bowed himself out in his most finished style.

Down on the street at the first news stand he purchased a theatrical weekly and verified an association he had been conscious of ever since he had identified Francesca Penrose as the Francesca Penrose of the much-discussed Theatre League play now on tour. Just as he thought . . . that play had been in Cincinnati for a week. Consequently Dick dispatched a detailed message to a fellow operative in that city. Then he set out for the Lindenwood address of the Harris Latimers, wondering if the unknown relative whom Cubbage had not recognized might prove to be Francesca Penrose.

A car was waiting in the drive as he approached the house. It was a smart, dark blue coupé, and when Dick observed medical insignia on the windshield he made an automatic note of the license number of the car. A maid, crisp in black and white, admitted him and bore off his card, upon which he scribbled a few words. Nor did he fail to note that the maid had read this notation before she vanished from his sight.

The maid reappeared shortly and showed him into a small, rather formal drawing-room. "Mrs. Latimer will be in soon," she parroted. Removing the lid from an extremely decorative inlaid box, she revealed an assortment of cigarettes and then withdrew. Again Dick was aware that the black-and-white maid was interested either in him or in the purpose of his call.

There was nothing that he could do but wait. The house, a charming place, was silent. The curtained doorway that led to the hall was no barrier and from it Dick deliberately reconnoitered. Still there was no sound of interest. Then quite without warning a door swung open a little further down the hall. He could see nothing more than that, but he heard:

"—to worry about, darling. You're a precious little fool."

This was followed by what sounded like a faint rush, and then the unmistakable little rustles and murmurs that accompany a certain stage of love making. About that Dick Stowe considered himself quite competent to judge. . . . The only other words he could distinguish were spoken in a light, quick feminine voice. "But I can't imagine where I left my gloves. It's worrying me. . . ."

When, shortly after, masculine steps issued from the opened door, Dick was no longer at his post of vantage; he was at a better one. From one of the long windows of the little drawing-room he had an excellent view of the waiting coupé and of the man who stepped briskly into it. Dick stood looking after the departing car in fond contemplation of a little new idea. Then a high, sweet voice greeted him and he turned to meet Mrs. Harris Latimer.

The woman to whom he addressed his skillful apologies was, if she had just participated in a passionate farewell, at this moment completely mistress of herself. As she listened assured in manner, she gave the impression of one whose regret at the death of a respected elderly relative was as conventionally proper as the occasion demanded. Katherine Latimer was a decorative, silvery blonde; Stowe thought her beautiful. He explained himself briefly and she listened with grave attention.

"My first question, Mrs. Latimer, is a very simple one. When did you last see your aunt?"

She sighed softly before she spoke. "We were not particularly attentive to Aunt Eugenia. Indeed, she had made it rather plain that we annoyed her, bored her, what you will. She was an eccentric. You must not forget that, Mr.

Stowe. But as for your question, I was driving by Windward Hill yesterday and ran in to inquire. She seemed just about as usual to me—had little to say. But then, she was never given to small talk."

"Were you driving alone? In your own car?" asked Dick, mindful of what Mrs. Banney had said.

"Yes—that is, no. How stupid of me. I was driving with Dr. Stuart. I am under his care—my wretched nerves. He thinks fresh air will help to steady me."

Katherine Latimer's serene poise had vanished. Her face sharpened tensely as she contradicted herself and she bit her lips in exasperation.

The young man who observed her went on with his business smoothly. "My second question is one that I do hope you can answer. The household at Windward Hill is so limited. . . . What can you tell me about the man Cubbage?"

"Aunt Eugenia's butler? I'm afraid I can't qualify to give him a reference, if that's what you mean."

"That's not what I mean—unless you mean that you have some definite reason that would prevent your recommending him." Dick was as conscious as his hostess was that they were playing for position.

"His manner of opening a door is abominable, and I don't like the way he waxes floors, but aside from that— At any rate, he must have pleased Aunt Eugenia if for no other virtue than his economy with coal."

"How long has he been with your aunt? Where did she get him? Were his references looked up?"

"With such a generous list of queries to choose from I ought to be able to tell you something—but I'm afraid I can't. A year ago, when I left for France, the man was not in my aunt's employ; when I returned early in October he was—that's all I know. I never discussed him with Aunt

Eugenia." She paused a moment and chose a cigarette. Her poise had returned tenfold. "Your questions call for facts which unfortunately I do not possess, but may I share a suspicion with you? I have seen this servant of my aunt's only three or four times since my return last fall, and I must admit that on those occasions I gave him the most casual sort of regard. But I have seen him other places —I'm sure it was he! Or else he has a most remarkable double." Again she paused.

Stowe was patient.

"Early in December I was a guest at a rather intimate little supper party that was given in honor of Fells Lothrop—the English poet, you know. It was one of those arty affairs where no one is introduced, but one of the guests was my aunt's butler—or else his son!"

Dick Stowe rather wished that Asher had not assigned him so definitely to the Marrender relatives. His immediate attention might better have gone to Cubbage. What Mrs. Latimer was saying made that only too clear. "Why do you qualify your identification?" he asked.

"Because the man at the party was certainly much younger than Cubbage. Otherwise the resemblance was perfect."

"You saw him again?"

"Yes, not more than a month ago. A group of us were slumming—this town has so little to offer in the way of night life. We had gone to a dinky little café out on the West End. The food was good, but aside from that we were pretty much let down. At a table next the wall I was certain that I saw Cubbage. The lights were dim, so I can't be sure that he looked his age, but it was his voice that attracted my attention this time. I heard him speak in that perfectly intoned accent of his. It's not one commonly heard from a servant in the Middle West, you know."

"I'd like to make a note of those two dates, Mrs. Latimer, if you can tell me exactly."

"Not offhand, I'm afraid, though I'm sure I can figure it out from my engagement book. I shall be glad to let you know later, if that will be of any help."

"Quite. And now for a third item. I understand that your cousin, Eugene Tracy, makes his home at Windward Hill. Can you tell me where he could be found now?"

Katherine Latimer's eyes, green with the lustre of old turquoise, narrowed swiftly. "Oh, no one ever knows where Gene is or what he's doing. He's the nonconformist of the clan. Whenever he's in funds, he's off; when he hasn't a cent, back he comes to Windward Hill. Frankly, I never understood his status with Aunt Eugenia. I suppose she tolerated him because he was by way of being her namesake, yet I've often felt that she was afraid of Gene. There was a poisonous hatred between them—don't ask me why. I don't know."

Stowe started to speak, but Katherine Latimer interrupted with a quick appealing gesture. "Please—I shouldn't have said that. You'll think I have no sense of family loyalty. My beastly nerves. . . ."

Stowe's friendly smile was as disarming as he meant it to be. "There's just one other matter I'd like to ask you about. What was there at Windward Hill that would attract, thieves?"

"At last you have asked me a question that I can answer definitely." The voice that answered him was again even and cool. "There is nothing of value at Windward Hill. Aunt Eugenia lived very simply indeed, for a woman of her wealth. The house is shabbily furnished. I'm sure it hasn't been redecorated for twenty-five years. There are a few fine Early American pieces, but the linen, silver, china, and so on are quite commonplace. She never cared for jewels;

she sold the only valuable piece she owned a few years ago—a gorgeous emerald. I don't mind saying it should have been given to one of her nieces. But she would have kept things like that down at the bank along with her papers and securities. My cousin William Marrender insisted on that several years ago." She smiled brightly. "I have no theory to account for the little gallery being entered last night. That's what you're getting at, isn't it?"

Dick tossed a half-smoked cigarette into the fire and rose to go. "All this, my dear Mrs. Latimer, is really a futile sort of busy work until the nurse is brought back. Her story will, no doubt, make short work of the apparent mystery."

"The nurse? Oh, yes. . . . But—her motive?"

"Oh, I dare say she and the butler have some sort of racket." Dick spoke indifferently, but his eyes were alert.

Just as he was withdrawing from the room, the maid who had admitted him announced Marrender.

Mrs. Latimer murmured explanations, rather unnecessarily. "My cousin and I must assume the responsibility of arrangements—out at Windward Hill, you understand."

7

RETURN OF GENE TRACY

Apparently Dick Stowe had paid little attention to Katherine Latimer's announcement that she and her cousin were going out to the bleak house on Windward Hill, for from the Latimer establishment he went directly to the Marrender address on the Levee Drive. He asked, however, for Miss Sara Marrender. The servant who opened the door informed him, stiffly, that Miss Marrender did not reside there.

"Where can I find her?" Stowe's watch was shot into view, as if to indicate that time meant money.

"I can't say, sir, where she might be at the present, but I presume that her business address remains the same."

That did not enlighten Stowe. The servant rather grudgingly emitted an address and then added as though, after all, it was not his shame, "It's a store called after her—Sally's Shop, or something like that."

Sally's Shop! Dick whooped silently. Sally's Shop, of all the priceless luck. Off he went. He did not have to be told how to find Sally's Shop. But wasn't he the social innocent not to know that Sally of the Shop was Sara Marrender in person?

On his way to the not quite aristocratic address of what the Stowes called an old-fashioned general store gone modernistic, Dick made hasty arrangements with himself to be perfectly frank with this scion of the Marrenders. He remembered how astutely she had sold them a chest the Stowe *ménage* had not exactly needed. . . .

It was late when he reached the Shop. Sally's assistants, both old enough to be her mother should she ever need two, demurred singly and in duo when the importunate young man demanded to see Miss Marrender. Unless, compromised the pudgy one, he was the man about the hanging oil lamps that were to be shipped up from Brown County. Obligingly, Dick was. . . .

When he opened the closed door at the back of the two square old rooms that once had been front and back parlors in the simple seventies, he found Sally unpacking a barrel of old dishes. Before she could sink from her knees to a more comfortable position on the floor, the wily young investigator plunged into his business.

"Maybe you recognize me, Miss Marrender. I hope you do. My wife and I about furnished our whole apartment from your last rummage sale. What you don't know, I suspect, is that I am a detective—not a divorce snooper. Lately I've been working almost altogether with the local authorities, though officially I am not of the police. At the present moment I am investigating the murder of your aunt—"

"The murder of—my aunt! Aunt Genie! How gracefully you break news."

The words were flippant, but Dick Stowe could have no doubt that Sara Marrender had not before known that her aunt had not died a natural death. The bright hazel eyes with their straight dark brows looked squarely into his. He watched the flicker of caution in their depths.

"I had a message early this morning that she had died, but I've had to be out of town nearly all day. And then these shipments came in that I had to check over at once. That old crook down in Georgetown thinks I don't know my marbles. . . . I'm closing the shop of course till after the funeral. But murder—Just what do you mean?"

When Stowe had given the gravely attentive girl a succinct account of what had transpired at Windward Hill, her only comment was: "Why have you come here to tell me this?"

"Because I must have the cooperation of every member of Miss Marrender's family if I am to be so fortunate as to solve the mystery of her death without involving the Marrenders in a lot of screaming publicity."

"That wouldn't be so bad for the shop, so you can't chill my blood like that. . . . Oh, I mustn't talk in that beastly way. Aunt Genie wasn't exactly popular with us, but I needn't stick that juicy bit down the public throat. You must believe me, Mr. Stowe, I want to be of assistance to you. I'd say, from what you have just told me, that it was the nurse and the doctor that did the dirty work."

"The doctor? That's an interesting idea. How did you get it?"

"Just plain cattishness, I'll have to confess. I don't like Perry Stuart much, that's all."

There was something suspiciously discreet about the frank expression. It led Dick promptly to his next question. "Does Mrs. Latimer share that feeling with you?"

"Kaye? So you've heard that dirt too."

Dick plunged boldly ahead. "I've heard that there's a divorce in the offing."

"No, you haven't heard that. Kaye couldn't bring action against Harris Latimer in a thousand years, and if she should let her foot slip so that he could sue her, she'd not get alimony, and without money Stuart would be a fool to try to handle Kaye."

"Thank you for so clearly pointing out the doctor's motive."

Sally cast him a wry smile. "I advise you to think that over again. In my own simple way I can see a crack in your premise."

"When did you last see your aunt?" Thus Dick waived her challenge.

"Strangely enough, yesterday morning. I hadn't been out to Windward Hill since the Sunday before Christmas. I was out trailing a corner cupboard on the Brookboro road and on my way back I ran in to see Aunt Genie. She acted like an old she-devil, too, and I don't mind saying it." Sally's eyes blazed with sudden anger.

"If she said or did anything that might throw any light on what was to happen to her, I hope you won't mind saying that also."

"Not at all." There was a curious dryness about the girl's reply. "When I came in the nurse asked me to stay with Aunt Genie for a few minutes, so there I was, planted. She started to quiz me right away about my business here—she's never approved of it, and the first thing you know we were quarrelling. Bill's attitude toward me may be positively medieval, but he's a grand brother, and I couldn't let her say what she did about him."

"What did she say?"

"Why—er—that as a guardian for little sister he wasn't so hot and a lot of tripe like that."

Sally's floundering reply was not convincing but of that Dick Stowe gave no outward sign. Instead he asked, "How did the nurse impress you?"

"Just as a good-looking girl who knew her business. I saw her only for a few minutes when I first came in. I got so mad at Aunt Genie that I walked out without waiting for the nurse to come back."

"What can you tell me about the butler?"

"Nothing at all. I didn't get even a good look at him— the hall at Windward Hill is a murky hole."

"What do you know about your cousin Eugene's status with your aunt?"

"I like Gene! He's my favorite relative, usually. He has never fit in with the Marrender traditions—not that I hold that against him. Anything but! I wish Gene had been at home when all this happened, for he's awfully keen. Really, I can offer no better suggestion than that you talk this whole mess over with Gene. He'll be back, of course, the minute he hears. He's been in New York. I had a note from him last week. He went to peddle his new score. He expects to revolutionize musical comedy some day."

"You haven't answered my question. How did he rate with your aunt?"

"Relentless, aren't you? All I know is that they let one another politely alone for the most part. She had no patience with his musical ambitions. Why, she wouldn't even let him have a piano in his own room. . . ."

"Your brother remarked that it was understood that Eugene was to have anything he wanted from the little gallery. What do you know about that arrangement?"

"Bill said that? He's been little-girling me again. That's something that has been kept from baby sister—I never heard of it before. I say, are you trying to frame Gene? That's my inspiration for today."

"Try to have another one—do! Anyone who runs a shop like this ought to be an authority on what there was of value in your aunt's house that would explain the ransacked room."

Sally Marrender rose to her feet and dusted her hands deliberately. "All right, listen to the expert then: if every stick of stuff in that house was being auctioned, I wouldn't even read the handbills. Windward Hill is perfect 1880 throughout, and we've a long way to go before marble tops and scroll-saw trims bust into fashion. But—papers are valuable sometimes, you know. What do you bet it was something of that sort that the thief was after?"

Gravely Dick allowed Sally Marrender to believe that she had presented him with a brand-new idea. He thanked her gratefully and left the shop. After a thoughtful dinner at George and Al's he climbed the drafty wooden stairs that led to the Inspector's office. Asher had left, but there was information waiting for him.

First, the autopsy had revealed a .38 bullet. The viscera showed traces of morphine, but in quantities that agreed perfectly with the opiate being administered under medical direction. The medical examiner's considered opinion on the approximate time that death had occurred was in keeping with Dr. Stuart's earlier estimate—not earlier than midnight nor later than three o'clock.

Second, Lieutenant Radge, in charge of Bertillon files and finger print records, reported that the photographs and other tests made of the window and door frames in the little gallery, the box of ammunition found in the nurse's room, and the edge of the open drawer in Tracy's room showed no distinct finger prints, only blurred smudges such as would have been left by gloved hands. At this, Dick was reminded that a nurse would undoubtedly have been supplied with rubber gloves, that a butler with a fastidious accent might not always have worked barehanded, and that anyone coming in from outside on a winter night would naturally have been gloved. On the medicine bottle, however, very clear prints had been revealed. They corresponded with quantities found in the nurse's room.

Third, so far Headquarters had not caught up with the Randall girl, but the police at Paloma were waiting for her the minute she stepped off a train. If she is really guilty, thought Dick, she will have gone off in another direction. The best proof in the world that she isn't mixed up in what happened here is for her to appear in Paloma. She'll have negligence to explain—criminal negligence maybe—but not complicity in the death of Eugenia Marrender.

Fourth, Asher had gone out to Windward Hill and Stowe was to meet him there before the evening was over.

An obliging underling just going off duty gave Stowe a lift as far as the last quarter of a mile that led to Windward Hill. The house stood on a gaunt bluff that overlooked the lower reaches of the river that looped its way through the city. The spectral grey-white sycamores that lined the climbing drive creaked in the winter wind, and the three twisted pines that shielded the house from the full force of the blasts threw black shadows across its face. Stowe had almost reached the narrow portico that marked the main entrance before he could detect glimmers of light from any window. The upper rooms were in darkness; the curtains below carefully drawn.

A familiar signal stopped him. It was Tim Asher. "That you, Dick? Good boy! The family's inside—some of 'em, and the lawyer. I had to tell that old bird where to get off. They had the idea that if they said so we'd just drop the whole business. They still think they're going to step on the newspapers. But, listen, they've kindly consented to let us investigate discreetly. That means you're elected— no kiddin'. There's nothing discreet about me, and as I'm the temporary boss I'm wishing it off on you. And Heaven help you, Dick, if you let me down!"

"Tim, you call me a White Hope at your own risk. What are you up to now?"

"I'm browsing around on the chance of catching Tracy. If he should come in tonight from New York, it will be the 8:52. One of the boys that knows him by sight is down there to tail him, but it's my bet that he's going to drop some other way."

"Who's inside?"

"Relatives. They're talking funeral arrangements now— that's why I thought it was safe to blow for a little while. As soon as they go, I wish you'd give the dump the dou- ble-o."

"O.K. with me. And I'd like a look at Cubbage."

"Right. Got anything to smoke?"

As Dick shared his cigarettes he asked, "Is the Banney woman still around?"

"At the back of the house somewhere. Try to get some- thing straight out of that old hen—just try!"

"Cheer, Timmy. Nobody's going to ride you if this case isn't solved by morning."

Stowe slipped off in the darkness and followed a bricked walk that led around the house to the left. According to Asher's report it was the second room on this side that had been entered. Long narrow windows like these would offer no difficulty to anyone determined to enter. The sills were close enough to the walk to make it a simple matter for anyone not completely disabled to step up and into the room. Yet Asher had also stated that the windows were fastened with the best sort of locks—not completely im- pregnable to a burglar, but a kind that could not have been easily forced. Furthermore, the locks had not been forced. That meant that the intruder had not found the windows locked, or else they had been opened from within. Why two windows, anyway? Dick propounded in the darkness. One exit ought to be enough for any self-respecting burglar.

He groped his way on toward the kitchen end of the house. A dusty, low-powered bulb swinging from a black- ened cord dimly lighted a screened porch, the door of which was fastened back against a supporting post. Dick took a long silent step across the porch to a window and peered within.

A shapeless, middle-aged woman sat at a high, zinc-covered table, a generous pot of tea at her elbow. She was talking; Dick could see the soundless motion of her lips. At first he could not see who it was she was addressing. Then a younger woman crossed the line of his vision and began to hang towels in a row behind the stove. This woman said nothing, but jerked her head in what looked like angry dissent from time to time. In a moment, just as Dick was about to knock at the door to announce his presence, the woman at the table leaned forward as if listening alertly and held up her cup in imperative caution. A second afterwards, a door swung open and a man appeared.

Cubbage, labelled Dick promptly. Tall and thin and slightly stooped—that was as far as Dick got in inventory before the man withdrew through the door by which he had entered. He had deposited a tray of empty coffee cups upon the table. Six of them, Dick counted.

Mrs. Banney—Dick concluded that the woman at the table must be she—listened stiffly for a moment and then plunged again into peremptory argument. This time she illustrated her remarks by something which she drew out of the pocket of her apron. Dick had some trouble in seeing that this object was a bit of fine-linked chain. It interested him so extremely that again he raised his hand to knock on the door.

Once more his purpose was delayed. A sound reached his ears. A sound from without, not within, a sound that was coming to him from below. Swiftly he leaped from the porch and ran across what by daylight might be a drying green or a kitchen garden. The ground sloped away beneath his feet. If his one remembered view of Windward Hill by daylight was serving him well now, the bluff upon which the house was built overhung the river steeply at this point. There must be some sort of path leading from the tow path below to the house above; undoubtedly someone was stumbling upward through the darkness.

Stowe darted back to the shadow of the porch and crouched behind a colony of refuse containers.

Eugene Tracy had walked the long river way out to Windward Hill. By the time he began to climb the rutted path that led to the back of his aunt's house, his head was mercifully much clearer. He had not elected to walk for that purpose, much as his head needed that sort of attention. He had walked because there was, so strangely, no money in his pockets. And the last thing that he could remember was that there had been quite a surprising lot of money . . . money and the flashing eye of a jewel. Maybe Esme could explain about the emerald. The little devil. . . .

God . . . . but he was tired and hungry. He mounted the last rise before the path swung round the tool house to the kitchen door. This dismal old house was the worst place in the world for him to come back to after what he'd just taken, but who was he to crab about that? If only he could catch the little nurse, she'd rustle a bit of supper for him. She'd be glad to, if he knew his Eves. . . .

He stumbled against the steps that led to the porch and steadied himself by clutching at the screen, which protested rustily and must have announced his arrival to those within. The door swung open. Mrs. Banney's voice reached Stowe's eager ears.

"Here's Mr. Gene now. They been expectin' you, you poor boy, you. It's like this—your poor old auntie, she passed away unexpected like. . . ."

The door closed and Dick heard no more. Within Mrs. Banney went on talking . . . talking, but to Eugene Tracy her words did not make sense. He hadn't thought Aunt Eugenia would die. . . .

8

FRANCESCA PENROSE

When Dick Stowe opened his eyes next morning at the insistent command of an alarm clock, he was immediately conscious that extra sleep ought to be coming his way after the night's work that Asher and he had put across. True, they had not got much out of Tracy, only his persistent refusal to explain his movements for the past twenty-four hours. They had kept at him until he collapsed, but they would begin again this morning just where they had pinned him down last night. . . . He'd have to talk, after that melodramatic accusation of Cubbage. Cubbage had been good, really superb. Dick complimented him in retrospect. . . .

"Explain!" Tracy had screeched. "I can explain myself perfectly. Just as soon as I can remember, I tell you! But till then, there's the man who must explain. He—he knows something!"

And then Tracy had fainted like a neurotic woman. Cubbage had picked him up and laid him on a couch. Then he had turned to Asher and himself. "Gentlemen," he had intoned, "the poor lad's secret is safe with me until he himself gives me permission to speak. Till then I have nothing more to say."

And by the Lord Harry, he hadn't said another word. Asher had third-degreed him till after two, but he had

stood up under it like a man of iron. They had been obliged
to call Dr. Stuart to quiet Tracy's jumping nerves and the
doctor had suggested a bromide for Cubbage, but the man
had refused it, chastely requesting only a glass of water
after his ordeal.

Thus Dick stretched himself out of his pajamas and under a shower. At the most impossible moment of this rite a
night letter arrived. The message was from Cincinnati and
informed him:

> ON NIGHT MENTIONED SUBJECT LEFT
> CITY BY MOTOR AFTER PLAY STOP DID
> NOT RETURN TO LIVING QUARTERS TILL
> LATE NEXT MORNING STOP HAS BEEN
> OPENLY TRYING TO RAISE FUNDS BUT
> UNABLE TO DISCOVER PURPOSE STOP
> SHALL I CARRY ON? PEEDEE.

Dick whistled gayly. There were motives springing up
all over the lot, except for the two who most obviously had
had the best opportunity for staging the crime, the nurse
and the butler. Any moment now ought to bring word
from Paloma, and that would mean a showdown of sorts
for the nurse. As for the relatives of the dead woman, it
might be interesting to know if they were informed about
the terms of the will. There was Katherine Latimer . . .
two hundred thousand dollars would make an alimony-
less divorce no barrier at all. Yet why hurry a matter that
through Dr. Stuart she could not fail to know would be
consummated naturally within a few months of waiting?
Nor must he forget that Asher had reported that Stuart
had given a satisfactory account of his movements on the
twenty-first. And the Sally kid had cheerfully admitted to
quarrelling with her aunt about something that concerned

her brother. That was an interesting thought . . . he'd hold
it for a while. There was the fact that William Marrender
had tried to sh-ush the police in their investigation of the
murder. Decidedly he must cast an eye on William Marrender. Then there was PeeDee's line on Francesca Penrose,
who'd been trying to raise a lot of money in a hurry and
hadn't been home on the night in question. A chat with
Francesca must go on the program too. Hold on . . . she
couldn't be the unidentified caller. At that hour she had
not yet left Cincinnati.

Aside from what Cubbage had said, there was more
than one reason for considering Gene Tracy's position.
His own inexplicable behavior . . . Mrs. Latimer's remark
about the strained relations between him and his aunt . . .
Marrender's fury when he beheld the state of the little
gallery. Sally was the only one of the clan, so far, to speak
of him with sympathy. Yet the Marrender money could not
be a motive in Tracy's case, for he was the only one of the
group who was not to inherit. Wait a minute . . . what had
Dexter said about an agreement that would come to light
after Miss Marrender's death? Dick's whistle sank to a faint
pianissimo. That was it! That was the document that had
been searched for in the little gallery. With that agreement
out of the way, the disinherited one could claim his legal
rights. The Marrender million would have to be split five
ways instead of four. Tracy looked clever enough to work
out an elaborate plot. If he had pulled off anything like
that, no wonder he had gone on a bender afterwards.

These setting-up exercises of Stowe's ended with a call
at Headquarters. There was nothing new, though they
were expecting any minute to hear that the nurse was on
her way north from Paloma. Asher had gone directly from
his home out to Windward Hill to relieve Downer, who
had been left to chaperon Tracy and Cubbage. That meant,
thought Dick, that the butler was in for another grilling.

Asher was welcome to the job. . . . Consequently Dick decided to take the next bus down to Cincinnati. A frenzied call from Windward Hill came in to Headquarters just after he left, but that interfered not at all with Dick's placid enjoyment of the trip.

Upon his arrival in Cincinnati a call to PeeDee from a pay station just off Fountain Square furnished him with the necessary address. It led him to a studio suite in an apartment hotel. A little colored maid admitted him and took his card to which he added an explanatory line. For nearly a half hour he saw nothing more of the maid nor of anyone else.

Dick Stowe had never seen Francesca Penrose act; he was not even sure that he had seen her picture in the periodicals that feature young actresses who are beginning to make the grade. Yet the moment she entered the room he knew he was facing a personality of extraordinary possibilities. Her beauty was not stereotyped. There was something sharp and thin about her youth that suggested that not yet had its metal been finally tempered. Her eyes were long, dark grey, full of restless light. Her hair was fine and straight and a glorious silver-gilt. Her lips were mobile and finely cut; in fact Stowe decided that her mouth was her most beautiful feature. There was a slight reminder there of the woman who was her sister, Katherine Latimer, though perhaps the straight haughty nose revealed the kinship more distinctly.

Her words came with husky rapidity. "I was rather expecting you—someone. But I made you wait because I was deciding what I should tell you."

She stopped speaking as suddenly as she had begun and the narrowed dark eyes swept Stowe speculatively. "It's not that I am afraid to talk, please understand. I intend to tell you exactly what I did the night my aunt was killed. You'll probably not want to believe me. . . ."

Still Dick Stowe was silent. If she intended to stage a scene, let her go to it, he was advising himself.

After a moment the husky voice went on. "On Tuesday night at the close of the play Mr. Galeotti and I left the city immediately. Galeotti was driving his own car. We took the Dayfield road, but my destination was Windward Hill. It was nearly two o'clock when we arrived, as Galeotti was not familiar with the route. At the entrance to the drive I got out of the car and went on up to the house alone. I ran around the side of the house to the gallery window, pushed it up, and stepped inside. I had brought a flash light, of course, and it did not take me long to get what I had come for. It was just where Aunt Eugenia had told me it would be. . . . Then I left the way I had come and rejoined Galeotti. We drove on to Columbus—Galeotti had an engagement there. After a bite of breakfast together I came back here by train."

She paused again, as if she expected to be interrupted, but Dick said nothing. She went on more slowly. "I'll confess that Will's—my cousin's telegram was a shock. All he said was that Aunt Eugenia had died. It was not till later that I was informed that she had been shot. At first I thought I shouldn't mention my visit to Windward Hill, but—I have been very frank, haven't I?"

Francesca Penrose leaned back in her chair perfectly at ease. Her eyes, limpid and untroubled, rested confidently upon the young man whose amazement was only too evident. Her attitude announced that she had done her complete duty.

Stowe bit back the words that he was tempted to say and thanked her punctiliously for her information. "However, Miss Penrose, you must appreciate that I cannot quite consider your statement complete. I shall have to ask you—"

"Of course, Mr. Stowe. But your questions will probably touch upon details of the situation at Windward Hill of which I am completely ignorant."

"I think not. . . . For instance, what was it you entered your aunt's house to procure?"

"Oh! That was careless of me. Of course you would want to know that. There were some papers which Aunt Eugenia had given me permission to use. She had already told me where I should find them. You see, I had made these arrangements with her previously."

"What was the nature of these papers? In what way could you make use of them?"

"Do you have to know that?"

Dick's steady eyes demanded an answer.

"They were—negotiable securities and I have already used them as I needed to. I see no reason for telling you why I had to make this arrangement with my aunt. It was a bit unusual, but perfectly clear between us. I left a receipt just as she asked me to do."

"Left a receipt? Where?"

"Where I found the securities. My aunt had requested me to keep that information secret, but I dare say that now—she doesn't care. They were in a heavy envelope which was wedged between the fourth and fifth volumes of *The Decline and Fall* on the bottom shelf of the corner bookcase. It was a fantastic idea of Aunt Eugenia's, but she was being so good to me—"

"When were these arrangements made with Miss Marrender?"

"Last week—just a week ago today, to be exact. There was no matinee and I drove myself up and back in the afternoon. I had a frank talk with my aunt and she finally said that the only thing she could do for me was to let me use—this envelope. She said it was something she had that happened to be nobody's business but her own—in other words, that Will did not know about it. She told me where I should find it and even suggested how I should get in—said she'd guarantee that I'd find a window unlocked."

"But, Miss Penrose, why all this secrecy about it? Why didn't she send you down to the little gallery right then and there to get the securities?"

Francesca Penrose hesitated a moment. "I know—it does sound frightfully absurd. But you must remember that Aunt Eugenia was—well, queer. She said she didn't want Cubbage to be asked to open the gallery door for a relative of hers. So when she proposed that I slip in at night through a window, I—humored her."

"Did she know exactly when you were coming?"

"No, she didn't. I said that I couldn't get away again that week, and she said that was all the better, that everything would be in readiness by the first of the next week—this week."

"I wonder," mused Dick, as if to himself, "how she arranged to have a gallery window unlocked. Obviously not Cubbage. There must have been another key beside his. . . ."

"I don't know, but if Aunt Eugenia had had another one that afternoon, I think she would have sent me down to the little gallery to get the envelope."

"Whoever had one was someone she could count on seeing within the next few days, and that eliminates—" Dick did not finish that sentence but directed an apologetic smile at Francesca Penrose. "I'm not trying to insult you, Miss Penrose, but how can you verify what you have been telling me?"

"I see what you mean. Unfortunately for me, Aunt Eugenia is dead. There's the receipt I left."

"Ah, yes . . . the receipt," murmured Dick thoughtfully. "Why don't you refer me to Galeotti? At least you could provide him with an identity."

"Gallo Galeotti! It's quite evident you're not—"

"I'm only a detective, Miss Penrose." Dick grinned cheerfully.

"Galeotti's etchings are rather well known. He's exhibiting here just now. We are good friends." A new note vibrated in her husky voice. "All that he could tell you would be about the drive from here to Columbus and the fifteen-minute stop at Windward Hill. I'm sure I did my little errand within that time."

Abruptly Stowe dropped the subject of Gallo Galeotti. "In what condition did you find the little gallery when you entered it?"

"Just as I last remembered it. Aunt Eugenia never shifted furniture about. Of course I didn't stand about taking inventory. I made a bee line for the book case."

"And in what condition did you leave the room?"

"Just as I found it, of course. But what do you mean?" The actress in Francesca Penrose was not responsible for the puzzled look that swept across her face.

However, Dick countered with another question. "You said Mr. Marrender informed you of your aunt's death. May I see the wire?"

"If I still have it." Her hands, small and delicate, darted capably through a heap of odds and ends on the table at her elbow. She tossed him a yellow envelope. In eight impersonal words William Marrender had announced his aunt's death.

"Later you heard—?" prompted Dick.

"My sister, Mrs. Latimer, called me by long distance just as I reached the theatre for the matinee. She told me that Aunt Eugenia had been shot, and that it looked like murder. And what should she do? My sister Katherine is like that . . . excitable, you know. I did what I could to quiet her, but I couldn't talk long—I had barely time to make up and go on. Of course I searched the evening papers. There was nothing but a death notice, for which

I was grateful. I mean, no sensational headlines. Then I called our lawyer myself and Barty, the old lamb, assured me that there was going to be the least possible unpleasantness for the family, and so on. Now what is there, that I don't know?" she ended.

"Evidently you have not been informed that the little gallery was broken into and turned upside down, as if the intruder was searching for something. Both windows were found standing wide open yesterday morning and everything in the room had been gone through."

"Then—my receipt!" gasped Francesca.

"I don't know. It may still be there. But let me tell you one thing—if your receipt has disappeared and if it can be used against you in any way, my guess is that you'll hear about it in pretty short order. If that should happen, get in touch with me at once—at once. Will you promise?"

"Yes, I promise," she agreed flatly.

"Another thing, while you were in the little gallery did you try the door that leads into the hall to see if it was locked?"

"No, oh, no. I had just one thing on my mind, Mr. Stowe. Only one thing."

"Do rally round, Miss Penrose. During that short time that you were at Windward Hill did you note anything at all that might help us to understand what happened? Sounds—lights—wasn't the well-known feminine intuition sparking any static or anything?" Dick was boyishly insistent.

She shook her head almost sullenly. "You say that both windows were found open? I've been so childishly frank with you. . . . How can you believe me when I say that it was the left-hand window that I found unlocked, and that when I left the room I drew it down again just as I found it? You'll build a marvelous circumstantial case against me—"

"Please, Miss Penrose, you've been splendid! Surely you see that it's the nurse and the man servant who are going to be in the tightest hole. By the way, you must have seen those two last week when you called on your aunt. How did they impress you?"

"I didn't see the man. A heaving creature in a dirty apron answered the bell—"

"Sounds like Mrs. Banney," labelled Dick.

"The nurse said I might stay about fifteen or twenty minutes and disappeared. She was a usual type—more than pretty, but out of sorts about something, I thought. I can imagine that Aunt Eugenia was a trying patient."

"When did you last see your cousin, Eugene Tracy?"

It was plain that the question had not been anticipated, yet the actress's answer came suavely. "Two months ago in New York. Just before this League play went on tour."

"On what terms were he and his aunt living together?"

"Please, Mr. Stowe, I'd rather not discuss Gene. He— he resents what little success I've had. It's not that I'm trying to conceal anything from you, only—Gene would loathe being discussed by me."

"I see. . . ." (He didn't at all—not then.) "There's just one more thing on my mind. Since your aunt confided in you about the securities, maybe she mentioned other valuables that might have been hidden in the little gallery. There must have been something at Windward Hill worth breaking in for."

Francesca answered with quick laughter. "I'm so glad you spoke of that. At last I can give you the melodramatic sort of information the occasion calls for. There was Aunt Eugenia's emerald brooch. I never knew she had such a lovely thing till that afternoon last week. She told me where to find it in her bureau drawer, but I decided it was too complicated a process—" She fell silent in dismay.

Dick completed her sentence. "—raising money quickly on a thing like that."

She nodded and a second later shrugged her shoulders.
"It's worth a tremendous lot. What a gorgeous pendant it
would make! I never saw a bigger emerald and there was
a double row of diamonds outlining it. But I put it back,
and then Aunt Eugenia thought of the bonds."

"Do you mind telling me where you replaced the
brooch?"

"Not at all—heaven grant you find it there! I realize
how I am hanging myself. I returned it to the place where
she had told me to look for it, in the middle drawer of
her bureau in the corner at the back on the left-hand side.
There's an old-fashioned velvet handkerchief case there
and down among the handkerchiefs wrapped in a little
twist of wrinkled white tissue paper you should find the
emerald brooch."

After Stowe had gone, Francesca Penrose continued to
sit motionless in the chair in which she had faced his questions so gallantly. Her bright head drooped . . . perhaps
so that the trouble in her clear grey eyes need not be betrayed.

9
DEATH COMES AGAIN

From Francesca Penrose's apartment Stowe went directly to a dealer's and obtained Galeotti's address. Fifteen minutes later he was being shown into the artist's hotel sitting-room. The appearance of the Italian was not as exotic as his name had led Dick to expect. He was inclined to be explosive as Dick explained his business; then he calmed surprisingly and answered questions with a docile promptness.

First Stowe assured himself that Francesca Penrose had not forewarned her friend by telephone. Galeotti glared at the instrument accusingly and insisted that not once had it summoned him that morning. Then Dick set to work to verify the actress's story. It was quite as she had said—the times, the route, the brief pause at the old house.

"Just two o'clock while I waited there for the signora. She would not permeet that I go with her. But not long was it that I wait. She must have run back, that one. She pant and shiver and breathe queeck when she return. Almost I theenk she have been frightened, but no, she say not so. We drive on and Francesca"—he used the beautiful Italian pronunciation—"warm her cold shaking hands in the pocket of my great coat."

"Where were her gloves?" Stowe asked quickly.

"That careless one, she have drop them somewhere. She had them when we leave the theatre." Galeotti went on to speak of the subsequent miles to Columbus, and Dick could see no reason to doubt the actress's story. He was ready with another question to start the fluent voice again.

"While you were waiting at the entrance of the drive did you observe anything that I might find interesting?"

"How do I tell what you find interesting? It was a very black night, you understand, and there was much wind. I try to watch the signora as she hurry along the drive, but in one little minute I can see nothing. I look toward the house where the ancient aunt lie so ill. All I can see that indicate there must be a house up there in the blackness is one faint little light. That must be in the apartment where is the seeck woman, I tell myself. The road is silent also. One car only go by."

Galeotti paused. He appeared to be considering something in a new light. "I am glad I recall this car. Perhaps you find it of interest. It come from direction of the town to which we have almost arrive. It slow as if to enter the drive and then swerve out and pass on, perhaps because my car was observe. I wait without lights, you understand, as Francesca request."

"What sort of car? Who was in it?"

Galeotti shrugged wearily. "How you tell those things? All I know is that I see the white blur of faces in a small closed car."

Further questions on Stowe's part led to nothing, and when a prospective purchaser of etchings was announced he was content to bring the interview to a close. Thanks to his own long legs he just managed to catch the next bus for Dayfield. During the journey he sorted out impressions, warm with self-satisfaction over his morning's work. He'd tackle Cubbage next. . . . It was only a hunch, of course, but what if Cubbage had himself staged the confusion

in the little gallery? He might have witnessed Francesca
Penrose's unconventional entrance and for purposes of
his own, so far unrevealed, be keeping silent. Thus Dick
Stowe theorized happily, but the fond pride with which he
regarded his acumen was soon to be deflated.

He was still sitting on the world when he reported at
Headquarters. Just wait till he told Asher about the receipt and the emerald. . . .

"Asher wants to see you, Stowe," yelled the desk-sergeant the instant he entered the first office. "And don't let
that guy Carney wiggle in when you open the door either."

A ubiquitous police reporter grinned and lighted another cigarette. "Don't raise your blood pressure over me,
Freddie. I get my tips from the higher-ups, and I'm sticking, see." He winked jovially at Stowe as the latter opened
the Inspector's door, but his quick eye, Dick observed,
leaped to the vista afforded by the briefly swung door.

It was a wild-eyed and flushed Asher that jammed a
telephone receiver back upon its hook and turned to greet
him. "For the love of Lulu, Dick, where have you stuck
yourself? It's all over but the trimmin's—"

"Why the lack of poise, old horse? Have I missed something?"

Asher's gesture was indescribable. "It's Cubbage. He's
bumped himself off."

"So that's the answer. . . . Well, talk it all out, and
you'll feel better, honest you will." Dick's facetious manner served for the moment to cover the chagrin which en-
veloped him. The hours he had spent in Cincinnati should
have been spent with Cubbage. How cocky he had felt not
five minutes ago. . . .

Asher gulped down a cup of coffee long since grown
cold and scummy and plunged into details. "When I got
out to the Marrender house this morning I had about decided to run those two bozos, Tracy and Cubbage, down

here to see if that wouldn't make 'em a little more chatty. Downer lets me in, see, and I knew right off that he was up in the air about something. Seems they had just tried to rout Cubbage out and couldn't rouse him. When they broke in his door they found him dead in his bed."

"Like the other—shot?"

Asher shook his head and swallowed the last of his sandwich. "Nope—just dead. Nothing in his room to show what happened, either. You and I were both with him till after two and we know he was all right up to then. Downer was in the hall all night and no one went near the room. The only thing—he had maybe a dozen morphine tablets in his vest pocket. Well, we rushed an autopsy and Doc Shade just now phoned me that it was a shot of some new stuff—a bird named Benssen worked out the formula. Doc says it's a slow poison and that Cubbage hadn't been dead more'n two hours or so when Downer found him. Sure looks like suicide, huh? But he might have left a confession." Asher sighed.

"So you'd say Cubbage's suicide explains Miss Marrender's murder." Stowe stood with his hands in his pockets and his feet wide apart. "That would be neat and satisfactory—just what the Marrenders could endure, besides giving us a lot more rope."

"Listen, Dick, it's got to be Cubbage. You know that imprint of a gun I told you about? Well, it faded out right away, but I put a gun on the same soft stuff and left it there twelve hours and the mark hasn't smoothed out yet. Cubbage must have fixed up that exhibit just to show me. Take it from me, this case is open and shut."

"Then be careful you don't get your fingers caught. What else happened? What about the nurse?"

"Sure, she's in it too. And why? Because she did not show up at Paloma this morning. Every train down there has been traced and she sure didn't go bye-bye that way, that's all. We had to start all over again from this end. She sure went somewheres."

"Maybe she will prove to be Cubbage's letter of confession—when found. How about Tracy?"

"We rode him all morning—they just hauled him out before you blew in—and he won't crack a damned thing. All he says is he can't exactly remember what he was doing night before last. The doctors have looked him over and they say he's on the level mostly about being blotto. But it's about time it was the morning after for that baby, I'm telling you. Anyway, you're it for the next session with him."

"Thanks. I'd have horned in regardless. But about Cubbage—you're sure there was nothing of interest in his room?" Dick was thinking of the emerald brooch and Francesca Penrose's receipt.

"A few clothes, but no papers or anything to give a line on the chap. Mrs. Banney says she saw him carrying an armload of trash down to the furnace late yesterday afternoon—stuff from his room. I was a fool not to arrest him yesterday morning, but I didn't know what I had on him then."

"Timmy, my lad, I grant you that it surely looks as if what Cubbage knew died with him. Sounds like common sense to say that he went crazy and killed Miss Marrender and then himself, but—it's too tame to be interesting. Heigh-ho, at least we can hope on, hope ever till we hear what the nurse has to say. By the way, what's been done about the little gallery?"

"Nothing. It's locked—everything left inside just as it was."

"Good. Here's why. . . ." Dick gave Asher a colorless account of his talk with Francesca Penrose.

Asher rumpled his stiff fair hair. "I get you, Dick. Cubbage's suicide will do to tell, but there's a damned lot we

don't know yet. I've a notion to beat it out there with you
to be in on the look-see for the emerald—"

"I'm on my way this minute, Tim."

Before Dick Stowe had turned the handle of the door in
exit the telephone bell rang. What he heard Asher saying
stopped him.

". . . sure, I'll tell him. He's here now. . . Your office?
I'll send him right over."

He swung round to Dick. "That was Dexter, the family
lawyer. He's all het up about something. Says he must get
in touch with you at once. Suppose you drop around there
while I'm O.K.-ing these reports. I'll pick you up in fifteen minutes and we'll run out to Windward Hill."

Obediently Stowe presented himself at the office of
Bartholomew Dexter and Son. The earnest young clerk
lost no time in admitting him to Dexter, *fils,* who gave
every sign of perturbation.

"It's this, Mr. Stowe. Most amazing, really." He waved
a letter about but did not offer it to Dick. "It occurred to
me that you might find it of interest, as it purports to be
a message from the late Miss Marrender.

Stowe's gesture was peremptory, but still Dexter did
not relinquish the sheet clutched in his hand. "Shades of
the spirit world," thought Dick, "what's going to break?"

Dexter, it appeared, wished to marshal his information
in an orderly recital before he permitted his caller to read
the letter. The envelope bore the local postmark and the
current date. The twenty-second was a legal holiday, the
little man carefully emphasized. The letter itself was dated
the twenty-first. It had been delivered at his office this
morning, the twenty-third, but Dexter himself had seen
it for the first time little more than a half hour before.
His liver had not been quite normal, he explained, and his
wife had thought it wise for him not to come down to his

office at his usual hour. Thus it was that a letter written some time on the twenty-first had not been read until the middle of the afternoon of the twenty-third. Then and then only was Dick Stowe allowed to take the epistle in his hands. He read:

> Windward Hill
> February 21, 1928
>
> My dear Mr. Dexter:
> Miss Marrender requests that you call upon her at your earliest convenience, as she has a matter of business that demands attention.
> Yours truly,
> Doris Randall

"Written by the missing nurse," was Stowe's first comment and for some minutes his only one. His next was the inevitable question: "Have you any idea what she wanted to see you about?"

"Naturally not," Dexter sputtered, "except that I recall that the last time I was in conference with the late Miss Marrender—the occasion was the drawing up of the will about which you have already inquired—she remarked to me that, unless she should wish to alter the instrument, that was very likely the last business I should need to perform for her."

"Then there's the possibility that it was something of that sort that she wanted to see you about, isn't there?"

"A possible reason, I grant you, but one not very solidly founded."

Which Dick granted him, also. "I say, Mr. Dexter, were any of the heirs acquainted with the terms of Miss Marrender's will?"

Dexter bristled. "Not through this office, sir. Miss Marrender herself told me that she had never given any of the young people reason to expect a cent from her. A woman of strong character, sir."

"If I could find out who knew she might be changing her will," Stowe was beginning when Asher's unmistakable signal rose from the traffic below. He bade the lawyer a polite good afternoon and departed, neatly forgetting to return the letter. On the way out to Windward Hill he appeared to be more interested in letter boxes than in Asher's elegant and improving conversation. When he had spotted the box nearest the entrance to the Marrender house, he jumped out of the car and made a note of its scheduled hours of collection.

The cheerless house on Windward Hill was in charge of the police, although Mrs. Banney and Mabel still held their ground in the kitchen. They were reinforced by a cub from the department to keep back reportorial initiative, against which the women's friendliness could never have coped. So, without delay, Asher and Stowe found themselves within the little gallery.

Many of the books ranged upon the shelves of the corner case had been tumbled to the floor, but those on the lower shelf, were not noticeably disturbed. All but the first volume of the row of Gibbon were still in place. Dick marched directly to them and pulled out the fourth and fifth volumes and lifted them apart. No paper fluttered to the floor.

"She was stalling, Dick. You might have known—"

"Maybe, and yet—well, it occurs to me that the receipt could be used rather skillfully by the villain in the piece."

"Don't kid yourself. No such paper came to light when the mess was searched—and the boys did a good job."

"All right, let's not waste any more time down here theorizing about it. The jewelry's next."

Again the door of the little gallery was closed and locked. The two men climbed the flight to the upper hall

and unlocked the door of the room where Eugenia Marrender had died. Within an orderly peace prevailed. The
curtains were drawn, the furniture ranged sedately against
the walls, the wide bed covered only by an old-fashioned
heavy white spread. The drawers in the marble-topped
black walnut bureau were not locked. Slowly Stowe drew
out the middle one and saw at once the velvet handkerchief case which Francesca Penrose had described.

He folded back its quilted flaps and thrust his fingers
into its depths. They closed about a bit of tissue paper.
But his fingers told him before he looked that the twist of
paper was empty. The emerald and diamond brooch had
disappeared.

10

PEN IN HAND

Excerpt from a letter written Thursday evening, February 23rd, by Richard Stowe to his wife Laura:

". . . so it's going to do to say the butler murdered her. But before I can quite believe it I'd like to know more about Cubbage. I could kick myself from here to you for not concentrating on him from the first, but Asher wished the relatives on me. It looks as if the man had destroyed everything that could give him background, and that fits in with the suicide theory, all right, but the pocket full of morphine is the reason that idea isn't on the up and up with me. Here's my slant on it—I think Cubbage was thinking of suicide but somebody beat him to it. It just about adds up to this: if Cubbage killed himself, then he must have murdered Miss Marrender; if somebody else killed Cubbage, it must have been because he knew who the real murderer was. Ergo, the same murderer did for both of them.

"I'm hoping I can get something out of Gene Tracy about Cubbage. I understand I am to see him the first thing in the morning and, of course, he'll quail before Dick the Deadly, eh, La La? Just the same I'd like to know why the rest of the Marrenders have such a snooty attitude toward cousin Gene. 'Tain't right. Maybe it wasn't Will Marrender's secretary who saw Tracy Tuesday morning, but I have a hunch that dame will spill something yet.

"Who was searching for what in the little gallery? The agreement that stated the case between Tracy and his aunt? Francesca's receipt? Or something so far unknown? Francesca had a flash light, but somebody else left a trail of burnt matches. Said matches are unlike any variety stocked at Windward Hill, so Asher's cohorts report. I'm willing to go on record that F. told me the truth—but not all of the truth. Could she have had any other experience during her visit to the house that would account for her shaken state when she returned to Galeotti? Oh, I know . . . what she had told me she had done would have made any girl slightly breathless.

"Then there's a mess of little items that keep annoying me. Two pairs of missing gloves ought to be checked in somewhere. Both Mrs. Latimer and the fair Francesca seem to be minus a pair. For some reason, too, I'm curious about the length of chain that Mrs. Banney pulled out of her apron pocket last night. I'll get after that tomorrow when I go out to talk to Tracy. Another pet idea I have is that the visitor whom Cubbage couldn't or wouldn't identify might not have left the house until much later in the evening. If I do say it, La La, that's a swell hunch.

"Time out, just at this point, Laura. Headquarters called with the latest dope. Asher's
line now is that the nurse might have gone to
Chicago. There was a westbound train waiting
to pull out at the same time the Cincinnati
train left. Dr. Stuart's office girl says that
Doris Randall stopped there on her way to the
station Wednesday morning, and Stuart says
he met her at the station and explained that
her reservations would be waiting for her in
Cincinnati. He put her on the right train himself but left immediately afterward, as he was
pressed for time. So she could have switched
trains. Furthermore, the doctor's reservation
was not called for. Asher checked on that.
If she took the Chicago train, she got there
about six last night and so has a twenty-four
hour start on us. The doctor's girl gave us a
crackin' good description of the nurse; Stuart's was as dumb as a man's usually is.

"After all, the whole case hinges on this:
what is the nurse's story? My bet is, over and
above everything else, she walked off with the
emerald. Asher is fine-combing all the fences
on his list, however. . . ."

Dick finished his letter and as a final inspiration
affixed an air-mail stamp to it, for his conscience told him
he should have written the night before. Three days later,
when Laura Stowe read the letter, she straightway wired a
discreet, impersonal inquiry which was not addressed to
her distant partner. But in the meantime . . .

11

TWO PIECES OF CHAIN

Before nine o'clock the next morning Dick Stowe was again on his way to Windward Hill, specifically detailed to interview Eugene Tracy. Mrs. Banney admitted him. One of Asher's men, Benny Parks, lounged sleepily in the hall. "Go right on up," he whispered. "That bird's no more pie-eyed than I am this morning."

Mrs. Banney lumbered ahead of Stowe. At the top of the flight he put one question to her. "How many of the family do you know by sight?"

"All of 'em. Why, me an' Mabel . . ."

"Fine. I want a talk with you a little later, Mrs. Banney. You're a woman of judgment. . . . Is this Tracy's door?"

Mrs. Banney creaked down the back stairs. Her self-esteem deserved another cup of coffee. Anyways, there was no sense wastin' all that double cream. . . .

A slender figure, not quite of average height, stood looking out of a window down upon the wind-blown dregs of a last summer's garden. He turned as the door opened and closed, and gave Stowe an enigmatic glance. Then he gestured abruptly toward the only comfortable chair the room offered and laughed mirthlessly. "I thought you'd be a hard-boiled old precinct captain," he said, not too distinctly.

Stowe's first impression of Eugene Tracy, the night he
had stumbled into the kitchen, had not been favorable.
This morning he felt as if he were facing a different man
altogether. He was still white and weak, but his eyes were
clear and his person fastidiously in order. He thrust his
long slender hands, artist's hands, down into the pockets
of his shabby dressing gown and perched himself with an
attempt at nonchalance upon the foot-board of the bed.

"Well," he challenged, "why don't you produce the
thumb-screws?"

"Just as you say," Dick returned amiably, "but the fact
is that the man Cubbage's suicide makes most of the questions that I was popping with the other night look a bit
silly now." As he spoke he watched Tracy intently, but
had to conclude that the mention of the butler's end had
caused no flicker of expression. "Of course, there's one
big question that he left unanswered—the one you yourself raised. Just what was it that Cubbage could have explained? You said he was the one who knew something."

"Did I? How I must have raved. . . . Did I say, also,
that I knew what it was? If I did, then I surely was all the
way off my nut."

"Yeah? After you passed out the other night, Cubbage
was very grand and noble about declaring that your secret
was safe with him. What secret, f'rinstance?"

"The one that's still safe with him, I should say."

"You force me to be crude. Where's the gun that you
kept in that drawer?"

Dick pointed to the chest where an imprint of a revolver had been found.

"You should have asked Cubbage that. But I'll volunteer this much—I never knew I kept a gun in that drawer.
I have never owned a gun."

"That," said Dick, "is a statement I am inclined to
accept without proof."

"Thank you very much," mocked Tracy. "Next?"

"Next I should like to understand your position in this household. I prefer your explanation, to be exact."

"You must have found the cousins quite frank. I'm the black sheep, the prodigal, the waster, the family failure—what you will—and always, the family poor relation. When I left college—my mother's little legacy had educated me—it was agreed that something must be done about me, but I was tactless enough to turn down the jobs that the Penroses and the Marrenders could arrange to open for me in the various Big Businesses that they controlled. There was something else I wanted to do. . . . I tried to pull it off on my own, but after a long bout with typhoid I was so shot I crawled back here and accepted my aunt's terms. She felt she owed me something because I had been named for her, she said, but I happen to know that she always considered that my mother had taken a liberty."

Eugene Tracy paused and fumbled for a cigarette. Dick watched his thin face with interest. It must be true, he was thinking, Tracy had hated his aunt.

"Briefly the agreement was this: she'd stake me for the next three years, not beyond the dreams of avarice, I might say, but adequately, if I would sign a paper waiving all claims to her estate when she died. If I hadn't got anywhere at the end of the three years I could go jump in the lake. However, I could always live at Windward Hill during her lifetime, though I must promise never to touch a musical instrument under her roof.

"I got around that by taking a ratty little room downtown. I had a second-hand piano there and I'd hole it when I felt like working. Another thing that helped was that usually I was careful enough with the funds she allowed me so that I could go to New York a couple of times a year. The only catch in it all was that my aunt's time limit was nearly at an end and I—well, I know now that I had the wrong idea about myself all the time."

There was that on Tracy's sensitive face that bespoke genuine suffering. Dick thought of what Sally Marrender had said about her cousin's ambitions in musical composition. If this long-cherished hope had gone on the rocks . . . but how could that sort of disappointment have any bearing upon the deaths at Windward Hill?

"This statement that you signed," Dick went on, "do you know where your aunt kept it?"

"I see . . . the rumpus in the little gallery. Maybe she kept it there—I don't know. It was in that room that I had my first, last, and only glimpse of said document. It was spread out on her desk in there when I signed it, nearly three years ago. No, Stowe,"—Tracy's eyes sought Dick's frankly—"I was not the person who ransacked that room with the idea of destroying the paper in order to claim my cut of the money, no matter how the damned will read."

"Perhaps you were attempting to choose something—I understand your aunt had said you could have whatever you wished from the little gallery."

Tracy flushed angrily. "If my aunt meant what she said, which I doubt, I should never have chosen that way to claim her promise."

At this point a certain theory of Stowe's went under without a trace. With no attempt at finesse he shifted the topic. "What's your line on the nurse?"

"She hadn't been on the case long before I left for New York, but I'm telling you, she had everything. I understand you sleuths are tracing her. What do you bet she'll let Stuart know where she is? She's ga-ga about him."

"Here's hoping she can spill something about Cubbage."

"Hasn't it occurred to you that as a name for a butler Cubbage is too good to be true? Wodehouse ought to hear about a butler named Cubbage. I can tell you just two facts about Cubbage and they both may be innocent duds—but you're advertised as a detective. The first is that soon after he began to buttle for Aunt Eugenia Ma Banney bolted into my room one day with a pile of laundry. In just a few minutes she caromed in again and said that one of the new man's hankies had got mixed with mine—her mistake, et cetera. She pawed around and mumbled something about its being marked with an M. Naturally I concluded that our little Cubbage had been christened Moses or Montmorency, until not long afterward I happened to notice a package that had been delivered to him from a clothing store. It was addressed to John Cubbage."

Dick Stowe had listened to Tracy's story without betraying his inner satisfaction, not so much at the information there might be in it as at the change of attitude taken by the speaker. Tracy's antagonism was waning. Consequently Stowe's only comment was: "I'm quite prepared to agree with you that Cubbage wasn't really Cubbage. Your second fact, please."

"Whoever he was, he was a much younger man than one would think, seeing him slink around here. I saw him one morning out in the garden in a full blaze of sunshine. He thought he was quite alone and he was—himself. His stoop was gone and there was no grey in his hair . . . but that same day at luncheon both those details were much in evidence."

"Tracy, are you sure you don't know what it was that he could explain?"

The two young men looked at one another, eye to eye, for a long minute. Then Tracy shook his head. There was bewilderment in his eyes, but they did not waver.

"Then if we've exhausted that topic," Dick resumed briskly, "we come at last to what you declared you'd tell just as soon as you remembered it—"

"An account of myself for Tuesday and Wednesday." Tracy took the words out of Dick's mouth. "I'm afraid I was pretty well lit, but I'm ready to talk—on one condition only."

"And that?"

"—is that you ask each one of my cousins to establish an alibi for the whole of Tuesday night."

"I find your condition stimulating. Go ahead."

"I had been in New York. My business there had—not gone well. I mention that fact only to account for my state of mind. I left there on Monday afternoon, a day earlier than I had planned, and reached Dayfield the next morning on the Queen City. I didn't come out here. I went to that room I spoke of and holed myself in. Unfortunately there was something to drink there. I'm one of the asses that can't carry much. I try to be sensible, but—well, I was sunk. Early in the evening I went around to a little joint to get something to eat. Some chaps there were playing a pretty hot game and I sat in. The last thing I remember was that I was winning quite surprisingly.

"Now here's where I spoil everything. . . . I suppose I passed out. All I know is that in the morning—that would be Wednesday morning—I was back in my room. Somebody had just gone out. I mean, I think I remember hearing the door close. Then I went under again . . . and the next time I came to it was dark again. The damn room was cold and I was hungry, and I didn't seem to have a cent in my clothes; and so I started to walk out to Windward Hill—and you know what I walked into."

"Not so good, Tracy, not—so—good. Who was it that left your room Wednesday morning?"

"I tell you—I haven't the slightest idea. I'm not even sure that I heard the door close. Perhaps it was only my landlady. She has the soul of an overseer. I'll give you her name and address, and the names of the chaps I played with."

"Right. But see here, Tracy, are you sure you've 're-membered' everything?"

"I'm not at all sure. I'll admit that was an awful bender. But I've told you everything that's at all clear in my mind at the present moment."

"If you can't remember anything more than that, how are you going to prove that you weren't up here at Windward Hill at some time between Tuesday night and Wednesday morning? You made an awfully positive statement a moment ago about not being the one who went through the little gallery. How do you know you weren't?"

"Call it an inner conviction of innocence. . . . . It's the sort of thing I don't do." Tracy's jaunty words did not match the look of strain that appeared in his eyes, and his glance, for the first time since the talk had begun, wandered away from Stowe's steady regard.

"You were drunk that night, Tracy. How do you know what you did?"

"Then it couldn't be a first-degree charge they'd bring against me . . . but we're forgetting—it was Cubbage who killed Aunt Eugenia. However, I rather expect to be formally arrested myself, probably after the funeral."

Again a new personality, bitter and mocking, flashed from beneath his guard.

"I can't say what will happen after I have checked up the alibi you have given me. That will depend—"

"Upon the other alibis which you have agreed to investigate also."

And with that Dick Stowe withdrew. The upper hall was deserted. During the fifteen minutes which elapsed before he too chose the back-stairs route to Mrs. Banney he examined with growing interest a curtained alcove in which the upper hall ended. The only article of furniture behind the curtain was a patently decrepit divan covered with an old-fashioned pieced silk quilt. One of the squares had already fallen into rags. From between the shreds of material and the stouter fabric that formed the lining of the quilt, Dick pulled out a few inches of gold chain.

Promptly thereafter he descended to the kitchen and cajoled Mrs. Banney into sharing her coffee. She proffered him the contents of ice-box and pantry as well, but Dick was eager to get to his questions. He wanted to know the last time she had seen Miss Marrender's nieces and nephews at Windward Hill.

"Before she passed away, you mean?" Mrs. Banney stirred another spoonful of sugar into her cup and considered. "Gene, he'd been gone close on to two weeks, I guess, and the day he left for wherever it was he went to was the last I see of him. Then, lemme think now. . . . that little one, Sara her name is, she come runnin' in a Tuesday morning. And say, her and her aunt had a lively set-to about something. That Sally's a little spit-fire, if ever there was one. Mis' Latimer, she was in that afternoon, but I didn't see her—"

"I remember. It was you who recognized her laugh."
"Yes, uh-huh, I heard her then, but that night I seen her."
"Here?" demanded Dick.
"On her way up here, looked like. I was leavin' an' I passed her down by the gate. It couldn'ta been no one else but her."

"What time was that, Mrs. Banney?"
"Nearer eight than seven-thirty, which is the time I'd ought to be through with the supper work."
"Was she alone?" persisted Dick.
"I didn't see nobody else." Mrs. Banney's answer was suspiciously brief, but Dick allowed her to go on. What

could have been Cubbage's motive in denying he knew her,
he was asking himself.

"The other Penrose girl, the one that's a actress, she
was here last week one day. I remember that plain enough
because I don't know when she'd been here before. She
don't live in town no more. That leaves Mr. Will." She
paused impressively and drew in her flabby lips. "The last
time I seen him here was two weeks ago this coming Sunday. He was the only one of the family that did right about
comin' to see the old lady."

For an instant Dick was conscious of a vague disappointment. There had been something about Mrs. Banney's last report that made him think he was about to
hear something startling about—of all persons—William
Marrender. Then he realized he had indeed learned something. If Marrender was a regular caller, it was he whom
his aunt had chosen to unlock the window preparatory to
Francesca's coming.

"I say, Mrs. Banney, there's something else I'd like to
ask you about. Wednesday evening just before Tracy came
home, I happen to know that you were interested in a bit
of chain. Where did you find it? What became of it? Why
didn't you want Cubbage to know about it?" The nice-
boy smile that more than once had served him well was
brought into action.

For a moment Mrs. Banney's face was blank; then she
nodded her head in vigorous recollection. "That there
piece of chain, mister—why, it ain't worth nothin'. I got
it here right now in my purse somewheres. If it was long
enough to do anybody any good, I'da give it back to Cubbage when I found it, but he was throwin' it away anyways, and so I kep' it."

"Throwing it away?"

Again she nodded insistently. "Cubbage, he took a notion late Wednesday afternoon to clear out his trunk or

something, and he carted off a lot of stuff down cellar and pitched it in the furnace. I picked up this here piece of old watch-chain off of the floor right there by the cellar door after he went down, and I just slipped it in my apern pocket. If he'da knowed I had it it woulda only been something else for him to jaw at me about."

"May I see the bit of chain, please?" Dick's tone was abstracted. He was thinking hard.

A scuffed and peeling hand-bag was opened, and a piece of old gold chain dragged up from the little inner pocket that once had held a mirror. Dick ran its length through his fingers. He must ask one more question before he dared leap at a certain fascinating conclusion.

"By the way, Mrs. Banney, in your work this week have you done any sort of cleaning in that alcove in the upper hall?"

"No, I ain't," she apologized almost contritely. "It's so shut off an' all. I mopped in there last Tuesday an' that's the last—"

But Dick was no longer interested. She had told him what he wanted to know. He drew out of his watch pocket the short bit of chain he had found up in the alcove and compared it with the piece that Mrs. Banney was sure had been dropped by Cubbage. The two lengths matched exactly.

12

TRAILING ALIBIS

As Dick Stowe left Windward Hill after these talks with Tracy and Mrs. Banney, there were so many leads to follow that he felt like flipping a coin to see which should come first. However, he wisely began his follow-up work by reporting to Asher the gist of his morning's experiences, and asked that those in charge of Cubbage's body examine it carefully for signs of disguised age.

Stowe had made an agreement with Eugene Tracy and he meant to keep his word. In fact, he had already begun a check on what the various Marrender relatives had been doing during the course of Tuesday night, though of that he had said nothing to Tracy. Francesca Penrose's statement had been largely substantiated by her friend Galeotti. To her credit it could be said that she had made no attempt to conceal her presence at Windward Hill on the night and dangerously near the hour at which her aunt had been shot.

Mrs. Latimer, Stowe recalled, had been quick to volunteer references to her own activities that night, but she had said nothing about a second stop at Windward Hill. It might be a good idea to have a chat with the black-and-white maid at the Lindenwood house. She had a look that indicated a smoldering grudge against someone.

Dick set out for Lindenwood, determined to make the most of the next few hours. The Marrender relatives would be safely out of the way, for after the funeral service, set for eleven, they were to be in conference with Bartholomew Dexter.

The black-and-white maid answered his ring. With the devout hope that it might be her mistress who was responsible for the girl's sour look, Dick promptly tested her with as large a bill as he could afford at the moment. It worked. She answered all his questions, venomously.

Had Mrs. Latimer been at home last Tuesday evening?

"No, she got all dressed up and went out to dinner somewheres."

Had she gone out with Mr. Latimer?

The girl shook her head and gave her generous caller an oblique look. "Him? No, he was in Dee-troit on business."

Where had she dined?

"She said"—there was a deliberate emphasis for which Dick was watching—"she *said* she was going to the Art League dinner."

As a rule, suggested Dick, there were cards of admission for public dinners.

"Yes," agreed the maid. "She still has them tickets, too."

How did she know that interesting fact?

"I seen 'em—in Mrs. Latimer's beaded bag. She sent me there herself this morning just before she left for the funeral. She thought maybe a pair of gloves she wanted might be in it. They weren't, but the tickets was."

The tickets, Dick pointed out, were now worthless. Would she get them for him?

The black-and-white maid thought of the windfall that had just come her way and gave value received. Dick professed mild wonder about there being two tickets, but the girl said nothing beyond the statement that Mr. Latimer had been called out of town rather unexpectedly.

At what time had Mrs. Latimer left and had she gone in her own car?

"It was maybe ten minutes past seven when she went away. Somebody stopped for her—I don't rightly know who, but I don't mind guessing it would be the same car that stops here nearly every day. She says she's sick. Sick . . . her! Love sick, that's all."

When had Mrs. Latimer returned?

"At ten minutes after three exactly. I know that because I was up just then—something I ate. She come back in the doctor's car, all right."

Dick considered that he had got his money's worth. From Lindenwood he went to the house on the Levee Drive. The fact that it was not the same servant who had admitted him Wednesday afternoon determined his approach. He declared himself a business caller and was breezily disappointed when he was informed that Mr. Marrender was not in.

"Say, he's never home, is he? I called the house last Tuesday evening and you or someone says he was out. Was that on the level, or were you kiddin' me along because I'm new at the business?"

From vastly superior heights; the servant condescended to explain that Mr. Marrender had been working late at this office on that Tuesday evening.

"Well, to tell you the truth, I hung around on the corner thinking I'd catch him the minute he got back even if it was late, but I must have missed him. He sure must have been working late."

"I have no idea at what hour Mr. Marrender returned. He would not need to ring to be admitted." The door closed resolutely, but Dick felt that he had picked up a crumb of information that might be useful sooner or later. He went jauntily on to his next port of call, Marrender's office in the United Utilities Building.

It was Marrender's secretary whom he wanted to talk to, but she had just left for lunch. A youngster whom he had not seen on his previous visit was the only person about the suite when he entered. It was evident that she had assumed full responsibility for the vice-presidential duties. Within four minutes Dick learned that the young lady's name was Bettina, that they were kind of taking things easy today because the boss was at his aunt's funeral—that rich old lady that got shot—and that she for one was glad when the boss wasn't around though that was maybe because she was new here. Yet he must have got Miss Wilcox's goat too, for she had thought some of quitting, but the boss had raised her salary. Janet Wilcox had all the breaks—why, she'd even seen the man who murdered the old lady that got shot.

"Miss Wilcox is Mr. Marrender's secretary, is she? How could she possibly have known who that man was?"

"Why, his picture was in all the papers yesterday, and Janet said this morning that it was the same man she had seen up here to see the boss."

"When was that, Bettina?"

Bettina did not know. They had transferred her from the auditor's office just the day before yesterday. It seemed that the auditor's staff considered her hopeless with a comptometer. Much Bettina cared. . . .

Just as simply Dick acquired a little information about the secretary's evening routine and withdrew before there was a chance that he might meet the young woman coming from lunch. Before he left the United Utilities Building, however, he had a chat with the elevator starter, and learned how a record was kept of employees or executives who were in the building after closing hours. Thus he saw for himself that Marrender's butler had told him the truth: Marrender had been in the United Utilities Building on Tuesday evening from eight until ten-twenty.

After a hasty bite of lunch for himself, Stowe set to work on Tracy's story. The address of the rented room he found without any difficulty. It was a frowsy house on Burden Street with a "Rooms for Rent" card displayed between the glass and grimy fragment of lace curtain of the front door. As he opened the door a sharp-eyed, curveless landlady emerged from a room at the end of the smelly hall.

"I'm to wait for Tracy. He said you'd let me in," said Dick, hoping he looked musical.

"You can go right in. He never locks his door." Her words came readily, but she watched him with an air of habitual suspicion.

The door she indicated was indeed unlocked. Dick stepped inside and closed the door behind him. The room was so dusky that he had to switch on a center swinging lamp before he could conduct any sort of accurate examination. That a composer of music could work in such a place seemed unlikely. Yet there was his piano, a battle-scarred grand of excellent make, and everywhere there were scraps of music manuscript. There was a violin, but its case was covered with dust. On the floor under the piano there were several shabby portfolios containing, Stowe discovered, finished scores in manuscript.

One corner of the room was roughly boxed off to form an inadequate closet for clothes; another corner held a cot, uninviting with its tumbled army blankets. A table and a single chair near the only window completed the furnishings. On the table were an empty whiskey bottle, an unwashed glass, and a heap of cigarette ends and ashes. These Dick examined quite carefully, though he was not at all interested in determining what brand they were. He concluded that all but two of the cigarettes had been smoked by the same person. That two were different he deduced by slight reddish stains he found upon them.

Lipstick, undoubtedly. Those stubs he carried away with him.

There was some music spread across the piano. Some of the pages were loose and slipping wryly out; others were upside down. Instinctively tidy, as Laura rejoiced, Dick set to rearranging the scattered pages and so came upon the most interesting discovery that the room was to offer him. Between the pages of the "Battle" symphony the face of a woman confronted him. It was an unmounted photograph, perhaps nine by twelve inches and beautifully finished. As Dick studied the face he was almost sure that he was looking at a picture of Marrender's secretary, Janet Wilcox, the girl who had said she knew nothing about Tracy. He left the picture where he found it.

Lastly he examined the baggage that Tracy must have brought back with him from New York. A Gladstone bag was easily opened but yielded nothing of importance. The other piece was a brief case, strapped but not locked. It contained a complete manuscript score. On the top page was written "The Blue Princess, a Musical Play in the Modern Manner, by Gene Tracy." But the score told its own story. In great handsful it had been seized and torn almost across, and then smoothed out sufficiently to stuff into the case.

"No takers . . ." murmured Dick.

Out in the hall the thin little landlady was alertly waiting. Stowe asked her to come into Tracy's room and then they both rose above what he had told her about waiting for his friend.

"Tell me what you saw of Tracy Tuesday and Wednesday," he began.

"He came in before ten on Tuesday morning and I never saw no more of him all day. About eight that evening, maybe, he went out again and when I seen him go I knew all right why I hadn't heard him at his pianna all day. It

musta been stuff he brung along back with him. Mr. Tracy's
as nice a gentleman as I've ever had in this room, but
once in a long while—you know . . ." There was an air of
infinite understanding about the woman that implied that
in her world men were all alike.

"I heard him come back not long after midnight—he
made enough noise for three people. That's all I could tell
you about Tuesday. Long about the middle of the next
morning—that would be Wednesday—I looked in here and
he was still dead to the world. He stayed that way, too, till
after dark. Then I heard him moving about some and later
on he went out and I ain't seen nothing of him since."

"Who else was with him at any time during those two
days?" Stowe was conscious of the possibilities in the landlady's account.

She looked at him patiently. "Say, you must think I
ain't got nothing else to do. Not a soul was in to see him
that I took notice of. But then, I wasn't settin' watching
over him all day long."

That was quite true, Dick silently agreed. Aloud he
asked, "Is there anyone else about the place that might
have noticed whether he had any callers?"

If Tracy's landlady attempted an answer, Dick Stowe
never heard it. He had opened Tracy's door and was about
to step into the hall. At the same moment the street door
swung open and a girl appeared. For the merest fraction of
time she poised in the doorway, her eyes fixed in alarm on
the unfamiliar figure emerging from Tracy's room. Moreover, her heavily reddened lips parted and one hand jerked
automatically upward toward her throat. Then she stepped
outward and backward and her hand dropped just in time
for Stowe to catch sight of a glowing green jewel.

So sure was he that this unknown girl was wearing
Miss Marrender's emerald brooch that he bolted from the
landlady's restraining clutch and made for the street door.

Unfortunately the door opened more stubbornly from within than from without. It delayed him no more than a minute, yet when he reached the street there was no sign of the girl.

There were a dozen places in which she could have sought cover, he concluded and withdrew to a chain grocery on the corner just below. There he established himself in the angle of the display window, where he could watch the dingy length of Burden Street in both directions. For a half hour he consorted with heads of lettuce and bunches of bananas, but he saw nothing of the girl who had so whipped his imagination.

Admitting finally that he was camping on a cold trail, Dick moved on to Mike's Chile Parlor, where Tracy had said he had spent a large part of Tuesday evening. Mike proved to be non-existent, but a bald-headed man named Charlie McGruder, who claimed proprietary responsibility for the bowls of chile and the little back room where the right fellas were always welcome, discoursed cheerfully on the subject of Gene Tracy. When he had finished, Stowe was convinced that Tracy's movements up to midnight could be satisfactorily accounted for.

Sally's Shop was next on Stowe's list, but he took enough time out for a telephone chat with Asher. He wanted somebody to verify the stories of Tracy's fellow players, and he reminded Tim that on Wednesday morning Tracy had found himself with empty pockets, though at the close of the play on Tuesday night, according to Charlie McGruder, he had all the money there was. Also, he submitted a description of the girl he had so momentarily caught sight of at the lodging house and asked that the boys keep their eyes open for her. Lastly, he suggested that Tim drop around to the Stowe apartment about ten that evening for a powwow.

Sally's Shop would be closed for the day, Dick knew, but the girl had told him of her bachelor quarters in the rooms above the littered little place. He found her in and alone. Her snapping wood fire and her cinnamon toast and coffee were inviting, but Dick was conscious of the reserve in her manner.

"I'm going to tell you frankly why I am here, Miss Marrender. You see, I've followed your advice about talking to your cousin Gene Tracy, and in the course of our conversation I made a little agreement with him. He told me what he had done on Tuesday night on the understanding that I should acquire similar information from his other cousins."

There was a little pause. Sally Marrender's square boyish face grew very white. Even the flickering rosy light of the fire could not conceal her pallor. After a minute she spoke, but her voice was unsteady. "So . . . my advice was good, was it?"

"That's a little hard for me to be sure of so soon. I'm—"

"You're here because it's my turn. That's fair enough."

Dick hoped she would go on speaking without waiting for his questions, but she refused to take the initiative. Even after his first direct query she spent some minutes poking the fire before she replied.

"Tuesday night I stepped out with one of the boyfriends. We had dinner at the Decatur and then went dancing at the Golden Roof. We didn't stay there long—the music was particularly rotten. Jim—it was Jimmy Towne I was with. Of course you will want to know that. We came around here and I sent him home right away, because my brother rang me up to say he was coming in. It was after eleven then, but when Bill wants to talk business nothing stands in his way." Her pixielike face crinkled into a sudden smile.

"Whose business were you discussing, his or yours?" asked Dick.

"Oh, mine," she answered without reluctance. "Talk about the strangle hold of family ties. I'm always being told how to run the shop."

"How long was your brother here?"

"We talked till after three or some such ungodly hour, and then I put him up for the rest of the night. I scrambled eggs for his breakfast, which he insisted he must have at eight-forty-five, as usual."

Dick frowned at the fire. His ideas needed rearranging. He was beginning to see the possibility of some astonishing new patterns. "I see, Miss Marrender. . . . You establish your brother's alibi and he yours."

"Bill will tell you the same," she insisted ingenuously. "I have no doubt of that." The level quiet of this acquiescence again drained the color from Sally Marrender's face.

Dick Stowe glanced at his watch elaborately and got to his feet. "I must be on my way. I've a dinner engagement."

This was quite true, although the lady he had in mind was not yet aware of the occasion in store for her. He hurried away from the shop to the lower lobby of the United Utilities Building and watched the descending elevators discharge their loads of clerks and stenographers. At last he saw the girl he wanted.

13
DINNER À DEUX

He stepped forward, hat in hand. "Miss Wilcox?"

The girl he thus addressed turned her head sharply as she heard her name, so sharply that Dick could see her teeth close upon her under lip, an artificially reddened under lip. He saw also that she recognized him.

Yet so diplomatic was he in his opening moves that she agreed to listen to his business with her over a bit of dinner. She herself chose the place, a not too popular grille where their business dress would not matter.

Over the soup Dick confessed that since his chat with the Marrender lawyer a day or two before, he had been given a most interesting commission. The relatives of Miss Eugenia Marrender felt that something ought to be done, in a perfectly quiet way, to unravel the history of the mysterious servant who had in all probability been responsible for the death of their aunt. The man was entirely beyond earthly justice now, but the nieces and nephews would like to know whatever could be found out.

The expression on Janet Wilcox's thin, intelligent face showed undisguised interest but she said very little. It was not until Stowe took a wide chance and told her that Mr. Dexter had suggested that she could be of as much service to him in the matter as William Marrender himself that a

certain reserve melted from her cool grey eyes. They dark-
ened surprisingly, and it occurred to Dick that perhaps she
was relieved to have the talk swing to another member of
the family.

"I've been learning," he led on, "that Cubbage came
to see Mr. Marrender not many days ago. Did he give his
name and business? I gathered the other day that it isn't
a particularly simple process to walk into conference with
Mr. Marrender."

In spite of herself, Janet Wilcox smiled and Dick decided that there was something about the girl that he liked a
whole lot.

"No, he didn't, and it isn't, but while I was trying to
find out his business with Mr. Marrender, it happened
that Mr. Marrender walked out of his inner office, saw this
man, and invited him in."

"Then how did you know the man was Cubbage?"

"I didn't then, but the pictures in the papers since—"

"I see. What was the reason for Cubbage's call? As Marrender's private secretary you might have some idea, you
know. I do hope you are going to be perfectly frank with
me."

She shook her head firmly and broke another roll. "You
couldn't possibly wish more than I that I could answer
that question for you, Mr. Stowe, but—I can't."

Dick labelled that answer ambiguous and went on.
"Were they together long?"

"For nearly an hour. I had to remind Mr. Marrender
that he had an important meeting."

"Did you see Cubbage as he left?"

Janet nodded.

"How did he look?"

"Very smug and self-satisfied, now that I think of it."

They finished their salad and for a minute or two de-
bated desserts. Dick was not satisfied with his progress. He

determined upon a skillful threat. If he judged the girl's intelligence rightly, she would not fail to get his point.

"The Marrenders and the Latimers and the rest of the relatives ought to be very grateful to the crazy old chap for admitting his guilt by suicide. Otherwise—"

He interrupted himself to offer Janet Wilcox his case before lighting a cigarette for himself.

"Thank you, no. I don't smoke," she said impatiently. "Otherwise what?"

"Otherwise it would be the easiest thing in the world for the police to build up a nasty case against Gene Tracy. He himself confesses that he doesn't know what he was doing on Tuesday.

Warily Dick was watching Janet Wilcox. Her eyes dropped, but the hand that lifted her demi-tasse did not tremble. His score was blank for that play.

"When did you learn of Miss Marrender's death?" For an instant hot suspicion flamed in the girl's eyes, but her answer came with level promptness. "There was a telephone call from Mr. Marrender Wednesday morning, just after I reached the office."

"Did he call from his home?" asked Stowe, thinking of Sally's story.

"He must have been at his home, for I recognized the voice of the servant who put through the call. Mr. Marrender never calls a number if there is someone about to do it for him."

"What time did you get this call, Miss Wilcox?"

"It was before nine. I think I came in about a quarter of that morning."

"Did he tell you that his aunt had been murdered?"

"Oh, no. Don't you remember that the newspapers said they didn't know for a while that she had been shot? He just said that he'd had a message that his aunt had died and that he wouldn't be in."

"I certainly appreciate your frankness, Miss Wilcox," said Dick expansively, "and I shall appreciate even more the lack of any spoken curiosity as to the meaning of some of these idiotic questions. You must remember that I am decidedly an amateur sleuth and I canvass a situation rather bluntly, I'm afraid." He paused while the waiter presented the check. "Mr. Marrender knew, of course, that he was to be the executor of his aunt's estate?"

"Mr. Marrender seldom referred to personal or family affairs, but I recall hearing him say one day that he hoped he hadn't let himself in for trouble when he agreed to settle his aunt's estate for her."

"Trouble?" asked Dick alertly.

"The man he was talking to was telling about a family lawsuit . . . that's all." She picked up her gloves and indicated that she was ready to go.

There was no excuse for lingering longer. But not yet had Janet Wilcox given him the lead he had gambled for. He helped her into her coat and suggested a vaudeville programme or the new movie house. He was determined to stick around until the subject of Gene Tracy could be brought out into the open.

But Miss Wilcox insisted that she must return to her rented room, and the only thing that Dick could do was to call a taxi and escort her to a distant suburban address. Even then he loitered hopefully, but Miss Wilcox said good night with such dispatch that he had to admit that he had lost his bet. She had made no further reference, nor allowed him to, to the man in whose room he had found her photograph.

Stowe and his taxi did a double quick back to the apartment, where he came upon Asher pushing the bell just as he stepped into the lower hall of the building. When they had made themselves comfortable in the Stowe living room, not quite at its best without Laura, Dick stretched his long legs and grunted wearily.

"Gosh, Tim, but I'm tired. I've been on the dog-trot all day and I don't think I've turned up anything so hot for all my footwork. Let's just take a little time out and use the good old beano—unless you have something good to spring."

"My report's soon made, Dick. We've traced the nurse to Chicago all right—and lost her. She might as well have jumped into the lake for all. we know. I've got a man watching Tracy's room on Burden Street, but so far nobody's come near it, nobody like that thin red-head you described, I mean. The fellows that played with Tracy Tuesday night all tell the same story. It's straight, I guess. . . . The only thing to the good is that we did what you asked us to—about Cubbage, and I'll say your hunch was damn good. When his hair was washed and the whiskers shaved off, it all showed up pretty plain. Then the doc looked him over again and he says there can't be a doubt. . . . That Cubbage bird was about thirty-five. Can you beat it! He looked fifty— But, I ask you, where does that get us?"

"Where indeed?" Dick murmured obligingly.

"I'm telling you, Dick, it's damn lucky for the department that we can let the case ride. There's a mystery there, but the two people most concerned are dead—"

"The murderer of Cubbage isn't dead."

"Wh-what did you say?" Asher leaned forward, awkward in his surprise.

"Tim, I can't prove a thing, but I can't help feeling that somebody killed Cubbage to keep him from springing something that would have jammed the works for someone else. Maybe after he'd told what he knew he would have killed himself—there's all that dope he was carrying around. But that wasn't the stuff that poisoned him. He could have taken it himself, of course. It acts slowly, re-member. Or somebody else could have given it to him." Dick's head was tilted back and his gaze rested on the ceiling.

"You didn't kill him and I didn't nor Downer," he went on dreamily, "so it must have been Stuart. He was at Wind-ward Hill that night."

"Good night, Dick! You're crazy," Asher exploded. "So was Tracy there, and Marrender, too, almost as long as we were, and Ma Banney—"

"Ruthless, Timmy, ab-so-lutely ruthless—that's you. Stepping all over my nice little theory. But let me tell you one thing, I've gone far enough checking alibis for the whole damn family to see that it would be possible to get every one of them in a hole. As for motive, same thing, though I have to confess I'm a bit hazy about why Sally Marrender is smoke screening big brother Bill—"

Here Asher interrupted with a long whistle that sig-naled a jogged memory. "A hot tip inkled in today, Dick—you should have had it before this. Marrender negotiated a personal loan last Wednesday morning for eighty thou-sand."

"But Wednesday was a bank holiday—"

"That's all right, too. It wasn't exactly a bank loan, see."

"On his prospects as his aunt's heir, I wonder," mused Dick. "And if we were to learn that he offered a fine, old-fashioned emerald as security, it would be bigger and better, wouldn't it, Timmy me lad?" He fumbled with a fresh pack of cigarettes and operated his lighter precisely. Then he wagged his head in exaggerated dejection. "Have it your own way, Tim. Maybe my hunch about the doctor isn't so hot."

"Another thing, Dick—better see Dexter tomorrow about how the family acted when the will was read. Tracy's signed agreement with his aunt turned up with her papers at her bank, so I understand."

Just as Stowe opened his mouth to reply, the telephone blared forth a summons. An official voice wanted to speak to Deputy-Inspector Asher.

All Dick could hear was a series of exclamatory comments, mainly profane, but as soon as Asher had received the report he relayed it to his host.

"It's a gun," Asher began, his voice high with excitement. "We've been tracing .38's—sale, registration, permits, and so on. Guess who bought one about three months ago?" It was a purely dramatic question. "Sally Marrender!" Asher looked almost apologetic as he made the announcement.

Before Dick could slip in a cool "Well, what of it?" Asher went on. "But that's not all. We're tailing Tracy, you know, and the man on the trick reports that Tracy has left the Latimers', where he'd been for dinner, and is heading for an address out in Edgefield. He picked up a girl there and the two of them seem to be headed for Windward Hill."

"What address in Edgefield?" Stowe asked mechanically. He expected the answer he received. It was the address to which he had lately escorted Janet Wilcox.

"Come on," snapped Asher. "Get your hat and let's see what he's up to."

Dick got his hat.

14

Night Scene at Windward Hill

On the way out to Windward Hill Dick Stowe passed on to Asher his knowledge that a girl had been with Tracy at some time during the two days that he had spent in his room on Burden Street. He still thought, he explained, that the girl might be Janet Wilcox, although his test with the cigarette had failed. It was more likely that she was the other and so far unknown girl, the one he had seen so momentarily at the entrance of the rooming house. There had been that tantalizing flash of green at her throat.

Asher grunted with disgust. "Don't spring another missing girl on me, Dick, or—say, maybe this second girl's the nurse. That would be a swell ending, I'll say. She got to Chi, see, and then beat it back here. Let's get a picture of the Randall girl and see if she doesn't look like the one you caught sight of this afternoon."

"Not such a bad idea," agreed Dick absently and let Asher work out its possibilities without further argument.

At the entrance to the drive they left the police car and slipped quietly up the slope toward the dark mass of Windward Hill.

"Tracy and the girl must have used a taxi," Asher whispered, "and Ben trailed in another. He ought to be around somewhere to give me the high sign."

He was. As the two men paused uncertainly at the front of the house, a shadow detached itself from the unbroken darkness and approached them. It was Ben Parks, and he reported that Tracy and the girl had gone in by the front door and were now in the little gallery. He had been keeping an eye on them from without the windows. Asher returned him to that position and said that he and Stowe were going in.

"Just a minute," begged Dick. "I want a look through the gallery windows myself." He rounded the corner of the house at Ben's heels and applied a cautious eye at the place where a pencil of light marked a carelessly drawn curtain. The room was still in the disorder in which it had first been found. In the midst of the confusion stood Eugene Tracy and Janet Wilcox. They were facing one another, a table between them, and they were talking earnestly. It was the girl who was doing most of the talking and it was apparent that Tracy was protesting. He kept shaking his head stubbornly and once he made a peculiarly imploring gesture. But Dick spied no longer than to assure himself that he could hear nothing of what was passing between them.

He rejoined Asher and together they tiptoed down the hall to the door of the little gallery. "You'll get the drift of the show all right," he whispered. "Just follow my lead."

He opened the door. The two within had had no warning. Yet there was no trace of guilty surprise as they whirled to face the two men who filled the doorway. However, Dick was interested in the air of suppressed desperation that he noted in the demeanor of Janet Wilcox. On the other hand, Tracy was remarkably suave and assured.

"In what way," he asked graciously, "may I be of assistance to the police?"

Janet shot a glance of enlightenment at Stowe as Tracy said "police," and Dick knew that his carefully assumed role of the earlier evening had gone by the board.

He replied with equal aplomb. "I confess I'm a bit curious about the reason for this rendezvous."

It was the girl who answered his question. She spoke with deliberate firmness so patently directed to Tracy that Dick promptly interpreted it as a warning to her companion.

"There's no reason why you shouldn't be told. I thought that if we went over everything right here on the spot, he might remember better. I tell him and tell him, but he can't remember—and he's worried. It's not true—what he's afraid of." Her head lifted proudly.

Before the detectives could question her astounding statement Tracy spoke. "What's the use, Janet? I'll tell them why we came out here tonight."

"Gene, dearest, you don't *know*—honestly, you don't!" Impetuously she turned to Stowe. "From what you said this evening I know you have discovered that Gene was— that Gene doesn't know what happened on Tuesday night. But I know and I'm going to tell you, and oh, you must believe me—you must!"

Before the emotion that throbbed in her voice Tracy dropped his head between his hands and groaned. There was a look in the girl's eyes that Stowe felt he had no right to watch. Then she faced him bravely.

"When Gene came back to his room on Tuesday night, I was there waiting for him because I—I thought he might be needing someone who understood. A serious disappointment had just come to him. Those things do knock one out, you know. I persuaded him to go home—out here to this house, I mean. We left his room together and at the corner picked up a taxi. On the way out to Windward Hill I saw my opportunity to be of genuine help to Gene. You see, I knew about that agreement with his aunt and, frankly, I felt that it was grossly unfair. We got inside the house without any trouble. Gene had a key and I used it, and thanks to the thick old-fashioned carpets everywhere we got down the hall without making a sound. The door of this room was bolted on the outside. I got him inside and then—he collapsed. He was in that chair—" she pointed, and Dick saw that her finger did not tremble.

"Just a minute," he interrupted. "Was the room in order at that time?"

"Yes, in perfect order. All I wanted was a key and I thought I knew where to find it—in the drawer of this table. I was searching just as hard and fast as I could, while Gene wasn't noticing, but I couldn't find it. So I started to look through other drawers, but just then I heard something that—that frightened me, and I decided we'd better get out right away."

Again Stowe opened his mouth to ask a question, but Janet Wilcox spoke on so rapidly, and what she said was so amazing that he postponed his intention.

"I rushed over to the door and turned the handle, but it would not open. Someway—somebody had bolted it again on the outside. I thought for a minute we were locked in and then I hurried to the window—that one to the right. It went up at my first push; it wasn't even locked. I made Gene understand that he was to follow me and we both tumbled out and slipped away down the drive. We walked all the way back to Burden Street and I saw Gene safely back in his room. And I know you'll not want to believe that we never saw a soul—it's all of three miles, isn't it? Except a milkman just as we turned into Burden Street. It was after four by that time, but still pitch dark."

Her voice dropped matter-of-factly as if she had come to the end of a normal recital. Asher gave a long whistle of skepticism. Tracy huddled in his place, eyes still downcast. Dick gave the girl a look of genuine friendliness, but his words warned that he did not intend to be misled.

"You can't stop there, you know, Miss Wilcox. There are questions you will have to answer—a lot of questions."

"Yes. I'll do my best."

"Your best truth-telling. First of all, let's clear up the element of time. When you left Tracy's room to come out here, what time was it?"

"A little after midnight," she replied. "Almost too late to be conventional, I know, but conventions don't matter sometimes."

"What taxi service did you use?"

"It was one of Vic's cabs, but I couldn't identify the driver if you tried a million years."

"You say you were looking for a key. What key, and why did you want it?"

It was as if she sighed before she answered. "I'll tell you that, too, though that will probably let me in for more explanations. I was after a key to a safety-deposit box and I intended to use it to do something for Gene, something that he never would have dreamed of doing for himself. Honestly"—here her astounding poise broke for an instant—"honestly, I don't know whether I could have carried it through or not, but just then I thought I could. I—I had to do it for Gene." She spoke as if Gene were not listening to her.

"You mean you were attempting to steal the key to Miss Marrender's safety-deposit box in which she kept her will and other papers of importance." Dick Stowe spoke slowly, as though he were thinking his way along.

"Yes. But I didn't find it, remember."

"Miss Wilcox, how did you know that there was such a key in this room and that its possession would win you—what you wanted for Gene Tracy?"

For a split second the girl's defense was down. She drew a sharp breath, but her answer came patly. Yet something

told Stowe that she had cast about desperately for a necessary lie. "It was something that Gene said to me once. I
can't remember the circumstances."

"And I suppose you had considered the problem of
getting access to Miss Marrender's box? Banks are rather
particular, you know. Your experience as a business man's
private secretary would have taught you that."

Her head nodded in unconscious acquiescence before the
full import of Stowe's comment flared in her eyes. Yet her
spoken answer was delightfully candid. "I must admit that
I hadn't thought that far. It was a quixotic scheme, really."

Dick went smoothly on to another question. "You said
you were interrupted by a sound which frightened you.
What was it and where did it come from?"

Janet Wilcox lifted her head highland looked squarely
into Stowe's face as if quite aware of what her words would
precipitate. "I heard what sounded like a shot in the room
directly above."

"Boy!" muttered Asher, but let Stowe keep his lead.

"And the door had been rebolted from the outside.
. . . What else did you hear? Surely there must have been
some other suspicious sound," Stowe demanded in growing
excitement.

"Not a sound. I swear it. Anywhere. Neither before nor
after the shot. Except the wind. It was a rough night."
Janet's tense accents whipped the skepticism of the men
facing her.

Asher yielded first. "Thick carpets everywhere, Dick,"
he offered.

"See here," barked Dick, "what time was it when you
heard the shot?"

"I—I don't know. I didn't look at my watch."

"But you must have reached Windward Hill by
twelve-thirty. How long had you been in this room before
you heard the shot?"

She shook her head in confessed helplessness. "I don't know. It couldn't have been long, though. I had just looked in the one drawer."

"More or less than an hour?" Dick suggested in brisk helpfulness.

"Oh, less—certainly."

"I see." Dick looked as if something had clicked neatly. "And the window was unlocked through which you left this room. Did you close it after you?"

The girl shook her head as if pleased that again a detail presented itself about which she could be exact. "No, I remembered when we got down to the road that I had left the window open. I was sorry—I thought of the curtain flapping out, but it was too late to go back."

"Isn't it strange that it took you at least three hours to walk back to Burden Street?"

She glanced significantly at Tracy, but made no specific answer.

"You have told me that you had persuaded Tracy to return to Windward Hill, his home. You escorted him yourself, with some difficulty, I can imagine. I can understand, too, why you entered the house so surreptitiously. You wanted the chance to search this room. Well, then, granted that you were frightened away, as you have just told me, why didn't you march around to the front door after you had crawled through the window, ring the bell, and deliver Tracy to Cubbage? Eventually he would have answered the bell."

Janet nodded in alert agreement. "I wish I had, Mr. Stowe."

"Instead you were taking a three-hour stroll toward Burden Street. What did you do after that?"

She gave an embarrassed little laugh. "I went to the railway station and pretended I was waiting for the 5:10 train. Fortunately it was an hour late. I managed a nice nap."

That part of the girl's story was true Stowe had no more doubt than that some of it was the purest fabrication. But he could not be sure which was which. . . . For instance, if Janet Wilcox were telling the truth about the time, then Francesca Penrose and Galeotti were lying. He'd been rather banking on the actress's story, too. According to it, at two o'clock the windows were unlocked but closed, and Francesca had closed them after her when she left. According to Janet, no later than one-thirty the right-hand window had been left wide open. Certainly something didn't hitch, but the discrepancy was one that could be nailed down eventually. What was much more interesting to Dick Stowe was the hypnotic way in which Eugene Tracy had listened to the girl's narrative. Tracy had been drunk on Tuesday night. That was a fact no one had denied at any point. And yet—if he had walked through the coldest hours of a February night, his mind could scarcely have been a blank at the end of the three miles, no matter how addled he might have been at the beginning. Stowe was just on the verge of calling attention to that fact when he had what he was later to describe to his wife as the inspiration of a lifetime.

Shifting his position so that he could watch the faces of both Janet and Tracy, he put his question. "Since you were the woman who was with Tracy through certain hours of Tuesday night, why haven't you mentioned the emerald?"

Stowe's deliberate reference to a woman's being with Tracy got under the guard of Janet Wilcox, just as he had anticipated, but it was the queer look of enlightenment that flashed momentarily into Tracy's eyes that the detective found most satisfying. It was his mention of the emerald that had called out that look. Equally plain was the girl's blank ignorance. The Marrender emerald meant nothing to Janet Wilcox.

A sound at the doorway wherein Asher had been lounging broke the tension. The three within the room whirled
simultaneously just in time to see Asher leap backward
into the gloom of the hall. They could hear his feet thudding down the passage. A door banged with a crash. Their
own scene forgotten, the three huddled in the doorway for
an instant and then Tracy and Stowe hurried after Asher.
They were just in time to see him burst through the door
of the room at the far end of the dark corridor—Cubbage's
room. Sounds of struggle followed; then Tim Asher's high
voice rose triumphantly.

"Leggo yourself. I got you now, you young devil!"

15

ANOTHER PAIR OF GLOVES

It was Tracy who found the switches and flooded the hall and the butler's room with light. At that moment Ben Parks came panting upon the scene. The sudden exodus from the little gallery had been too much for the curiosity of the sentinel posted without.

Asher was sitting on the edge of the bed and almost upon the writhing figure of a slight youth. The lithe form squirmed mightily and achieved a sitting position, though Asher's hands were still firmly gripped upon his wrists. He shook his dark hair out of his eyes and gazed defiantly at the group that had followed Asher into the room. They in turn stared in amazement and well they might, for it was the face of Sally Marrender that they looked upon.

The hypnotic lethargy that had gripped Tracy throughout the scene in the little gallery had disappeared. He was now the first one to speak. "Sally, Sally, you weren't expected, you know."

Asher chanced his recognition of the name and released his hold. The girl slipped to her feet and shook herself. They could all see now that it was the riding clothes that had given the impression that Asher had captured a boy. Never had Sally Marrender's square brown face looked more stubborn. Her eyes glowered at them from beneath the straight black brows.

To Asher the prolonged silence demanded explanation. "I heard a noise in the kitchen and then I saw something slide across the hall down there and into this room. Ghost or no ghost, thought I, here I go. Whoever it was banged the door smack in my face and tried to hold it shut, but I've still got my strength. I burst in and the two of us had a little set-to before the round ended in my favor."

Tracy continued to eye his cousin speculatively, or so it seemed to Stowe. Ignoring Asher's explanation, Tracy again addressed the girl. "What did you come for, Sally?" he asked softly.

"To do a kind deed. Can't you see I'm a boy scout in disguise?" The words came flippantly, yet Dick wondered just what she was trying to tell her cousin.

"Did it have to be done in this room?" he asked.

"No," she said, and her voice had lost its first note of defiant fright. "I merely intended to lie by until I had the house to myself. I didn't expect you either, you see."

"Does our presence still embarrass you?" Tracy persisted.

"I'm afraid it does. In all likelihood the kind deed will be postponed indefinitely."

Stowe stepped forward with authority. "Miss Marrender, will you tell me what brought you here tonight?"

"I will not." The answer was insolent.

"Tracy, what do you know about your aunt's emerald?" The cool way in which Stowe swung his investigation from the angry girl to her cousin amazed them all. Tracy's answer was equally astonishing.

"Not a damn thing—that I'll tell you."

"Miss Wilcox,"—the girl's gasp of dismay was pitiful—"did you strike any matches while you were in the little gallery?"

She shook her head dumbly; then her stiff lips managed to say, "No, I lighted the lamp on the table."

Dick was like a teacher giving out words to a row of spellers. "Miss Marrender, were you by any chance coming to look for this?" He tossed a small object to her which she caught adroitly. Her mouth tightened as she bent over it. The others could not see what it was she held cupped in her hands, though Asher and Ben Parks were in grave danger of a general dislocation.

"Thanks a lot," murmured Sally. "How clever of you to guess what I wanted." The hand that held the spoil plunged deep into the pocket of her tweed coat.

"Tracy, to what extent can you verify the story Miss Wilcox has been telling us?"

"To what extent can you accept the word of a man who was as far under as I was on that occasion?" The counter question did not trouble Stowe. He turned gravely to Janet Wilcox.

"Why did you wait until tonight to search for that key? The contents of Miss Marrender's safety-deposit box were examined this afternoon when the family lawyer read the will."

"Oh!" she gulped and her lips trembled in agony. Her lie had gone for nothing.

Again Stowe faced Sally Marrender, who was now regarding him with growing respect. "How do you explain the fact that the guest who breakfasted with you on Wednesday morning held a telephone conversation—two telephone conversations, I suspect—from his own home at approximately the same hour that the eggs were being scrambled?"

Again Sally's square, wholesome face lost all of its natural color. Yet her answer came bravely. "Then I must have reported the time very inaccurately to you."

Eugene Tracy was awaiting his next question with ill-concealed nervousness. Perhaps for that reason Stowe spaced his words deliberately. "Suppose it should become gravely necessary for Miss Wilcox to establish an alibi for herself. How could you help her?"

"I'd move heaven and earth to give you the surprise of your life." The reply came like a challenge.

"Miss Wilcox, are you sure you don't smoke?" He smiled at Janet as he spoke.

The question sounded so easy. . . . "To tell you the truth, I've never even experimented."

"Where's your gun, Miss Marrender—that .38 that's on the permit records?"

"On the shelf just below my cash register in the shop," she answered and there was a disconcerting lilt in her voice.

Dick aimed his fourth question at Tracy with an oblique eye upon Janet Wilcox. "If Miss Wilcox's story was the truth, then you can scarcely deny that when you returned to your room on Burden Street early Wednesday morning after a longish walk through the cold, you must have been sufficiently your own man to know what was going on?"

Janet awaited Tracy's answer with clenched fists. When it came it did not completely satisfy her. "No doubt, no doubt," he returned airily, "but I promptly lost all that I had gained. I think you understand me."

"What is your theory, Miss Wilcox, to account for the disappearance of the money that Mr. Tracy had won at Mike's that Tuesday evening?"

For the life of him Dick Stowe could not be sure whether this was the first time the girl had heard of Tracy's empty pockets. Her reply he judged another valiant attempt to fend danger from the man she loved. "Maybe he dropped it on our way back, or perhaps someone robbed him during the next day. What has the money to do with this, anyway?"

"Exactly my own attitude," murmured Dick. Imperturbably he swung once more toward Sally Marrender.

Without warning, the girl who was Marrender's secretary and who loved Gene Tracy, began to sob—a long, shuddering, tearless sobs that bespoke intolerable strain.

At that Sally Marrender stormed into action. "Mr. Stowe, you probably know what you're doing, but we don't. We've been idiots to answer your questions—anything we say may be used against us. Isn't that the litany? Now let me make you a proposal. Maybe the others will want to make it hold for themselves too. Before I answer another one of your questions, will you answer one that I shall put to you?"

"Why, certainly, Miss Marrender." Dick regarded the girl narrowly.

Tracy frowned but said nothing. Janet's choking sobs continued.

"Here's my question, Mr. Stowe: How did this article come into your possession?" Sally's hand still hidden in her coat pocket indicated what she meant.

"I found it in the upper hall of this house," he answered promptly.

"Thank you. Now, Gene, use your head." Her terse words might have conveyed a warning.

Tracy flashed his cousin a wry smile and launched his query. It landed with a jolt. "Stowe, have you seen my aunt's emerald?"

"I'm afraid I can't give you a positive answer, Tracy, but I can tell you that I suspect I have seen it."

Stowe's reply brought out a look of decision upon Tracy's thin face. He bent tenderly towards Janet. "Haven't you a question you'd like to ask the detective, dear?"

During the question and answer that had passed between the two men the shaken girl had forced herself to a measure of control. Again Stowe was convinced that the references to the emerald were wholly mystifying to Janet Wilcox. Now in answer to Tracy she faltered out her question, "Are—are you going to arrest Gene?"

Sally watched the girl in quick sympathy, as did the police officials, yet they were all conscious that Tracy's shamed eyes had dropped.

"Not until I have direct proof that he was concerned with the shooting of Eugenia Marrender or with the theft of some of her property." He paused a long minute after his grave answer while his eyes rested first on one and then on another of the three strained faces that watched his so closely. "And now I shall tell you frankly what I intend to do. I have learned certain things tonight which I shall follow up in my own way—follow to their inevitable end, whatever that may be. In the meantime, if any of you conclude that it would be the better course for you to assist me with more frankness than you have given me tonight, I shall expect you to come to me. If not, then sooner or later you may each expect me to come to you—and I can't promise you that it will be a particularly happy moment. That's all for tonight, as far as I am concerned. I'm going to ask one of the boys here to see you each home. I don't advise further conferences with one another. They might be overheard, you know."

"I came out in my own car," snapped Sally, who plainly did not like the idea of an official escort.

"Excellent," beamed Dick. "The four of you can go back in it and Asher and I will follow in the police car a little later. If you will tell Ben where to find it, he'll bring it around.

"Scarcely." Sally's, laugh was short. "It's down on the river road and it would take a good half hour to come around to the drive. If you'd handcuff us together we might get down the path without attempting to escape."

"Don't be silly," drawled Tracy. "Stowe's no bonehead. You girls get along down with your chaperon. Stowe will take me down himself, if he wants to, but first I have something I want to whisper in his shell-like ear. . . ."

Don't worry, Janet, I'm not going to confess to anything yet."

Sally Marrender turned briskly toward the kitchen exit, but as she passed Stowe she managed to inform him through her teeth, "I'm keeping it. See me tomorrow."

Janet stumbled after her, casting Stowe an imploring look as she did so. At the outer door she paused and called back in a tight, determined voice, "Gene, remember—" The door banged shut.

Tracy's slender hand was eloquent as he indicated the unseen speaker. "Don't hound that girl, Stowe. God knows I don't deserve what she's trying to do for me, but I can't let her in for anything like this. All I can say now is that I swear to you I don't know how she could possibly have hit on the line that she tried to hand you tonight. . . . Wait a minute, out there, I'm coming."

Tracy disappeared in the darkness and Asher slipped after him and trailed the party down the dim path that led to the River Road. When he had seen them on their way back to town in Sally Marrender's car escorted by Parks, he came back to Windward Hill. He knew that Dick would be waiting for him. He found him in the front hall gloomily surveying the little gallery.

"Well, Timmie me lad, what did you think of my third degree? It was quite my own invention."

"Yeah? Maybe you think it got you somewhere." There was nothing rapier-like about Asher's repartee.

"But I've got myself somewhere. Look here. . . ."

Tim Asher looked. He saw Stowe pull from his pocket a limp pair of gloves.

"They're a woman's gloves, Tim, and they're marked K.M.L. And I found 'em just now—this will be the cue for your department to hang its head—I found 'em in the pocket of Cubbage's overcoat between his own not quite shabby pig-skin mittens."

"What of it, huh? What do you say the Marrender kid planted 'em tonight? You told me yourself she was kind of catty about the doctor and Mrs. Latimer. But if Parks or Downer slipped up on a thing like that, they ought to be broke for it."

"Sorry, Tim, I don't think they were planted. Listen here. . . ."

Tim Asher listened.

". . . so that's why I gave the impression that there would be nobody here the rest of the night. You and I will now make ourselves as comfortable as possible on the chance that the kid will come back."

But the black hours ticked by till morning and the old house on the hill let slip no more secrets.

16

THE DEAD HAND OF CUBBAGE

The two men stepped into position the next morning as snappily as though the trap they had watched throughout the night had yielded them the spoil they had hoped for. Stowe's first move was determined for him by a telephone call which came just as he was entering Headquarters.

A voice which he at once recognized as Janet Wilcox's informed him politely that Mr. William Marrender wished to see him at his office at once, if convenient. Dick replied that he would be there within fifteen minutes and admitted to himself that the girl had her points. In transmitting her employer's message she had given no sign that they had shared an amazing evening.

When he entered the Marrender suite and the secretary stepped forward as if to inquire his business—the not-to-be-counted-upon Bettina was fortunately still gossiping at the water cooler—she made it yet plainer that what had happened the night before was not to be referred to in any way. Which did not displease Dick Stowe.

Two minutes later Stowe had entered Marrender's private office. He faced the man with interest, aware that this was the only one of Miss Marrender's relatives with whom he had not talked, and he noted the man's powerful shoulders and the brutal line of his jaw. Then his attention was commanded by what Marrender was saying.

"I understand that you are the brains behind the local authorities in their so-called investigation of the death of my aunt. Dexter tells me you know your business, but— why haven't you talked matters over with me?"

Stowe's answer was suave, and he gave no sign that he observed the pen point that was being jabbed viciously into the expanse of blotter beneath Marrender's hand. "Frankly, because certain lines that demanded immediate investigation did not lead to you. Then came the butler's suicide—self-explanatory, in a sense. Nor did I consider yesterday the occasion to intrude. I assure you, I should have presented myself today."

Marrender nodded jerkily. "So you people are satisfied with the butler theory, are you?"

"It satisfies the public. Also the relatives of the dead woman."

"What do you mean by that?" Marrender's words leaped savagely.

"If Cubbage did not commit suicide, he was murdered. If he was murdered, he did not kill your aunt. If he did not kill your aunt, he knew who did. If he knew that, he knew too much for someone's peace of mind." Stowe spoke with deliberation, his eyes fixed intently on the man opposite him.

"You don't know?"

"Not yet."

"In that case—"

"Don't misunderstand me," interrupted Stowe. "I know that Miss Marrender's death prevented her from changing her will. I know that you, for instance, within a few hours after her death arranged to borrow a not inconsiderable sum for some unknown personal use. I know that you might find it difficult to establish your alibi for the hours of that night. I know that you were at Windward Hill late enough the next night to have administered to Cubbage the dose that killed him. Those are some of the items that I know which affect you personally." The friendly warmth in Stowe's voice would have done credit to the fulsome close of a eulogy. He gave no indication of the risk he was well aware he was running.

There was a long moment of silence. The only sound was the muted jangle of office machinery from the other side of the third vice-president's closed door. Like a hawk Dick was reading the emotions that shifted over Marrender's jutting face. It was not until a faint flicker of humor lighted his torpid eyes that Dick's secret tension relaxed.

"I conclude," Marrender said at last. "That you would not have said what you have if you really thought me guilty of either death. For that back-handed expression of confidence—I thank you." He laughed abruptly. "You say you know this and that detail which might conceivably embarrass me. Go ahead, young man, go ahead. I want you to understand this: as head of the Marrender family I hereby instruct you to follow any clues you may have, no matter where nor to whom they may lead. I stand willing this minute to answer any questions you may wish to put to me."

"Thank you, Mr. Marrender. Your attitude is very fine," replied Stowe, adding to himself, "and I'm finding out right now whether or not you're bluffing." Then aloud once more, "I should like to know about the loan."

Before Stowe could go on Marrender began to speak. "You're barking up the wrong tree, if you're thinking of that as a possible motive. The facts are these: arrangements that had been in the making for a week or more happened to culminate on the afternoon following my aunt's death. There was no possible connection."

"But your present position as one of the heirs to a large fortune must have facilitated those arrangements."

"If so, it was an attitude over which I had no control," Marrender countered blandly. Then he hunched himself

forward across the desk. "See here, Stowe, I'd like to convince you that I'm playing straight with you. I shall go as
far as to tell you that I had tried to borrow the money I
needed from my aunt. She refused pointblank. Now make
what you can of that."

"Therefore I'm barking up the wrong tree. Q. E. D.,"
murmured Dick. "Your sister was in your confidence in
this matter, was she not?"

"To some extent," Marrender admitted grudgingly.

"On Tuesday night you were working here in this
office. It was after ten when you left, and from here you
went around to your sister's apartment. Where did you go
from there?"

"We talked so late—my sister is quite a competent business woman, you understand—that she put me up there
for the rest of the night."

"Were you still there or at your own home when you
received word that Miss Marrender had died during the
night?"

"At my own house," Marrender answered as promptly as
Dick expected him to do. "I went around bright and early
Wednesday morning. Sally never eats breakfast, but I like
my meals."

"I'm right with you there." Dick's laugh was genial,
though the reason for that Marrender would not have
found particularly comforting if he had been aware of it.

Apparently the very fact that the young detective was
not subjecting him to a rigid catechism was beginning to
have its inevitable effect. For a space the blotter under
his hand was again viciously attacked by his pen. Then he
spoke. "About Cubbage, Stowe—you must be wrong there.
The man was a mental case, absolutely. Delusions of grandeur and all that rot. Let me tell you something. . . ."

Distinctly to Dick's surprise, Marrender plunged
straightway into an account of the visit that Cubbage had

paid him earlier in the week, the one Janet Wilcox had already reported to him. "He came in here last Monday afternoon—said he must see me. I recognized him but thought he had come up to relay some sort of message from my aunt. But when I got him in here, all he did was sit and stare at me. Of course, I couldn't let him take my time like that and so after a decent interval I suggested that if he couldn't remember what he had come for, he might just as well run along. That seemed to be all right with him—he walked out as quiet as a lamb, but, my word, he just about gave me the heebie-jeebies—the wild look in his eyes."

Stowe listened in silence. Marrender's story lapped perfectly with what Janet had told him, except for one detail. She had said that the two men were together for the best part of an hour. He decided to chance the question. "How long was he with you before you told him to go?"

"We-ell, maybe I can't hit that exactly. There was some work lying on my desk and until his half-cracked manner got on my nerves, I kept at that, and perhaps the time went faster than I thought."

"Mr. Marrender, do you call behavior like that delusions of grandeur?"

"Used the wrong word, eh? All I meant was that the chap acted damn queer. I don't know another thing about him, but I've always had a feeling that he hadn't started out as a handy man. He could sling the language like a blurb writer and all that. It seems to me he'd be just the type to go off his nut and kill someone."

"I agree, Mr. Marrender, that almost everything in connection with these deaths at Windward Hill could be satisfactorily explained on the basis of Cubbage's guilt, and yet—well, we must hear the nurse's story before we close the case. For instance, I'd like to know what she knows about the missing emerald brooch."

Marrender's eyebrows shot upward in interrogation. "Do you mind telling me, Stowe, just how you knew that my aunt possessed such a jewel and how you learned that it was missing? I understood that she had sold it some years ago."

"A member of your family told me she saw the stone not many days before your aunt's death. Asher and I failed to find it in the place where it had been secreted."

"Who told you this?"

"Miss Penrose. Miss Marrender had shown her the brooch the last time she called on her aunt."

Marrender started to say something which he choked back. His second effort brought, "Yes, no doubt the nurse must have known where it was. But it strikes me as rather strange that my aunt made no mention of the emerald in her will."

"It's possible that Miss Marrender intended at the time she drew her will to sell the stone, as she had told some of you, but for some reason changed her mind—but not her will," suggested Stowe.

"Perhaps that is the explanation," agreed Marrender. For a minute or two he played nervously with the pen in his hand. Then he leaned across the desk and addressed his caller with a new earnestness. "I've already begun to regret what I said to you a few minutes ago. About following your clues, no matter where they led. . . I'm regretting it for the sake of one of my cousins. . . . I suppose I must be candid. Well, then—"

But there was an awkward pause. Dick waited in polite silence.

"It is quite likely," resumed Marrender at length, "that you have already discovered that my cousin Mrs. Latimer is a highly neurotic woman. I shall go further than that and say—an extremely erotic woman. She and her husband have never been particularly happy together, but Harris Latimer has an unusual antipathy, for a non-religious man, for divorce. That coupled with his extraordinary patience has saved us from scandal more than once. Don't think that I enjoy exhibiting a family skeleton, Stowe, I must tell you this to keep you from stirring up a particularly hideous mess. Mrs. Latimer's name is already linked with Dr. Stuart's among the gossips. If your investigation should give the slightest opening in his direction, her name would inevitably be dragged in. I beg you, let your discreetest judgment guide you."

There was a stiff, artificial cast to Marrender's final words, of which Stowe was quite conscious. "What you have just told me," he replied, "verified a rumor I had already picked up concerning Mrs. Latimer and Dr. Stuart. Also, I happen to know . . . the doctor and Mrs. Latimer were together until quite late on Tuesday night."

Marrender frowned and looked worried. He leaned still closer to the detective. "My cousin told me about that. I see I have no choice now but to repeat her story to you. She had been somewhere or other with Stuart that evening. They were on their way home in his motor. It was rather late, I dare say. They had some unforeseen trouble with the car at a particularly inconvenient spot and were delayed for several hours. She told me all about it on our way out to Windward Hill the other day. But she seemed to have no idea of the—unpleasant position she might find herself in if she were asked to account for herself during those hours."

Stowe said nothing in so pointed a manner that Marrender's eyes shifted restlessly and in a moment he added, "I mention that circumstance to show you how embarrassing matters might be for my cousin if—anything should lead you to—er—to a too hasty conclusion."

"Ah," murmured Dick in tones of agreement and rose to go. He had accumulated a dozen fascinating possibilities that he wanted to rush right after. But Marrender put out a restraining hand. At the same instant the door opened and Janet Wilcox appeared.

"Has another mail come in?" he asked his secretary.

"I have it here, Mr. Marrender." Janet Wilcox laid a neat stack of opened letters upon the desk and withdrew. Dick could see that on the top of the unfolded sheets were several envelopes whose flaps had merely been slit.

"Just one minute, Stowe—" As he spoke Marrender picked up the envelopes and immediately stiffened with curiosity. "By the Lord Harry, that's Cubbage's handwriting!"

No need now to beg Dick Stowe to linger. Marrender jerked the letter out of its envelope and flipped it open. Together the men read it.

> *"This is to inform you all that dead men tell no tales. May the living as well as the dead rest in peace.*
>
> *"J. C."*

"Crazy—crazy as a bedbug!" Marrender's voice was tinged with disgust.

"You're sure this is Cubbage's writing?" barked Dick, scrutinizing envelope and letter sheet.

"It's like bits of his writing I've seen from time to time—but then, I'm no expert."

"But, see here!" Dick's excitement was growing. "Cubbage would have had to write and mail this some time on Wednesday. He was dead at getting up time on Thursday. This thing's postmarked Thursday night, see. You should have received it yesterday morning."

"Maybe I did, at that. I wasn't in yesterday. The funeral, you know." He buzzed for his secretary. "When did this letter come in, Miss Wilcox?"

Judicially the girl looked at the envelope. There could be no doubt that she remembered something about it, for it was on flimsy paper, hand written in very black ink, and marked "personal."

"Yesterday afternoon," she answered slowly, and gave Stowe a long level look. "On the last delivery."

"Keep this to yourself, Marrender," commanded Stowe and strode to the door. "I'm taking care of this," and he tucked the letter into his pocket.

This time William Marrender made no effort to detain his caller. He recognized that urgent action was afoot. But the palms of his hands were clammy with sweat. . . .

Dick Stowe reached the corridor just in time to miss a down-going elevator. He jabbed the bell impatiently, but the next down car went on without him because by that time he had darted back to beckon imperiously, to Janet Wilcox. "Answer just one question," he directed. "When Cubbage was with Marrender the other afternoon, could you hear them talking together? The sound of their voices, I mean?"

"Yes," she said, and her voice was cold and even. "Yes, they talked steadily all the time he was there."

"Thanks. That's all I wanted to know." And Dick hurried off. He wanted to see Dexter and Katherine Latimer and Sally Marrender and Dr. Stuart and Gene Tracy, and he hardly knew which pull to answer first.

17

CONFIDENTIAL TALK WITH MRS. LATIMER

As it happened, wisely he went first to the office of the postmaster. There was something significant, he was beginning to think, in the appearance of two letters from dead hands. The coincidence was remarkable, or else—and this was what he really hoped—somebody was overplaying his hand.

Dexter's letter had been written by the nurse at the direction of her patient. There was no reason to doubt this. If it had been posted in the box nearest to Windward Hill later than four-twenty in the afternoon, it would not have been collected until the next morning. However, Wednesday had been a legal holiday, always punctiliously observed by the postal authorities. Dick had already informed himself that the box near Windward Hill was scheduled for no collections on holidays. That would account, therefore, for the letter not reaching Dexter until Thursday.

The first letter was in all probability bona fide. Before he could be as certain about the one this minute in his pocket he had a few questions to ask someone.

Within the next ten minutes, accordingly, he was told that every day brought in its quota of letters addressed to the postmaster which were only covers for other letters which their unknown writers wished to go forward with greater anonymity. It was a nuisance, surely, but when these enclosed letters were properly addressed and stamped, what could be done? Furthermore, the envelope with its heavy black superscription in which Marrender's letter had arrived was recognized by one of the mail clerks consulted. It had gone through his hands the day before.

Yet when Stowe endeavored to trace the letter further he came against a dead end. The letter might have first arrived in its covering envelope Friday or Thursday. Mail addressed like that never commanded immediate attention. However, the civil servant promised faithfully to see if the janitorial force could trace the basket that had held the discarded envelopes.

If the envelope should be found, if it bore the same heavy black writing, then Dick might learn where and when it had originally been mailed, a point upon which he had to be certain. If the letter had been mailed after Cubbage died, then somebody else might demonstrably have written it, and that somebody else would be a most necessary person to uncover. If it was genuinely Cubbage's epistle, then Dick agreed heartily with William Marrender—Cubbage was as crazy as a bedbug.

Dick dropped in at Headquarters again long enough to supplement his string of directions to Asher, and to ask if anything had come in about the missing nurse. Nothing had. Then he hurried around to the office of Bartholomew Dexter.

His business there did not take long, for he found the fussy little man more amenable than before. He gave Stowe a clear account of the reading of the will the afternoon before, and was willing to be as endlessly detailed as the detective desired. Certain points Dick found particularly interesting. Francesca Penrose had not been present, her professional duties interfering. Eugene Tracy had not appeared until after the will had been read but before the contents of Miss Marrender's safety-deposit box were checked over. Among the various articles contained in said box was the agreement drawn up between Tracy and his aunt.

That last item Dick found especially stimulating, though he made no comment to the lawyer. That agreement was certainly not the reason for the turmoil in the little gallery. Still, if Tracy and Janet hadn't known that it was not there, that might have been the reason for—no, it couldn't have been. . . . Tracy knew that the document had come to light that afternoon! What in thunder was the reason for their late visit to the little gallery the night before?

Dick dragged his attention back to Dexter, who droned on about presenting the will for probate and added that since the one cousin was not included in the division of the estate, he personally greatly admired the spirit shown by William Marrender, who suggested to the other heirs that the modest pension heretofore paid Tracy by their aunt should be continued jointly by the others. The proposal had been opposed first by Tracy himself, quite naturally, and also by Mrs. Latimer, who showed the strain of the recent events quite sadly, in Dexter's opinion. Miss Sara Marrender said nothing at all, he concluded, and as Miss Penrose was not present, nothing definite was done.

"What's to become of Windward Hill?" asked Stowe, edging toward the door.

"It is to be sold and the proceeds will establish a series of scholarships in a denominational college in which Miss Marrender was always much interested," explained Dexter. "And that reminds me—you should be informed of this contretemps. The will specifically reminds Eugene Tracy that he is entitled to whatever he wishes that is in the little gallery. In due order he stated to me in the presence of the others that there was nothing at all in the room that he wished. Unfortunately, Mrs. Latimer again lost control of herself and accused him of having already overhauled the apartment. In considerable indignation Tracy left the conference."

"Yet he dined at the Latimer house last night. I wonder . . ." He took an abrupt departure, leaving Dexter murmuring vaguely. Lindenwood must be the next stopping place.

Dick Stowe was rather glad that another maid admitted him when he reached the Latimer house, a maid who mumbled something about Mrs. Latimer's being unable to see anyone just then. Dick flashed a badge and the girl scuttled off. He slipped along at her heels. She had no more than gulped out, "But it's a policeman, honest to Gawd, Miss Latimer," than he stepped into the lady's boudoir.

"Awfully sorry and all that to intrude like this, but it's tremendously important, as you shall see," he explained with portentous gravity when she had waved the maid out of the room.

Upon Stowe's unexpected appearance Katherine Latimer had half risen from a great fire-side chair, the soft fur rug thrown across her knees clutched in one hand. He was aware that she had assumed a forced nonchalance but that she was also taking his measure with practiced feminine eyes.

"Really, Mr. Stowe, I was just about to give you a ring— to report about those two times I had seen Cubbage, you know. Not that it matters now, since the poor fellow has done himself in."

For the moment Dick permitted her to think that was indeed the chief object of his call. He produced a notebook and poised his pencil expectantly.

"It was the 26th of January that I thought I saw him out at that grubby place in the west end. The place was run by a woman named Quinn. Had I told you that? And the little party for Lothrop occurred on the 9th of December." She finished with a quick breath.

"Who gave the party?"

"Of course I'll tell you, Mr. Stowe, but I must ask you to be careful about involving others in our personal and private affairs." She spoke as if from a great height.

Stowe assured her with appropriate meekness.

"The host was Dr. Vincent Rhand," she then pronounced.

"Name some of the other guests, please."

She sighed patiently. "It's been rather a long time, you know. The usual crowd from the Arts and Letters Club, of course, and the doctor's sister—"

"Dr. Stuart's sister?"

"No, he didn't get there—he hasn't a sister—I mean, Miss Bessie Rhand, of course. My cousin Gene Tracy was there, too." She checked herself hurriedly, but she was aware that she had made a slip about Stuart's name. Stowe followed it up.

"Was the man who looked like Cubbage there when you arrived?"

"No, I don't believe he was. As I recall it, I didn't observe him until I was thinking of leaving, and then I looked about for Gene, meaning to call his attention to the strange resemblance, but by that time Gene had gone."

"That reminds me, Mrs. Latimer, of something Bartholomew Dexter intimated to me this morning. I hope you will answer me frankly. Why did you object to the proposal that Mr. Marrender made yesterday concerning the continued payment of Tracy's so-called pension?"

Katherine Latimer leaned toward him with an air of worried confidence. "Indeed, I do intend to be frank with you. It may be a beastly thing for me to say, but I know myself well enough to realize that my nerves are going to torture me until I share my hideous suspicion with some-body! It must have been Gene who went through the little gallery that night." Her voice sank appropriately and her eyes misted with tears.

"What makes you think that, dear lady?" Stowe knew exactly what he was doing when he so addressed Katherine Latimer. It had just the effect he had anticipated.

"If I tell you that, I shall have to trust you very, very much indeed," she murmured and stretched out a beseech-ing hand. "But I do trust you—oh, infinitely. But first, you people of the police are satisfied that it was Cubbage who shot poor Aunt Eugenia? I mean I'd never breathe a word of this if I thought you'd try to implicate Gene in the murder, too. I myself am quite convinced that he could have had nothing at all to do with that. He could have had no motive, for one thing. His agreement with Aunt Euge-nia came to light, as you know. With that in existence he had nothing to gain one way or another."

If Dick Stowe found Katherine Latimer's exegesis of Tracy's motive for murder sounding rather patly memorized, he gave no sign. Instead he agreed with no audible reser-vations that Cubbage most certainly must have been guilty of the killing of Miss Marrender. And he was just ever so happy to think that she trusted him so implicitly. . . .

"I want to tell you, really I do. My conscience will be clear, though a wee bit embarrassed, I must confess. But it's much better to be straightforward about things, isn't it, than to have them pop out later and perhaps compro-mise one." She fluttered appealingly. "And so I have decid-ed that I'd rather be embarrassed now than compromised later."

She paused to offer Dick another cigarette. Encouraged by his quick sympathetic smile, she went on. "You see, on Tuesday evening, rather late, I'm afraid, I went for a little airing with a friend. I've been sleeping so wretchedly this winter and my doctor prescribed motoring. In fact, I happened to be with my doctor on that evening."

There was just a hint of a side-long glance as this coy admission came out, but Dick was blind.

"It was a glorious night, really, wild and stormy. I mean the way the wind blew. Perhaps you remember? It stimulated me, intoxicated me. And then, just as we were on the home stretch, what do you think? We had a break-down—some sort of obscure engine trouble. Dr. Stuart is awfully clever with machinery and all that, but nothing did any good. At last he decided that he'd have to go for help.

"It was while he was gone that the thing happened that I feel I just must tell you about. I forgot to say that we were on the River Road just below Windward Hill, as it happened. Maybe you've found out—detectives see everything, don't they?—that there is a rocky little path that leads from the back of Aunt Eugenia's place down to the River Road. I huddled in the car alone, and scared to death, though I knew there was a—though I wouldn't have admitted that to the doctor for worlds."

She smiled frankly into Stowe's eyes and continued. "All at once I distinctly heard footsteps crashing down the path, stumbling and running, you know. It was ever so dark, but in a minute a shadow lurched out into the road and began to run toward town. As the figure passed the car, I recognized Gene—I mean, I'm almost certain it was Gene. There's something about the way he swings his shoulders, you know. . . ." Her-voice trailed off. "If you only knew how I loathe myself for telling you," she sighed.

But in a moment she went heroically on. "Not knowing what was happening at Windward Hill, I really thought very little of it—until the next day, and since then it's worried me—oh, dreadfully. At first I decided to say nothing about it—you recall I told you I had no theory about the looting of the little gallery."

Stowe, the perfect confidant, nodded gravely. Sympathy vibrated in his voice as he asked, "Did you tell Dr.
Stuart about your experience when he returned?"

"Yes, and he said he had passed a man about a half mile
below, but he hadn't recognized him. So I said nothing at
all about my idea that it was Gene. You can't blame me for
that, can you?"

Of course Dick couldn't. . . . But had the doctor found
a garage mechanic?

"No, he had no luck at all, poor man. But what do you
think? When he got back to the car, the very first touch he
gave the starter, everything began to work perfectly. Aren't
motors inexplicable! But at that it was ever so late when I
got home. I was quite ashamed of myself."

"Now if you'll tell me as accurately as you can about
the times . . .?" encouraged Dick.

"It was nearly eleven when we started to drive and I'm
afraid it was after one when we found ourselves stuck on
the River Road. And we were at least an hour tinkering
with the car before we got under way again."

"So it was probably two or after when you saw Tracy. . . .
Um-mm. . . . By the way, during your wait there did you
by any chance hear the shot?"

"You mean—oh!" Katherine Latimer's exclamation was
shrill. "That was probably happening to poor Aunt Eugenia at that very time," and in spite of her fur rug, she
shivered. "No, I heard nothing—nothing. The wind. . . ."

"Since you were so close to Windward Hill, why didn't
you go up there and call for help? The all-night service
stations in town would have had a man out in a jiffy."

"I know, but it was hardly the thing to disturb a sick
woman's household at that ungodly hour, was it?"

"So you advise me to ask Tracy to account for his actions on Tuesday night, or rather, Wednesday morning.
May I use your name?"

"If you find it necessary." Dick thought her particularly good at the martyr's stake.

"I sincerely hope for your sake that it will not be." Dick patted her hand reassuringly, and her smile quivered bravely back at him. "Now there's just one more little matter that I'd like to clear up and, please, don't let it excite you. Personally I think it's all part of Cubbage's machinations, but you must be told of it."

The blue eyes widened and the color deepened almost to purple. She shrank back into the depths of her great chair. "Tell me," she murmured.

"By the way, these belong to you, do they not?" Carelessly Dick slipped his hand into his pocket and drew forth the suede gloves. "I took a chance on the initials," and he tossed the soft wad into her lap.

"They look familiar—I'm always mislaying gloves." She dismissed them impatiently. "But you were going to say—

"The gloves were found among Cubbage's possessions after his death. I have reason to believe that you may have lost them last Tuesday. What can you tell me about the circumstances?"

"Cubbage—had them!" she gasped. "That sounds too silly," but the grip of her fingers on the edge of the fur rug did not relax.

"But you were at Windward Hill Tuesday afternoon," Dick reminded her innocently.

"So I was. I must have left them then—"

"Or early in the evening when you returned. It was Mrs. Banney who saw you then. I want you to tell me about that second visit, Mrs. Latimer." Dick leaned forward compellingly.

"No, no. I can't. . . . It's a lie—I wasn't there . . . no, no. . . ." Her slender body tensed with hysteria and her choking sobs brought the strange maid running.

18

Dr. Stuart Reports a Loss

As Dick made his way out of the Lindenwood house, he kept his eyes open for his friend the black-and-white maid. Katherine Latimer's attack upon her cousin Gene Tracy, deserved or undeserved, had been so plainly calculated that Stowe was curious to discover what might have taken place between them the day before, after the scene in the lawyer's office. Asher had reported that he had dined at the Latimers' and from there had gone to Janet Wilcox. Another thing that might be profitable to learn would be just how frequently Mrs. Latimer and Marrender had been in conference.

But he saw no sign of the black-and-white maid.

His next interview must be with Dr. Perry Stuart. A query telephoned in to the doctor's office assistant informed him that at this hour the best chance of catching the doctor was at the hospital. On his way there Dick's thoughts raced restlessly around the appalling mixture of stuff that he had so hypocritically allowed Katherine Latimer to tell him.

The night was wild and windy; everyone spoke of that. Yet she said she heard stealthy footsteps descending the path. . . . There were those unused tickets for the Art Dinner. Soon now Asher would have checked up on that and they'd know definitely whether or not she'd been there. And his statement that Mrs. Banney had seen her at Windward Hill early Tuesday evening had precipitated the hysterics. . . . Consequently it had been no trick at all for him to retrieve the gloves he had handed over to her. The gloves probably meant nothing; she could so easily have left them in the afternoon. Hold on there. . . . He mustn't forget that she had told Stuart she was worrying about the gloves. . . . The joker was that Tracy had been at Windward Hill on the night in question. But if Janet's story were true, he had not left the place alone nor by the path down to the River Road. Was it just blind chance that Mrs. Latimer had dragged him in or had she actually seen him about somewhere? After all, he had only her word that she had remained in the car while the doctor went for help. . . . That was damned odd, anyway, come to think of it. Under no circumstances could he imagine a woman like Katherine Latimer being left alone on a deserted road in a stalled car between one and two in the morning. She would be just the type to tag the doctor. . . . Wait a minute, she'd made a little slip about something. . . . Yes, that was it. "Though I knew there was a—" she had said. "Though I knew there was a gun in the car." Was that what she was going to say? It was up to him to find out, all right. If his luck would only hold so that he could find Stuart's car in the hospital parking space, he might make some kind of start. . . .

However, his luck was not particularly good. He managed to spot the doctor's car without much difficulty and one hand thrust through a narrowly opened window had explored one side pocket, but he felt nothing that could be a weapon. Then his wary eye saw the doctor hurrying out of the surgery wing.

He darted back among the other cars to hail the physician cheerily a minute later. "Just a minute, Dr. Stuart. If you'd be willing to give me a little lift back toward town, it would save your time and mine. I'm after a little expert information—I'm trying to straighten out the Marrender mess, you know."

"Hop right in. Glad to help in any way I can. I'm on my way to an out-of-town call—something that doesn't happen very often. It's out on the Hollandville road, so I'll be cutting clear across town and you can go as far as you like—both geographically and officially."

As he settled himself, Dick was speculating on his chances of examining the pocket on his side of the car and wondering what would happen to the doctor's frank cordial manner if he were to say, "You know, old top, it might have been you who did for Cubbage."

Instead of that he said, "You know, of course, that in a sense the case is closed. The butler's suicide satisfies the family and the public, though we all admit that we can't quite put a period to it till we round up your missing nurse. Then there are a few other little details that keep me a bit restless."

"Doris Randall—I confess, Stowe, that I don't know what to make of that girl. She's a crackin' good nurse, speaking professionally, and a damned attractive little piece, speaking every other way. But just between you and me she wouldn't have had sense enough to disappear as she has done—if she's involved in what happened, I mean. Here's my theory—take it for whatever it's worth. I asked her to go on that Florida case and she seemed tickled to death. I wired down to Cincinnati for her reservations and saw her on her way myself. She didn't get that far. You police think you traced her to Chicago. I think someone kidnapped her."

"Not Cubbage?"

"Certainly not. He was under someone's eye all of that day. Likewise, it could scarcely have been any member of the family, except—those who were not in town on Wednesday."

Dick whistled in pleased surprise.

"You see what I mean?" The doctor's attention was on the traffic lights, and Dick's right knee was engaged in cautious exploration. "As I see it, the burglary of the house and the murder of Miss Marrender have no connection. Doris—the nurse knew nothing about the shooting. If she had, she never would have been able to conceal it from me. I know that girl's type, I tell you, Stowe. But either she did know something about the room that was entered, or somebody thinks she does, which amounts to the same thing."

"Does your theory include the idea of possible foul play—that the girl's to be suppressed permanently?"

"You're kidding me, I dare say, for butting in on your own affairs," laughed Stuart genially, . . . "and yet when the girl is found, or if she is found, her story will be damning to somebody. That's the way I look at it."

Dick nodded in agreement. "Perhaps that somebody will be herself." It was a grave pronouncement, and for a time both men were silent. Then Dick spoke again.

"However, I wanted particularly to ask you about something else. You've been in and out at Windward Hill with considerable regularity. What did you make of the butler?"

"Cubbage? He was a bad actor, if that's what you want to know." The words were exhaled with relief, or so Dick interpreted the emotion from which the physician relaxed. "Frankly, I never paid any attention to him until I caught on to the fact that he was worrying my patient."

"That's interesting. Go on."

"It's nothing specific—sorry to disappoint you. But I'm sure his influence over her was growing. It was apparent to me that he controlled matters at Windward Hill. There was no need yet for another nurse, partly because Cubbage was so skillful in relieving Miss Randall. I think he may

have wanted to postpone the appearance of another constant presence in the house—"

"I say, Stuart—Cubbage himself mentioned something
about plans being under way for the nurse to sleep in Miss
Marrender's room. It looks as if that fact and the necessity for another nurse before long hurried up things, what?
Had you said anything definite about that to him?"

"Come to think of it, I had. I'd talked matters over
with Miss Randall on Monday morning, if I recall the time
correctly."

"I see. Well, it gives me something to think about, all
right. Now another matter, doctor. Did you discuss the
situation at Windward Hill with any of Miss Marrender's
relatives?"

"No. There is only one member of the family whom I
know beyond the bowing stage—Mrs. Harris Latimer. She
happens to be a patient of mine too just now, and professionally I knew she oughtn't to be worried with anything
that was as nebulous as my suspicion about the butler."

Dick marveled somewhat at the technique that had so
skillfully introduced the topic that could prove embarrassing for the doctor, but all he said then was: "Your
suspicion about the butler—I do wish you could be more
definite, doctor. I don't mind telling you that the chap has
sunk himself without a trace."

"But it's hard to translate hunches into words—a detective ought to appreciate that. You see, he nearly always
made a point of stopping me as I would be leaving after
a visit to ask me rather specific questions concerning the
patient's condition. He led me to believe that he answered
a good many telephone queries from members of the family and friends in town, and, I say—I've just remembered
what he asked no later than last Monday morning!" Stuart
looked triumphantly around into Stowe's face as if to add,
"I'll hold you now!"

"Shoot!" grinned Dick.

"He inquired about Miss Marrender's mental condition—whether as the disease advanced her mental processes would tend to become clouded and so on."

"Did he, by any chance, use the phrase 'of sound mind'?" Dick inquired.

"The very words. Now what do you suppose the old ghoul was up to?"

"He may have had the humanitarian idea that a sufferer from an incurable malady should not be allowed to die by inches," suggested Dick disarmingly.

"It was a *faux pas* for him to drop out without leaving a confession. I don't see how you are ever to be certain of anything."

"How aptly you put it, doctor. And that reminds me—how about that shot of Benssen's #3 that Cubbage took? Wasn't that an unusual poison for a servant to possess?"

"Absolutely. Only—well, you yourself have been intimating that not much is known about Cubbage."

"And Benssen's #3 is so uncommon that the source of this dose is not going to be difficult to trace," Dick ventured.

"That's true . . . it's not as if it were a staple in *materia medica*. In fact, all I know about the stuff is that it has some obscure commercial use. I heard one of the chemists from United Utilities mention it in a speech once."

"You did, did you?" noted Dick to himself. Aloud, he blandly changed the subject. "I'm glad you mentioned Mrs. Latimer a moment ago. You see, I've just been talking to her and she tells me that she was with you on Tuesday night."

"I hope she included the tale of our embarrassing moment." Again the physician's manner was easy and urbane. "Damned awkward for us both, at that, in the light of what has since transpired."

"She seems in a highly nervous condition."

"Indeed she is. In fact, if you can assure her that she needs to fear no consequences, it would do her a lot of good. Her neurotic imagination is torturing her, to tell you the truth."

"Consequences? I'm afraid I don't follow you."

"It's utterly baseless, but I can't seem to convince her of that. She is worrying for fear her name and mine will be dragged into your damned investigation. We were stalled on the road just below Windward Hill at a bad time, you know."

"If I should say that if your consciences are clear you both know you have nothing to worry about, you'd throw me out on my ear, here and now, wouldn't you?" The way Dick drawled this comment suggested the utmost personal confidence in the integrity of his companion. "But I assure you I understand your position; no matter how innocent the situation, you don't want to be involved in this other matter. The only danger for Mrs. Latimer is if something should come of what she told me about seeing a man emerging from the path that leads down from the house. By the way, I can rely on that detail, can I? Not a case of nerves, eh?"

"No, her story is straight. You see, I saw; the man too—and I think I recognized him." The doctor spoke with guarded emphasis.

"Meaning you haven't shared your impression with Mrs. Latimer?"

"Under the circumstances, no. In her condition it would be cruelty. You see, it involves the family. I think the man was Eugene Tracy."

Were they playing neatly together, or not? Dick could not be sure. . . . On only one thing would he bet, and that was that the whole family were expert liars.

"Neither you nor Mrs. Latimer have anything to fear from Tracy." He stopped abruptly, as if he had spoken rashly. "I am going to ask you, however, if you were with Mrs. Latimer earlier in the evening."

An old woman was indecisively crossing the street ahead; perhaps that was the reason that the doctor did not answer Stowe's question at once. When the pedestrian had gained her goal, he spoke. "Yes, I was attending Mrs. Latimer professionally."

"Where?"

"In my rooms down-town. I went up for something—it was not an office-hour night—and found her there. She had been on her way to dinner somewhere and felt one of her nervous attacks coming on and stopped on the chance of finding me. She needed attention, all right. It was a couple of hours before she was calm enough to leave in my car."

"What time was it when you found her in your office?"

"About eight, I believe. I can't be positive. . . . Now if you want to go all the way out the pike with me, say so. I can step on the gas from here on, you know."

"No, this is the end of the car-line, and I'd better hop on the one that's coming and get back on the beat. You have told me a lot, Stuart, and I thank you. And for heaven's sake, if you hear from your wandering nurse, bust a button getting in touch with me, or we shall begin to think you're mixed up in the mess too. So long!"

"Wait a minute, Stowe. I forgot something." Stuart had already started his car, but he stopped again and thrust a grey-capped head through the lowered window. "Would you mind reporting to the proper person at Headquarters that the .38 I'm legally permitted to carry with me in the car has been stolen? It must have been swiped this morning while I parked for twenty minutes down on Garfield Street. It was there when I left the garage. . . ."

The roar of his departing car drowned anything else he might have been saying.

19

AND SALLY DISCOVERS ONE

All the way back to town and Sally's Shop, Dick's next port of call, he entertained himself by checking over the devious ways by which every member of the Marrender circle had blurred the issues with suspicions against one or more of the others. The doctor had been particularly good. Well, maybe his hunch about the nurse's being kidnapped wasn't so bad. . . . and his line about Cubbage had been hot, all right. And was his report about his stolen .38 straight, or was that merely an artful announcement that he had been aware of his passenger's surreptitious search of the side pockets of the coupé? Speaking of hunches, his own was that there was something not quite convincing about the double story of Tracy's being seen on the River Road . . . unless the Wilcox girl were lying her head off. Janet Wilcox made him think of United Utilities and United Utilities made him think of what Stuart had said about Benssen's #3, and Benssen's #3. made him think of the death of Cubbage, and the death of Cubbage made him think of William Marrender. . . . By the time Dick had thought about this new arrangement of United Utilities, Benssen's #3, and William Marrender, he entered Sally's Shop wondering how to test the answer that had presented itself.

Sally's eyes directed him to the room at the back of the
shop. Within a few minutes she followed him, first skillfully completing the sale of a cherry and ash spool bed
to an over-upholstered customer who had shown signs of
wanting to dicker.

Deliberately Dick waited for Sally Marrender to speak,
but at last he had to prod her with, "This is tomorrow and
here I am."

"Oh, yes . . . about the piece of chain." She thrust her
hand into the pocket of her smock and produced a fragment of old-fashioned gold watch chain between three and
four inches long. "This is what you handed me last night,
isn't it?"

Dick nodded.

The girl's left hand went down into the other pocket
and emerged with fourteen similar inches of chain at one
end of which swung a distinctive charm. "Would you say
the two pieces are alike?" she asked.

Carefully Dick matched them. Even to the casual glance
there could be no doubt that the pattern of the links was
exactly alike, but Dick was concerned with something
else. With scrupulous care he was examining the broken
or cut ends of each piece that had been produced when one
old-fashioned watch chain had by design or accident been
pulled apart. . . .

"My short piece shows a recently severed end. Your long
bit ends with a link that shows no fresh scar of any sort,
though originally it must have been pried open. What have
you to tell me about it?"

"The long piece with the charm belonged to my grandfather, Robert Rufus Marrender. I was only a kid when
he died. Because he was the eldest grandson, he left my
brother Will some of his own personal things. In the lot
was his first watch. With it was this piece of chain, broken
just as you see it now. Will treated the ancient relic with

respect and all that, but he really didn't give two hoots for it, and when I began to show symptoms of this"—her hand indicated the indescribable jumble that made up the shop—"he let me take it. It's been in my cabinet of Mid-Victorian jewelry ever since—not for sale, of course. When you flashed your piece last night, it struck me that it was a missing part of Grandfather Marrender's chain."

"A missing part?"

"Yes, another length is needed to restore the chain as it originally was."

"Well, what of it?" asked Dick, as if the missing bit was not already in his possession, kindness of Mrs. Banney.

"As you say, what of it? When I first started the shop, I nagged Aunt Genie for the rest of the chain and she informed me in her own final manner that I needn't bother, that she had positive knowledge that the other part of the chain was no longer in existence."

"Hm-mm, yet I found my bit in the upper hall of your aunt's house yesterday morning. Was any other member of the family interested in the chain?"

"If they were, they concealed it beautifully. But if the two severed ends don't match exactly, maybe that means—"

"It could mean a lot of things." Dick broke in almost rudely. "See here, Miss Marrender, did you go to Windward Hill last night to search for this piece of chain?"

Sally's hazel eyes flashed stormily. "You would come back to that. But listen, I—will—not—tell you about last night."

"I'm supposed to be good at finding out things for myself, remember. I've found out that you and your brother did not breakfast together Wednesday morning, for instance."

She laughed spontaneously. "Everybody knows my clocks are never right."

"Your clocks have nothing to do with the fact that you told me your brother breakfasted here with you and he

says he ate at his home. Was that lie necessary, Miss Marrender?"

"Yes. I may be minus zero as a cook, but I still have me
pride." Her answer was flippant, but her eyes were somber.

"I'm afraid you were lying about something else, too. It
was your brother's business, not yours, that you discussed
so late on Tuesday night . . . and you quarreled with your
aunt about his affairs on Tuesday morning. You have pointed out to me a grave possibility, Miss Marrender."

That told, but in a way that increased Dick's caution
rather than his satisfaction. Her mobile face indicated,
on the whole, that an unexpected turning had presented
itself.

"Someway I can't forget that peculiar scene between
Kaye and Gene up in Mr. Dexter's office yesterday," she
murmured dreamily. "I must tell you about it—"

"I'm already informed." Dick was brusque. The girl's
device was disgustingly transparent.

"Then you don't think my cousin— But then; everything points to Cubbage, thank goodness."

"If Cubbage murdered your aunt, I can't understand
why everyone of you goes to such elaborate trouble to get
me all hot and bothered about some other member of the
family. According to one or another of you, each of the
others is under the gravest suspicion. That means just one
thing to me: every last one of you is hugging a bit of guilty
knowledge and trying to finesse the other fellow into the
open. And I propose to take the tricks myself."

"Go right ahead and have your own fun. After all,
there's only one thing I know: neither my brother nor I
had anything to do with what happened at Windward Hill
that night." Her declaration was low-voiced but defiant.

"So? Then—how about your .38? It was a bullet of that
caliber that was found in Miss Marrender's body. We've
identified a recent sale of such a gun to you."

"My revolver is in the next room in its usual place. Would you like to examine it now?" She rose coolly as if eager to demonstrate. "It's merely a gesture on my part. It's never even been fired."

"Just one minute, Miss Marrender. Are you prepared to prove to me that the gun has been in its usual place continuously from Tuesday on till today?"

"Which means that you can't take my word for it. The rules of your game, no doubt. . . . You could ask my two assistants; they might know something. And another thing, Mr. Stowe. You assume there was only one such .38 in existence. Didn't I hear the men from Headquarters talking about a trace they had found of such a gun in Gene's room? You can't prove that the shot that killed Aunt Genie came from my .38. That's silly!"

"Can't we? We have the bullet, you know." But Dick realized that the significance of this meant nothing to Sally Marrender.

"I see no need to prolong the discussion." A strange dignity possessed her. "Let me show you my revolver."

Dick followed her back into the main room and across the floor to the corner where so modern a contrivance as a cash register looked slightly conscious among the lyre-backed rosewood chairs and hand-blown glass flasks. Imperiously she called to the tall, puffy woman whom Dick had noticed upon his first official visit.

"Mrs. Morrison, will you please show this gentleman where we always keep the arsenal?"

"Right under here," began Mrs. Morrison chattily. "There's a shelf, you see, and in case someone should try to make us open the register, Miss Marrender has always told us to think quick and—"

As she talked she had thrust her hand along the shelf groping for the protecting weapon that should lie ready. But the startled way in which she had stopped speaking and the blank look that slid over the soft expanse of her face told their own story.

"It's not there, Sally!" she gasped.

If Dick had not been watching Sally Marrender's square dark face he probably would never have believed it; but as it was, he knew he could have no doubt. Sally Marrender had honestly expected her revolver to be in its proper place . . . and it was not there.

"But it was here—this morning—the first thing. I looked!" Then she pulled herself together. "You're sure you haven't touched it?" she demanded of the quivering Mrs. Morrison.

"No, no, my dear child. You know how I've always felt about knowing it was under there, liable to go off at any minute."

The other assistant, the thin, wiry one, tap-tapped back to collect candle sticks for a customer who had just drifted in. She beamed maternally at her employer.

"I mustn't forget to tell you, Sally dearest, that a gentleman was in a few minutes ago who wanted to see you rather particularly. But you had said you weren't to be disturbed in case this—er—this person came in."

At that slip the hazel eyes glared balefully, but Miss Trent chirped on. "He waited a few minutes and then went out. It was somebody you know—he's been here before, a tall, good-looking man. He wore a grey tweed cap."

"Just where did he do this few minutes' waiting, Miss Trent?" It was the very question that Dick would have asked if Sally had not worded it first.

"He was back here looking at the brass fire-sets when I first spoke to him, and well—I really didn't notice him anywhere else. He liked the andirons. He knelt right down on the floor to look at them."

Dick and Sally looked at one another. Both had leaped to the same conclusion, but before Dick could pin Miss

Trent down to a more detailed description of the recent caller who might have stolen the gun, Sally asserted herself.

"Just a minute, please, Mr. Stowe." Imperatively she waved the assistants back to their customers and addressed Dick.

"A tall, good-looking man," she repeated significantly. "I'm afraid I know who that was—Perry Stuart. I had been told that he wanted to see me—"

"But, Miss Marrender," interrupted Dick, "I happen to know that Dr. Stuart—" He stopped himself abruptly. "If your weapon has lain here undisturbed all week, why should you be so eager to fasten its present disappearance upon the doctor?"

"Let me tell you all I know about being sure that it was here all the time," she proposed after a curious little pause. Stowe's last direct question was ignored. "I know the revolver was here on Tuesday morning. I was hunting all over the place for something a customer wanted and the shelf here was one of the places I searched. The gun was there. You were here for the first time late Wednesday afternoon, weren't you? I didn't even know then that Aunt Genie had been shot—remember? Well, after you left, I suppose because of the association of ideas or something, I came in here, and my revolver was in its usual place. This morning I looked again and everything was all right. I suppose it was on my mind just because of what you said last night."

She had been speaking in a rapid, low voice and now as she concluded with this oblique reference to their strange meeting at Windward Hill the night before, Dick recalled the assurance with which she had answered his question then. As if to himself he murmured, "But I still wish I knew why you went to Windward Hill last night."

An angry flush told him something.

"You're welcome to third-degree Mrs. Morrison and Miss Trent about my gun, or anything else," she said after a minute, during which she might have been counting ten. "Mamma Morrison's the kind that you can make say anything that's helpful, but Trent's nobody's fool. In the meantime shall I call—the regular police about the theft of my .38?"

Dick wanted to laugh at the angry girl, but he answered gravely, "I'll be glad to report the matter for you, Miss Marrender, but first if you will allow me to follow your own suggestion about your assistants. . . ."

So while Sally Marrender carried on quite pointedly with the customers from whom the two women were temporarily recalled, Dick Stowe learned for himself that their employer had rated them quite accurately. Mrs. Morrison was so skittish about anything that might go off with a bang that she would have allowed battle, murder, and sudden death to be done rather than touch the hidden weapon. Consequently she was very vague about when she had last seen the gun. She had, however, observed Miss Marrender searching about on the shelf a number of times recently.

Miss Trent had noticed the same thing. Miss Marrender had made no explanation of her search. This was somewhat odd, thought Dick. Moreover, Miss Trent always kept her purse in the far corner of the shelf in question and she was prepared to swear that the revolver was in its proper place this morning. She admitted that she hadn't thought about it the other days—Wednesday and Thursday, that is. The shop had been closed the day of the funeral. . . .

Then Dick referred to the tall, good-looking man. Miss Trent's additional details certainly did not rule out the possibility of Dr. Stuart's having been the caller, in spite of Dick's certain information that he had been on his way to pay a professional visit out on the Hollandville road. She confessed, however, that she did not know Dr.

Stuart even by sight. Dick thereupon risked a test . . . a test which left him more uncertain than ever.

Did she know her employer's brother, Mr. William Marrender? . . . Since she did, had she noticed when he had last been in the shop? . . . This very morning—was she positive?

Indeed Miss Trent was quite positive. He had come in quite early, about ten, and after a few words with his sister had left immediately. Another member of the family had been in that morning, too, volunteered Miss Trent. The week had surely been a difficult one for the Marrenders, but it moved Miss Trent deeply to observe such fine, old-fashioned family solidarity. . . .

Brusquely Dick reversed Miss Trent's digression and listened to an accurate, unmistakable description of Eugene Tracy. He had not been in the shop long either, she reported, but he had gone directly to the back room as if searching for his cousin, who chanced to be out at the minute. He had left no message.

Dick meditated. The "tall, good-looking man" who wore a grey cap might have been Dr. Stuart and he might have stolen Sally's .38, in some strange impatience to replace his own . . . but in that case his trip out the Hollandville road had not been taken. Instead he must have turned back to town immediately upon discharging his passenger. Why . . . why? But the revolver could have been stolen at any time during the morning after the opening of the shop . . . and Marrender had been in and Gene Tracy. . . . Some mess, thought Dick.

He chanced a final question that brought an amused glitter into Miss Trent's black eyes. Could one get to the shop from the apartment above without going outside and using the main entrance?

A thin shoulder blade lifted itself expressively. There was a door in the back room. Sally was a darling, but she often forgot that overtime for the rest of them meant late trips home. All she had to do was slip up those back stairs. . . .

Dick left Sally's Shop and made for the nearest public telephone. There was much to report to Asher. Extra eyes must be trained on the doctor, and he wanted information about United Utilities and Benssen's #3; and the police must know that two .38's had mysteriously disappeared during the last few hours and Mrs. Latimer's two leads about Cubbage ought to be followed up. That man was more mysterious dead than alive. . . . But perhaps first he ought to have another chat with Tracy. Tracy had "remembered" something last night the instant he had mentioned the emerald, and Dick ought to get after that before Tracy "forgot" it. After all, Dr. Rhand and his party and Mrs. Quinn's quick-lunch counter could wait. . . .

All these thoughts filled the interval of waiting for his call to get through to Asher. What Tim had to say took the decision about the use of his next hours beyond his choice.

"And say, Dick, guess what now?" came Tim Asher's high voice over the wire. "Tracy's beat it. Better drop around a minute, huh?"

20

Nettie Quinn's Place

Since Cubbage's death the spotlight at Headquarters was no longer playing solely upon the Marrender affair, yet the deputy temporarily in charge of detectives had been more than willing to allow Stowe to go ahead with the matter in his own way. So when Dick stuck his head around Asher's door, the latter promptly transferred his attention from the latest news about a cross-country chase after two youngsters who had held up a suburban bank that noon to discuss the newest development in the Marrender muddle.

"Smart trick, I must say, letting Tracy give you the slip like that," scoffed Dick.

"Who said so?" Asher ruffled up instantly. "We know where he went all right."

"My mistake, Timmy, my mistake. But did you send somebody after him?"

"Let me tell you. He spent the night at his dump on Burden Street. Parks had his eye on him, hoping to see that girl, like you said, but nothing doing. This morning he had breakfast at Mike's and then strolled back through town to his cousin's shop. He came out right away with Miss Marrender and the two of 'em went around to the morgue—to take a look at Cubbage, I guess. On their way back to the shop some guy picked Tracy up in a car. For a while they just cruised around town. Then all of a

sudden the roadster headed out of town on the Dixie. Parks
was all out of luck; he followed but ran out of gas. So he
'phoned down the line to check up on the car as it went
through the various towns. It was set for Cincy, all right."

"And so that makes you think you can put your fingers
on the boy just any time you want to—oh, Timmy, Timmy!"

"Keep your shirt on. We got the number of the car and
who he's with and all. We can pick him up any time. And
he may show us the way to something we don't know yet."

"Yeah? Here's where I have a little chat with PeeDee
just the same."

When that had been accomplished, Stowe felt better.
Asher then listened with becoming admiration and respect
to his exposition concerning the missing weapon in the
Marrender case. When he had theorized at some length,
Asher interrupted heavily.

"But listen, Dick, you really haven't got a thing on the
Marrender kid, even if it was her gun—you're only guessing that that was what she was hunting last night at Windward Hill. If she really thought it was where it belonged
this morning, then that means that she must have found it
somewhere out there last night, and for the love of Lulu,
Dick, I don't see how she could have put anything like that
over on us. Then if Marrender, Tracy, and possibly Stuart
each might have walked off with the thing this morning,
well, it's about got me tied. And you say that the doc had
a .38 of his own. . . ."

"The only way to prove which, if either, of the two
guns was used is to lay official hands upon them and if we
can't do that, where are we, I ask you?"

"You think the girl's not wise to the way we can tell . . .
when we do find the guns?"

"No, she evidently doesn't go in for thrillers." He
frowned and shook himself impatiently. "Everything you've

been saying is true, Timmy, and a whole lot more. The case is more a muddle than ever. Even if half of what they've told me are lies, they've all come across with enough to embarrass every one of them. I guess that's what I'll have to do sooner or later. Line 'em all up together and make 'em all tell on each other. That way they'll help me spot the lies. . . . The way I size it up now, all five of 'em were at Windward Hill the night the old lady was killed. Sally and Will Marrender haven't admitted as much yet, but each is alibiing the other, and you know what that amounts to. I can hang knowledge of the unlocked window on Marrender. Lord, I wish the nurse would show up."

"She'd have been found within two days, if we could have turned the newspapers loose on the story. But that was the heavy hand of the Marrender money."

"There would have been a thousand of her found, and you know it. Mysterious glimpses of her would have been seen everywhere. It looks to me, Tim, as though the Marrender family don't want the nurse to appear to tell her story."

"Your hunch about Cubbage must be right . . . the whole damn family act so guilty—"

"Which brings us around once more to the matter of Benssen's #3. I want some detailed information from that side kick of Radge's—that chap that knows so much about poisons, I mean— Here, I'll leave a memo about it. I want it done in such a way that nobody at United Utilities will associate it with this business, you understand." Dick scribbled a few notes on a card and handed it across the desk to Asher.

Much as the deputy inspector might have desired to ask questions, he was given no further opportunity, for Stowe lounged away, his mind mulling over the enigmatic Cubbage. He was telling himself that it was about time that he sat down by himself and spread out all the bits of the puzzle so far collected, and try various ways of assembling them. But first he'd see what he could round up about Cubbage from Mrs. Latimer's information and maybe he ought to have another round with Tracy, provided the faithful PeeDee returned him safely, and, then he promised himself that he'd take a day off from this fruitless running around in circles and think the Marrender case through. A program which, to some extent, he was to carry out . . .

Within the next hour he ascertained that Dr. Vincent Rhand was a dilettante in medicine and a devotee of all the arts. As a critic he quite fancied himself, according to the professional who reported local aesthetic progress for the *Herald-Press*.

Therefore, as one eager to learn at first hand an authoritative estimate of the real contribution of Fells Lothrop to modern *vers libre*, Stowe sought audience with the oracle. He had no difficulty, office hours being of small importance in the doctor's schedule. Thereafter he promptly lost his enthusiasm for ultra-modern verse that had so impressed his host during the preliminaries. Skillfully he fanned the doctor's curiosity.

Mrs. Latimer had told him a surprising thing about that so charming occasion when he had entertained the distinguished British guest. She had been quite convinced that one of his guests had been her aunt's butler—the one who had insanely attacked and killed Miss Marrender. Could the doctor recall accurately just who his guests had been?

The doctor could and would. . . . It had been a very select group, just sixteen, including his sister and himself.

Rapidly he named the people who had been his guests, names that Dick knew could be easily identified, but he counted only twelve names and Mrs. Latimer's had not been mentioned. When that was called to Rhand's attention he explained that in a sense it was fortunate that his friend Perry Stuart had been detained. With a trace of embarrassment Rhand became involved in detail. There had been a disastrous accident to one of the plates of salad which Miss Rhand had ready to serve, and she would have been distressed beyond all words if she had been obliged to substitute a plate of a different pattern. She was that sort of hostess. . . . So with the addition of Mrs. Latimer, his sister, and himself, the party had been only fifteen. He knew absolutely, because after the accident in the pantry there had been only that number of Wedgwood plates.

But the guest who looked like Cubbage had left early, Dick explained, not long after the arrival of Eugene Tracy. Dr. Rhand remembered distinctly how late Tracy had been, and yet he was sure there had been but fifteen who had eaten supper.

That must indicate, Dick pointed out, that there had been an extra guest who had slipped out early, but Rhand's mind was a blank on the subject. His attention had been completely centered on his guest of honor, as was quite natural. Such a rare privilege. . . . Yes, perhaps Miss Rhand might remember something more. She'd be glad to help in any possible way, when she returned. She had gone to Indianapolis for the weekend.

Labelling his call on Rhand a dud, Stowe travelled to an entirely different milieu. Nettie Quinn's place in the far West End had stirred him not at all when he first heard it mentioned. Even now it was his sense of duty, not the urge of enthusiasm that carried him along the dingy street that led to the eating-house.

He experimented with a bowl of Nettie Quinn's famous noodle soup and found himself soothed. A stumbling old man served him and explained huskily that Mis' Quinn she'd gone to git her plate fixed. By the time Dick woke to the fact that a trip to the dentist was meant, he had become so attached to the shuffling little fellow that he prolonged the conversation.

The waiter's name was Jake, and he was on duty most all the time on account of he didn't have nothing much else to do and anyways the folks that come in and out always give him plenty to think about.

So when the noodle soup had given way to pumpkin pie and a second cup of superb coffee, Dick had concluded that Jake would serve his purpose better than a more cautious Nettie Quinn. He produced the newspaper print of the man known as Cubbage.

"Ever see this chap in here, Jake? You say you always notice your customers."

"That's right. I always remember faces that have et here at Mis' Quinn's, but that feller now, I don't never remember seein' him in here. I was real interested too in what was in the papers about that there, and I'll tell you why. Y'see, oncet I worked for old man Marrender, and you know how them things kinda give you a interest."

They gave Dick Stowe an interest also.

Gently encouraged, Jake indulged in reminiscence. He'd been hired—and fired by Robert Rufus Marrender himself, years ago now. Jake recollected that he must have been just about twelve years old. Something about the way he emptied waste-paper baskets and handled the heavy old letter-press in the Marrender office had not found favor, or maybe it was because the boss caught him chewin' tobacco. Anyways, he was fired so quick he didn't know which end he was on. At that, Jake had always liked the old man. He was the whole works in them days, long before he went in with them other big concerns and made so much money for his children to spend. And now none of 'em was left. Two sons and three daughters he had. This one that had just been killed was the last one.

"Two sons?" Dick questioned.

Yep, the first one of the family that died was a son. A fine young feller, not married nor nothin'. And then the two girls that married so grand had died, and the old-maid one, this Eugenia, she and her dad lived on in the old place on the hill and bossed the rest. The other son, he died just a few years after his daddy. Folks said sometimes that the grandson, the only one that could carry on the name, Will Marrender, looked so much like his granddad, but Jake couldn't see that a-tall. Funny thing, though . . .

It was an off-hour at Nettie Quinn's, and Jake's husky voice had chatted on without interruption, but now another customer demanded soup. Dick wondered whether Jake's recollections were worth another wedge of pie, but of his own accord the shambling figure again leaned confidentially across the oilcloth-covered counter and resumed his discourse.

"Funny, ain't it? When you ast me if I ever see that feller, I says, no, and that's right, I ain't. But that got me to thinkin' about old man Marrender, and just now I remembered how oncet I seen a feller that did look enough like him to be his own son."

"Who was that?" Dick asked dutifully.

You could search Jake—he didn't know who the guy was. He'd only come in the once, but there was just something about him that made Jake think of old Robert Rufus himself.

Dick took the leap boldly and once more drew forth Cubbage's pictured face. "You're sure this wasn't the man?"

"Him?" Jake gave a kind of strangled snort that registered utter disdain. Dick thought with exceeding great regret of the very different looking Cubbage that only that morning had been buried with the sketchiest of Christian rites and no mourners. He continued to ponder over various combinations of possibilities, and held no further talk with Jake beyond asking him to keep an open eye for a possible reappearance of this man who so remarkably resembled the elder Marrender. This Jake agreed to do, first correcting Dick by reminding him that this feller he seen didn't exactly look like the old man—just made him think of him, sort of. . . .

Nettie Quinn returned as Dick was leaving, giving visible evidence as she answered his few perfunctory questions that the plate had been successfully repaired. Mis' Quinn remembered, as through a glass darkly, however, the night that bunch of swells had busted in, but she was rather belligerent about denying that there were any bums playing poker in her place at the time. Not if she knew it, they wasn't. . . . Dick dropped his inquiry and returned to his own establishment, still arguing with himself about the tomfool idea that Jake had guilelessly given him.

It had been a long, full day, and Dick Stowe was tired. He resolved to stay put for the rest of the evening and the next day, unless he should hear something from PeeDee about Tracy. It was high time he was seeing what the various digits in the Marrender problem added up to . . . and he wanted to write to Laura. He hadn't had a minute in the last two days. The youngster would be suing him for gross neglect.

There was a telegram awaiting him when he let himself into the quiet apartment that was only a place to send laundry from when Laura was away from it. He'd better do as much of that thinking as he could tonight, for tomorrow was already being commandeered. He read the message again:

WILL BE WITH YOU SUNDAY MORNING FOR INTERVIEW STOP EXPECTED DEVEL-OPMENTS. FRANCESCA PENROSE.

It was the phrase "expected developments" that Dick found most entertaining about the wire.

If Richard Stowe had been a certain recognizable type of detective, he would have spent his evening painstakingly writing out endless notes about each member of the Marrender circle, setting down the pros and cons that involved every one of them. There would have been, in addition to the five sheets for the five nieces and nephews of Eugenia Marrender, a dossier for Dr. Stuart, one for Janet Wilcox, one for Cubbage, one for the vanished nurse, and one for the girl with the emerald.

Perhaps Dick's method ought not to be held against him. He talked the case over aloud, quite like the verist moron. He asked himself questions . . . and answered them—some of them. One of his favorite answers, he began to notice, was: "That's something the nurse ought to know about." If he had been making notes, the nurse's page would have been overrun.

He demonstrated that he could formulate a case of a sort against any one of his eligibles, singly or in combination, and yet in each instance at least one question would intrude that undermined the whole careful fabric. At last he disposed of this collection of questions by launching them upon Laura's distant head. Consequently there was a businesslike paragraph incorporated in the midst of an otherwise luxurious epistle.

Dick yawned hugely and slipped out to the letter slot in bathrobe and slippers to start Laura's letter on its long journey. La La was bored, out there doing her daughterly duty, and this would give her something to think about. There was really no way for Dick to know that by the time Laura's eyes rested on his questions, the Marrender case would have been solved beyond all doubt.

His telephone called him back. "PeeDee, the old wheelhorse," he thought as he padded across the hall and back into his own quarters.

But it was not PeeDee. It was Tracy who was calling him.

"That you, Stowe? I'm just back from Cincinnati. . . . You probably knew I had gone, unexpected as it was. . . . I'd like to see you tomorrow. Something to your advantage and all that, you know. . . . Well, as soon as you can get away then. . . . I'll be out at Windward Hill, if the watch-dogs will let me in. You'll come? Right. . . ."

21

STOVE VIEWS A PORTRAIT

Having thought to some purpose, or so he flattered himself, before he went to bed, Dick wasted none of his sleeping time in idle tossing about. He slept with such abandon that the next morning he had barely time to shave and dress before a ring at his door announced Francesca Penrose.

"I thought I'd come directly here," she explained, "for in a hotel or club someone would be sure to recognize me. Out here it won't matter. I don't want the relatives to know that I've been up, you understand."

She gazed frankly about the Stowe living-room, admiring Laura's hangings, and suggested coffee herself. "This is ever so early for me, you know. Couldn't you do with another cup of coffee yourself?"

That having been satisfactorily arranged for, she lost no time in coming to the occasion for her conference with her impromptu host. "I've heard from my receipt," she announced, "and now I know how it feels to be blackmailed."

"So that's the line. . . I thought it would be. It may sound heartless, but I'm tickled pink to hear it," replied Dick.

"Because you think it will lead you to the murderer? Well, maybe—but let me tell you what happened and then judge for yourself." Just in time she rescued the next two slices from the toaster and applied butter liberally.

"Quite late yesterday afternoon I received an anonymous telephone call. It was a man's voice, but it was obviously disguised. Yet, some way, there was something vaguely familiar about it. What he said was just a sort of blanket threat. It doesn't worry me for a minute, because I know exactly where I stand in that wild night's work. But you wanted to know if I heard, and so here I am."

"Aren't you going to tell me exactly what he said?"

"Of course I am. First the voice asked if it was I and so on and then said, ever so pleasantly, that it was the holder of a certain little paper that I had left on my aunt's book shelves who was speaking, and that all he wanted was to remind me that a skillful introduction of that paper could involve me very embarrassingly with those who were investigating my aunt's death. That was all. On second thought, it isn't true blackmail, is it, unless you promise to leave unmarked bills in the stump of the old lightning blasted tree at the cross roads in the dark of the moon? I've been let down." She laughed and poured Dick another cup of coffee.

"That may come in due time, Miss Penrose. Was it a local or long-distance call?"

"A local call and from a private telephone, too. At least there wasn't the usual palaver that goes with a pay-station call. Should I have traced it?"

"You could have tried, I suppose, but I doubt that you would have got much. Whoever made the call had probably arranged matters carefully. Now I wish you'd be wholly frank with me—you said a moment ago you knew exactly where you stood in the affair. How could that receipt be used to embarrass you?"

"It could be used to show that I was at Windward Hill the night my aunt met her death, but—"

"But you've not denied that to me."

"Exactly. And it could force me to publish certain business matters that have to do with the Theatre League and a little deal I'm interested in would flop. I'd lose money rather inconveniently, but if my unknown friend meant to insinuate that the receipt could prove that I have guilty knowledge of my aunt's death, I just can't imagine how he plans to do it."

"By which you mean that if necessary you can throw the light of publicity upon your last business arrangement with Miss Marrender?"

"Yes . . . but I also mean that I'm not going to be scared into doing it, for the matter has absolutely no connection with what happened to her."

There was something convincing about Francesca Penrose's statements, Dick admitted to himself and, in a minute, to the lady herself. "My suggestion now is," he added, "that since your conscience is so clear you play your unknown friend along. We'll see then whether there's a slip somewhere that you haven't thought of or whether he's up to something himself—more likely that. Sooner or later he'll give us a lead to himself. Maybe he thinks you know something—or he's afraid you know something." Dick stopped short. He had reminded himself of a certain little detail. Now was his chance.

"Miss Penrose, which window did you use to enter the little gallery?"

"The first one I reached—the one nearest the front of the house—the left-hand window from without, to be painfully exact."

"And it was unlocked?"

"Yes, I pushed it up and stepped inside. I told you all this once."

"I know." Dick's smile was apologetic. "And when you left?"

"I pulled it down just as I had found it; I couldn't lock it from the outside."

"Thank you, Miss Penrose. Next I should like to know whom you met or saw during your trip from the car up to the house and back."

She looked at him stonily, as if trying to fathom how much he knew. "I saw no one." She answered slowly and the stubborn look in the depths of the grey eyes might have meant that she had assumed a position from which she did not intend to budge.

At any rate, Dick made no attempt to follow the matter beyond the bland remark, "That's right; it was dark as a pocket that night."

For an instant only, Francesca Penrose registered extreme annoyance.

"I'm about to change the subject, Miss Penrose," he went on. "I hope you won't say the topic is none of my business. I'd like to be set right on a point or two concerning the Marrender family history. Your grandfather had two sons, I've been informed. The elder one died as quite a young man?"

His interrogative tone brought a careless nod from the actress.

"Are you sure he left no children?" That question provoked a distinct interest.

"I'm not the family oracle, Mr. Stowe, but we children were all brought up on the tale of the tragic death of the young uncle whom none of us had ever seen. He was drowned while he was still in college—eighteen or nineteen years old. If the young Galahad that he was, traditionally, left an heir, he would have no legal standing. But there's small chance of anything so romantic. The lady in the case would have stepped forward long ago."

"So as far as you know, you and your sister, Will and Sally Marrender, and Eugene Tracy are the only descendants of old Robert Rufus Marrender?"

"Of course we are. The Marrender men have never been that sort. At least, they've never been caught—unless you've unearthed something scandalous."

"Not yet. . . ."

Francesca Penrose demolished the little mound of toast crumbs that she had carefully accumulated as they talked and rose to go. "It's a pity, I've often thought, that Aunt Eugenia couldn't have lived now. I mean, she was never the type of the sweet young thing of her own girlhood. She'd have made a gorgeous Wild Young Person. Yet, I don't know . . . if she had wanted a fling, she would have—"

"—flung," Dick completed with great gravity.

"You'll not forget, Mr. Stowe, that no one is to know that I came up to have this chat with you this morning. I'm rather in disgrace with Will because I didn't attend the funeral. Poor old Will . . . the publicity of all this is torture to him."

As she stood in the door talking idly while pulling on her gloves, Dick made his last attack.

"What became of the gloves you lost last Tuesday night?"

"I'm sure I can't imagine," She answered promptly with unconscious candor, and then her eyes flared with surprise as candid. "Why, how did you know I lost my gloves?"

"I didn't know it, and I haven't found—your gloves left anywhere as a suspicious clue against you. Let's call it just a simple exercise in deduction on my part. We detectives must do our scales regularly, you know."

When Francesca Penrose had gone, Dick took a moment to wish that his reasoning about her lost pair of gloves, which had nothing to do with the case, could be applied to the other pair, the ones that certainly were Katherine Latimer's, the ones that so oddly had appeared in the pocket of Cubbage's overcoat. If he could only risk as lightly and successfully certain deductions concerning the man who had called Francesca Penrose . . . or reveal some

hitherto unknown chapters in the family archives of the
Marrenders . . . or surprise her into telling who it was she
knew or suspected was at Windward Hill at the time of her
own unconventional call. . . .

As it was, Dick felt quite positive of one thing and
afraid of another. It was clearly not Francesca Penrose who
was lying about the hour of her visit to the little gallery
and the condition of the windows. Therefore it must be
Janet Wilcox. That was the item he was quite sure of. The
one he was afraid of was that the caller whose voice sounded slightly familiar and who had made a futile attempt to
frighten Francesca into some desired course would very
likely prove to be Eugene Tracy. Poor Janet, she was playing a losing hand.

But he must be on his way to Windward Hill. Tracy
had asked for it, and Dick had a big notion to let him
have it straight. Suppose he gave that engaging rascal to
understand that he had been seen that night. . . . Well, his
course would depend somewhat on the opening that Tracy
might give him.

The house, at Windward Hill was cold and deserted
looking, save for one thin curl of smoke. That came from
the kitchen chimney, Dick soon discovered, and it was in
that room that Tracy was waiting for him. He was, indeed,
chatting cozily with the man from Headquarters who had
dogged him, not too willingly, out from town.

"Run away, Parks, I'll carry on now." Dick slipped into
the flat-bottomed chair behind the range and grinned
cheerfully at Tracy. "If we're not careful, we'll have you
thinking we don't quite trust you, what?"

"If I weren't such an indifferent beggar I could be raising the devil about my constitutional rights or whatever
you call 'em. I'm not under arrest nor detained as a material witness, and yet I'm not exactly being ignored by the
police." Tracy's soft voice droned on in similar style for a

minute or two longer, and then there was no sound for a longer interval save the purring of the coal fire.

"I'm waiting," hinted Dick at last, "to hear what else you have remembered. Especially about the emerald."

"And I'm ready to tell you a thing or two that ought to get you somewhere, but on just one condition."

Dick gave Tracy a cynical look. "What, again?" he murmured.

"Oh, I know what you're thinking. Who am I to set conditions? But this one ought not to cramp your style a lot."

"All right, what is it? I don't mind telling you that I've got to get somewhere soon."

"I'll talk . . . if you'll tell me what you've got on Miss Wilcox."

"Beyond the fact that she keeps telling me stuff that isn't true, I haven't a thing on her—not a thing. And that line of hers doesn't worry me because I understand her motive." He looked Tracy straight in the eyes, a look which made Tracy's lips twitch nervously.

"I know," he muttered. "I'm not worth it."

"I might ask on my part, what has she on you?" Dick pressed.

"I wish to God I knew—for sure."

Dick nodded his head in slow agreement. "Suppose you tell me what you do know—for sure."

Tracy pulled himself together, but in spite of obvious control his voice shook as he said, "I know—for sure—where my aunt's emerald is."

There was delighted surprise in Dick's steady grey eyes. "Yes?

"At Jupe's in Cincinnati," Tracy answered slowly, and Stowe took that moment to speculate about the hitherto faithful PeeDee. Why in thunder had he heard nothing from him since his commission yesterday?

Tracy thought Stowe's silence skeptical and went heavily on. "If I could have raised the money I'd have brought it back myself, but you people ought to know what to do."

"Also, we know what the usual explanation is when anything like that appears at Jupe's. . . . What's your story?"

"It isn't my story; it's the truth." Tracy's reply showed a faint resentment. "Now, Stowe, get this straight. I was drunk last Tuesday night and most of Wednesday—completely squiffed, but I'm clear about a couple of things. I remember that once during that time the emerald brooch was in my possession, but by Wednesday night when I got back here I didn't have it, nor the money I'd won at Mike's. I remember a long walk in the cold and darkness that Janet—that Miss Wilcox told you about . . . the last part of it anyway. I think she was with me then, but if it would do any good I'd swear that it wasn't she who was up here at the house—"

"Who was the other girl, Tracy? I'd figured that far myself."

"You're welcome to find out, Stowe, if you can," he replied wearily.

Whether Tracy were quibbling, Dick was at a loss to know. "Well, go on about the emerald. What made you look for it in Cincinnati?"

"I went down with one of the boys, just for the air as much as anything—and to annoy you and your friends. The chap I was with had a business errand to do, and while I waited I was loafing down there in that section below Second Street. I saw the bloomin' thing in Jupe's window. That's all."

"Not on your life it isn't, Tracy. I'm no child, even though I have an honest face. If it's true that Jupe has the emerald, you just didn't happen to see it; you knew exactly what you were looking for and where. . . . Why, my lad, do you think for one minute that bird would keep a stone like that in his window? Permit me one refined ha ha!"

"You'll find it there, nevertheless, unless he gets the wind up. And another thing—you'll not find that it was I who left it there in the first place." Apparently he had abandoned his first story. "As for the other details, work out your own explanation."

"Which is exactly what I shall do, I promise you," retorted Dick grimly. "As for Miss Wilcox, she can't lie for you forever."

"Stowe, you're not a complete simpleton. Surely your mighty mind has considered the fact that if I broke into this house on the night my aunt was killed, the whole place would have been aroused. I couldn't have pussyfooted—the state I was in."

"Granted without further demonstration. But where are the three people whose alibi for you I'd be willing to listen to respectfully? Your aunt is dead. If you came when Miss Wilcox says you did, it is very likely that Miss Marrender was still alive. At the moment I can not be certain that she was still living when you left. . . . Cubbage is also dead. I'm willing to bet that Cubbage saw and heard you and maybe helped put you out. But, as I said, Cubbage is dead, unfortunately. . . . The third person who was legitimately present that night was Miss Randall, your aunt's nurse. I ask you, where is she? Believe me, when we round up that girl, she's going to precipitate some embarrassing moments, or she can just turn around and go back where she came from. And not for herself nor you only. There are others who—"

"Do you know, I am beginning to suspect that myself. My cousins are—jumpy." Tracy stopped abruptly.

"Go ahead, 'Remember' some more."

But Eugene Tracy lapsed into sullen, dour silence. Stowe tried another approach. He tossed a length of chain across, the piece that he himself had found.

"Take a look at that, will you? You've lived here at Windward Hill for some time. Ever seen anything like it around the place?"

Tracy spent a deliberate period looking at the bit of watch chain. "No, I can't say that I ever saw this particular piece, but I've seen one of similar pattern, and so have you—if you're any sort of detective."

The way he spoke made Dick's blood hot. "Yes, I know," he said hastily. "It matches the chain left on your grandfather's watch."

"That may be, but that's not what I meant." Tracy looked across at Dick's disconcerted face with some pleasure. "My late lamented aunt always wore a chain like this. Didn't you examine the body? But this isn't her chain. Hers was still intact and in its place the day she was buried."

"I see . . ." said Dick thoughtfully, but made no exposition of what he saw.

For a minute or two he busied himself twisting the fragment of chain about one of his lean brown fingers. Then with bright conversational zeal he asked, "Had your aunt always lived here? I've been told she was something of a recluse even before her illness. Had she ever been away from home for any extended time? Travelled, you know . . ."

Tracy permitted himself a quizzical smile as if to go on record that though he was quite aware that this move of Stowe's must mean something, he was personally not much concerned. "Not since the World's Fair, if the family legends can be depended upon. Or thereabouts. Maybe it was a year or so later that she spent sixteen months going around the world. I've always been thankful that she didn't collect curios. When I think of the junk that she might have brought back with her. . . . But don't, take my word as authoritative. All that giddy jaunting must have been before the little stranger came from the everywhere into the here. I've only seen thirty summers."

Dick looked at his watch and rose as if to go. "Say the word, and I'll run you back to town."

"No, thanks, old chap. You might absentmindedly run me back into a cell or something. Call back your guard, if you want—I shan't mind. I really have no devious purpose for being out here, except that I prefer this to the Lindenwood establishment or to the one on the Levee Drive. At that, Will and his wife are out of town. I'm waiting till evening to call on Miss Wilcox. Police tip gratis—hope you appreciate it."

Dick grinned in spite of himself. "By the way, you saw Cubbage before he was buried. Any—er—reactions?"

"I could never have recognized him—as Cubbage."

"Could you have recognized him as anybody else?"

"Come with me," ordered Tracy. "I'll show you."

He led the way from the kitchen down the length of the chilly hall to the drawing-room. Curtains were pushed aside until enough light fell obliquely upon a dark, heavily framed portrait.

"My grandfather, Robert Rufus Marrender," announced Tracy tonelessly. "Judge for yourself. My grandfather was not yet forty when this was painted. I thought the resemblance startling, myself. So did Sally. Though I can't understand why she should hold that against me. . . . I had planned to kill time with her today—"

"Are you telling me anything, Tracy?" demanded Dick.

"What quick wits you have, grandfather. . . ."

22

MESSAGE FROM PEEDEE

Compelling as were Dick Stowe's impressions and ideas
after his talk with Tracy, he had to push aside their inter-
pretation for matters more objective. Tracy's story about
the emerald must be checked immediately. Asher could
send a reliable man down and he could act with PeeDee.
Queer, why PeeDee hadn't reported. . . . And he himself
would have a session with Janet Wilcox. Poor girl, no matter what the eventual answer might be, Janet's chance for
happiness with Eugene Tracy did not promise much.

At Headquarters a bored desk-sergeant informed him
that he wouldn't find Deputy-Inspector Asher at his home
for the excellent reason that he was right here on the spot.

"Why not say so in the first place—in sign language,
if necessary," sputtered Dick, and walked in on Asher's
quiet conference with himself and a stack of departmental
reports.

Asher listened to everything that Dick had to say, which
was not quite all that he had learned that morning, and
relieved his mind about his agent.

"You've been called a couple of times this morning by
that buddy of yours in Cincinnati, but he won't spill a
thing to anybody but you. I told him I'd have you call
back— Say, why shouldn't you and I both go down to see

what's in this Jupe business? You know I had a report on that fence yesterday morning, and nothing doing."

"I think Tracy planted it there himself and he didn't get down till the middle of the afternoon. But say, Timmy, what for you gyp me about this chain?"

With puzzled attention Tim Asher examined the length of chain that Dick handed to him. "Gyp you? Me? Wait a minute—I'm on now. There was a piece of chain like this around the old lady's neck—"

"You'd not let me hear about it, would you?" exploded Dick. "Not that it matters now. Except that I wish I could have seen for myself that her chain was like this."

"Take it from me, kid, it was. Got a hot idea?"

"A crazy one—and it will keep. Anyway, until I've called PeeDee."

From the resulting telephonic complications it soon became evident that the dutiful PeeDee was trying just as frantically from his end to call Stowe, and as the little man in Cincinnati was more persistent and less imaginative it was Stowe who stood by patiently and allowed the call to come in to him.

When the connection was at length established, Pee-Dee's news reversed their proposed program, though it was Dick who snatched first innings. When PeeDee had been told about Jupe and the emerald, the wire clicked with PeeDee's determined interruption.

"Say, listen, Stowe, I'm telling you. I've found a girl down here, I'm on my way up with her right now. . . ." The line went dead.

"The nurse!" Dick chortled and invented an intricate dance step on the spot with the useless telephone as a partner. "It won't be long now. I know what PeeDee can do with a car."

"Maybe there'll be time enough for you to take a squint at these reports," said Asher, showing no signs of excitement. "It's stuff you've been howling for."

Dick dropped into the chair opposite Asher's and addressed himself to the sheaf of papers that the deputy-inspector pushed across the table to him. For a time there was no sound in the stuffy room except the rustle of pages and the regular scratching of matches as one cigarette after another was smoked. When Asher had finished his task, he surveyed the young man whom his superior thought so highly of.

Dick glanced up to meet the steady gaze and quirked an eyebrow. "Not so bad, this dope, eh, Timmy?"

"I'd like to hear what you make of it, old son, particularly that jargon about Benssen's #3."

"Oh, that!" Dick laughed. "I'm out of my depth there, too, but I've managed to gather one comforting fact from it."

"What, for instance?"

Dick shuffled papers busily for a minute and when he spoke he ignored Asher's question. "Whose picture is this?" he demanded, separating an unmounted print from the litter of material spread before him.

"There should be a memo attached. You're sure it's not your Burden Street dame?"

"Not a chance. She was like a slat."

Asher sighed dolefully. "One grand hunch gone to pot. That's a picture of Doris Randall."

"Cheer up, Tim. What do you bet we'll be seeing her in about an hour? Three cheers—when did this report come in from the post office?"

"Just this morning. Service, huh?"

"I'll say . . . and I'll also say, Timmy, that their report puts a period after one item all right, all right."

"Don't overdo yourself spilling anything. . . ."

"Aw, Tim . . . you read the report, didn't you? And you can see this envelope addressed to the postmaster, can't you? Well, then, since it bears the postmark of the twenty-fourth, Marrender's letter from Cubbage was mailed at least twenty-four hours after his death, which means that

my guess was right—Cubbage was murdered. Whoever
wrote the letter must have killed the man."

"And your guess about that?"

"Don't embarrass me, Timmy. Um-mm, this everlasting list is the names of those who turned in tickets at the
Art Dinner, is it? Just as I thought—Latimer and Stuart
were not among those present. In fact, they've never insisted that they were. Only . . . someone in a car stopped
for Mrs. Latimer about seven that Tuesday evening, and
a little before eight Mrs. Banney saw her at Windward
Hill, and at eight or thereabouts she was receiving Stuart's
professional attention in his offices downtown; and after
eleven they were driving together; and between one and
say, two-thirty, they were stalled on the River Road just
below Windward Hill, and— What I'd really like to know
is: What happened at Windward Hill during the eight
o'clock visit? Two people who knew are dead, and the third
person—well, we'll see what PeeDee drags in. I say, Mr.
Inspector, what about the doctor's .38?"

"He's got an ad in today's Losts and Founds."

"The devil he has! Tim, your department ought to help
him find it."

"Sa-ay! What about you being all steamed up about the
doc snitching the Marrender girl's gun yesterday? We gave
him the works all right, but not a thing. For once, your
foot slipped, I'll say."

"Right you are, Tim. If Stuart had procured a substitute
for his own supposedly missing gun yesterday, he would
not have bothered to advertise today." Stowe picked up
another paper hurriedly. "Somebody did a neat job about
the milkman."

"That was Downer. I thought you'd be pleased."

"Yes, it's about the first break in their favor. . . . Since
a milkman has been found who saw a man and girl turning
into Burden Street a little after four a.m., I hope more of

Miss Wilcox's story is true than at the present time I dare
believe."

"So that's your weakness now?"

"No, Tim, but I am trying to be fair. Tracy's going to
be in a nasty jam, I'm afraid, and yet—I gotta feelin' that
he did not kill his aunt. He could have had no conceiv-
able motive. You see his signed agreement with his aunt
appeared safely just where it should be. But there's that
arrangement by which he was to have whatever he wanted
from the little gallery, so he might have been the one who
tore that place upside down. It's the sort of trick a drunk-
en man would do, Tim . . . or is it? I keep thinking about
both windows in the room being open. Damned odd. . . .
And if Tracy walked out of Sally's Shop with her revolver
yesterday morning, think of the scads of chances he had to
dispose of it for good and all between here and Cincinnati.
Oh, Lord. . . ."

"What got you all steamed up about that piece of gold
chain, Dick?" asked Asher after five minutes of uneasy
silence.

"I said it was a crazy idea, Tim, and I'll have to investigate family history a bit further before I can be sure I'm
on to anything. I may never be able to prove a thing, but
I'm betting with myself that maybe the old chain will help
clear up the mystery of Cubbage's identity. If it should,
it's going to score pretty heavily against the Marrenders."

"Meaning Sally and Will?"

Dick shot a keen, quick glance at Asher, but made no
answer.

"Sure, Dick, listen. . . . They were each doing this
and that during the earlier part of the evening. Then they
got together and what happened after that we're supposed
to take on faith. They could have beat it out there and
pulled off most anything. They could have been in the
car that Galeotti saw change its mind about turning in to

the Windward Hill drive while he was waiting for his girl
friend. And I'll tell the world this much—Marrender was
a damned cool customer Wednesday morning when the sad
news was broke to him. I saw his face, remember. And the
girl was up to some kind of funny business Friday night.
If you're right about her gun, then her own brother could
have made off with it yesterday morning. What do you bet
that guy is on to what the marks on a bullet can tell?"

"Motive?" queried Dick, regarding Asher with interest.

"Money." The answer was dogmatic. "You've not forgotten about the loan that Marrender pulled off the very day
after his aunt was killed, have you? And Tuesday morning
the girl quarreled with her aunt. Looks to me as though
she had asked for something which she didn't get, and so
she and her brother made their own arrangements for the
evening. Maybe the old lady announced to her that morning that she was going to change her will. Remember the
letter that Dexter got. . . ."

"Very neat, Timmy, ve-ry neat. Moreover, according
to this,"—Dick indicated the formidable report from the
poison expert—"the stuff that killed Cubbage could have
been administered at the hour Wednesday night that Marrender was there—and Stuart and you and I and Downer,
as I have remarked before." He ran his eye along the typewritten lines again. "This does little more than verify
Shade's first report. There's nothing here about United
Utilities yet."

"No, you'll have to wait till tomorrow for that."

"Frankly, the only relative that I feel comparatively confident about is Francesca Penrose. She's told me a
straight story except for one detail. She heard something
or saw someone while she was doing her stuff in the little
gallery. I believe I could make a guess. . . . You see, Miss
Penrose is not the sort to rhapsodize over her relatives, but

I can't imagine she'd willingly give her own sister away. Therefore, I'm forced to conclude that she ran into something that she associates with Mrs. Latimer. Galeotti said she was all to pieces when she get back to the car."

"Even you could have your leg pulled."

"I'm not that susceptible to blondes, Tim. But if Miss Penrose suspected one of her cousins of being at large about Windward Hill, she wouldn't be quite as edgy as she is. If it was Mrs. Latimer whom she met, well—I can't make it seem necessary. It was only a question of time before Miss Marrender would have died in the natural course of events. Stuart knew that. Why wasn't she—or he—or both of them—content to wait? After Mrs. Latimer had safely inherited two hundred thousand dollars, not getting alimony from Latimer wouldn't have held her back for a minute, and Stuart could then have taken on a wife who could pay her own expensive way—"

"Maybe she figured that if she waited the doctor would have changed his mind."

"Timmy, you darned old torch-bearer, that's it exactly. You've got the doctor's number all right. Why didn't I think of that myself? Why, I remember somebody saying something about the doctor and the nurse. . . ." He narrowed his eyes and consulted the Western Union clock that tick-tocked between the windows whose grimy panes did so little to illumine the office of the Inspector of Detectives.

"After all's said and done, maybe Cubbage did kill the old lady." Asher stirred restlessly in the Inspector's swivel chair.

"When we hear from Jupe, perhaps we can arrest Tracy, and that may start something with the others. Don't worry, Asher; the responsibility for giving this juicy bunch of suspects so much rope is all mine. Hello, that sounds like action out there. I wonder if PeeDee—" Both men turned alertly toward the door. It opened and the slim, compact figure of one P. D. Simpson stepped inside.

"I got here, Stowe, and I brought the girl-friend, too. The matron will trot her in in a minute. Business of powdering the nose, see. And somebody up here will have to explain to a constable down the road between Hebron and Middleville. . . . Sorry, I don't think this dame connects up with the emerald, but she does with Tracy all right. I followed him yesterday—sure I did, but all he did was hunt this skirt up and have a long chin about something. Then he came back down-town and got himself a bite to eat and loafed around until his friend picked him up again. I saw 'em out of town, and then I came back to see what I could start with the girl he'd been talking to. I trailed her around the rest of the evening but at last I pinned her down and—well, this morning she decided she'd tell somebody something, and I figured it might just as well be you, Stowe."

PeeDee stepped backward to the door and swung it open. "Here, you, step inside," he commanded.

A slight, nonchalant figure crossed the threshold. The resulting introduction was a masterpiece of gallantry.

"This here's Esme Croft. She says she's an actress."

The instant Dick Stowe's eyes rested upon the girl's set face he knew that at last something was going to unwind. For Esme Croft was the girl whom he had seen in the hall of the shabby rooming-house on Burden Street . . . the girl who had been wearing the Marrender emerald.

23

Memorable Experience of Esme Croft

Esme Croft took Stowe's measure with cool eyes and waited for him to speak. Dick waited also, but his sinister deliberation had no effect upon her. PeeDee reluctantly withdrew to explain his hurried arrival to a still skeptical traffic man, but Asher remained in his seat of authority.

Just as Dick was concluding that though Miss Croft might be a trained actress she was undoubtedly a natural-born adventuress, she smiled in slow disparagement. "Surely it hasn't taken you all this time to remember that you've seen me before," she drawled.

"Certainly not! I've just been wondering whether you could tell the truth."

"I might begin with a genuine sample and—after that, you'd have to decide for yourself."

"You were in this city last Tuesday night?"

"Yes. All day, in fact. I came in from New York on a morning train. I spent the evening with Miss Eugenia Marrender."

"What!" It was almost a shout; certainly Stowe had never expected to hear that.

"I promised you a sample of truth-telling. This is it: she didn't know I was there. I was waiting for Gene Tracy."

"Then you're just the person we've been looking for. What do you say happened at Windward Hill that night?"

"Unfortunately I was not occupying a box seat." She was astonishingly suave.

"Tell your story and tell it straight," he commanded.

The smooth finish that so far had distinguished her manner slipped abruptly off. "I couldn't let him play me for a sucker, could I? When Gene showed up at that dump of his, see, he hadn't kept his promise, so I marched him up to that god-forsaken house on the hill."

"You mean you were waiting for him at the Burden Street room when he turned in there before midnight. I see. . . . Now his promise about what?"

"Aw, do your own guessing. You're not that dumb, are you?"

"How did you make the trip from Burden Street to Windward Hill?" Dick was imperturbable.

"Taxied."

"What time did you get out there?"

"A little after one, I think. Gene had a key and we slipped into the house. He parked me down in the hall while he went upstairs to get—what he'd promised me. It took him longer than I thought it ought to, but just as I was all set to go up after him I heard someone coming from the back part of the house. Honest, I was so scared for a minute that I did a darned fool trick. According to what I've read in the papers since, it must have been that crazy butler. Anyway, I dodged out of the hall through a partly opened door. It was that first room on the left, a kind of living-room, as near as I could tell in the darkness—and, believe me, it was pitch black in there. I waited there for quite a while without hearing a sound. At last I thought I could take a chance on stepping out into the hall again, but, say—I couldn't get out!

"Somebody had locked me in. It's a wonder I didn't scream bloody murder, I'm telling you. But, believe it or not, I was scared stiff. I didn't even try to get out some other way or hunt for light buttons or anything sensible like that. I just sat there on the floor and shook—my god, it seemed like hours . . . and then after a million years I heard the door being unlocked and the handle turn. The door swung in toward me and I could hear someone breathing. Don't ask me how I lived through it. . . . Then a graveyard voice said, real low, 'It's all right now, Miss. You'd better be off before it gets light.'

"I didn't say anything—I couldn't. I got to my feet, though, and stood in the door trying to see who it was. Much good it did me! Then I felt a wave of cold outside air and that awful voice said, 'I've opened the door, Miss. If I were you, I should leave immediately.'

"Well, that's what I did. I was fed up with that nightmare, and I don't mean maybe. Once I got started I went out of that house in a hurry; but not quite fast enough not to have something wished on me, at that. This old devil that kept whispering to me through the darkness pushed something into my hand just as I went through the door and said, 'From Mr. Eugene, Miss,' and then he laughed like a fool.

"I hung on to whatever it was and beat it down the drive and then along the road. When I'd got out of sight of that awful house, I came to enough to figure that I was running away from town rather than towards it, but I kept on anyway. I walked for about an hour before I came to the first village and then I found out that it was almost five o'clock. By that time I knew I wanted to get as far away as I could, so I took the first way I saw—an interurban trolley loaded with milk cans. I stayed with it till it got to Cincy, too. After I got on the car I had my first chance to see what my parting gift was. Do you need three guesses?"

"The emerald pin," said Asher and Dick as one.

"Yes, that damned emerald." Esme Croft sighed and said nothing more, as though she had finished her story.

"If you've told me all you will of your own accord, I can think of two, no, three questions I must ask you." Stowe leaned forward confidentially.

"Is that all? Don't stint yourself." The girl's first hardness echoed in the words.

Before Dick could launch his attack, a long-distance message called Asher out of the office. He was loath to go, for he knew that Dick would go ahead with his examination of this astonishing story. As he departed he heard the first of the three questions.

"While you were locked in the drawing-room, what at any time did you hear?"

"I heard a shot . . . and not long after that I heard steps coming downstairs, only not the front stairs—I don't *know* that there's a back stairs to that house, you understand—and something like a door shutting." Esme's pale green eyes regarded him without a flicker. "I almost called out then, but I knew they weren't Gene's steps, and so I kept still."

"You heard rather a lot, didn't you? and you knew they weren't Gene's steps?"

"Is that the second of your three questions? I always recognize people's footsteps—one of my many native gifts. I had never heard these steps before, so they weren't the person's who had locked me in."

"This isn't number two either: can you venture a guess about the time?"

She shook her head. "No, only that it seemed midway during that everlasting time I was shut up. I must have been in that locked room nearly three hours, don't you think?"

"Yes, I dare say you were. Here's my second question: had Tracy promised to give you the emerald?"

"If I say yes, you'll want to know why, and that's this li'l gold-digger's private business. But I will tell you this much, which you won't want to believe—I thought till yesterday that the emerald actually belonged to Gene."

Dick nodded in agreement, well satisfied. "In that case, what brought you to his Burden Street place the other day?"

"After what he let me in for at Windward Hill, some sort of show-down was coming to him."

"You wore the emerald very openly. Your naturally reckless temperament, I presume."

"Go ahead and kid me—I don't mind. I'll admit that was careless. I thought my scarf covered it. At any rate, you scared me off."

"So you saw nor heard nothing from Tracy until yesterday? Go on with your story from there, please."

"How about that third question? I've lost count."

"Later . . . later, Miss Croft."

"You dicks haven't been supervising his mail evidently. I dropped him a card with a Cincinnati address after I failed to make connections with him the other day. He appeared yesterday, as you seem to know, but it wasn't an arranged meeting. We had a good old heart-to-heart. Gene wasn't crystal clear about his part. He thinks he sat down to rest when he got upstairs and fell asleep, and he tried to tell me that I walked all the way back to Burden Street with him. He looked sick when I showed him the emerald pin. I let him think he'd given it to me himself, see. Then what does the piker do but tell me it wasn't his to give away. I wasn't going to hand it back to him, just like that, so we—er—compromised. I told him I'd take it to this joint down by the wharves. After I'd realized a little something on it, I didn't much care who got it."

Dick Stowe's eyebrows twisted in a frown. "I confess I can't understand your generosity, Miss Croft."

"I'm rather proud of it myself," she mocked.

"Did Tracy tell you about his aunt's will?"

"Yes, I asked him."

"Miss Croft, are you by any chance in love with Eugene Tracy?"

She shrugged her thin shoulders. "Not even before I heard that he didn't inherit, and now—he hasn't a chance. I've got to look out for little Esme."

"There's another girl, you see."

"I know. She can have him, and welcome. If you think it might make her any happier, you could tell her that he didn't wander of his own accord. Me, I'm going back to Broadway."

Dick shook his head regretfully. "Not immediately, I'm sorry to tell you. Your frankness has been very delightful and I'm going to reciprocate with a warning as frank. Watch your step, Miss Croft. You know without being told that you can be held as a material witness. In other words, be around when you're wanted and don't babble."

She gave him a friendly, impudent smile. Her heavily rouged lips sent him to fumbling in his pocket for a certain token. He untwisted the fold of paper that protected it and displayed the lipstick marked cigarette end.

"You see, I knew all along that you were in the Burden Street room." Dick looked at Esme Croft as though he expected a fulsome compliment.

"Then why didn't you know that I was shut up in that black parlor, too? I smoked everything I had—I had a lighter that worked. That was the only way I could tell what sort of hole I was in." She shuddered reminiscently.

"Cubbage must have removed every trace. He meant something by every move he made . . . if I only knew what."

Dick followed his questing thoughts till Esme moved impatiently. "Your third question?" she hinted.

"How drunk was Tracy when you were with him?"

"Oh, he'd been drinking, some. That's why he'd slipped up on getting the emerald for me earlier in the evening— or so I thought. But by the time he rounded in to Burden Street the worst was over."

"You are sure of that, Miss Croft? A lie just now would be dangerous to everybody concerned."

"When he left me standing in the hall at Windward Hill he knew exactly what he was doing, and that's straight, Mr. Stowe."

The girl's shallow green eyes were candid.

Dick was conscious of a great desire to proclaim to someone what a smart boy he considered himself at that moment. The continued insistence upon Tracy's befuddled condition had for some time, Dick had been thinking, sounded forced. It was an excellent shield to keep from telling what ought to be forgotten . . . and yet, Esme herself apparently accepted Tracy's story about not knowing what he had done after he left her in the lower hall. What if Cubbage had—drugged him? Nice little solution.

Asher at that instant yanked the door open and strode inside. "For the love of Lulu, Dick, the emerald's gone! Report just now came through from the boys in Cin—"

"Try and hang that on me—just try it!" squawked Esme.

"No, so help me, it's another woman. Wouldn't that tie you!" Asher groaned helplessly. "Has your PeeDee started back yet?"

"No," replied Stowe. "Take it easy, Tim. How do you mean—gone?"

"Jupe's story clicks with this dame's about bringing the pin in early Saturday evening, though he claims it wasn't worth near what she thought it was."

Esme sniffed, but Asher was talking directly to Dick. "Then early this afternoon a stylish blonde lady, according to the way he described her to the boys down there, dropped in and asked to see old-fashioned jewelry. She didn't pay any attention to the emerald pin, but he missed it, all right, after she left. That's his story and he's sticking to it."

"Hm-mm, a stylish blonde lady . . . it's a pity that Jupe's not better at description," mused Dick. She was obviously not Sally Marrender. That was as far as he felt safe. She might have been Katherine Latimer . . . or Francesca Penrose. She might even have been Mrs. William Marrender, he thought generously, recalling the tidy little mouse-blonde creature who had once been pointed out to him as the wife of the most rapidly advanced executive in United Utilities. But why was he assuming that she had to be one of the ladies of the family?

"Let's round up PeeDee," he concluded, and Miss Esme Croft found herself once more parked with the police matron.

In short order a fully commissioned PeeDee was making a return trip to Cincinnati, late as it was, and Dick was hailing a taxi and giving the driver Janet Wilcox's Edgefield address. After hearing Esme's story it was more important than ever to have a talk with Janet before Tracy kept his proposed engagement with her.

The recent events at Headquarters had stretched over more time than he realized. Miss Wilcox had gone out for the evening, he was told. . . .

To steady the jumble that his thoughts were in, Dick walked back to his own diggings. He found himself again mulling over the masterly brain wave that he hadn't had a chance to spring on anyone. No doubt he was a fool to try to prove that Cubbage was a Marrender, but somehow the idea was annoyingly persistent. A handkerchief marked with an M . . . the fact that the man had disguised his appearance slightly and his age more than that . . . Jake's maunderings about having once seen a man who reminded him of old Robert Rufus—the portrait hanging in the drawing-room at Windward Hill . . . the impression created by Cubbage's dead face upon both Tracy and his cousin Sally . . . a broken length of old chain—what did they *prove?* Then there was the sinister way in which the man had acted as stage manager on the night of the crime, provided Esme's wild story could be relied upon. Some way he felt that it could, in spite of the endless varieties of lies that the others had offered him. Cubbage had so obviously pointed out evidence involving both Tracy and the nurse; he had as plainly screened Mrs. Latimer's call early in the evening . . . yet why had he mentioned a caller at all, and why had her gloves appeared in his coat pocket? After all, wasn't it infinitely easier to assume that Cubbage was guilty of everything?

Dick sighed; he was tired. Then suddenly a new thought chilled him. Janet Wilcox was not at home. Would the unsavory Jupe, whose forte was clearly not description, report a girl like Janet Wilcox as a stylish blonde?

Help was coming, but Dick Stowe did not know that, nor expect it. Neither did Asher, Deputy-Inspector of Detectives. In fact, it was an underling at Headquarters; who received and answered in a routine manner the non-committal inquiry from a jumping-off place called San Barto for full details concerning a certain witness of importance.

24

REVISED VERSION

As a consequence of his fruitless expedition of Sunday
evening, the next morning Stowe lost no time in seeking
out Janet Wilcox at her post of duty with United Utilities,
only to be informed that she had not reported. Someone
had telephoned that she was ill. . . . Sorry, but Mr. Marrender had not yet arrived.

At that point Bettina asserted herself. Bettina had
plenty of time to be chatty. Too bad about Janet . . . she
wasn't hardly ever sick. No, the boss wasn't sick. He'd had
to take his wife down to Cincinnati on Saturday—Bettina
had heard him talking about it over the 'phone. There was
some doctor down there that Mrs. Marrender wanted to go
to, but the boss said he'd be back by Monday noon sure.

Dick thanked Bettina gravely and once more set out for
Janet Wilcox's Edgefield address. Rather interesting information, that, about the Marrender's weekend in Cincinnati, he thought and whistled softly throughout the trip.

Suppose Janet too had disappeared, he thought as the
doorbell shrilled under his thumb, but the landlady's se-
date little ten-year-old daughter took him for the doctor and ushered him without question up to the lodger's
room. Dick was no diagnostician, but when he stepped
inside he knew that the girl within was sick with worry
and fear. Perhaps his visit would do her more good than a

legitimate practitioner's. For her part, when she saw who it was, she made a brave attempt to appear displeased at her landlady's carelessness, but her underlying panic could not be concealed.

Dick began as though no explanations were necessary. "Since I saw you last, Miss Wilcox, I've had a very interesting talk with the young lady who accompanied Eugene Tracy to Windward Hill last Tuesday night. I thought you might like to hear about it. I'll be glad to tell you what I can, if you'll straighten out that story of yours. . . . You were there yourself, I believe, but not as an actor. Right?"

Eyes wide with frightened attention, Janet nodded. She tried to speak but could not risk her control.

Dick's hearty voice went on. "This other girl—she's resigning. In other words, she didn't hanker after the boy-friend for himself alone, so that's one thing you don't have to worry about any more."

He paused diplomatically. Time out was needed for the faint pink to flood and recede from Janet's thin cheeks. "I hope you don't mind admitting to me that it was nothing but jealousy that made you trail after them the other night."

This time she managed a very small "I suppose I ought to die rather than agree with you."

"But afterwards, you were glad that you had because of what happened. Gene never needed you more in his life. . . ."

"You have found out—?" Again, the words were blurred and choked with fear.

"Not everything yet," he answered, seemingly unaware of the devastating emotion that shook the girl. "That's why I think you and I should have an understanding—in Gene's interest. Suppose you begin with his return Tuesday morning."

"He had been in New York seeing about his big score. A plan that was almost agreed upon unexpectedly didn't go through. It was a shocking disappointment. Nobody knows about that—nor cares, except me. That's why he came back here sooner than he had planned. He didn't even let me know, but I happened to see him as he came from the train that morning. A girl was with him whom I had never seen before. All day I expected to hear from him, but I didn't . . . and I was a little worried.

"I don't suppose I have to tell you that Gene and I are engaged. We could get married just as well as not—the way I look at it, I'd keep on with my job, but Gene won't hear of it till he's proved he can make money from his music.

"By evening I was so worried and uneasy that I did something I'd vowed never to do—I called the Windward Hill place. I suppose it was the butler who answered me. All I said was, Had Mr. Tracy got back from the East yet? The man said no—"

So that was the explanation of Asher's hunch that Cubbage was lying when he declared there had been no telephone calls on Tuesday evening, thought Dick. But why? What game had the man been playing? Ah, he must listen to Janet.

"So then I went around to the Burden Street room. He wasn't there . . . and so I went to a movie by myself. When I came out of the picture show I couldn't bear to come out here without knowing . . . so I went around to Burden Street again. This time I slipped into his room and waited. In just a little while I heard him coming and I—could tell that he had been drinking. I thought maybe one of the men that were with him might come in, so I stepped behind the curtain that shuts off the space he uses for a closet. The men didn't stay, but before I could come out the door opened and a girl came in—the same girl I had seen with him in the morning.

"There I was—I had to listen to what she said. It was terrible—for me, I mean. I could tell that he had been seeing something of her when he'd been in New York, and that he'd got in some sort of mess. She was insisting that he keep his promise about something. At last he said, 'All right, come on. I'll show you,' and they went out together.

"I followed them—the girl couldn't have recognized me, and Gene—Gene hardly knew what he was doing. I heard her tell a taxi man where to go, and for some reason that made me mad clear through. As long as I've known Gene Tracy he's never taken me out to Windward Hill. I made up my mind to tag along, but there wasn't a taxi anywhere. The best I could do was to take the street car, but at that I made pretty good time. The empty taxi was just coming out of the drive when I came in sight of it. But by the time I got to the house there wasn't a sign of life anywhere—"

"Just a minute," interrupted Dick, "when you told your other story you said it was about one o'clock. Does that still hold?"

"Yes. I couldn't see my watch, but I'd been on the last trolley and it was twelve-thirty then."

"All right. Then what?" It occurred to Dick that the conductor on the car could be found to verify that much of the story, if necessary.

"I tried the front door, but it was locked. There was no light in the lower hall and I couldn't see a thing distinctly, though once I thought I saw a shadow moving at the farther end. I prowled around on the outside and went back down the drive far enough to look up at the upper windows. As far as I could see there was a light in only one room and that was very dim. It was Miss Marrender's room, I suppose. I was beginning to think that maybe Gene and the girl hadn't gone in after all when something happened that made me forget about them for awhile.

"I was about halfway to the entrance of the drive and well hidden in the shadow of a clump of dwarf cedars. No one coming up the drive could possibly have seen me. So when I heard the sound of running steps I just stayed where I was. A woman came scudding up from the road. All I could tell about her was that she was a woman and light on her feet, and taller than the one who had been with Gene. I watched her flying shadow till she swerved around the house and out of sight. Then I followed. I cut up across the lawn to the side of the house. All I could see was one swinging beam of light coming through a window, add then I realized that someone was coming out through this window. It was the same woman, I'm sure, though she didn't use the flash-light again. She turned around and pulled down the window, and just as she started away she made a funny little sound almost as if she spoke to someone, but I couldn't see or hear anyone else there. The woman began to run again, back toward the road, and I followed a little way, but it was so black under the trees that I couldn't see her long. Anyway, a few minutes after I lost sight of her, I heard a motor start up. That's all of that part."

"Good Lord, is there more?" exclaimed Dick. What a priceless alibi for Francesca Penrose, who didn't need it!

It was doing Janet good to talk. Her voice was now firm and her eyes clear and steady. The wave of terror that had gripped her so pitiably before she had lost herself in this astonishing narrative had ebbed completely. There was even a glint of humor now as she said, "Now I must incriminate myself. The bright idea that I told you of the other night really did occur to me—I saw a fine chance to do something for Gene that he never would have done for himself. If I could put my hands on the extra key to Miss Marrender's safety-deposit box I knew I could—"

Again she stopped just as abruptly as she had the night Dick had confronted the two of them in the little gallery, and again Dick's mind fumbled blindly with the hidden reason for her pause.

"You see, I knew I could get into that room too, the same way that somebody else had just got out of it. So after waiting awhile longer and arguing with myself about it, in I went. It was just as easy. . . . The only catch in it was that I had no flash-light. I was awfully afraid I'd stumble over something in the dark. It was quite a while before I had courage enough to snap on a light. I pulled the curtains close over the windows and hung my hat over the doorknob so the light wouldn't show through the key-hole. By the way, that's when I found out that the door was locked on the outside—not later, as I told you last Friday night."

"I hate like everything to interrupt,"—and Dick meant it—"but I must know about the time. You've said over and over that you waited awhile and so on."

For an instant Janet Wilcox reverted to the efficient secretary that she was. "It's only a rough estimate, but you can have it for what it is worth. I must have put in a good hour and a half snooping around in that shameless fashion since my first appearance on the scene. I wandered around outside ever so long before the woman came up the drive. I was—pretty much sunk about Gene and that girl. But when I got inside the room what happened was just what I told you before, except that I was—alone. You can see for yourself why I said Gene and I were together." There was frantic question in her eyes.

"I take it that as long as you did not know what Gene was doing in the house that night, you were chancing an alibi of sorts for him." In spite of the pleading eyes, Dick could not as yet honestly give the girl the assurance that an alibi for Tracy was unnecessary. "And then what?"

"I was still searching for what I wanted when I heard the shot. I was frightened, though I associated it only with Gene and the girl. Gene has a nasty temper, and of course I hadn't liked the looks of the strange girl. There wasn't a sound anywhere—the shot wasn't getting the house excited, I mean. But I wanted to get out and get out quick. I snapped out the light, grabbed my hat, and climbed out of the window faster than I had got in."

"You really left the window open, just as you said?"

"Yes, wide open."

"It was the window to the right from the inside? To the left from without?"

"Yes."

"And was the room in good order?"

"Yes, quite. Everything was stiff and prim and not-lived-in looking, except that whoever had been in just before I came had evidently forgotten her gloves. There was a pair lying on the table nearest the book shelves."

Dick wanted to burst into applause. "Did you leave them there?" he asked.

She nodded. "Yes. I thought afterwards I might have found out who the woman was from them, but I suppose the police did that."

Officially Dick Stowe was non-committal about that point; privately he was wondering what the devil had become of Francesca Penrose's gloves. Could there be an error about the pair found in Cubbage's overcoat being Mrs. Latimer's? Aloud he began to thank Janet for her remarkably clear account of her unconventional evening.

"But I haven't told you everything yet," she murmured.

"That's all right with me. I was hoping you hadn't."

"I tumbled out of the window and raced down the drive just as fast as the first woman had, but when I got to the road I stopped to get my breath. The road was awfully dark, and suddenly I felt afraid to go back to town alone.

I'd lost all my nerve by that time—I felt I'd just as lief freeze to death by the side of the road as walk on through that blackness alone. Then I heard steps coming down the drive, slow and stumbling. There was something dreadful about them, but I wasn't afraid. I knew they were Gene's.

"He was a lot worse than he'd been earlier in the evening, but I couldn't smell liquor on his breath. He didn't know me—not at first, anyway. He was awfully groggy and mumbled and moaned to himself as he lurched toward me. I thought the best thing to do was to keep him going and we started off down that black road towards town. I forgot all about being afraid.

"After awhile I could tell that I had done the right thing, for the cold air brought him around, but even though he got so he could answer my questions, things were all the worse for me. Gene didn't know what had happened back there at Windward Hill . . . and I began to think—pretty terrible things. You see, there was no sign of the girl. And there was the shot I had heard. . . . Once he called me Esme, that must be her name. All he knew was that he had stopped for a drink and must have fallen asleep—"

"I am beginning to think that was just exactly what happened. Have you had any experience with people who have been doped? No? Well, never mind . . . go on."

"The rest is just as I told you the other night. We walked all the way back to Burden Street and we didn't see anybody except one milkman. I left Gene and went to the railway station—I told you all that. I was frightfully worried about Gene—he was awfully queer. And then later on that day when I heard what actually had happened to Miss Marrender-—oh, I can't talk about it. . . .

"The more I thought about it, the worse it looked for Gene. And afterwards, I couldn't get in touch with him for a secret talk until Friday night. There was somebody from the police around all the time. When we met at last—he still didn't seem to know what he had done that night. God in heaven, I thought I'd die . . . till I thought of a plan. So I told him, and later you, my version of what had happened that night. For a little while I believed my plan was going to work, till you began to ask about the emerald, and then I realized there were things I didn't know about. Last night all Gene would say about the emerald was that the mystery about it would soon be cleared up." Again Janet looked at Dick questioningly.

"I'm not so sure of that, though after all the emerald is not Tracy's party." If she could scrape any comfort from that, let her, he added mentally.

Again her anguished eyes sought his. "I—I can't stand much more. Please tell me—is anything dreadful going to happen to Gene?"

"If you have told me the whole truth at last, Miss Wilcox, why are you still so obsessed with fear for Tracy? You are convincing me that you are suppressing some one detail which you fear would involve irretrievably the man you love."

White-faced, the girl shrank back into the depths of her chair. "No—no." Her stiff lips formed the words, but she could bring forth no sound.

"It's worth trying at any rate," he murmured to himself and rose to go. At the door he turned briskly. "By the way, Miss Wilcox, you struck no matches while you were in. the little gallery?"

She shook her head mutely.

"I thought not." He bade the girl a polite good-day and set out for Headquarters.

25
WHOSE .38?

At Headquarters Stowe stopped only long enough to annex a cub assistant who drove a police car where he was told with no outward curiosity. The youth permitted himself one question as he parked his car at the railway station.

"You going away?"

"No, there's a parcel at the check-room that I want." Dick's reply was discreet. He knew very well what it was he wanted, but he was taking a long chance on knowing where to look for it.

After a brief interview with the station master, a cryptic order was handed to the man in charge of the check-room which resulted in Stowe's admission behind the counter. Up and down the narrow aisles he marched, inspecting the baggage-laden racks. Several times he paused to examine more closely a parcel or a box. The acolyte trailing at his heels gave promise of a future by observing that pieces of regular luggage were never noticed.

At last a grease-stained shoe box still redolent of luncheon, was taken down and carefully untied. All that the cub could see when the lid was lifted was a bundle wrapped in lengths of paper toweling. Cautiously Stowe's lean fingers poked and prodded. A grin of Cheshire proportions dawned on his face.

"Come along, you. I'm willing to take a chance on this." His voice was jubilant. "Back to Headquarters and step on it."

Like a whirlwind Dick made for the Inspector's office. "Open this, Tim, open it—and break it gently to me if I've pulled a boner."

Asher was provokingly deliberate. He was particular about knots and he fingered the checking tag still looped about the cord. "Dated 2-22," he observed. "The day after the party, huh?"

Dick jerked off the lid and lifted out the paper-swathed object. With fingers that shook a bit he unrolled the wrappings until what was hidden lay revealed.

A .38 caliber revolver.

"For the love of Lulu, Dick! Where did you pick it up?"

Quickly Stowe ran over the high points of Janet's latest story. "Everything she told me this time checked with what I'd been suspecting might be the explanation of the curious discrepancies of her former story. She reported much that sounded like straight dope, but there were gaps that did not click at all with facts I had reason to be pretty certain. about. Change her from actor to spectator and you can see why she drew blank about some things."

"Call her a spectator, do you, when she crawls through a window and overhauls a room?" growled Asher.

Dick went on blandly. "Her insistence that she had left the window open, and Miss Penrose's statement that she had closed it after her when she left was a mighty plain lead."

"Anything that actress says you take for gospel, I've been noticing." Asher was critical.

"Miss Wilcox's new version only strengthens Miss Penrose's position, if I may point that out to you, Timmy, as well as my feeling that Francesca Penrose is still holding out something," he added as if to himself. "It was easy enough to see that Janet Wilcox was acting only to shield Tracy, and I could tell from her whole attitude that there was something . . . somewhere that made her fear that sooner or later he would be accused of murder. I looked at the situation from her point of view. What would she consider the most incriminating fact that could be brought against him? If she knew, for instance, that he had a gun on him when he left Windward Hill. Apparently Tracy himself remembered nothing about a gun. What had become of it? The girl could have hidden it . . . but where? From Burden Street she had gone to the railway station. What commoner place to park what you don't want to carry around? There was no use, I thought, to look for a piece of ordinary baggage. She had to use a make-shift, cast-off container. So when I told the station master what I had to do, I decided I'd bother only with the bundles and such-like. That wreck of a lunch box looked like a pretty good bet and sure enough—but that was just a lucky break for me."

"I call it damned good logic." Asher was painfully solemn as he delivered his tribute to the young detective's ability.

"At that dreary hour of the early morning the chances are that no one noticed what she was doing. Even the matron was probably dozing. Since the gun was wrapped in paper towels, I gather that she might have transferred it from her hand-bag to the box in the wash room. She used the towels to keep the thing from bouncing about in its hiding place. And now—"

"Yeah, I know what's next all right. The gun and the bullet will be tested immediately. If it turns out that it was fired from the Marrender girl's gun, then what?"

"If it's Sally's, then the problem is, how did Tracy get the Marrender gun?"

"But, listen, Dick, we got to give that Marrender chap the works sooner or later. That is, if you're still interested in Benssen's #3. Take a look at this." He shoved another report across to Stowe.

Dick's eyes raced through a half page of pale blue single typing, and then he turned the pages of an advertising booklet that proclaimed the merits of United Utilities products. "This part of the exhibit?" he demanded.

"I'll say it is. . . ."

"Um-mm, this must be it," Dick mumbled and had nothing more to say for a few minutes. He did not look up again until he checked with his pencil certain items in the booklet which he must have considered especially illuminating, for he said, "So it was William Marrender who influenced United Utilities to undertake the practical demonstration of the industrial possibilities of Benssen's #3. I find this booklet downright intriguing. Did you read it all, Asher?"

"Not all the way through."

"I thought not. I say, there's one thing I keep wondering about . . . if the Wilcox girl wanted to find and use the key to Miss Marrender's safety-deposit box, the idea must have come to her because she had had access to it before as the properly accredited agent for—only one person and that is—"

"Marrender. Sure thing, Dick. He had the other key, acting as his aunt's business representative. Remember I told you how he acted from the very first."

"Since you're so keen on the idea, Tim, here's one thing you can do about it. Find out what sort of matches the chap uses. I'm getting curious about those matches. Miss Penrose had a flash-light. Janet Wilcox struck no matches. And you and I know the matches stocked at Windward Hill are not at all like those burnt ends you picked up in the little gallery."

Asher nodded. "Say, listen, Dick. You seem to think that girl this morning told you the truth, but I don't know. . . . Who tore up the room if she didn't?"

"The person who left the matches, maybe." But Dick's smile was skeptical. "By the way, have you heard from PeeDee?"

"Yes, and how! Jupe's story changes every time he tells it but he's still playing up the stylish blonde lady. He's a little too insistent that the stone wasn't worth much. I think the old boy was counting on a nice turnover. Anyway it's gone, all right. Of course if it was lifted by a common jewel thief, it will turn up somewhere. Everybody's looking for it."

"And if it was not a common thief . . ." Dick was thinking of the various women who undoubtedly had a more personal interest in the Marrender emerald than a professional thief would have. "I must be getting on my way. Shoot me the big news on the gun as soon as Radge finds anything."

"Sure. You're going to pin the girl and Tracy down to it, aren't you?"

"Thanks, Timmy, for reminding me that they may deny everything." Yet Stowe did not say that he was on his way to confront Janet Wilcox with what he had found in the check-room. Instead, he tucked away in his pocket the typewritten report about the poison that had killed Cubbage and the United Utilities booklet that discussed in such a one-syllable fashion its industrial uses. At the door he turned as he flipped up the collar of his overcoat. "Has Dr. Stuart found his stolen property?"

"Hr-umph," Asher mumbled.

"Too bad. Really, your department should strive for increased efficiency." Quickly he slid through the door but tactfully refrained from banging it behind him.

The first thing that Dick Stowe did after leaving Headquarters was to learn by discreet inquiry that Sally Marrender had indeed viewed the body of Cubbage before
burial. She and Tracy had come to the mortuary together.
Mrs. Latimer had not seen the dead man, nor had her sister. There remained only Marrender to be checked up on
this point. For the time being, Dick did not wish to see
William Marrender.

The next thing that he did was to attempt an interview
with Miss Rhand. She had not yet returned from Indianapolis, he was informed. Evidently Miss Rhand's weekends
were elastic.

Nor did the third matter concern the two items he had
checked in the impressive United Utilities booklet. He
may have been thinking about them, but what he did was
to resort to the work-out room of his favorite public gym-
nasium. There he put himself through an elaborate program of exercises and a series of baths. By that time it was
late enough to consider dinner. He went to George and
Al's where his steak set a new record. After he had walked
back to his apartment, he told himself that he was now
ready to bring the Marrender case to the mat.

But before he had settled the master mind to its evening of cogitation, he received a message that indicated
that such heavy mental effort might be unnecessary. His
telephone announced a Western Union call. Mechanically
he jotted down the words as they came precisely spaced
over the line:

DO NOTHING RE MARRENDER BRINGING
BACON QUICKEST ROUTE WATCH EVERY-
BODY LAURA

26

JOYFUL REUNION

The telegram from Laura Stowe had been filed in Los Angeles that noon. If it meant what it said, and Dick knew that a dictum of Laura's must be treated with respect, she could scarcely be expected earlier than Thursday night or Friday. "Unless the kid's insane enough to stow away on a mail plane," he groaned to himself.

Again and again he read the telegram, each time with shifting emotion. Its first command was as clear as it was imperative. The one point about it that irked him was the intimation that anything he might be moved to do about the case would be wrong. All she knew about the affair was what he himself had written her. The phrase that followed hinted at something that filled Dick with giddy hope. Resolutely he forbade himself to feed upon it unduly. The last two words, he concluded, might not be quite as blanket-like as they sounded. He must watch everybody in order that a particular someone should not be overlooked. . . . In any case, he was glad that Laura was coming home.

As exactly as he could, he obeyed his commanding officer's orders. Fortunately, Asher was not too curious. He was so engrossed with his own contribution to the Marrender case that he had little time to discuss theories. Astutely he had set about collecting sample matches from Marrender's home, his office, his clubs, even from the gadgets with which his automobile was equipped. Triumphantly he reported a set that was similar to the ends picked up in the little gallery.

More important than that was the report from the ballistics experts that the bullet that had killed Eugenia Marrender had been fired from the revolver found in the check-room. The characteristic scratches left upon every bullet fired from that weapon could not be questioned. However, the ownership of the .38 could not be settled so scientifically.

The clerk at the sporting goods shop who had sold a .38 to Sally Marrender was not sure. . . . The gun he was asked to inspect was just like the one he had sold to the young lady. Sally herself denied its ownership flatly, firmly, but on the whole, magnanimously. Patiently she reminded Mr. Stowe that she had told him that her revolver had not disappeared until Saturday morning, and that the one at the station had been checked there the morning following its alleged use. Moreover, hers had never been fired, she repeated. Dick in turn rather pointedly did not remind her that she had not yet told him what she had gone to Windward Hill for on Friday night.

Dr. Stuart was also magnanimous and almost insolently polite when he was called in to inspect the unidentified .38. It certainly was not his. His had a peculiar scratch along the length of the barrel by which he could identify it at once. Indeed, he was beginning to fear that his stolen property would never be returned to him. His advertisement had brought no results. Evidently the police were sadly lax in rounding up gun toters—there was a city ordinance that covered such offences, he believed. . . .

Thus Tuesday dragged by and most of Wednesday. Laura Stowe's restraining wire restricted her husband intolerably, for Dick now felt that he knew in which direction to jump. Concerning that he said little, even when Inspector

Peyton returned late Wednesday afternoon and called him into immediate conference. The Inspector listened to Asher's reports and Stowe's guarded statements, and agreed that as long as no one was pushing the department they were safe in letting the problem work itself out.

He looked at his young friend shrewdly. "So you think there are answers to these—er—contradictory details that you have rounded up?"

"To some of them—yes, though to date I have no explanation for the little gallery being found in confusion nor for the box of ammunition found in the nurse's room, nor can I state who took a .38 from the drawer in Tracy's room any more than who put it there in the first place—"

"I'm still betting on Cubbage," broke in Asher. "He was so darned afraid I was going to overlook her room."

"I must confess that I shall be disappointed if Cubbage is the eventual answer to everything," said Dick slowly, "and yet, if it wasn't for the silly melodramatic sound, I'd say that the dead hand of Cubbage is still pulling the strings."

Inspector Peyton's smile was brief. "Well, Stowe, suppose we let it ride. If anything breaks, just let it break. Don't worry; you can't solve all the mysteries, you know."

But Dick Stowe walked homeward rather stubbornly certain that here was a mystery that could be solved, even though the dead could not be recalled to life.

He fumbled at the contents of his mailbox and climbed the stairs to the Stowe suite. He unlocked the door and stepped inside, but before he could switch on the lights there was a rush of quick feet from the bedroom. Laura, no other. . . .

"We flew most of the way, old darling. I was so afraid you might do the wrong thing before we got here because—" She extricated herself from Dick's clutching arms and darted into the bedroom. "I want you to meet my travelling companion," she called back.

Two seconds later she reappeared hand in hand with a plump and pretty girl who in spite of her hostess's gayety was plainly harassed and miserable.

"Miss Randall, may I present my husband? He's awfully clever; everything will work out all right now." Again Laura swooped in flying embrace upon a flabbergasted husband. "Oh, Dick, aren't I just the smartest wife you ever had?" she crooned.

The immediate desires of these three people were quite contradictory. Dick wanted to hear just how Laura, in dutiful attendance upon a slowly convalescent mother, could have linked with the problem confronting him. Laura wanted the present state of affairs outlined to her. And the long-missing nurse, Doris Randall, wanted to be assured and reassured that when her story was known no one could possibly arrest her for anything.

At last the chaotic excitement subsided, and Laura's discovery of the nurse was first presented.

"No miracle about it at all, Dick; just a little manipulation of the well-known thinker. I got your letter Sunday—you sent it air mail luckily. My first bright

idea was that California was just as good a bet as any other resort—better, because of the long train trip intervening. So I wired Inspector Peyton for a detailed description of the vanished nurse—"

"What? Do you mean to tell me Headquarters knew—"

"Oh, it was just a run-of-the-mine inquiry and I used a new name for myself, but I got an answer all right," Laura explained airily. "When it came I rushed an ad to all of the L. A. papers for a nurse—one recently out from Ohio to minister to a mythical homesick patient. I spent Monday in town inspecting the people who answered and picked out this girl as the missing Doris Randall—just like that! She was all confused and worried—nothing had worked out right. She couldn't find the patient she'd been sent to and she didn't have much money. So she took my job like a little lamb, and then when I got her off by herself I confronted her with the little information I had. And, Dick, it was all a grand surprise to her. She didn't even know Miss Marrender had been shot. But the big news is this, Dick: it was Dr. Stuart who sent Miss Randall to California."

The Stowes looked long at one another. Doris Randall began to whimper.

"I told her she had to come back with me." Laura's dark eyes flashed and Dick knew what the set of her chin meant. "And I made her see what a nasty mess she was probably going to be in, but—she's quite sure that the doctor's reasons for sending her away had nothing to do with the death of Miss Marrender. Her professional loyalty won't permit her to be quite frank with me."

There was a significance to Laura's words that Dick did not miss. He turned politely to the weeping nurse. "Miss Randall, the only safe course for you is complete frankness. No person involved in this dreadful matter is going to sacrifice himself for you. Why should you? Suppose you tell me all about your experience at Windward Hill. . . ."

And so Doris Randall began to talk. Listeners far less acute than the two who were giving her such grave attention could not have failed to see that the pretty little nurse was in love with Perry Stuart. She told how she had gone out to Windward Hill in January, how dull and uninteresting the case was—nobody treated her like a human being. There were very few visitors. Doris couldn't even talk to her patient, for Miss Marrender never talked to anyone much except the butler, a creature who fairly gave the girl the creeps.

"Just how do you mean that Miss Marrender talked to Cubbage?" demanded Dick.

Miss Randall hardly knew how to explain, but nearly every day there would be a long conference of some
sort—she was always sent out of the room. Cubbage was
in charge of the house, but no doubt Miss Marrender liked
to feel that she was still running the place.

Dick was careful to ask about the callers of the last week
and found that his previous information was substantiated. The nurse recalled the visits of Francesca Penrose, of
William Marrender, and of Sally. The only new fact that
he gleaned during this portion of the girl's recital concerned the quarrel between Sally and her aunt on Tuesday morning. As usual, the nurse had left the room, but
she had heard loud and angry voices. She returned after
the Marrender girl had stormed out, and Miss Marrender
mumbled something about "He's a fool to send a boy to
the mill." She remembered that because her patient so seldom made any sort of personal comment.

"Did she say anything else?" Dick was eager.

"Yes. As nearly as I can repeat it, it sounded like 'My
money's still mine. Even after I'm gone . . .' and the rest
she just muttered."

Without mentioning names Dick next asked about visitors during the afternoon. Miss Randall knew of none.
She had gone into town to do some necessary errands, she
explained.

"Did you write the note for Miss Marrender before or
after this trip?"

For an instant the nurse looked blank and then apparently she remembered. The letter had been written at Miss
Marrender's request before she left for town. She was supposed to have mailed it on her way in, but it had slipped
her mind entirely until her return, when she had dropped
it into the nearest mailbox.

"What time was it then?" asked Dick, who wanted to
check a minor point.

"Nearly five o'clock."

Just as he had thought . . . the last collection for the day had already been made. That fact together with the intervening legal holiday accounted for the delayed reception of the letter summoning Bartholomew Dexter to Windward Hill.

Dick put his next question with a secret breathlessness. "Have you any idea what she wanted to see Dexter about?"

"No-o, except that she asked me while she was telling me what to say whether I'd ever witnessed anybody's will."

"Could any members of her family have known what she was up to?"

Doris Randall shook her head doubtfully. Laura had long since discovered that the girl was not the sort to make lightning calculations with twos and twos.

"Have you any reason to think that Cubbage knew anything about her purposes?" persisted Dick.

"We-ell, he went in to speak to her as I was leaving that afternoon."

"Fair enough . . . now let's hear about the evening."

Doris Randall's account of the events of that Tuesday evening corroborated Cubbage's report to Asher to some extent. However, she could not precisely remember that anyone had called while she was eating her dinner. In fact, the only thing she could remember about her dinner hour was that Cubbage was frightfully slow about service. She had waited and waited for her salad and dessert. From the time she went back to her patient at eight o'clock to ten-thirty, when she left her for the night, nothing had occurred. No one had called, nor had she seen Cubbage again, though once she thought she heard him at the telephone. The reason that she had paid so little attention to the rest of the house was that her patient had been unusually restless and nervous that evening—all unstrung. By

the time she had been settled for the night, however, her
nerves were normal again.

"What could have caused this nervous excitement?"
asked Dick.

The nurse had no idea. Her patient hadn't reacted like
that after Miss Marrender's visit that morning, when it
was evident that there had been a scene.

Doris Randall then began a reconstruction of the night
hours. Dick, of course, was the only one of the three who
knew how many conflicting purposes had centered about
the windswept house during the hours of that night. "Tell
me everything you can remember," he begged, "every sound
you heard or thought you heard, everything you did. . . ."

That ghastly night . . . could she ever forget it? Her
emotion was genuine as she told how restless she had been
when she first went to bed. The wind nearly drove her
wild; shutters creaked and banged everywhere. At last she
fell asleep. She slept heavily; she always did. The wind
was still at it the first time she roused. Just what time that
was she could not say, though she heard a clock strike one.
Everything seemed perfectly all right in Miss Marrender's
room, though she supposed she might as well admit now
that she hadn't gone across to the bed—she had just stood
at the door.

"Was it one o'clock or—it might have been half-past
anything for all you know."

Doris Randall said nothing contritely.

"So you couldn't prove that she was dead or alive then,
could you?" accused Dick. "The shot that killed her might
have been what roused you."

"I—I don't know," she faltered miserably. "Maybe it
wasn't the wind that waked me—I thought it was. I—I
guess I didn't want to frighten myself about it."

"Miss Randall, are you the sort of person who is sensitive to the unseen presence of another?"

"You mean—can I feel it if somebody is watching me? Cubbage made me crawl half the time by doing that."

"Well, then . . . did you have any such feelings at that particular moment?"

Laura Stowe knew that her partner in investigation could not be particularly proud of such leading questions, but she was also aware of what Dick was groping toward. The murderer of Eugenia Marrender could not have been far away at the moment when the nurse crossed the hall and stood looking into her patient's room.

"If I had felt there was anybody there, I know I should have screamed—I couldn't have helped it," insisted Doris. "I went back to my own room and got to sleep again without any trouble." Then she went on to relate that she had made the next inspection of her patient not long after four, and had at that time made the discovery that Miss Marrender was dead.

"Do you mean to say that your examination was so casual that you failed to see that she had been shot?" Dick's voice was drained of sympathy.

Doris blushed painfully. "People think that just because you're a nurse and all you're used to those things. Honestly, the cases I've been on—I mean, I haven't seen so many people die, and she looked so peaceful and the doctor had warned me about her heart and, of course, murder was the last thing in the world I had any reason to think of. . . ." Her tearful voice trailed off. Her negligence could not face the standards of her profession.

To propitiate she plunged on into a confession that could not directly involve anyone else but herself. "You see, I had the idea that she had killed herself."

When she had told about the little bottle of tablets and how their contents had become alarmingly less since ten o'clock when she had administered the bedtime dose, and the conclusion that had occurred to her, Dick Stowe's grey eyes filled with a light which she did not understand but which his wife considered promising.

"So you emptied the bottle in order to spare Dr. Stuart the annoyance of a coroner's inquest and went downstairs to find Cubbage. Then what?"

She recounted how she had called the doctor's man, how a little later she had received the doctor's urgent call to a new case, and how she had packed and left. She had been in such a hurry, and rather upset too, that she had paid almost no attention to Mrs. Banney's alarm about burglars, though she remembered that Cubbage had been at the telephone reporting something to the police.

"Do tell him about the gloves," prompted Laura, ready for a new sensation.

The word alone was enough to swing Dick's attention away from a new contemplation of Dr. Stuart's relation to these events to what he already knew about two pairs of gloves.

"I thought they were mine, you see, till I tried to put them on and they were too small. They were lying on the table in the hall and I know they weren't there the evening before. That's all, except that I have them—I mean Mrs. Stowe has them."

"That's fine, Miss Randall," Dick beamed. "Now if you'll explain why you went out to Los Angeles when you were supposed to be heading for Florida—"

The look of distress on the girl's pretty face indicated that she had not yet accepted the doctor's duplicity in the matter. For the moment Dick did not force his proof upon her. He allowed her to explain that Dr. Stuart had wired her about the stupid mistake he had made, and how he had urged her to stay out on the Coast for a little vacation. . . .

"There's no use being plain simple, Doris," Laura scolded. "You're only making it worse for yourself. She doesn't want to tell you that Dr. Stuart threatened her with the police if she didn't stay out there and keep out of any investigation here. He told her he might be charged with malpractice. She swallowed it too, hook, line, and sinker," Laura explained bluntly quite as though Doris were not there.

Dick next questioned the girl about such items as revolvers and small boxes of ammunition, until he had convinced himself that she could not be held responsible for what had been found in her room and in the drawer of Tracy's chiffonier after her departure.

"All right, Miss Randall. . . . Now, are you sure you have told me everything?"

And Doris Randall, loyally conscious of the doctor's fountain pen still hidden in the depths of her handbag, answered with fluttering breath, "Every single thing, Mr. Stowe."

27

CHIVALROUS ATTITUDE OF DR. STUART

The Stowe bedchamber was graciously turned over to Doris Randall; the Stowes could themselves manage quite well with the living-room davenport. That the rest of the night would be spent in an exhaustive analysis of the facts so far known in the Marrender mystery the Stowes did not mention to their guest. Whether or not they agreed exactly in all their conclusions was none of Doris Randall's business. They were, however, unanimous upon one point. Their decision to open their attack by an early call upon Dr. Perry Stuart was casually announced. That ought to worry the nurse. . . .

Accordingly, the next morning, after a telephone talk with Asher, the Stowes set out for the physician's apartment. On their way they picked up the obviously excited Deputy-Inspector, who insisted that it was only common sense to have one of the boys from Headquarters keep an eye on the nurse. What if she had promised till she was blue in the face . . . there was no use taking fool chances.

Scotty burred his uncertainty about disturbing the doctor while he was at breakfast, but even Scotty was no match for Asher plus Dick and Laura Stowe. They filed into the doctor's presence, rather neatly penning him into the windowed alcove where his breakfast was served.

"We've come to tell you that we've just had quite an illuminating chat with Miss Doris Randall," Dick began in a bright conversational tone.

"Poor kid, she's in rather a nasty hole, isn't she?" Dr. Stuart's manner matched Dick's expertly.

"As far as you are concerned, yes," agreed Dick. "Why did you scheme so elaborately to get her out of the picture? We know you wired her—more than once. So don't deny anything too flatly."

The right-about-face that Perry Stuart executed at this moment was almost visible. "Awfully ill-advised and all that—I see that now, but I was acting for her own good. You see, I was afraid that Cubbage would incriminate her—"

"Hold on, doctor. You must have had advance information. You created this imaginary case for Miss Randall very early on Wednesday morning."

Stuart hedged skillfully—so skillfully that Dick almost accepted his answer at face value, almost but not quite. "When I called my nurse for further particulars—she'd given her message to my man, you know—it was Cubbage who answered the telephone. He told me something that worried me and I followed the first course that occurred to me in order to make things easier for Dor—for the nurse."

"Ah," sighed Laura, "chivalry is not yet dead."

"What did Cubbage tell you?" snapped Asher, never quite at ease when the indirect methods of the Stowes were functioning.

"He said he was at a loss to understand why the young lady had waited so long to report his mistress's death and—well, he more than intimated that he considered it his duty to report her to the relatives for gross negligence." There was an echo of Cubbage's stately style about the doctor's words.

"A report to Mrs. Latimer, I dare say," murmured Dick, and the shot told.

It was Asher who had patiently followed the trail to Florida, and it was he who burst into protest now. "That won't go. You can't cover your deliberately misleading statements to the police like that."

"I hated to see the girl in a jam—she's a good kid." Stuart ignored Asher.

Laura wished that Doris could hear his patronizing tone. It would surely open her eyes, the little fool.

"Why did you withhold your lead about Cubbage? You had your good chance, if I know Deputy-Inspector Asher," said Dick.

"To tell you the truth, I intended to have matters out with Cubbage when I got to Windward Hill that morning, but the police were already in charge—the burglary, you know. Then my natural excitement at learning that Miss Marrender had been shot crowded that out of my mind. Later I determined not to interfere."

"Hm-mm, so that's what you call it," said Dick as if to himself, but he was remembering that Asher had been certain that the doctor's shock was genuine when he saw how Miss Marrender had met her death.

"I shall go further," added Stuart, "and tell you exactly why I was so startled when I realized that Miss Marrender had been killed. I knew what medicine had been prescribed and while I stood at the door of the room speaking to you,"—he turned with elaborate politeness to Asher—"I saw that the bottles of medicine were empty. I knew then that Doris—that the nurse was in for a nasty bit of explanation. I expected you chaps would question me about it, but that was something you slipped up on, eh? We're all fallible, of course. . . ."

"I scarcely see how that fact alone put you in such a stew about Miss Randall's position. No, Stuart, I'm going to let you have it straight; I don't believe you. Too many stories go back to Cubbage—now that Cubbage is safely

dead and buried. You catch my meaning?" This question
Stowe addressed not to his opponent but to his allies.
"Another thing—you rationalize with extraordinary speed,
don't you? I am so crass as to doubt that Cubbage had time
to tell you anything over the telephone that morning, but
that's something I can soon straighten out. Listen in, if
you want to."

He turned to the doctor's telephone and called his own
number. In a minute the quavering response of the nurse
reached his ear. The others could not hear what she said,
but they were welcome to make what they could out of his
side of the brief conversation.

"You were drinking coffee in the kitchen when Cubbage called you to the 'phone. Did you hear the 'phone
bell ring? . . . You're sure? Good! Was there any conversation before you were called to the 'phone? . . ." There was
a longer pause here. Dick listened intently and then said,
"I wish I could say the same to you about him. . . ."

He swung about to face Stuart. "Miss Randall informs
me that Cubbage came for her within two or three minutes after the bell stopped ringing and that all she heard
him say was 'Yes?' and, 'Just a minute, please.' So I can't
believe that on that occasion Cubbage discussed Miss Randall's shortcomings with you. You had your plan to whisk
the nurse out of range of any embarrassing inquiries—
embarrassing for you, not for her necessarily—before you
heard that Miss Marrender was dead. More than that, you
were expecting to hear something from Windward Hill,
and my guess is that your belated motor trip with Mrs.
Latimer had a bearing on that expectation."

"Yes, your guess . . . but how about your proof?" The
doctor's manner was still frigidly polite.

"Here's something we want to hear you laugh off."
Apparently Asher wished to demonstrate his right to be on

the plain-clothes squad. "What made you so busy getting rid of a gun of the same caliber that killed the old lady?"

Afterward the Stowes paid due tribute to the masterly ambiguity of that question.

"You can't expect me to answer a silly question like that, can you?" Stuart could retort debonairly, but Asher's query had found some obscure chink in his armor. Yet if it had indeed been he who had walked out of Sally's Shop with her .38, it had not since been in his possession, as Headquarters could have admitted with appropriate chagrin.

For another half hour the fruitless sparring continued. No matter what went on in the doctor's agile mind, his three opponents slowly became certain of three separate convictions. Dick's was that there was no real reason that he shouldn't assume that both Katherine Latimer and Dr. Stuart had paid a late visit to Windward Hill during the time that their car was supposedly stalled down on the River Road. Asher's was that no matter who bumped off the old lady, Stowe's hunch about its being the same one who did for Cubbage was surely the right answer. Cubbage knew too damn much. Laura's was that Dr. Stuart was lying about two women to save one at the expense of the other. Doris was a fool. . . .

It was Laura's conviction that broke the deadlock, though she herself could claim no credit for it. Scotty was heard in rolling argument, which was cut short by the determined entrance of no other than Doris Randall. Resolutely she wrenched her eyes from the doctor's. Fumbling in her bag she produced a slender green object which she thrust into Laura's hands.

"I don't know—I can't understand," and her ready tears began to splash. "I thought I loved him enough to keep still, but you frighten me so—I've got to tell everything. I found that pen on the floor by Miss Marrender's bed that

morning after . . . and I'd have to swear that it wasn't there
when I settled her for the night. But I can swear too that
the doctor wasn't at Windward Hill after his usual morning call."

Laura Stowe looked deep into the tortured eyes of
Doris Randall, and knew that at last the girl had told her
everything. Not at any time since she had found her four
days before had she had that confidence. Asher and her
husband, for their part, were watching the hypnotic fixity
of Stuart's gaze upon the pen in Laura's hand. Asher was
thinking that they had that bird now, but Dick was concentrating on the completely baffled expression that was
congealing the doctor's features.

"You can't explain the pen, is that it?" he asked quietly.

Stuart passed his hand across his forehead and through
his hair as if to convince himself that he was not seeing double. The other hand fumbled in the pocket where
a fountain pen could have been anchored, but was not.
"You're right, Stowe; I can't," he muttered, still dazed.

Then he pulled himself together sharply. "But I can
damn well see how you're going to frame me. All right, I'll
talk—I'll tell you everything I know. I've already told you
whom I was with during the course of the evening—I'll call
her my patient. On this evening she was in an extremely
nervous state. Professionally I should have no hesitancy in
saying that for several hours she had no control of herself
and could bear no responsibility for her actions. While she
was in this condition she attempted to carry out a dreadful impulse from which she and her victim were saved by
what I then considered the providential interference of
the man Cubbage. It was he who informed me of what had
occurred—I was waiting in my car at the lower end of the
drive—and he agreed with me that nothing need be said
about my patient's—er—break-down."

Asher shifted his position restlessly. Stowe might think this yarn sounded like something, but it didn't make sense to him. "Aw, say it with flowers, why don't you? Sounds like a lot of blah."

"Am I to understand that you called for your patient to escort her to a dinner engagement but instead drove out to Windward Hill? I see. And you did not enter the house, you say, but your patient ran up to see her aunt, presumably. Please be frank about what she did at that time?" Dick was checking off more than one unexplained item.

"Cubbage said—I have only his word for it," and Stuart gave Stowe a cool glance, "Cubbage said that he followed her upstairs just in time to keep her from dumping half the contents of a medicine bottle into the medicine glass. It would have been a lethal dose, though Miss Marrender was quite conscious of what the scene meant and would, of course, have resisted to the limit of her own weakened condition. Cubbage told me that she herself insisted that nothing be made of the incident—"

"That must have happened while I was eating my dinner," broke in the nurse. "I told you I thought her decidedly upset when I went back on duty." For the moment it was evident that Doris Randall was not thinking of herself.

Stuart continued to talk directly to Stowe, ignoring the others. "Cubbage got my patient out of the house and down to my car, and I took her back to my office. You understand the slight discrepancy of my former statement, I trust? After such a horrifying collapse she needed my attention. I tended her for several hours, and then we drove for miles until eventually a satisfactory degree of control had been gained. Then occurred that distressing delay on the River Road—that is just as I had told you.

"My story from then on still stands, except for this addition. When I left my car to go for help, like a sensible

man I went to the nearest place—Windward Hill. I said
nothing to my patient then, nor have I since informed
her. I came up from the road by the steep path that brings
one to the back of the house. I knew that the butler had a
room on the ground floor and my idea was to knock on his
window and rouse him, but I mistakenly turned to the left
instead of the right—his room is on the right, I believe.

"At once I saw something I could not account for.
Someone was in one of the rooms on the left side of the
house, or I should say, I saw a light there. The light at that
moment went out and a woman stepped through the window. Because of the scene earlier in the evening I myself
for a moment was insane enough to fear that this woman
coming out of the window was my patient. But it wasn't,
because I hurried at once down the path and there she was
in the car just where I had left her."

There were varying degrees of skepticism on every face.
Stowe and Asher knew the identity of the woman whom
Stuart had seen; now they could understand Francesca
Penrose's one reservation.

"You addressed this woman by your patient's name, did
you not?" demanded Stowe.

"I may have—I was—er—startled."

If Francesca Penrose had been mistaken for her sister,
thought Dick, then no wonder she had feared that an unknown person had expected her sister to be at Windward
Hill that night. That much could be rubbed off the slate,
at any rate. But how about the story that Mrs. Latimer had
already told him about the man who came crashing down
the path? Should he not now be identified as the doctor
himself rather than Tracy? If so, then Katherine Latimer
was indeed informed concerning the doctor's late visit
at Windward Hill, no matter how smoothly he had just
stated the opposite.

Just as smoothly the doctor was concluding his recital. "I tinkered at the car again and the damned thing started—that's all."

"Oh, no, it's not!" It was almost a full chorus. "You haven't explained the pen."

"You heard Miss Randall say where and when she found it and that I hadn't been in that room since the preceding morning." Dr. Stuart spoke slowly, as though he were groping for the truth. "I believe I could produce witnesses to prove that I had the pen at later times during Tuesday—patients at my office, for instance. I'm trying to think back to be sure. . . . I have been aware since that I had lost it or mislaid it somewhere, but I paid no attention to its disappearance. Let me see . . . the last time I remember using it on Tuesday was at my club. Four of us were finishing a rubber and I was totting up the scores when I was called to the telephone. I must have left my pen lying on the table."

"What club and whom were you playing with?" Stowe's query was mechanical.

"The Anthony. The other players were Major Odell, Bill Marrender, and that little red-headed engineer who's running the Power Dam now—I forget his name. I might say, however, that I called the club secretary the next day to ask if my pen had been picked up. It hadn't."

"Thanks. That helps a lot," drawled Dick.

Stuart glared angrily. The nurse sniffled and blew her nose, and afterwards did things with an enameled vanity compact.

"See here," Asher broke in, "I want to go back to one thing. What was the reason that your—er—patient attacked Miss Marrender?"

"I have no idea." The doctor's reply was judicial. "Remember that it was the act of one who could by no means be held responsible—"

"Old stuff," grumbled Asher.

"In connection with what the Deputy-Inspector has just now referred to, doctor, what did you think when the nurse telephoned that Miss Marrender had died?" Dick Stowe's question was not laced with anything except honest inquiry.

"You can understand that I was not keenly surprised—the incident the evening before had been a shock, and I knew the condition of her heart. There was absolutely nothing about Miss Randall's report to create any suspicion—"

"If that is so, why did you hurry her off to a distant case and deliberately misinform the police about her destination?" Dick had cut in with the question before Asher had a chance.

"Because I was afraid to risk Miss Randall's discretion."

There was something about the way Stuart made the statement that infuriated the nurse. She leaped to her feet and confronted the physician. "You were afraid I'd expose you and your 'patient.' I'd seen you together and God help me, I can understand why she would have committed murder if it could mean marrying you! I knew when I saw her that I didn't have a chance . . . but just the same I was willing to perjure myself to keep you out of trouble, and you—you—" Her gesture of abandonment betrayed that the spell the man's personality held for her was still potent. "You wouldn't as much as trust me to protect you!"

She turned upon Dick. "Mr. Stowe, if he had been at Windward Hill that night, wouldn't I have known it—felt it?"

"I'm sorry, Miss Randall, but I am inclined to accept the main points of the doctor's story." Dick's words were soothing, but Laura as well as Asher looked displeased. "However," he added, "I quite agree with you that he has so far failed to reveal his real motive for sending you upon that long unnecessary journey. Let us hope that the doctor's—er—discretion will make him a bit franker about that before long. In the meantime, there's another matter—the weapon in the case."

The pause that followed was so interrogatory that Stuart gave under its strain. "What do you mean?" he mumbled.

"Finish your story," commanded Dick.

The doctor's words came rapidly, and so low that the others had to lean forward to distinguish what he said. "You're not going to believe this, you know. . . ."

His challenge was so genuine that Dick knew it must be backed by the truth.

"I said that I hurried away from the house and down the path to the River Road. Just as I was about to round the corner of the house and strike out for the path something whizzed by my head and thudded into the heavy, winter-matted grass. I stopped long enough to grope around and—I found something. It was a revolver, and it must have come from one of the windows at the back of the house. I stood right in my tracks, rather stupidly, and then the kitchen door was thrown wide open and the light caught me plainly. There was that damned butler and he saw what I was looking at. Almost before I knew what had happened he had taken the thing from me, gone back into the house, closed the door, and snapped out the light."

"Didn't he say anything?" asked Laura in the voice that her husband knew meant she was thrilled.

"Yes, he said something," replied Dr. Stuart, and his voice was lifeless. "To atone in some way to Miss Randall, I suppose I should not hesitate to betray another woman. Cubbage's vile whisper was: 'For God's sake, give that back. It's Sally Marrender's!' . . ."

28

STOWE ADMITS UNCERTAINTY

Asher and the two Stowes were snatching a bite of lunch after their surprising moment with Perry Stuart. Over hot meat sandwiches they had all talked at once with superb inattention to anyone's lines but their own. Now over mince pie and coffee the others were listening to Dick.

"Don't forget that Stuart says he heard no shot. I have two witnesses to prove that the shot came some time after two when Francesca Penrose left by the window."

"Two witnesses, Dick?"

"Well, one corroborates the other in a way. Janet Wilcox saw Francesca leave; the Croft girl only heard the shot."

"All right, that leaves Cubbage with the gun and the old lady hasn't been shot yet." Asher dumped another spoonful of sugar into his cup and stirred the whole until it splashed.

"Yes, but—now see here, someone must have thrown the gun out of the window. You'll admit that it could scarcely have come from the windows in Miss Marrender's room if it landed where Stuart says it did. And if Cubbage popped out the kitchen door almost immediately, how could he have thrown it out? He's one grand mystery man, but he couldn't have been that limber."

"Call the roll, Dick. Who was in the house at that time?" Laura was not equal to lightning deduction after the strain of the last few days and next to no sleep the night before.

"Gene and Esme Croft, and by that time Janet must have crawled into the little gallery and, of course, the sick woman, Miss Randall, and Cubbage."

"Will and Sally Marrender say they were at Sally's apartment," put in Laura with meaning.

Dick shook off that suggestion impatiently. "The two girls declare they were locked in. Miss Randall was asleep—I'll say she must have been lost to the world!—and Miss Marrender was helpless in her bed. Cubbage must have been in the kitchen or not many steps away. That leaves Tracy at large."

"But if Cubbage had drugged Tracy. . . . That was your own bright idea, remember."

"Then there must have been somebody else roaming around that night."

"You bet there was," agreed Asher. "Stuart and the Latimer woman."

Dick stared at his cigarette absently. "Frankly, I'm of two minds about his story. It may be that he's given us the stark truth—it wasn't a pretty yarn to make up against himself. And yet . . . they both lied about seeing Tracy, and Mrs. Latimer must have made a hundred per cent. recovery if he left her sitting by herself in a stalled car on a deserted road between one and three in the morning. And he slipped up badly when he said that first of all he went up to Windward Hill. Why should he have thought that the woman leaving by the window might be Mrs. Latimer?"

"She couldn't have got to the house that quickly if he had just left her in the car," mused Laura. "If only Cubbage had spilled a thing or two before he was done for—"

"By the way, you noted the regular appearance of the unknown factor again in Stuart's story? Another story which only Cubbage could prove . . . and you know what

happened to Cubbage. My guess is that that chap was planning an extensive program of blackmail. His statements
against any of the others would have carried weight. There
was something impressive about Cubbage, eh, Tim?"

Asher nodded glumly. More action and less talk would
have made the Deputy-Inspector more his own man.

"I'm trying to be fair to Stuart. Cubbage was no doubt
his reason for saying nothing to you when he arrived
Wednesday morning. If he had mentioned the gun, Cubbage presumably would have retaliated by telling how Mrs.
Latimer had tried to kill her aunt the evening before. And
I think he sent the nurse away rather than give anyone else
a chance to talk to her. He might well be worried about
what Miss Marrender might have let slip to her about Mrs.
Latimer's insane attack upon her. . . . You see, Miss Randall had so little to do with what had happened that she
wouldn't have had the sense to keep still about anything."

Asher grunted, unconvinced.

"I know it's not water-tight, not by a long shot, but it's
not all apple sauce." His eyebrows met in a level twist and
he sighed gustily.

"'Smatter, Dick? Are you having a little theory?" Laura's impish smile braced him.

"No, I'm just reminding myself that there are sever-
al items between us and that little theory we were about
to hand ourselves. It would be slick all right to say that
Stuart came back to Windward Hill to finish what Mrs.
Latimer tried to start earlier in the evening, and that Cub-
bage knew it and that therefore Stuart later had to silence
Cubbage, but—but the fact that the weapon that killed
Miss Marrender was disposed of by Janet Wilcox would
wreck any case brought against anybody except Eugene
Tracy."

"Oh, Dick, let's backslide or something. It must have
been Cubbage who killed her. Why not let it go at that?"

"You're tired, La La."

"Look here, folks, I've just tumbled to something darned peculiar. The doc came across with his story about picking up a gun that Cubbage said was the Marrender girl's—when? I ask you, when?"

Stowe grinned happily, but let Asher have the floor. "Not till Dick here said, 'What about the weapon in the case?' And then the doc starts right in like a lamb with that rigmarole about Sally's gun. And why? Because he had a .38 in his car at the same time, and he knew we knew it. Call the gun Sally's right away, before anybody could suggest any different, huh?" In triumph Asher planted his elbows on the table, and looked at Stowe as one expert to another.

"A plus on that, old-timer. I was beginning to think I'd have to diagram it."

"Aw . . . but you got to admit I knew what I was doing when I put Parks on to watch that guy. He'll be arrested too before—"

"No! Tail him all over town if you like, but wait— We've got to round up Will Marrender and his sister first." Dick waved an airy hand. "Listen, my children, and you shall hear my plan of procedure with Sally dear. . . ."

Empty pie plates were pushed aside, and ribbons of smoke merged in a single spiral above the three heads knotted in conference over their table.

A half hour later when Sally Marrender saw Stowe enter her shop she greeted him with easy nonchalance, and ushered him immediately up to her own apartment. They used the stairway at the back, and thus Dick saw for himself the position of the inside approach and exit from her quarters.

"You look so deadly serious, my staff couldn't have survived another conference downstairs. They're still agitated over your last descent upon me and your mysterious interest in my arsenal."

"I gather that your cash register has remained unprotected in the interim. . . ." Dick was chatting lightly, trying to account for the air of easy assurance that possessed Sally Marrender.

"Yes, but the police assured me that the thief would be promptly pursued and my heavy artillery returned. I'm thinking of viewing the situation with alarm in a letter to the newspapers." She cast another log on the fire and then seated herself before the blaze.

"I shouldn't do that, if I were you, not unless you can account for the presence of your revolver at Windward Hill on the night your aunt was shot," warned Dick.

Sally Marrender made no pretense of not understanding the full purport of his words. She shook the thick black hair back from her forehead and clasped her hands about her knees. She had chosen to sit on a low stool, and to meet Stowe's eyes as they talked she had to look squarely up. She did this with complete and sober frankness.

"How did it get there?" she demanded. "I told you it was where it belonged on Tuesday morning. It was there late the next afternoon. How could it have been at Windward Hill? You police have been saying, and we're believing, that Cubbage killed Aunt Genie, but you suspect every member of our family, don't you? Your professional conscience won't let you believe that my brother and I spent the night here, all because I was silly enough to say that I got breakfast for him and he told you that he ate at home. I'm sunk to think that I let Will down that way, but it was the stupidity of innocence, I assure you—"

"Slow up a minute, Miss Marrender. I ask you to account for the presence of your gun at Windward Hill and you thrust the same question back at me. Shall I tell you who I think could have gone up to Windward Hill armed with your gun?"

She met his insinuation calmly. "I'm sorry, but Will and I must sink or swim together. Besides, if we had known we should need the perfect alibi, we would have arranged for one—and I never, never would have slipped up on the breakfast detail."

"Your brother was pressed for money . . . and you had a lively quarrel with your aunt on Tuesday morning . . . and we have not yet learned any fact to spoil our idea that it was your gun that was used to kill Miss Marrender." He checked off one item after another. "It's not surprising that it occurred to me that you or your brother might have made a swift, secret trip to Windward Hill and back again to accomplish your own answer to the problems that were confronting you, problems which your aunt would not help you to solve. The gun could have been used and put back in its place. It was there Tuesday *morning* and late Wednesday *afternoon.*"

"Will or I murder Aunt Genie for money! You fool . . . you fool!" And Sally Marrender drew back from Stowe with loathing.

He winced within himself but took the scene in his stride. Later she might listen, if he succeeded in accomplishing what he was slowly working toward.

"Then what took you to Windward Hill on Friday night? Especially when you say you knew beyond a shadow of a doubt that your .38 was parked down here in your shop."

"I shan't tell you, Mr. Stowe." She spoke the curt words as placidly as though her emotional outburst a few minutes before had not been.

Dick rose from his chair and crossed the room to a window. He stood staring down at a traffic-thronged street until Sally's eyes had ceased to follow him. Then he shifted his position just enough to enable him to make an oblique survey of the surface of Sally's writing table. What he saw of paper, ink, and pens decided him further. He turned from the window and slid into the desk chair and spoke.

"I confess, Miss Marrender, that I can't quite dismiss my impression that when Asher was so rude as to jump on you last Friday night during your invasion of Windward Hill, you had already gained whatever point you had in mind. You came in through the kitchen and got no further than Cubbage's room, as I remember." As he talked he watched the girl narrowly, but his hand was busy making senseless scrawls on a pad of paper, first with one pen and then another.

Sally stirred nervously but said nothing.

"There's another point I consider extremely odd—when I talked to you the afternoon after the death of your aunt, it appeared that I was the one who first told you that it was a murder, not a natural death. You heard first through your brother, I suppose?"

She answered with exaggerated patience. "Yes, and I told you at the time that I had been out of town during that day—out of touch with any of my relatives. My brother was extremely occupied and the others assumed that he had already told me. But no doubt you can read some sinister meaning into that very natural situation."

"You're quite right. Miss Marrender. Would you like to hear it?" Crumpling the paper upon which he had been aimlessly scribbling and thrusting it into his pocket, he got to his feet and faced the girl's taut figure. "Your brother dreaded your knowing that murder had been committed at Windward Hill because he knew—he knew that you would have grave cause to think him guilty."

His words dropped into the sudden stillness of the room. The girl at whom they had been hurled regarded him stonily, her eyes dark with anger or fear or surprise, Stowe could not tell which.

At last she sighed, as though her patience or her resistance were exhausted. "No, I tell you, no! My brother could not—would not have killed my aunt. That would be unreasonable—unthinkable. Why, I should sooner believe that he murdered Cubbage!"

"I should add, perhaps, that I also believe that likely."

"That Will—my brother Will killed Cubbage?" The words were almost soundless.

"It was a dose of Benssen's #3 that killed him. Must I remind you that it is a compound used only in one of the industries under your brother's control? I can as easily demonstrate that he had both the motive and the opportunity to bring about Cubbage's death. Then there is the detail of the pen found in your aunt's room. The pen is not your brother's, but its presence in her room will be a nasty bit of circumstantial evidence for him to refute. . . ."

But it was not the moment for logic. Sally was not listening. Her dazed attention had heard nothing since Stowe's second accusation of her brother.

She took a step toward him with an impulsive, pleading gesture. "But nobody murdered Cubbage. I just said that. I didn't really mean it. He committed suicide—you've said so all along." She spoke like one who was arguing with herself.

"Somebody did murder Cubbage, Miss Marrender."

"But not Will—oh, don't you see—don't you understand . . . there was no need to worry about Cubbage after Aunt Genie—" She caught back the words, too late, yet even in her extremity her defiant spirit did not fail her.

"Thank you, Miss Marrender." Dick's voice was gentle. "I quite agree. Your brother probably did not kill the man Cubbage, menacing as he must have been, but I am sorry to say that I am not yet certain that he did not murder his aunt."

29

An Indiscretion of the Mauve Decade

When Dick Stowe at length left Sally's rooms, it was with the conviction that one more pull of the thread would straighten out the tangled knot of the Marrender case. There was one point upon which Sally remained implacably stubborn. If, as Dick suspected, that matter had a bearing upon the identity of Cubbage, then he might have to accept defeat on that score. Always to guess, never to know, the truth about that inscrutable personality . . . to leave the matter thus did not please Dick Stowe. What if he had discovered who had brought death to Windward Hill? To leave an ultimate question about the man Cubbage meant something less than complete success.

He swung into the street and headed toward Bartholomew Dexter's office, only to find Asher falling into step beside him.

"Thought I might catch you on the fly," he explained. "There's a woman waiting to see you and nobody but you, up at Headquarters. Quite a dame, believe me. Her name's Rhand."

Dick hesitated. Her story could wait, but he might need the rest of the afternoon to convince Dexter. "All right," he concluded. "It's not much out of my way, but she's got to cut it short, and, Tim—keep Parks on Stuart and put somebody just as good on Marrender. So long!"

Three minutes later, in Inspector Peyton's inner office, Stowe was facing Miss Bessie Rhand. She was older than her brother and her fluttering, breathless manner spoke unmistakably of the mauve decade.

"Vincent—my brother tells me that you wished to consult me. Something tells me that I know why—so I have lost no time. I—I have never been to a place like this before." Her voice sunk apprehensively and she drew a violet-decked fur scarf more snugly about a throat too plump to be wrinkled.

"That's right, Miss Rhand, I had wanted to see you. It's mighty thoughtful of you to come to me. It's not a matter of the first importance, really—had your brother mentioned it to you?"

"Yes." There was a marked significance to the reply that should have aroused Dick's attention.

"Then I needn't detain you long now," said Dick, thinking of Dexter. "Mrs. Latimer tells me that she saw a man among your guests the night Fells Lothrop was with you whom she believed to be Cubbage, her aunt's butler. Was there an unaccounted for person present that night?"

"I'm sure I wasn't aware of it at the time, but when my brother mentioned your call to me I recalled distinctly that Mr. Tracy arrived very late and refused all my offers of refreshment—and yet, the fifteen plates of salad had all been served. I declare, it's most puzzling," and she soothed her perturbation with a silver-topped *vinaigrette*." No, I am quite sure that I did not observe the person we have in mind—on that occasion."

Dick waited politely.

"However, I had occasion to observe Miss Marrender's man—and with no little interest, I assure you." She paused abruptly and bent a frosty blue eye upon her listener. "Young man, I am no gossip and my Christian duty as a gentlewoman is to let the secrets of the dead lie with

them. Does justice demand that the name of Eugenia Marrender be scandalized?"

Eugenia Marrender . . . was that the answer? Dick's
attention leaped in triumph. "If you know any fact that
might clear away the mystery of her death . . . otherwise,
those who are innocent may suffer unjustly. You were saying that your attention had been called to Cubbage—"

Miss Bessie Rhand's feathered turban jerked in assent.
"I knew Eugenia Marrender all my life. We went to the
same school. I was her junior by—er—a number of years.
I admired her very much—the usual school-girl adoration,
you understand. In fact, I admired her so much that she
never knew, nor did anyone else, that I knew something
about her that no one else in this town could possibly have
believed to be true."

The *vinaigrette* waved her listener to silence and the
neat, well-bred voice went on. "In fact, I had known this
fact so long and had thought about it so little of late years,
that when the matter was recalled to me I suffered from
nervous headache and insomnia for days afterward. The
occasion was this:

"One day early in the autumn I drove out to Windward
Hill to call on my old friend. I had heard she was not well.
I was admitted by the butler and as he opened the door
the outdoor light caught his face squarely, I looked up to
speak to him and in a flash the whole miserable story came
back to me—I declare, I hadn't thought of it for years. He
showed me into the drawing-room, and while I sat there
waiting to hear whether Miss Marrender felt able to see
me, I tried to figure out, as one will, what there was about
that servant that had brought to life my old memory. It
was his eyes, I was thinking, when the maddest, most fantastic idea flashed into my mind. What if this should actually be the man, the one who—you know . . . and then I
looked up from where I was sitting directly at the Lumley

portrait of old Robert Rufus Marrender, and I give you my word, young man, I saw the butler's eyes again!"

Miss Rhand's laughter rippled faintly. "And then I knew that I was being perfectly ridiculous. If the butler had been the—one I had thought of, he couldn't possibly have resembled Eugenia's father, you see. Though he looked the right age. . . ."

Her voice fluttered into silence and she restored the little cut-glass bottle to its place in her substantial handbag.

"My dear Miss Rhand," Dick began carefully, "do you realize that you have left me completely in the dark—this story about Miss Marrender that came back to you so surprisingly?"

"Oh, oh. . . ." Miss Bessie Rhand relapsed wholly into the Nineteenth Century. Her eyes dropped and a faint color transfused her face. "No one knew, unless it was her father. It was all so long ago. . . . The poor girl was—an unmarried mother." Her last words were almost lost in the violets under her chin.

"How could an event like that be kept so secret? And how did you happen to know about it?" Dick's questions were briskly Twentieth Century.

"It must have happened while she was travelling—we thought she was travelling, that is. She was gone almost a year and a half. I learned about the baby quite by accident. It was at an orphanage in Pennsylvania. My father was called there for a consultation—he was a physician also. He took me with him. I remember that he thought a little change would do me good. He was detained there several days and I amused myself with the children, especially the babies. The nurse in charge of them took quite a fancy to me and told me all sorts of interesting things about them. There was one baby boy whose story sounded ever so romantic, and before I left the nurse showed me the clothes and other articles that had been with the baby when it was brought to them. There was one object that made me turn cold and sick because I knew I had seen it before, many times. It was a piece of chain with an old watch charm on it—"

"Like this?" asked Dick softly, and drew out one of his lengths of chain.

"Yes, quite like that." And in a very lady-like manner Miss Bessie Rhand began to weep.

"Who left the child? You asked, of course?"

"Yes, oh, yes. It was a man. The name she mentioned was strange but her description of him told me that it must have been—Eugenia's father." Miss Rhand produced a fragrant handkerchief and wiped her eyes. "That was the story that came back to me that afternoon at Windward Hill. I'd often wondered about who the—the child's father was, but of course it was silly of me to imagine that it might be Cubbage, for the—er—father of Eugenia's child could not have resembled her own father."

"Cubbage looked like a man in his fifties, I should say," Dick ventured.

"Yes, indeed. All of that. . . ."

When Dick had thanked Miss Rhand and assured her that her statement would be most discreetly used, she snapped the fur scarf closely under her drooping chin and left the official precincts. She had no more idea of the vital part she had just played in solving the Marrender mystery than Dick Stowe ever was to have that her disclosure had been animated solely because of a barbed remark about the social status of the Rhands uttered by Katherine Latimer.

Before Stowe could get away from Headquarters Asher returned precipitately, "No use side-stepping action any more, Dick," he announced. "Parks has just wig-wagged that his bird's getting ready to blow out of town."

"Go ahead, old-timer—arrest him. It might just as well be today as tomorrow, but keep the other man on Marrender." Very casually Dick compared his watch with the office clock.

"But if you've got the dope on the doctor, what's the big idea about Marrender?"

"I'm not so sure, Tim, but I do know this—the charge against Perry Stuart will be the murder of Cubbage."

"How do you get that way?" howled Asher. "Marrender's the guy that could get hold of that Benssen stuff. He was there that night—"

"But he was not the only person who was there. I believe I remarked once before that it was evident that you had not carefully perused the attractive advertising booklet put out by the United Utilities Corporation. If you had been diligent enough to follow its pages to the end, you would have observed that the staff of physicians retained by the factory to minister to the bodily needs of its employees was headed by no other than Perry Stuart, M. D."

Abruptly Dick ceased to mock. "You yourself, Tim, will probably take the stand to testify that Stuart prepared a bromide for Cubbage that Wednesday night. Cubbage refused it, saying that the only restorative he desired was a glass of water. You remember that the doctor took the glass of water from Mrs. Banney as she brought it in from the kitchen. That's when he dropped in his few crystals of #3. . . ." He thrust his hands deep into his coat pockets while his gaze rested on his nonplussed colleague. Then his own expression became slightly like Asher's. "I say, Tim—"

He drew his hand from his pocket and thrust a crumpled bit of paper at the deputy-inspector. From an inner pocket he produced the letter that Will Marrender had found in his mail the preceding Saturday morning. "I say, Tim, have Radge or some other of your hand-picked experts get the low-down on this. I have an idea that the paper and ink are alike and I'm darned sure that one of the pens used on this paper wrote the letter, but then, I'm no expert."

"Whatever you think you're doing, there's one thing you can't pin on Marrender. He and his wife were in Cincinnati over Sunday all right, but the whole outfit at the Gibson can alibi him if necessary. He certainly didn't pinch the emerald."

"Ah, Timmy, you make a new man of me. What I'll be like by the time you get Stuart arrested—"

When the door had slammed after Asher's irate departure, Dick made a second attempt to get away also and a second time he was detained. It was a telephone call that stopped him. Janet Wilcox's voice came over the line.

"I must see you, Mr. Stowe—I must. There is something that I must explain—"

"It is I who can explain, Miss Wilcox, the reason that you did not find the parcel that you had checked at the station when you went for it."

Dick heard a strangled gasp. He went smoothly on. "I shall be only too glad to explain. Suppose you come up to my apartment this evening. My wife is home and she wants to meet you."

He hung up the receiver and this time succeeded in getting away. He hurried around to Dexter's office only to be informed that the lawyer was already on his way home. Crisply Dick instructed the anemic clerk to telephone the Dexter establishment that Mr. Richard Appleby Stowe would call in person that evening at eight-thirty.

That would give him time, thought Dick, as he made his way along a street already dusky with twilight, for a little talk with Janet Wilcox. If he went straight home now, he could plan out his campaign with Laura. That wasn't such a dumb idea. . . .

"It looks to me now," he expanded over dinner *enfa-mille*, "as though I really had the mess by the tail. Anyway, after what that Queen of England told me this afternoon, I'm going to chance the big show-down tomorrow. I sure could have kissed that old girl, feather bonnet included, La La. You see, no matter what I'd unearthed, and I surely had turned up a lot, I still had the feeling that I was up against three separate mysteries—"

"Who shot Miss Marrender?"

"Yes, and the identity of Cubbage—"

"And whether the disappearance of the emerald and the ransacked room downstairs had any connection with the murder," Laura finished.

"Exactly. Now I know that the man who masqueraded as Cubbage was the motive for the murder."

"But the emerald, Dick? And the condition of the little gallery?"

"It was Cubbage who handed out the emerald to Esme, remember." Dick attacked his second helping of chicken pie and frowned ominously, though not because his food displeased him. "Listen, La La, how's this? Cubbage's long-laid plans were dished when Miss Marrender was killed before she could change her will. Therefore, in a spirit of malignant revenge he set about to torture every one of her legitimate heirs by setting the stage so that each one could be made to feel that he was the villain whom circumstances were spotting. He had something on 'em all. I'll bet he rough-housed that room himself, but opening the second window was where he overplayed his hand. I sensed something phony about it from the very first."

"Dick! Were you here when Doris told me that she heard Cubbage moving furniture very early that morning? She thought he was cleaning, the little simp."

"Ah, ha, so papa guessed right, didn't he? Incidentally, La La, I love your enthusiasm for the captivating Doris. Now if I could only think what he did with the gun."

"In Gene's pocket, dear."

"I mean the other gun."

"You're running rings around me tonight, Dick, but I don't care. As a pedigreed dog in the manger, Cubbage wins the blue ribbon."

"Pedigreed, Laura? Not quite the accurate nor tactful word. But cheer up, old girl. If I weren't in the bosom of my adoring family, nothing could induce me to admit that the master mind fumbled a few straight leads from the take-off."

"How charmingly you say you missed your partner! Those first clues were awfully stagey though. I wonder what would have happened if Cubbage had been arrested immediately?"

"Even Tim thought they'd been planted. . . . What Cubbage might have done after the will was changed, I don't know, but until that happened Miss Marrender was safe with him. And if he had been arrested at once, he would have had the fun of telling on all the others."

"There were four heirs who stood to inherit under the existing will," said Laura thoughtfully. "If you had picked out the one who knew the aunt was going to make a new one—"

"Yeah? The nurse knew it, which means she probably spilled it to the doctor. Stuart also could have had his suspicions aroused by Cubbage's persistent questions. His knowing it of course involves Katherine Latimer, and you heard what a brain storm it stirred up in that quarter. Francesca did not know it. Funny how willing I am to believe anything that woman tells me—it's a darned good thing you're back on your wifely job, La La. I suspect that Sally knew it. It must have been the cause of her quarrel with her aunt that very morning. But if Will Marrender knew, it was Cubbage himself who told him."

"Then you don't think that Sally told him?"

"No. I think, rather, she'd have gone to any length to keep that information from him. He'd had all he could stand when Cubbage told him who he was."

There could be no more after-dinner loitering. At any minute now the bell would ring announcing the arrival of Janet Wilcox. Yet in the fifteen minutes before she appeared the Stowe telephone rang twice, and each time Headquarters relayed a report that pushed another detail of the Marrender case from the unknown to the known side of the record, and each time Dick ended his side of the colloquy with the words, "Tell Tim to keep his shirt on."

When Janet stepped into the Stowe apartment she could scarcely control herself while Dick introduced Laura, and then she burst into hysterical reproaches and denials. Their theme, as Dick had anticipated, concerned the parcel she had checked at the station.

Bluntly Dick silenced her. "Whether you and I know Gene Tracy to be innocent does not matter. We also know there is a web of circumstance that can entangle him in a charge of murder. Miss Wilcox, somebody else knows this too, someone who will not hesitate to pull this web to a strangle hold about him. Who this person is I am working to find out. You must help me."

"How can you doubt me, Mr. Stowe?"

"Tell me, then—if you had found the key to a safety-deposit box belonging to Miss Marrender, what could you have done that would have helped Gene Tracy?"

"Her will—it was against him."

"How did you happen to know where Miss Marrender kept her will?"

"Not through Gene Tracy," she flashed.

"I consider my question answered, Miss Wilcox, for I recall whose secretary you are. And now, if you don't mind, let me accuse you of lying. You told me that Cubbage and

Marrender were closeted together on Monday afternoon, but that you had no idea about the matter that brought Cubbage to Marrender's office. Later you informed me that they talked steadily the whole time. . . . Just why did you so suddenly announce your resignation to Mr. Marrender and afterwards reconsider it?"

This question seemed to have so little bearing upon the point at issue that Janet looked as taken aback as Laura looked surprised.

"I know now what you want me to tell you," breathed Janet. "I did hear something they said that afternoon—not much. And all of a sudden I made up my mind to quit. You see, Gene had the silly idea that if I kept on with my job after we got married his relatives would feel that they were handing out charity to him. So it wasn't what I heard that made me decide to stop working for Mr. Marrender. I wanted to marry Gene so much—and so my decision coincided with the interview that was going on. It was a lively interview— a regular quarrel was what it sounded like, though all I heard was, 'I'll show you—I'll show you! Come out—', and then in a minute, 'Very good, tomorrow night.' It was the caller's voice, not Mr. Marrender's.

"Well, when Cubbage went away, I told Mr. Marrender right away what I had decided, and it had the strangest effect upon him. He didn't say much about my leaving, but he kept asking me questions about whether I had overheard what his caller had said and so on. I—I told him I hadn't. It seemed to me that I had actually heard so little that I might as well say nothing. Then he begged me to stay on and almost doubled my salary. I was awfully surprised, but my common sense rallied around and I told him I'd stay. I was thinking that now I could furnish the apartment. . . . Mr. Marrender hung around a while as if he was really glad that I'd changed my mind, and pretty soon he suggested that I not mention his visitor's behavior as he was mentally unbalanced. After having a raise like that handed out to me what could I do?"

"You've done the right thing now, Miss Wilcox, let me assure you. And that's all for tonight. I haven't time to take you behind the scenes just now, but there's a chance that Tracy himself will tell you the whole story by—say, tomorrow night. Stay here and chat with my wife, do! But I must ask you to excuse me. There's a little matter of business to take up with Mr. Dexter."

Bartholomew Dexter dined at a later hour than the Stowes. When his caller was ushered in, he had just lighted his first after-dinner cigar and set out a test deal for contract bridge. Mr. Dexter was a text-book player who solemnly illustrated every lesson for himself.

Having been forewarned of Stowe's coming, he accepted the interruption with patience. Point by point he admitted the logic of the series of deductions which the ruthless young detective drew for him. A *laissez-faire* course would have been so much more dignified, but that was an opinion he could only regretfully keep to himself. However, he warned Stowe that a half-way clever defense could convince any jury that if Cubbage were that crazy he would have been crazy enough to shoot Eugenia Marrender, whether the will were changed in his favor or no. Likewise he pointed out that Tracy's testimony could never survive cross examination. On the other hand, the old lawyer did not appear shocked when Dick related the story told by Miss Bessie Rhand. He recalled, he admitted, a certain amount of rumor at the time of Miss Marrender's extended period of travel.

"What do you propose to do?" Dexter asked at length.

Dick Stowe told him. "If I'm wrong, all right; but I've got to give it a work-out and they must all be there. So if you'll agree to attend to that matter—"

Very deliberately Bartholomew Dexter produced a memorandum pad and a gold pencil. "The place?" His voice was as stern as that of the stern daughter of heavenly parentage whom he had never yet failed to answer.

"The little gallery," responded Dick.

"The time?"

"Eleven tomorrow morning."

"And the—er—occasion of my summons?"

"That a new will has come to light. That'll bring 'em all."

Dexter finished his precise jottings. "No doubt you feel justified in this deliberate misleading. In my opinion your position rests on one fatal weakness—you can produce but one weapon."

"If this were only Christmas Eve, Santa Claus might put it in my stocking. I have been a good boy. . . And now, before I go, let me suggest that you drop around at Windward Hill a little ahead of the others tomorrow. I'll have your last instructions ready for you by that time. You're still uncertain about your role in the finale, aren't you, old cautious!"

30

Stowe Arraigns the Marrenders

And so, on the tenth morning after the death of Eugenia Marrender, driven by conflicting emotions, the three nieces and the two nephews of the dead woman came to Windward Hill. Laura Stowe admitted them and announced that Mr. Dexter would meet them shortly in the little gallery. Laura secretly hoped that they accepted her as a temporary maid, nothing more. Inspector Peyton and Asher were lurking in the drawling-room opposite, while Dick and a visibly perturbed Dexter were in conference in Cubbage's room.

Sally Marrender and Tracy were the first to come. Laura noted the stubborn set of the girl's chin. "She'll never tell," thought Laura, "and Dick's no brow-beater." Tracy's manner revealed a nervous uncertainty. "And so should I," Laura meditated. "I could never pose as a serene spirit if I knew there was a gap in my conscious experience that corresponded alarmingly with the time at which murder had been done."

Will Marrender and Mrs. Latimer arrived next, though not together, Laura observed. There was a strained vivacity about Katherine Latimer that kept her high sweet voice echoing ceaselessly from the open door of the little gallery. Marrender fidgeted and looked at his watch repeatedly. His patience would not serve a prolonged waiting upon the tardy lawyer.

Francesca Penrose came careening up the drive toward Windward Hill in a cut-rate taxi. She jumped out and tossed a reckless bill at the driver. At the door she paused only long enough to commission the alert-eyed maid who admitted her. "If a Mr. Stowe is anywhere about the place—and I very much suspect he is—tell him at once that Miss Penrose has news about the emerald. He'll understand."

From Cubbage's room down the hall an inquiring head was thrust forth. Laura promptly gave the all-set signal. Within a minute or two Bartholomew Dexter emerged, and like a martyr advanced toward the half-open door of the little gallery. He cleared his throat and stepped over the threshold.

Laura and Dick in the hall, the detective officers in the room across—all could hear that the lawyer was carrying out his instructions. The heirs of Eugenia Marrender were first to be informed that they had possessed an illegitimate cousin, the son of their murdered aunt.

". . . I must admit to you that this surprising fact is capable of proof. Dates are known; the orphanage is known. It might even be that some one of you before me is not hearing this for the first time, but that point I shall not press for the moment. It can be demonstrated that this fact might account for almost every detail of the astounding situation in which you, as the relatives of the murdered woman, have become involved. However, before we enter upon a discussion of procedure, will you be so good as to give your attention to Mr. Stowe?"

At the words Dick Stowe entered the little gallery. Laura stationed herself demurely just inside the room, and Peyton and Asher lounged in the doorway. As he crossed the room Francesco Penrose was the only person who allowed her eyes to meet his. She did more. She laid an imperative hand upon his arm and whispered something to him rapidly, inaudibly. Dick listened, gravely attentive, and moved on to the farther end of the room. He turned and faced the group from between the two windows, the flying curtains of which had first announced trouble to Mrs. Banney. At his right hand were Francesca, Dexter, and Will Marrender. Directly behind the latter Laura hovered. Upon his left, Mrs. Latimer, Sally, and Eugene Tracy were seated. Dick slid his eyes from one guarded face to another. Francesca Penrose was not the only skilled actress in the family connection, he was thinking.

Stowe began to speak. "You have been called here to face a grave family crisis. Before you are asked to make a decision, you must all know all that is known. A part of what I shall tell you is already known to you all; parts are known to some of you individually; but none of you knows all the circumstances. What I must say will not be pleasant, at times, for any of you. That is the reason that Mr. Dexter is present. He will serve as a witness—a disinterested, unprejudiced witness, let us hope. There is some one of you who can corroborate every statement that I shall make."

Dick Stowe paused briefly, but no one in the room stirred except Marrender, whose fingers drummed unevenly upon the arm of his chair.

"Every crime," Dick's steady voice continued, "calculated or unpremeditated, has its roots in past events. You have just now heard for yourselves the remote cause of the violent death of Eugenia Marrender. It makes little difference now whether the man called Cubbage came to Windward Hill because he already had proof of his relation to its mistress, or whether he came in order to make his suspicion a certainty during the succeeding months. We may safely assume that the time came when he revealed himself to his mother. He led her to think of writing a new will in his favor. I cannot believe that she resisted his suggestion. In the course of my investigations I have gained a clear idea of the state of affection existing between each of you and your aunt. . . .

"Cubbage's plans for himself were sent crashing to ruin before they were accomplished. A murderer had foiled him. If Cubbage were alive and standing before you this instant, he would tell you that he did not know the identity of that murderer, and, ladies and gentlemen, I believe he would be telling you the truth."

A curious intentness of gaze marked his listeners, but no other emotion.

"If Cubbage had known who the murderer was, would he not have directed his attack upon one of you only? Yet it can be shown that all of you, and the nurse and Dr. Stuart as well, felt his malicious revenge.

"What else did I learn from my investigations? I shall spare you unnecessary detail, but I shall have to be blunt. Concerning Miss Penrose, for instance, I learned that she paid a stealthy visit to this room about the time that her aunt was killed. She carried away with her forty thousand dollars' worth of securities. Her arrival was witnessed by two people and her departure by three. At the present moment she is in possession of a valuable emerald, one time the property of her aunt. I do not know that Cubbage was aware of her presence that night, but I am convinced that it was he who attempted to confuse the issue by leaving the gloves, which she had forgotten to take away from this room, where he thought they would be immediately noticed."

No need now to fear that these people were indifferent to Stowe. Their eyes clung to him hotly. He continued.

"The part played by Tracy that night was much more melodramatic, I discovered. He arrived at Windward Hill about one o'clock accompanied by a young woman to whom he had rashly promised his aunt's emerald pin. Cubbage saw their arrival immediately and was sadly

inconvenienced by it. To save the situation for himself
he acted promptly. He followed Tracy upstairs and took
advantage of his maudlin state to offer him a generous
dose of Miss Marrender's sleeping tablets. For the time
being Tracy could safely be left on the couch in the alcove
at the back of the upper hall. At the same time he dropped
there a length of fine gold chain which eventually led me
to suspect that Cubbage was more closely related to the
Marrenders than they knew.

"The girl who had come with Tracy was locked in the
drawing-room to be held until called for. Two hours or so
later, when Tracy had been escorted to the door and sent
stumbling down the drive, he carried away with him the
weapon with which Miss Marrender had been shot. Not
long afterward the girl locked in the drawing-room was
freed, and as she left the house Cubbage slipped into her
hand the emerald pin, saying he had been asked by Tracy
to hand it to her. That, by the way, is a detail that per-
suades me that Cubbage was contemplating suicide after
he had set in motion enough wheels against you all. Otherwise, he would have salvaged the jewel for himself. The
next morning Cubbage called the attention of the police
to Tracy's room, where the imprint of a .38 revolver could
be plainly seen upon a flannel dressing gown. This imprint
was so lightly imbedded that it could not possibly have
been made by the gun in Tracy's possession when he left.
Please observe that curious fact. I consider it of the gravest importance."

Someone's breath was expelled sharply. Another's eyelids twitched. No one spoke.

"As I turn next to my discoveries about Mrs. Latimer,
justice compels me to point out that she could have known
that her aunt was about to change her will. For Dr. Stuart had come to quite correct conclusions about that. The
doctor's personality, I should also say, loomed as large in

the nurse's emotional life as in Mrs. Latimer's. The fear
of losing her share of her aunt's fortune, and thus her
advantage over other rivals for the doctor's devotion, impelled Mrs. Latimer to a dreadful attempt upon the life of
her aunt. This occurred early on Tuesday evening and was
prevented by no other than Cubbage himself. Dr. Stuart
will testify, though I cannot say what weight a statement
from him will have, that at that moment Mrs. Latimer
could not be held responsible for her actions. Whether it
was then or later that Cubbage possessed himself of Mrs.
Latimer's gloves, I do not know, but it is more than likely
that Cubbage saw in the episode another opportunity for
revenge, even future blackmail. But I prefer to dwell on
known facts. . . .

"Between one o'clock and some time between two and
three, Stuart and Mrs. Latimer were stalled on the River
Road just below Windward Hill. The doctor climbed the
path to the house to rouse Cubbage and telephone a service station. Perhaps the lady was left alone in the car
because the doctor's revolver was there, a .38. Stuart saw
a woman emerging from the window of this room, and a
few moments afterward narrowly escaped being struck by
a revolver thrown from one of the rear windows of the
house. Promptly, thereafter, the kitchen door opened and
Cubbage snatched the weapon from his hands, his only
explanation of the peculiar incident being that it belonged
to Sally Marrender. Stuart returned immediately to his car
and was greatly relieved to find Mrs. Latimer sitting within it, for he had, he said, a giddy moment of thinking he
recognized the woman coming out of this window as Mrs.
Latimer. Whether he ascertained at that time that his .38
was in its usual place in the pocket of his car, he has not
yet confessed. No doubt you are all aware that by the end
of the week he was publicly advertising the disappearance
of the gun. So necessary did a weapon appear to him that

he himself stole one the following Saturday from a place known to you all as Sally's Shop. That was not his only rash and ill-considered act. The turn of events pleased him so little that early the next morning he dispatched the nurse, Miss Randall, to an imaginary case on the California Coast, informing the police she had gone to Florida. The role taken by Cubbage during the course of that next day and evening he considered so menacing that for him he adopted less devious tactics."

At that a shudder ran round the entire group. Tracy, Francesca, and Marrender each attempted to speak, but something in Stowe's bearing silenced them. Both Sally and Katherine Latimer swayed toward him as if their wills were in his control.

"Wait, you must hear everything. Certain statements remain that involve Mr. Marrender and his sister."

Sally's dark head went back, but a groan burst from the brother. The sound caused his cousin Katherine to relax from the dreadful tenseness that gripped her, and at that Francesca sighed lightly.

"I have learned," Dick resumed, "that Cubbage had approached Mr. Marrender with his claim upon the woman whose servant he was. Mr. Marrender demanded proofs and it was arranged that he should go to Windward Hill late on Tuesday night to see them. The possibility that his inheritance from his aunt might be lessened, even entirely diverted from him, by this claimant whose power over his aunt, already sinister, increased the difficulty which Marrender was facing. He was obliged to borrow a large sum of money secretly and quickly, and he had been counting on his expectations from his aunt to swing the deal. His sister was in his confidence in this latter worry and she had tried to help by asking her aunt for a direct loan, which was brusquely, and I dare say vindictively, refused. On Tuesday night the brother and sister had a serious talk, and it was agreed that the first thing to determine was the exact strength of Cubbage's preposterous claims. In other words, Marrender must keep his appointment with Cubbage.

"I think Marrender went out to Windward Hill alone; I know he went armed with the .38 Miss Marrender kept in her shop. What Marrender's purpose was in entering this room I do not know, but I know he was here. I suspect Cubbage knew he was here. You can now understand that the unexpected arrival of Tracy threatened Cubbage's conference with Marrender. I do not know how far that interview proceeded; Stuart's experience with the gun would indicate that it had a violent ending. Marrender came back to town without the revolver. He left behind him also a fountain pen, a circumstantial detail which betrays his presence in the room where his aunt was shot.

"When his sister realized the significance of the missing weapon, she undertook to recover it. She reasoned, aptly, that it still might be at Windward Hill. Undoubtedly a gun of that description had been here on Wednesday, when Cubbage had made a curious use of it, as I have already mentioned. I think she found something which satisfied her that Friday night, but so far she has kept her own counsel. I have reason to believe that a .38 was in its proper place the next morning at Sally's Shop until it was stolen by someone equally interested in it. Marrender, Tracy, and Stuart were all at the shop during the course of the morning.

"That Mr. Marrender was as uneasy as any of you, I can point out by telling you that he resorted to a very crude red herring indeed to distract my attention, and that he indulged in threats almost as awkward against Miss Penrose. He must have been as relieved as anyone at the death of Cubbage, and, again I must remind you, he was among those present during the last hours of the man's life."

Stowe's voice fell as he finished his indictment. He looked slowly from face to face. After an interminable pause he spoke again. "Ladies and gentlemen, one of you here present is guilty of the murder of Eugenia Marrender. I have put before you every fact that has come to light and every deduction that might be drawn therefrom. The inevitable answer I have come to see clearly, but you must see it clearly, too, all of you—not only the one who this very instant knows with a dreadful certainty that he or she is the murderer.

"Mr. Dexter will provide each of you with a ballot. Write upon it the name of the person who is guilty. If your decision is not unanimous—but it can be nothing but unanimous. In the meantime, to permit you the freest private discussion, we who represent the police will withdraw."

31

Unanimous Decision

It was a bold move. It left the jury of five shaken and fearful of a trap. Slowly Bartholomew Dexter moved to the head of the room and stood gazing wretchedly across the tops of the heads before him. "What is your pleasure?" his stiff lips at last permitted him to ask.

"If we all write Cubbage's name on the ballot, what will happen?" demanded Francesca huskily.

"Until Miss Marrender had changed her will in his favor he could have had no motive." Dexter's answer came with automatic precision.

"So Stowe suspected all along that Cubbage was murdered too. Maybe his murderer has already been arrested." Tracy's restless eyes lingered just a second longer upon one face than upon the others.

Again Francesca Penrose spoke, so quickly as to ward off any possible comments on her cousin's suggestion. "Perhaps I should not have so much to say. . . . I honestly feel that I have not been under the blackest suspicion—I know I am innocent, you see. Yet I plead with you all to drag every secret out into the open if our souls are ever to know peace again. . . .

"When I stepped into this room on that dreadful night, I did not know that Will was here, but he saw me and drew quite correct conclusions as to what had brought me here." She turned abruptly to the man at her right. "My receipt did not do you much good, did it? I guessed it was you who had it, although all I told Mr. Stowe was that the voice over the telephone sounded familiar—he discovered later that you were indeed in Cincinnati at that time. Will, believe me, I did not want to implicate you in murder. You and Kaye. . . . When Dr. Stuart spoke to me as I stepped through the window, I was afraid—on her account. He thought I was Kaye. . . ."

Francesca's moving voice died away into a cold and heavy silence. Then Sally Marrender rose to her feet and made an unsteady rush across the room to her brother, who still sat with his head sunk on his chest.

"Will, Will," she sobbed, "say you didn't do it—oh, say it! What if you did take my revolver? When I found it, it hadn't even been fired."

Her pleadings brought no response from his abject figure.

"Do I understand you to say that you found a weapon, Miss Marrender?" Dexter inquired, his nervous fingers seeking his cameo ring.

"Yes, yes—last Friday night. Cubbage must have hidden it, for I found it in that secret drawer in the butler's pantry. Aunt Genie always kept old napkin rings and discarded spoons there—she showed me once, long ago when I was a little girl. I thought Cubbage might have discovered the drawer for himself and put his proofs there—about being Aunt Genie's son, I mean. They weren't . . . but my gun was and not one shot had been fired from it."

"But, Sally, are you sure it was your revolver you found?" For a moment Dexter's manner was fatherly. "I dare say you ignored the matter of finger prints."

"No, I didn't. Before I put it back on the shelf under the cash register I wiped it off with energine. Any finger prints found on it after that would all be mine."

"At any rate, Sally, we can agree that you are safely out of the picture, even if your .38 isn't?" Tracy cast another sardonic glance about the group. "That reduces the candidates to three."

Suddenly Will Marrender stood erect before them all, but he spoke only to his sister as if the others were not present. "Listen, Sally, I told you that I was going to Windward Hill, didn't I?"

Her quick, triumphant, decisive nod did not interrupt him.

"I told you why I had to go?"

"You had to see for yourself—for the sake of all of us—what right he had to say that he was Aunt Genie's son."

"I took your gun with me—"

"You took it because I insisted that you must. The idea was all mine. . . ."

Gravely Marrender bowed his head in assent. "And what time was it when I returned?"

"A quarter of three. I was waiting."

"What did I tell you?"

"The truth, Will. . . . I know it was the truth. That the interview with Cubbage had not gone your way—"

"By which I meant that his claim upon Aune Eugenia could be very clearly established. What else did I say?"

"You said—oh, Will, what a terrible meaning I thought it had! Not then . . . but when I heard what had happened at Windward Hill. If you had only told me yourself that Aunt Genie had been murdered! You said you saw a new way out of your trouble and that I wasn't to worry."

"That was your receipt, Francesca." There was a note of stiff apology in the words Marrender tossed to his cousin. "If you had access to forty thousand dollars, I thought I could persuade you to let me use the money for four or five days. That would have been long enough to swing me out of danger. You said we should lay everything bare.

This money business was just a personal mess I'd got myself into, but I'd have dished myself with United Utilities
if they had got wind of it. . . . And then the next day when
the news about the murder broke, I saw that I had run my
head into another noose. Any half-baked detective could
produce a damning motive against me. That's why I tried
some hocus-pocus of my own—trying to scare Fran with
mysterious messages about her receipt—"

"I couldn't have sworn to it, but I was so afraid I had
recognized your voice."

"—and writing a letter to myself as if from Cubbage,
but I very soon saw that the detective chap hadn't swallowed that." Marrender turned again to his sister and his
hands fell heavily upon her shoulders. "Sally, what did I
say about the gun when I came back? The truth, dear."

"You said you put it back where you'd found it."

"And you believed me?"

"I never dreamed of looking till late the next afternoon. Mr. Stowe's visit worried me."

"And then you knew that I had not brought the gun
back from Windward Hill. But, Sally, I did not kill our
aunt . . . nor do I know who did. All I know is that after
I had experimented with the window which the Sunday
before Aunt Eugenia had asked me to unlock, I came out
again and entered the house by the usual way. Cubbage
took me back to his room, and in short order put his cards
upon the table. I saw he had a case and so I attempted
to play an ace of my own. I knew you others would back
me up if I could get him to sign a sort of quit-claim paper—in consideration for value received, of course—but
he was vilely offensive. I saw red—that must have been
when he managed the business about the fountain pen. He
had taken it from me as if he meant to sign. It was Stuart's pen and I meant to return it to him the next time I
saw him—I'd absentmindedly walked off with it from the

Anthony. How it got—where Stowe says it was found later I can't explain, but no doubt Cubbage could if he were still living.

"As I was saying, the scoundrel infuriated me. I admit I tried to get at my gun, but he knocked it out of my hand. We clinched and struggled for a moment. Then he broke away from me and dashed out of the room, switching off the lights as he went. I fumbled around in the darkness, for I had a feeling that Cubbage was in ambush. Then I heard the shot. Someone was moving on the back stairs. I lost my head like a damned fool. Without stopping to investigate I got out of the house and back to you."

There was another pall of silence. Bartholomew Dexter turned his ring slowly and regretted his promise to that whippersnapper, Stowe. Eugene Tracy laughed in a strained, unnatural fashion. He started to say something about "and then there were two . . ." but only part of the phrase was audible. He tried again.

"Why be so damned polite? After all, I'm the most logical villain, and there are enough extenuating circumstances to keep me from a straight first-degree charge. In the first place, I was there. I wasn't quite myself. Isn't that the euphemistic term? And it appears that I was there with the avowed purpose of stealing the family heirloom. I dare say I shot its rightful owner when she opened her beady eyes and saw me as I tiptoed across her room to its hiding place. I can't prove that I didn't do just that even though Cubbage isn't alive to accuse me of it. That might do for a motive. God knows I've no particular reason for living—I've forfeited the respect of the only person who ever gave two hoots in hell for me. So, ladies and gentlemen, I solicit your votes at the polls."

Dexter's protesting hand went unheeded. Again Francesca murmured, "I insist that it must have been Cubbage." An interrupting voice silenced her, a high, shrill voice that had lost all of its loveliness. Grey defeat crept over Francesca's face as she listened.

"What—what was that you said about knowing who murdered Cubbage? It must be the same one who—who killed Aunt Eugenia. . . . Why don't we tell that to the men who were here? I—I don't think I can stand much more discussion."

"My dear Mrs. Latimer, I have been instructed to answer that question." The lawyer's voice trembled. "Dr. Perry Stuart was placed under arrest last night, charged with the murder of Cubbage. This morning he admitted his guilt and explained how he possessed himself of a revolver which he hoped might prove to be his—one he found in Sally's Shop. He further stated that he disposed of the weapon, when he had satisfied himself that it was not his, by throwing it into the reservoir north of the city. The police inform me that it has already been retrieved. Their examination shows that it is indeed a revolver that had never been fired."

"Then the one found in my pocket—" Something like relief surged through Tracy's hoarse question.

"—was Dr. Stuart's in spite of his first denial. However, he has not yet confessed that he killed Miss Marrender."

"But he didn't—he didn't, I tell you! Don't let him say he did it!" Katherine Latimer sprang to her feet and clutched wildly at Dexter's steadying arm. "They stopped me the first time, but not the second. It was the only thing I could do—Perry was slipping from me. . . . I was here that night. I followed Perry up the path. I had taken his revolver out of the side pocket of the car, but I was afraid . . . afraid. And when Cubbage opened the back door and came out toward Perry, I slipped inside and up the back stairs. I heard somebody breathing but I didn't see anyone—not then. No one could have stopped me—no one! She was a devil, I tell you. She said—only that very

afternoon she had threatened me—I must choose between
her money and her doctor. I made the gun go off—it was
easy. And then I heard the breathing again—out there in
the hall. It came from behind the curtain in the alcove. I
made myself look . . . that was a harder thing for me to do
than—the other." Her laughter climbed hysterically. "But
it was only Gene lying there. I thought he was drunk—"

"Of course!" Only Tracy could have interposed a comment in this torrent of confession.

But the frenzied woman was oblivious to the interruption. She swayed perilously yet her fingers did not relax
their grip upon Dexter's coat sleeve. "So I thrust the revolver into Gene's pocket and turned the corner down the
back stairs just as Cubbage or somebody ran up the front
way. I ran down the path to the road and there was Perry
looking for me. I wouldn't tell him where I had been, but
he guessed—he guessed . . . and he must have been afraid
Cubbage would tell, so that's why— Oh, don't you see—he
loved me more than I knew or he never would have done
it. I don't care— I'm not sorry I shot her. It made Perry
prove how much he loved me. I don't care now— Where—
where's Francesca—?"

In the hall without, the group of four waited. Asher
smoked in short nervous puffs. Peyton looked at his watch
every other minute. Dick Stowe did not find the set of the
Inspector's jaw particularly complimentary.

"All right," Stowe was thinking savagely, "if you're so
sure I'm giving them too much rope, go ahead with your
own rules. You know we've got the dope. . . ."

Laura spoke. "Don't you agree with my husband, Inspector, that they must convince themselves—as they are doing
now? Then you can step in and—"

"Of course, the woman will plead insanity, though the
doctor won't—he can't. There's been a swell lot of dirt

dished up." Further than that Inspector Peyton refused to
comment upon the wisdom of Stowe's course. His consent
to it committed him irrevocably, he considered.

"Dick, whatever did Miss Penrose mean about the
emerald?" demanded Laura.

"She was the one who snitched it away from Jupe. I
knew she was a possibility at the time, but I did not consider it a vital point. I mean the further adventures of
the emerald were leading away from rather than toward
the murderer of its owner. Miss Penrose's present idea is
to plant it somewhere in the little gallery and insist that
Gene find it and keep it for his—that fantastic promise
of the aunt's, you see, that Gene could have whatever he
wished from the room."

"Umph," snorted Asher, "that's not such a hot idea."

"Tracy, luckily for him, has a girl who will always do
his heavy thinking for him, if he has sense enough to give
her a chance to forgive him. Janet Wilcox will insist that
he choose to hold the receipt that Miss Penrose gave to
cover her borrowing of the securities. I rather think the
old lady kept them down in the little gallery purposely for
the wayward namesake to stumble upon."

Peyton's lazy eyes glinted with approval, but Asher was
still captious. He jerked a thumb toward the closed door
of the little gallery.

"You think you can trust Dexter to tell you—?"

"You forget I've got the drop on everything they're con-
fessing to one another this minute—everything except one
point." Dick's voice fell regretfully. "I don't know for sure
why Sally Marrender came up here Friday night. Stubborn
little devil!"

"And if she swallows a dose of poison just when she
comes across with her confession, then where are you?"

The door of the little gallery swung open. Bartholomew
Dexter appeared on the threshold, his plump jowls drained

of their fresh color. He tried twice before he could say what he must.

"I am instructed to inform you—" His legal formalities went down before a rush of human emotion. "Mr. Stowe, you were quite right. Katherine Latimer has admitted her guilt."

MURDER IN THE FRENCH ROOM

For Faith
whose name is not
just a word.

1
Fitting Room E

Joyce Terry scuttled from the cashier's desk across the taupe-carpeted expanse of the women's ready-to-wear department of Line and Hollis's and into the more secluded quarters of the French Room. She hurried on to the suite of fitting rooms beyond, where she had left her customer. She had been detained longer than usual at the desk because Mr. Knox, the floor man, had been trying to straighten out a tangle over a credit slip. Joyce's customer in fitting room E, she was thinking, would have lost all patience waiting for her to return to get name and address for the charge.

As Joyce whirled around the partition that led to the row of fitting rooms, she almost ran down a woman who was emerging. There was a murmur of apology to which the departing customer paid no attention, and Joyce hurried on. All she could remember afterward was that the woman was drawing on a pair of light-colored buckskin gloves. The glint of a jeweled ring just disappearing under one glove came back to her much later.

Joyce pushed open the door that led to the last compartment in the row. "I'm sorry to have kept you waiting like this—"

The words died away to a choked gasp. The door of the little room swung shut, concealing what she had been forced to look upon. With the back of her hand pressed tightly against her lips, Joyce fought back an impulse to let out a shrill, hysterical scream.

A pick-up girl appeared at the entrance of the corridor, her arms full of immaculate evening gowns. Joyce knew she must not allow the child to come any nearer. "Dottie," she made herself say in as natural a voice as she could muster, "go tell Madame Nordhoff to come here immediately. Tell her it's urgent."

Dottie backed out obediently. The look in her sharp little eyes seemed to say, "Who am I—or you either—to tell the Head to do anything p.d.q?" Joyce waited, her back stoutly against the closed door of room E. Voices were audible from other fitting rooms in the group . . . familiar tones . . . scraps of talk between saleswomen and customers. Business at Line and Hollis's droned on as usual in spite of the horror just within room E. A long shudder slid icily along Joyce Terry's spine.

Dottie must have found Madame Nordhoff, buyer for the French Room, reasonably close at hand, for within less than two minutes she too turned the corner that led to the fitting rooms. There was a cock to her eyebrows that Joyce recognized as a danger signal.

"What's your big idea, Terry? Just as if a customer like Mrs. Dunn Marlay could be left when she was about sold on a Lanvin model . . ."

Joyce interrupted ruthlessly. "Something terrible has happened to my customer in E here. I—I just now found her. You'll have to keep people out—"

Madame Nordhoff waited to hear no more. She had found the girl's whisper sufficiently convincing. She brushed Joyce aside and opened the door of room E. Joyce could not see her superior's face from her position behind her, but she heard the involuntary sharp breath that meant shock.

"You did the right thing, Joyce. Don't raise a row but get right out of here and send in a call for Miss Brooke. I'll stand guard here. It—it must be murder. And it's almost an hour till closing time . . . customers everywhere—"

But Joyce Terry did not stay to listen to the head of her department. Trembling and sick at what she had seen within the fitting room, she hurried off to summon the store detective to the scene. Mr. Knox must be told, too, but Joyce's flying glance did not find him. He must have gone back to the credit manager's office.

In an unbelievably short time she was on her way back to the fitting rooms, side-stepping prospective customers as she hurried along. There was no Madame Nordhoff waiting outside the door of room E. Oh, yes . . . there she was. What nerve Nordie must have, going right in that awful place like that.

Joyce said as much to the buyer as she rejoined her. "One look nearly finished me. That blood everywhere. . . . And she'd been laughing and talking with me all the time she was trying on—"

"You'll be into this up to your neck, Joyce. I mean, having to answer questions and tell who she was and so on."

The girl clutched the older woman in new terror. "Her name! That was just what I was coming to ask her when I found her—"

Authoritative heels tapped an approach. It was Jessica Brooke, seasoned personnel worker and store detective, a decided personality among the employees at Line and Hollis's.

"What's up?" she demanded, her immediate thought being that Nordhoff had caught one of her own girls dead to rights at something crooked.

"Take a look in E and you'll know as much as I do. Miss Terry here made the discovery. The chief thing is—no panic on the floor. My last numbers are moving slow enough now."

Madame Nordhoff stood aside to allow Jessica Brooke to open the door. Joyce was at the detective's elbow, determined to test herself with another look. Ah-h-h, just as before. A slight lovely, figure huddled across the fitting stand, blood everywhere—ghastly . . .

Jessica Brooke's day's work made many unpleasant demands upon her, but this was the first time she had come upon murder. For murder it undoubtedly was. One step beyond the door brought her to the huddled figure. Intrepidly, she stooped and touched one outflung hand. In a heap on the floor, trailing from the hand, was a dress.

"She must have been attacked just as she reached for her dress. It's hers, of course, for it's been worn, and she hasn't one on, and there's her coat and hat—"

Miss Brooke spoke softly as if the other two were not about. In fact, Madame Nordhoff was still standing in the corridor to forbid any salesgirl bringing customers to this group of dressing rooms. Joyce Terry had followed the detective into the little room, however. Her self-control was returning and she was conscious of a curious excitement.

"But I can't see what was used to kill her. Nasty wound, what?" Jessica Brooke directed her comment at a greatly impressed Joyce, as if she expected professional corroboration. Then she circled the spot where the dead woman lay in an attempt to see what she could without touching the body.

The victim had fallen forward on her face and lay across the fitting platform upon which customers mount to have skirt lengths adjusted. Until the body should be lifted it was impossible to see much of the woman's face. The short dark hair lay in what both observers knew were natural waves. The line of neck and throat was lovely and the skin, except where the hideous wound gaped, was fair and exquisite. The lingerie in which the still, slight form was clothed was neither cheap nor vulgar.

"No," said Jessica Brooke, "we can't touch a thing. The police and the coroner— Here, you're in on this already." Her swift glance, took Joyce's measure. "Hurry up to Mr. Galway's office and have him come down. But first tell him to send in a quiet call to Headquarters. I'd like Dan Bratton. He's their best man."

As Joyce Terry again left the French Room to make a hurried crossing of the main floor of the ready-to-wear, it seemed fantastic to her that customers could be so casually inspecting the latest models in afternoon frocks or sports outfits. Some of the salesgirls were no doubt wondering just why they were being shunted from the French Room fitting alcove to the much less impressive suite provided for purchasers of wares from the Economy Shop, but a story about a customer's being taken violently ill had been started by somebody and was going well enough. So far there was only a faint ripple of uneasiness to be felt in the ready-to-wear.

Joyce Terry's errand created a sensation in the office of the general manager. Galway paused only long enough to send in the call to Headquarters and then followed Joyce down to the department on the fourth floor. He was so close behind her as they entered the French Room that for a moment she thought the words she heard were addressed to herself. They came from a man lounging on a divan provided for bored husbands or inspecting fathers who sometimes accompanied shopping women folk.

"How are you, Otis, old man? So this is where you do your stuff, eh? Will they throw me out if I smoke? I'm waiting for the girl friend, and how . . ."

The man who drawled out these words was sleek and dark and too noticeably well turned out. Yet there was an insidious element of cheapness about him that matched his phrases. Joyce wondered how a man like Otis Galway, whom she admired very much indeed, could enjoy much of his society.

Galway murmured some sort of reply and stalked on in Joyce's wake. An anxious group was waiting for him in the passage leading to the fitting rooms—Jessica Brooke, Madame Nordhoff, and, by this time, Knox, the floor superintendent. The store detective beckoned imperiously. She murmured a word or two in his ear, and then he too was shown what lay behind the door of room E.

Galway backed precipitately out of the cubicle, looking shocked and sick. "What ought we do?" he muttered and wiped a fine steam of perspiration off his face.

"Do? It can't be done, if you ask me," snorted Jessica Brooke belligerently. "Whoever murdered that woman has had a thousand good chances to walk right out of this store unquestioned and unhindered. What chance have we of blocking all the exits and examining everybody under the roof? Why, there's not a chance in a million that the murderer will ever be caught—"

"Miss Brooke's a detective—she ought to know." Knox's words and quick, nervous laugh came with ill-timed face-tiousness.

"At least we can attempt to hold the people now in the department." Galway's suggestion lost its value as Jessica Brooke gave her smooth head a derisive shake.

"Like to see you try it. Women strolling in and out of the picture all the time. No, I did the only feasible thing. I'm holding the women that happened to be in the other compartments when the crime was discovered—that is, those I found after I came up. There's no use talking to them yet. Better wait for Dan Bratton to come. It will mean not hearing their stories twice."

Galway moistened his lips before he spoke. He still looked faintly green. "Who is the woman? She—she looks—a little like somebody I've seen. And who found her?"

"Number 82 found her—Miss Terry." It was Madame Nordhoff who spoke. "Why doesn't somebody ask her all about it? She must have been the last person—to see her alive."

2

JOYCE TERRY'S SHOES

Never had Joyce Terry felt more alone than she did in the pause that followed Madame Nordhoff's words. The wave of suspicion that eddied about her was like something tangible. Even Miss Brooke's friendly eyes narrowed formidably. Knox cleared his throat in obvious nervousness as the general manager turned upon the slight figure of the salesgirl. Then the arrival of Dan Bratton from Headquarters brought a curtain to the scene that more than one in the taut group now wished had never been precipitated.

Bratton was a wiry chap, not much above medium height. There was a spark of fun in his sharp blue eyes that few people who faced him were calm enough to discover. His secret weakness was for boutonnieres, but only after he had successfully brought a case through to a finish was he brave enough to face the underlings in his department so adorned.

A few words of explanation from Galway enabled Bratton to issue his first directions. He stationed one of his men outside the door of room E until the coroner should arrive. The salespeople and customers caught in the block of fitting compartments when the crime was discovered were marched off to Galway's offices on the ninth floor. Not one of the customers demurred, Bratton duly noted. Perhaps curiosity had triumphed over disgruntlement.

Before following them, Bratton turned to Jessica Brooke. After a word or two she hurried off to put a few quiet questions to the girls on the elevators and the attendants in the rest rooms and to station Daddy Baynes and his crew at the exit doors immediately. The chance was slight at best, considering the locale of the crime, but perhaps some circumstance might thus be reported that would lead to the trail of the escaping murderer.

Galway himself remained in the department to assist Knox in curbing the restless and constantly increasing excitement that these unexplained activities in the French Room were causing. Already a reporter had announced herself, but so far the story of a customer's sudden illness was holding her.

As soon as she had carried out Bratton's suggestions, Jessica Brooke made her way to the ninth floor. She wanted to watch Headquarters' best man in action. Moreover, this was her big chance to show Dan Bratton that his silently expressed respect for her good sense was not ill-founded. Her constant war against shop lifters brought her many contacts with the local police authorities and she knew that her private opinion of Detective Inspector Bratton's prowess was well grounded.

The store detective slipped into the general manager's suite just in time to hear the questions Bratton was asking Joyce Terry.

"Now I want the young lady's story—the one who was waiting on this woman," said Bratton. "Miss Terry?"

Joyce took a long breath and began to talk. At first her voice was small and shaken but the friendly attention in Bratton's eyes steadied her. The others waiting their summons to inquisition listened greedily. It occurred to Jessica Brooke to wonder fleetingly with what eyes each in the group saw the girl who was speaking. She herself saw Joyce Terry as young and eager and shyly pretty. Her soft dark hair was a curly mop and her eyes were a smoky violet. Her nose was as plebeian as her feet were aristocratic. Not the girl, Miss Brooke decided, to pass unscathed in spirit through the ordeal of publicity.

". . . she wanted to see afternoon dresses, Mr. Knox said, and after I had got out six or seven she decided to try several of them on and so we went back to the fitting rooms. She tried three, I think, before she settled on the beige chiffon velvet. It was to be charged. I hadn't brought my salesbook in with me, so I said I'd be back in a minute, and I went out, and at the desk Mr. Knox—he's our floor manager—stopped me, and I was detained longer than I expected, and when I got back to E . . ." Joyce had been speaking faster and faster. Now she stopped abruptly. Her eyes sought Bratton's like a frightened child's. "I—I found her all in a heap and there was blood—" An involuntary shudder ran over the girl's tense body and the faint green of nausea tinged her face.

"Can you tell me how long you were gone, hunting for your salesbook?" Bratton asked in a calm, everyday voice that helped her mounting nervousness.

"Five minutes, anyway. Maybe longer. I'm never very clear about time. Mr. Knox might—"

"Sure he will. I'll talk to him later." Bratton smiled as genially as though he had not obliquely announced that he knew how to run his own game. "Now tell me, whom did you see as you left the booth and returned to it?"

"When I went to get my book? Why, I believe that Ede—Edith Pike was taking a customer into F. That's the opposite booth."

A rotund, florid, more than middle-aged woman interrupted. "I was that customer, and I want to say here and now that Line and Hollis will have to explain to our lawyer why I have been so outrageously detained."

"Certainly, madame. Just one minute, and I'll be glad to hear your story." Dan Bratton stopped the red-faced woman temporarily. "You were saying, Miss Terry—did you see anyone else?"

"Only Dottie. She's the little girl that gathers up gowns and puts them back in their proper cases. She was on her way out ahead of me. I'm sure I didn't see anybody else as I left the fitting rooms." Joyce paused and Bratton made a careful memorandum. "And as you returned?"

Joyce Terry wrinkled her forehead before she replied. "I just sort of seem to remember that I passed someone as I turned in toward the fitting room alcove, but I can't be sure. Oh, isn't it annoying when you're just on the verge of re-calling something that won't quite come!" Joyce smiled at Bratton as if she had forgotten that he was a police detective.

"Umph! Sounds very convenient." It was the florid lady again. Once more Joyce Terry was conscious of the miasma of suspicion.

"Did you at any time observe that your customer spoke to anyone else, sales people or patrons?" Bratton asked.

"No, I'm quite sure she didn't while I was with her."

"I'd like to say something about that." It was Madame Nordhoff who spoke. A buyer for a department like French imports expects to be listened to. She was. . . .

"Before they left for the fitting rooms I had noticed what customer Terry was busy with—that's only part of my regular business, you understand. I saw the woman look at her watch and then out toward the elevators as if she was expecting somebody."

"Good. That's rather an interesting detail." Bratton smiled blandly. "Did she appear to recognize anyone?"

"No-o-o, not that I observed."

"Did you happen to see what—er—she's just men-tioned?" Dan Bratton's obliging forefinger indicated

Madame Nordhoff, but before Joyce could answer the buyer named herself suavely, and inserted further explanation.

"If I can trust my memory, Inspector, Terry had just
turned from her customer to get some models to show
her."

"If you can't trust your memory, Mrs. Nordhoff, you'd
better keep still." For an instant there was no twinkle in
Bratton's blue eyes, but the words he next addressed, very
pointedly, to the girl were warm with friendliness.

"Another question, Miss Terry, and then you may stand
by—till later. While you were with this woman, did she
do or say anything which in view of what was shortly to
happen to her might now have some special significance?"

"I—I don't know what you mean, exactly. . . . She didn't
do anything except look at dresses, and when we went into
the fitting room to try them on, why—she just tried the
dresses on, you know. All that we said to one another was
about the dresses—whether they were the right color and
line and so on, mostly—"

Abruptly the girl stopped. That something had occurred
to her was clear. She bit her underlip and then continued,
more timorously. "She did say one thing that—that makes
me creep now. There was a blue crêpe. . . When I slipped
it on her she took a complete turn against it. 'I wouldn't
want to be caught dead in that,' she said. That's just a
common expression, of course, and doesn't mean a thing.
But maybe this will help more. . . . When she had decided
on the beige number, she said something about a dress as
stunning as that ought to give any woman courage enough
to go out and break the seventh commandment."

The red-faced lady grew purple, but Bratton let the remark pass without comment. Instead he again asked with
studied swiftness, "And you say you didn't know your customer's name, nor recognize her in any way?"

"No, I was just going to take the charge when I—"
Again Joyce shuddered with nausea.

"Of course there's likely to be something on the body
that will help us out. We'll come to that later. Well then,
you sent for Mrs. Nordhoff." Bratton turned politely to
the head of the department. She bowed ever so slightly, as
though to indicate that while she was wholly at his official disposal she had no intention of volunteering further
information.

His questions brought out a clear, definite statement,
but one that added nothing to what had already been
learned. She had been busy with a customer when the pick-
up girl delivered Terry's message. She had come at once
and when she saw what had happened she had sent for the
floor superintendent, the store detective, and the general
manager. While she stood on guard outside the door of
booth E, waiting for the first of these three to arrive, no
one had left the alcove and she had need to shunt away
only one of her girls with a customer in tow who wanted
to try something on. The woman, she assured Bratton, was
a complete stranger to her. "Certainly not one of our regulars. I remember faces too well to be mistaken about that."

"I see. . . . How long have you been with Line and
Hollis?"

"It will be two years in January."

There were signs of imminent outburst from the florid
rotundity. Bratton, therefore, gravely invited her to be the
next speaker. Her story did not wait for prompting questions.

"I am Mrs. Ludlow Wilkinson. My husband is presi-
dent of the Bennett Memorial Seminary. We live on Cam-
pus Hill. I saw this salesgirl step out of the opposite booth
just as my clerk pushed open the door of the one I was to
use. We entered and I proceeded to try on the navy blue
georgette that I had tentatively selected. The entire hem

would have to be let out in order to bring the skirt to a decent length, I discovered. The only conversation that passed between me and the girl who was serving me was the necessary comment relative to that operation. . . ."

Did Jessica Brooke imagine it, or was that an authentic expression of relief that flitted across the face of Ede Pike, who had sold Mrs. Wilkinson the too-short georgette?

Mrs. Wilkinson went on. "I mention that only to show you that if anyone murdered anyone else across that narrow passage I should certainly have heard it. Furthermore I should have done something about it at once."

"I assure you, madame, there is no doubt about it. Somebody was murdered, rather hideously murdered." Bratton's voice was mockingly apologetic.

"Then why didn't I hear something? Those little bandbox rooms are only partitioned off with cardboard. They're not closed in at the top, and their entrance doors don't even go clear to the floor. Why, I'd have you know that I could hear every word of the story that was being told in the one next to mine—not that it had anything to do with this trouble you've stirred up, of course."

Mrs. Wilkinson's last words came a bit too hastily to escape the detectives' notice. Jessica Brooke tucked the item away for later consideration, and Bratton asked himself how if she was so busy listening to somebody spilling the dirt, she could be so positive that no disturbance issued from the compartment across from hers.

Edith Pike next verified everything that her stout customer had related and added that she was on her knees adjusting the hem of the blue georgette when Joyce Terry returned.

"How do you know that?" Bratton demanded.

"I recognized her shoes. The way I was kneeling there on the floor I could see under the door and I saw Joyce go in. I must have shifted my position some—of course I did, working around the hem like that—anyway, I didn't see her come right out, like she said. Or if she did, I never paid any attention to it."

Again Joyce Terry had the icy feeling of utter defenselessness.

"Let me get this straight," persisted Bratton. "Miss Terry was leaving, ostensibly for her salesbook, when you and your customer entered F. You saw her return, recognizing her by her shoes. You can not be positive that she bolted right out again. Now about the time interval. How long did it take to get this dress on Mrs. Wilkinson and for you to be on the floor fussing at the bottom of it?"

"Not long. Not more than ten minutes, but I have no way of being positive." Edith Pike's answer came decisively.

"I see," said Bratton cheerfully. Jessica Brooke thought she knew what that meant.

"And then what?" the inspector prodded.

"My customer and I left the booth together—I had to stay to help her into her dress instead of going ahead to the desk"—the look that Mrs. Ludlow Wilkinson launched at Ede Pike forecast a resolve never to buy another stitch at Line and Hollis's—"and there was Madame Nordhoff and Miss Brooke standing in the passage looking kind of queer and Miss Brooke asked my customer kindly to wait for her at the desk. At that I suspected something right away, because that always means just one thing with Miss Brooke, but I guess the lady wasn't on to that, so she waited."

"All right. Now the next one I'd like to hear from is whoever was in the fitting booth next to E—the middle one on the right, it ought to be."

Dan Bratton looked about expectantly. There was no sign of cooperation from the wary group. They were no longer particularly enjoying themselves.

Joyce Terry's shaking voice broke the waiting pause. "Maybe there was nobody in C. I know there wasn't when

I was looking for a vacant place for my customer. I pushed that door open first, but the lady said something I didn't hear and stepped into E herself. I followed."

"She said something—you say you didn't hear it? Are you sure you're telling me everything you know?"

Again Joyce was conscious of numbing isolation.

Another saleswoman's nervous gestures diverted Bratton's attention from Joyce. He pointed her out bluntly. "What do you know about it?" he demanded.

"There was someone in C when I came along," the girl said breathlessly. "I tapped on the door and started to push it open the way we do, and a voice called out, 'Busy.' Just then a woman left B and I took my customer in there."

This was definite enough to lead to instant question from the detective inspector. He learned that the salesgirl's name was Grace Ramby, that she had no idea whose voice had answered her, though she had assumed that it was one of her fellow workers, that the customer she had taken into B had found immediately that the dress she had taken in did not fit her and refused to stay to see anything else, so that they had both very promptly thereafter left the little block of fitting rooms and were nowhere about when the first excitement broke. However, Miss Ramby knew her customer well and gave her name and address to the official.

As Bratton listened, with a few pencil strokes he had blocked out a rough diagram of the fitting rooms and had checked against the ones about which he had secured at least a partial report. "All right," he proceeded briskly, "now let's hear who was in this first one—A."

For an instant no one spoke, but Jessica Brooke and Bratton were not the only ones who noted that two pairs of eyes rolled in anxious consultation.

"Speak up, Madge," prompted the store detective. "Evidently you know something. What about it?"

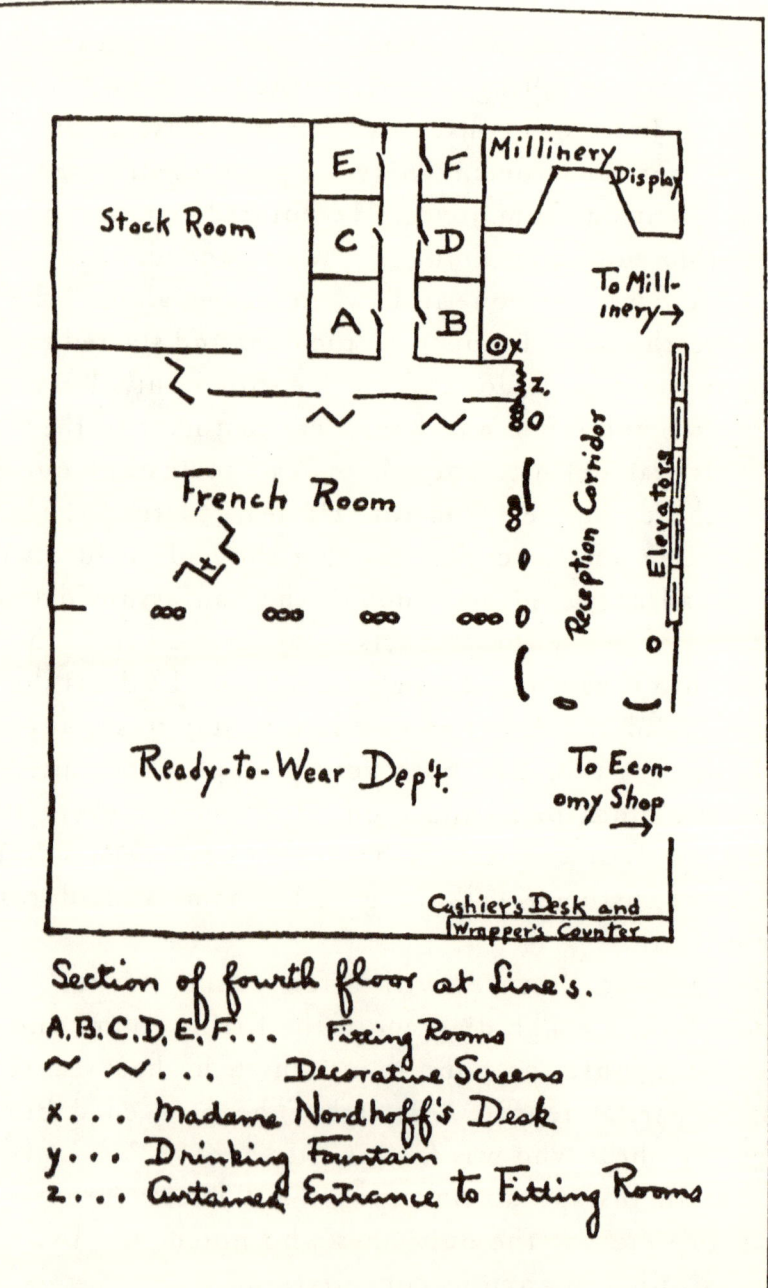

Section of fourth floor at Line's.
A.B.C.D.E.F... Fitting Rooms
~ ~ ... Decorative Screens
x... Madame Nordhoff's Desk
y... Drinking Fountain
z... Curtained Entrance to Fitting Rooms

Jessica Brooke addressed a very pretty young salesgirl whose blue eyes were round with fright. "Not a thing, Miss Brooke. Honestly, not a thing. Only I knew I and my customer had been in A when he asked—"

"What do you mean—not a thing?" Bratton pounced upon her to save time, for he could see that she was the type to tell everything she might know in one unrestrained gush at the first hint of intimidation.

"I was out hunting through stock for everything in green in my customer's size and when I got back I didn't notice one single thing out of the way anywhere no more than when I went in with my customer."

"That puts it up to me, doesn't it?" It was Madge Allen's green-hunting patron who spoke. Her accent echoed New England, and all the women looking at her were correct in deciding that it was a mistake for her to want to wear green. "I'm quite sure that I can contribute only one item that might prove of interest. I heard the person in the next compartment call out 'Busy,' as someone has just reported, but I heard nothing else to indicate that dresses were being tried on in there."

"But you did hear something, huh?"

"Frankly, I did. A peculiar sound, which I could not identify."

"Try to describe it."

"It was a sort of—thud, Inspector. It was quite like the sound one makes jumping off something. I realize I'm being quite vague, but I give you my impression for just what it may be worth."

"Are you sure this sound came from C?"

"Not at all. However, I do feel positive that it came from the side of the fitting alcove where I was. If I may see your diagram for a moment—" A gloved finger hovered over the inspector's crude sketch and then pointed out the spaces lettered E and C. "I should say that that was the general direction of the sound, but whether within the booths or in the passage, I could not say."

"Were you alone when you heard this interesting sound?"

"Yes, the girl that was showing me dresses had gone out to look for something else."

Bratton nodded his head and continued his thoughtful regard of the diagram. Then he called for a report from D.

Again for an awkward moment or two there was no response; then a thin, worried-looking saleswoman answered. "I had a customer in D not long before all this—happened. But she was the kind that was just looking. She tried on three or four models and did a little talking—"

Mrs. Ludlow Wilkinson snorted but restrained herself from any further comment, and Miss Millin went on with her report.

"No, I can't tell you the lady's name. As far as I know I had never waited on her before and she thought everything I showed her was too expensive, so probably she wasn't one of our regular patrons. No, sir, I swear I didn't see a thing out of the ordinary as I went in and out, and I know I didn't hear anything either."

Before Inspector Bratton could proceed further a message interrupted him. It concerned the unknown victim and those officials who were dealing with the cause of her death and it called him back to the scene of the crime. As he left he commissioned Miss Brooke to look after names and addresses and to permit those with whom he had already talked to go, with one exception.

Accordingly the store detective took charge. When the lady who should never have thought of wearing green—her name was Lavinia Spinner and she was on the faculty of the Municipal Junior College—and Mrs. Ludlow Wilkinson had at length been dismissed with reinforced warnings about discretion, it was obvious that only members of the sales force were left. In turn, Miss Millin, Grace Ramby, little Madge Allen, and Ede Pike were sent away also, as were the two stock girls, Dottie and Luella. There remained a group of saleswomen who had appeared after closing hours, by request. They were the ones who had been busy elsewhere in the department when Joyce Terry made her horrible discovery. Miss Brooke questioned them competently, first as to whether or not they had taken a customer into booth C, and then as to where they were and what they were doing just before the news broke. Then they too were allowed to go, having added nothing to the meagre store of known facts. No one was left but Joyce Terry, the head of the department, and the store detective.

Madame Nordhoff moved restlessly about but said nothing. Joyce huddled on a chair and tried not to think of what she had seen when she opened the door of compartment E. Miss Brooke looked over the slightly incoherent notes that she had scribbled while Bratton was in the lead and speculated again on the Inspector's willingness to permit her to tag along in the wake of his own investigations.

After fifteen minutes of this sort of time marking a telephone announced that Detective Inspector Bratton wanted Miss Brooke to come down to the French Room at once.

"Joyce, dear," Jessica Brooke turned just as she was disappearing through the door and addressed the girl gently, "do you mind waiting here? The Inspector may want to see you again."

Madame Nordhoff sent an acquiescent signal over the girl's head to her co-worker. Joyce nodded mutely and drooped on the hard chair still more limply. When the door had quite definitely closed behind the store operative, the buyer swung about and regarded the girl through lowered lids. "Are you sure," she asked at length, "are you absolutely sure that you have no idea who that woman is?"

There was no question whom she meant. That ghastly, outflung figure in booth E.

Joyce Terry began to sob hysterically. "I never saw her before this afternoon in all my life," she wailed.

Madame Nordhoff's elaborately coiffed head jerked with satisfaction. "I just wondered . . ." she murmured.

3

BRATTON AND BROOKE

When in response to the summons from Inspector Bratton Jessica Brooke reached the French Room, it was evident that the police authorities had the entire department in expert hand. One man was keeping an eye on the bank of elevators. Others were scattered about the great stretches of floor space, as though a careful search was going on. It was now well after the closing hour and otherwise the store was well cleared

As Jessica Brooke neared the group standing in the salon where the imported frocks were shown, a significant cortège made its way out of the awkward narrowness of the corridor leading to the block of fitting rooms. The body of the murdered woman was being removed.

Jessica Brooke hurried toward Bratton, the question in her eyes unnecessary.

Bratton shook his head shortly. "To the mortuary," he said. "Haven't identified her yet. I've got to see that girl again—the one who found her. You told her to wait, like I said?"

"Certainly. But can't you tell—weren't there cards in her bag, or something like that?" Almost did Jessica Brooke imply that if she had been given half a chance she would have had the murdered woman identified long before this.

"There's no sign of a bag, purse, or any other sort of thing you'd expect a woman to drag around with her," announced Bratton.

"Interesting, eh what?" murmured Jessica. "How far am I in on it?"

"The whole way, if you say so. I'm plenty willing to divide up on the puzzles. There's no sign of a weapon, either."

"What did the medical examiner say?"

"She was stabbed just below the neck. That it killed her was by way of being a fluke, I gather, but some way a vital spot was reached. The weapon used was not an ordinary knife or dagger. It was something much thicker and blunter, for it made an ugly broken gash and—well, you saw the bloody mess the place was."

Jessica Brooke's twitching lips silenced more of that sort of detail. Line and Hollis's store detective knew her stuff, Bratton was thinking, but murder was something else again. Still a woman wouldn't be a bad bet in a case like this. Then the determined approach of the general manager trailed by Knox, the floor man, claimed the attention of both detectives.

"I've just been talking to Mr. Line on long distance. He'll be back in the morning. Mr. Hollis of course is on his way to Japan. We'll have to remodel the whole place, I'm afraid." The general manager looked as if he wanted to resign.

"No woman will ever want to buy a dress here again," Knox groaned.

"But they'll come in hordes to see," Miss Brooke reminded him.

"Mr. Galway," Bratton spoke peremptorily, "I'll do my best to permit your business to go on as usual tomorrow morning, but you'll have to understand that various individuals will be called upon to cooperate with me first and perform their duties in the store second."

"Yes, yes, of course. Anything on earth that we can do—"

"I'm of the opinion right now that the murderer was out of the building and away within five minutes after the crime was committed. Doubtless there were nearly a thousand persons under this roof at the time. Your employees offer no insurmountable difficulties. I mean we can trace them and their activities whenever necessary. But after all a department store is a semipublic place. People go in and out at will, and no one could possibly be sure of everyone who might have been here at any given moment. In other words, it's not going to be easy finding out who killed that woman. I'd like to have you turn Miss Brooke over to me and give her a free hand with your rules and regulations."

"Certainly, glad to. . . . You people know as well as we do that she knows her business."

This unexpected praise from Galway rather surprised Jessica Brooke, though she would have preferred to know just how far the local police authorities agreed with the manager's generous statement.

Upon that matter Bratton did not commit himself at the moment. Instead he rather obviously dismissed the two store executives. "All right, then. I'd like a little talk with Miss Brooke first and then I must get to work on the identity of the victim. That's going to mean a lot of publicity, you know," he warned the harried manager.

At that moment a woman could be seen emerging from an elevator. Though the floor was not fully illumined at that hour, it was not difficult to recognize the characteristic carriage of the buyer for the department. Madame Nordhoff wanted a word with Galway and Knox.

When the three had withdrawn to the cashier's desk, Bratton turned with a sigh of relief to Jessica Brooke. "Now if she'll only keep those two birds off me for a while—they do nothing but twitter. Want to take one more look-see before you tell me any little thing that may have come to roost on your mind?"

Without waiting for her reply Bratton led the way to the narrow corridor from which branched the six fitting rooms that formed the radius of the crime. There he produced the rough sketch he had made while listening to the stories of the women who had been housed in the tiny cubicles.

"The occupants of E and F and A and B have been more or less satisfactorily accounted for. The customer in D is nameless, but her clerk gives a pretty straightforward account of her. It's C that strikes me as a possibility; especially when I think of what the green lady spilled. How about it, Miss Brooke?"

"I've already been curious enough to discover that not one of our girls had a customer in there during the time that's got to be accounted for."

"And if someone had been hidden in there, how could she have known that her victim was going to enter room E at any given moment?" Bratton looked at his adjutant as if he would soon be doing some twittering himself. Then he strode forward to the closed door of E. "The finger print men will be here any minute now and of course the mess can't be cleaned up till they've done their stuff. I'm not anticipating anything much though. There will be millions of finger marks everywhere. Every shopper in town— But if you think you can stand it, I wish you'd give the place the once-over again. I may have had a blind spot about something."

Some people would have said that was just Inspector Bratton's line, yet no one who had ever worked with him ever felt that his modesty was assumed.

He flung open the door. The little cabinet was mercilessly exposed under the glare of a swinging center light. Jessica Brooke's unflinching gaze deliberately circled the apartment.

"I saw her lying where she fell, you know. . . . You'd have expected some sort of identifying marks on the clothes she was wearing." Her thoughts had veered, but it was easy to follow them.

"No laundry marks; tailor's labels—nothing personal like that. We'll have to call in the public to help us out."

"They'll eat it up. As for finding the murderer—"

"Yeah?" challenged Bratton.

"If the guilty person escaped without blood-stained clothing, it was a miracle. And a more or less messy weapon had to be taken care of."

"Sure." Bratton's indifferent reply put a period to that topic. Jessica Brooke was never to know that her comment led the inspector, eventually, to the murderer. Certainly Bratton was not then aware that a logical conclusion was shaping itself somewhere in the back of his mind.

Jessica Brooke took the two steps across the little room that brought her to the hook from which hung the victim's dress and coat. On a little gilt chair just beyond lay her hat, crown downward. Its maker's label was thus plainly visible. "It's a Felix," she murmured. "As you said, that's no lead at all. I'm sorry, Inspector, but I don't seem able to call your attention gloatingly to any unnoticed clue."

"It's a mess, right, and the only thing that looks like sense just now, aside from starting the machinery to identify the woman, is to go after that girl—the one who found her," Bratton meditated as he backed out of the cubicle and led the way down the narrow passage.

"You say that looks like sense?" countered his companion. "How about whoever was in the next booth?"

Bratton nodded his head in bland agreement. "Sure, Miss Brooke, but the one woman's here and the other one isn't. Here comes the camera man now. While he's busy here, I'll go back up and have another talk with the Terry girl."

"That reminds me—I ought to have some interviewing to do too, if I had any luck at all."

Bratton looked his question.

"I thought some of the service people might have noticed something. I'll let you know if I start anything."

When the store detective entered her own small office she found three individuals waiting for her in various stages of impatience. She chose to speak first to the matron in charge of the public rest room for women.

"I done just like you said, Miss Brooke, kep' my eyes open for anything or anybody that seemed the least bit queer. But land! they's lots like that all the time. The on'y thing that might be what you want to know is that along about half pas' four a woman come in and had a real bad nervous chill. I wanted to send for the nurse, but all she'd let me do was call a taxi for her. She was awful upset about something, but I couldn't get a thing out of her what it was all about. She lemme give her a asp'rin, though."

"What did the woman look like, Emma?"

"She was a good dresser, all right, and nice and thin, too. Her eyes were big and dark—brown, I guess, but I couldn't see none of her hair. You know how hats are—"

"Did she say anything? It's important, Emma."

"Yes'm, Miss Brooke. No'm; she didn't say nothin' hardly. She just moaned and shook something pitiful, on'y once she let out a name, I guess. Sounded for all the world like Ross. Then she gritted her teeth and clinched her hands till she about busted out her gloves."

"Did you find anything unusual left in the rest room?"

"Nothin' that looked like it had been left on purpose, if that's the idea. They's always a mess of handkerchiefs and things like that—pocketbooks, too, but they always come back hotfoot askin' about them. And little packages, and of course umbrells. I turn 'em over to the Lost and Found first thing every morning."

"Maybe I'd better take a look before you do that this time. As for parcels, did the woman who had the chill have anything in her hands?"

"Now, lemme think. . . ." A process which required much eyebrow manipulation. "Her purse, for one thing. It was a flat under-arm bag, seems like. And yes—she had a flat package like a book, wrapped up in our paper, so she musta bought it here. That's the on'y thing I can remember, Miss Brooke."

Emma was then sent away and Jessica Brooke listened next to Chester Penn, who ran elevator number 3 in the rank of Down Only cars. Chester had the physique of a jockey and the dignity of an ambassador. His report was abrupt and startling. At twenty minutes after five, when he had stopped his car at the fourth floor, a man who acted scared to death crowded on the elevator ahead of all the women who were waiting. That breach of etiquette was not at all extraordinary in Chester's daily ups and downs, only this man, he explained, looked like such a swell—just the kind that would stand back and bow himself in two. When the car stopped at the main floor the man had been the first one out and he had gone off almost running in the direction of the Court Street entrance.

When Jessica Brooke had made a note of Chester's description of this gentleman in a hurry, she turned to Daddy Baynes, who had patiently nodded himself into a cat nap.

Daddy Baynes's crew at the various exits of the great store had reported nothing to him that stood out from

routine happenings. Jud Placer on duty at the Hamilton
Street door had had a little argument with a taxi driver
who insisted that Jud produce the fare that had sent for
him, but though Jud had been obliging enough to attempt
paging the arrival of the taxi nobody had claimed the cab
and the driver had been forced to move on to keep peace
with the traffic regulations.

That was a possible item, thought Jessica, and scribbled another memorandum.

A rapid knock sounded upon the door of her office and
Inspector Bratton slid quickly inside. "Good! You're still
here. Thought you might like a look at the reports my men
have turned in—not that they've raised anything much,
but— And say, Miss Brooke, that Terry girl had vamoosed
when I got up to her. What do you know about that?"

Jessica frowned slightly and shook her head. She didn't
know anything about that, except that Joyce Terry was the
kind of employee who did what she was told.

During the next two hours while various lines of procedure were being contemplated by the official in charge
of the investigation, Joyce Terry was sitting in her usual
place in the reading room of the public library waiting to
keep her date. But for the first time in the months that she
had known him, Phil Leonard failed to appear.

4

The House at Buckeye Heights

It was inevitable that the murder in the French Room at Line and Hollis's crowded all other news off the front page the next morning. But nowhere in the mass of detail devoured by a greedy public could be found the solution on the immediate problem in the case—the identity of the murdered woman.

In spite of the night-long activity of the police they knew no more the next morning than they had when they were first called in who the woman was who had been so brutally stabbed to death in the tiny fitting room of the town's most reputable department store. During the hours of the night Bratton's men had searched the great place exhaustively—elevators, rest rooms, lavatories, checking desks, outgoing deliveries, but no tell-tale blood stains nor a possible weapon had been discovered. Even the pay-telephone booths had been searched on the chance that the murderer might not have made an escape.

Nor had the first reporters on the case done any better, though more than one of them were conscious of a feeling that they had seen the woman somewhere before. It was Paula Pringle—that was the name she had evolved for press use—who was the first to associate an actual name with the pale sheeted body lying stark in the morgue. Paula was canny enough not to give a yelp of recognition.

Instead, she slipped quietly to the nearest telephone booth and called a Buckeye Heights number.

"Is Mrs. Rupert Thayre at home?" she asked sweetly.

Mrs. Thayre was not at home. Which was, so far, just what Paula fervently expected to hear. Nor could the maid say just where she was. . . .

"Where can I reach Mr. Thayre?" she suggested.

At this hour Mr. Thayre would be at his office. He was with the City Realty Investment Company down in the Meade Building.

In due time Paula found herself connected with the treasurer and general manager of the City Realty Investment Company. Bluntly anonymous she hinted to Rupert Thayre that if he hadn't seen the morning papers it was his duty to take a look at the unidentified woman at the mortuary and then hurried there to be on the spot herself when—or if—the great recognition should take place.

But it was more than an hour later before an attendant ushered a worried, frightened man into the clammy apartment where the woman's body lay—an hour which Paula had used so wisely that it was no trick at all for the *Bulletin* to be first on the streets with its astounding extra.

For Rupert Thayre had given but one choked, anguished cry and stumbled out again, "That's my wife," he muttered to Dan Bratton, who by that time had caught up with him, and collapsed. When he had sufficient control of himself to answer questions, what the husband had to tell did little to clear away the mystery surrounding his wife's death.

Thayre had last seen his wife alive the morning before when they had breakfasted together. He could not recall that she had said anything very definite about her plans for the day except that she had mentioned that she might run up to her mother's for the night. Her mother lived at Green's Mill, and as her health was not good, Vivian made a point of going up every week or so. Accordingly he had not given the matter another thought when he found that he was dining alone. The evening he had spent at his club playing contract.

Shaken as he was at the terrible fate that had come upon his wife, Thayre could only reiterate that Vivian hadn't an enemy in the world. Certainly the authorities could search through her effects, if they thought it necessary. He wanted to help in any way that would track down her slayer.

"And you say you hadn't seen the papers this morning—how did you happen to round in here then if you weren't suspicious?" Bratton asked, his own suspicion undisguised.

"I told you that once, didn't I? Someone called at my office this morning—"

"That's what you said. Who called you?"

"I don't know. It was a woman's voice—sounded like a kid. Just said I might be interested in seeing the body that was being held at the morgue and rang off."

"You're sure you didn't recognize the voice?" insisted Bratton.

"I've no reason to believe that I had ever heard it before. It was entirely strange to me."

"Humph! I'll be doggoned if. . . ." And thus until he had a spare minute to read the *Bulletin* extra, Paula Pringle innocently helped to prolong the mystery of the murder of Vivian Thayre.

The noon editions of all the papers carried as much information concerning the private lives of the Thayres as could be scrambled together without an interview with Thayre himself. The reporters had to wait until Bratton was ready to turn the man over to them. Rupert Thayre was well established in the business life of the Ohio city, though his real estate ventures had fluctuated alarmingly within the last year. That situation, however, had been offset by a phenomenal run of luck he had had on the market. At least, that was the general drift of financial gossip, though he did not appear to be doing business directly with any of the local brokers.

Vivian Thayre was his second wife. Some ten years before he had been divorced and shortly afterward he had married the twenty-year-old girl whom Mary Thayre had named as co-respondent. The first Mrs. Thayre had resumed her family name and left the town, of which she had not been a native. The girl in the case, Vivian Agnew, as the new Mrs. Thayre, might have had aspirations to enter authentic local society circles, but if so she had not attained her hopes. There was nothing markedly exclusive about the set she was soon allied with, though it was admittedly a group that maintained a certain flashy prominence.

When the message from the mortuary had reached him that morning, Dan Bratton had been at Line and Hollis's awaiting the arrival of Joyce Terry. He planned to examine the girl rigidly, for her disappearance the night before had not pleased him. Aside from her disobedience, which Bratton's kindly common sense had told him was only natural, and the slight evidence that an unknown person had been in fitting room C, no clue of commanding significance had been started from his investigations at the scene of the crime. Bratton gave Jessica Brooke a free hand to do what she could with the woman in C and hurried off to the mortuary.

The identity of the murdered woman established, Bratton determined to reapproach the problem from the standpoint of the victim. Accordingly, as soon as Thayre had pulled himself together sufficiently, the inspector and Jeff Gryce, a promising young subordinate in the detective division, climbed into Thayre's car and went with him to his Buckeye Heights house. It was one of the latest show places of the Heights. Indeed, it was everything that a leading realtor's residence should be—tapestry brick and minute sunken garden without and tiled sun parlors and wrought iron fixtures within.

"There's nobody here but one maid," said Thayre. "It's not likely she's—heard yet, and she never reads a newspaper. I—I'd appreciate it if you fellows would tell her. Her name's Milly. I'll go on up to Vivian's room. That's where you will have to start looking, I suppose," he groaned.

One jerk of Bratton's thumb and Gryce went on upstairs with Rupert Thayre. Bratton walked alertly through the rooms on the first floor. The furnishings were conventionally correct though they showed no trace of an arresting personality in invention or arrangement. In the kitchen he came upon Milly, perched at the top of a step ladder busily rearranging dishes on an upper cupboard shelf.

Milly proved to be a Dunkard girl, who dressed "plain." Startled by the silent appearance of a strange man, she drew her voluminous gray calico skirts decently about her and stared down at the intruder with slightly prominent pale blue eyes.

Bratton made his announcement briefly and concluded at once that there was no deceit in the terrified girl. He demanded first an account of Mrs. Thayre's activities the day before, as far as she knew them, but was content to let her tell what she would in her own way.

"Well now, mister, everything was just like always. I made breakfast for the mister and just as he was settin' down to it, why, Mis' Thayre, she come down and et with him. I nearly always take her up a little tray—she ain't the one to eat much. They set there and talked and laughed till the mister, he had to cut and run. And then she kinda trailed around the house—she had on one of them pretty floating wrappers of her'n. After the mailman come she went back upstairs and oncet I heard her talking on her telephone. I didn't see her for mebbe an hour after that till I come through to mop up in her bathroom. She was settin' in her room, shinin' up her finger nails and singin' kinda low to herself, like she was feelin' pretty good. Before I'd got my work done in there she called out to me not to make her no lunch, she was going up town. Then she started to git herself fixed up to go out and I went down to find the grocery list I wanted to show her before I telephoned to the store about it. It was after half past ten when she went away, and that's the last I seen of her, mister." Milly mopped her red-rimmed eyes and blew her nose.

"So Mrs. Thayre did not usually breakfast with her husband?" Bratton's remark was half question, half comment.

"Mebbe two-three times a month. She was one that liked to lay yet."

"What did they talk about yesterday morning?"

"Land sakes, mister, I didn't listen to 'em."

"Weren't you in the dining room at all?"

"On'y oncet while him and her was both there. The biscuits was all and I took 'em in a hot pan. The mister, he likes my bakin' fine. That there time she was tellin' him about some new clothes she was goin' to look for at Line's, and he says good, for her to go as far as she liked—she'd never broke him yet. Them two got along just fine, mister."

"Now, Milly, you heard Mrs. Thayre telephoning. What can you tell me about that?"

"'Mister, I'm one to mind my own business still. I just took notice she was talkin'. . . . I kinda recollect still she was sayin' something like 'All right, then, at four-thirty. Don't forget. . . .'"

Certain that he had picked up a thread of importance, the inspector's examination became more enthusiastic, but the girl stubbornly insisted that she could add nothing more about the telephone conversation.

Somewhat disgruntled he then asked, "Did you see what mail came?"

"No, mister, I didn't. The missus went out to the box herself. But long about noon I was doin' a little dustin' in the settin' room and I seen some papers and what all layin' on the liberry table."

"So you couldn't say whether or not Mrs. Thayre received any personal mail yesterday morning?"

Milly could not.

"When she left for her shopping trip did she say when she expected to be back?"

"No, but I mind she ast about dessert for their sup—dinner."

"So she didn't tell you that she was expecting to go to her mother's?" Bratton pounced the question upon the girl.

"No, hunh-uh. The mister, he told me when he come home that night."

Was that something to be curious about, Bratton wondered. That and the scrap of telephone conversation about a four-thirty appointment. . . . The two, items might bear thinking about. "All right, Milly, and thank you very much," he said in his most amiable manner. "Stick around; I may want to ask you some more questions before I go."

The inspector then joined the two men still waiting in the upper hall and together they moved toward the door to which Thayre nervously motioned. They entered a frippery, excessively feminine bedroom. There was nothing obviously out of order, and yet it was apparent that a woman had recently been very much at home there. For a minute or two Bratton looked about quietly without leaving his position just inside the door and then he stepped across to the dressing table. He stared down at the usual miscellany of feminine toilet articles and cosmetics. He pulled out the two shallow drawers but saw nothing except tidy piles of handkerchiefs and an astonishing assortment of bead chains and necklaces in the one and an equally

amazing quantity of neatly folded silk stockings in the
other. There was no reason to churn anything into disorder and Bratton was not the man to take needless action,
even to exhibit thorough-going method.

He allowed himself to look helpless before a many-draw-
ered chest and a closet hanging thick with women's dresses,
but he systematically satisfied himself that there were no
secrets in either place. He riffled the pages of a book lying
on the bedside table and threw back the lid of a lacquered
box but discovered nothing. There was a small fireplace in
the room, but despite the season its hearth was clean and
bare. Only one object of interest remained in the room—a
writing table. It contained quantities of supplies, expensive and correct, but very little in the way of actual correspondence. One pigeonhole disclosed a little sheaf of
bills, most of them unopened.

"She always kept everything till the fifteenth of the
month and then turned them over to me," Thayre explained through tightened lips. "Personal letters she always destroyed after she had answered them. I'd say those
stuck in there at the right were her few unanswered ones.
Go ahead and look at them, if you have to."

Bratton had to. . . . The first one he unfolded was
signed Gwen. "Who is she?" he asked.

"Some woman friend—lives in Washington, I think.
I've never met her, but my wife spoke of her often and
spent a week with her just after Easter last spring. I'll have
to let her know. . . ."

Gryce could tell that his superior was finding nothing
of importance in the blackly written scrawl that filled the
pages of Gwen's letter. He watched Bratton slide another
letter out of its envelope.

"I'd say from the color of the paper," offered Thayre,
"that Vivian's mother wrote that. Mrs. Agnew has always
been a voluminous correspondent—a long letter every

week, even with Viv running back and forth as often as she did."

"Hmph, right you are. It's signed Dora Agnew and seems to be all about a family dinner with one Cousin Theodoric Underwood. By the way, Thayre, just when was it that Mrs. Thayre spoke to you about going up to her mother's?"

Thayre cleared his throat abruptly. "Why, it must have been at breakfast, Inspector—really, I'm not just certain. It might have been the day before at that."

As if, after all, he was not particularly interested in the answer to his question, Bratton pulled out another envelope. It felt heavy in his hand, but there was no letter within it. A flexible bracelet slipped out into his palm. His years of experience had taught the inspector enough about jewels to recognize this one's worth. It was hand-wrought gold, he thought, and it was set with jade. But more interesting was the fact that the watching man beside him was plainly disturbed at the sight of the bracelet.

"You recognize this?" Bratton asked.

Thayre shook his head. "Didn't know she owned such a piece," he mumbled.

Bratton reversed the envelope and noted the postmark and date. It had been mailed in town the day before. The address had been written by a distinctly masculine hand in pale ink.

"That's odd," he said. "The bracelet certainly did not come in this envelope, but where's the letter that did?"

Once more he examined the fireplace and then poked into the highly ornamental little scrap basket, but it was as clean and as empty as the fireplace. There was no trace of a pearl grey letter sheet to match the envelope in which he had found the jade bracelet.

"See here, you chaps! What do you expect to find up here anyway?" It was as if Rupert Thayre's control had held as long as it could. "I have no reason to believe that my wife had an enemy in the world or a secret of any sort that could have had anything to do with this hideous thing that has happened to her. Why aren't you working from the scene of the murder? Some woman down there must have run amuck—what else could have happened?" Thayre groaned and clenched his hands in agony of spirit.

"Sure thing, Mr. Thayre. I grant you it could easily have been the deed of a homicidal maniac, yet there was a chance of coming on some little thing out here that would indicate that she went to meet someone, maybe. It's plain hell for you, I know. . . . Well, I'll just take another look through the rooms downstairs and speak to the maid again, and then I'll take your advice and go back to Line's to hear what's new by this time."

In spite of their reasonable sound there was something not quite soothing about Bratton's words. Furthermore, Gryce wondered whether Thayre saw him slip the bracelet and the envelope in which it had been discovered into his pocket.

The three returned to the lower floor and again Bratton walked casually through the luxurious rooms, the other two trailing him uncertainly. At the kitchen the inspector made an abrupt turn. "Just a minute. There's one question I want to ask the girl—by myself, if you don't mind." Which was an order no matter how placating it sounded.

Milly was sitting primly by her well-scrubbed kitchen table, but her pale eyes and doughy complexion showed that her distress had not lessened. Bratton smiled at her reassuringly and pulled out the jade bracelet. "Ever see this before, Milly?" He swung it back and forth before the girl's impressed eyes.

"On'y oncet I did. Yesterday morning when she set in her room fiddlin' with her finger nails I took notice it was on her wrist yet. I'd never seen it before though."

Bratton reentered the hall just as Gryce hung up the telephone receiver. "You're to get down to Headquarters as soon as you can make it, sir. Something big seems to have bust loose."

5

SCISSORS!

It was not Headquarters that wanted Detective Inspector Bratton; it was Jessica Brooke at Line and Hollis's. That young Jeff Gryce was adequately bawled out was of moment only to the culprit himself, though the resolve he made in his chagrin eventually had a minor share in solving the mystery of the French Room murder.

He found himself shuttled with rapidity into Miss Brooke's private office yet it was not evident that she had been walking the floor pending his arrival. However, she greeted him eagerly.

"Good morning, Inspector. Several items have just come to light that apparently bear upon what's happened but, frankly, I'm not so good at saying just how. I felt that I ought to pass everything on to you at once."

"Good girl! Go to it. No reason why I couldn't have a smoke while you're doing this plain and fancy passing, is there?"

Jessica pushed an ash tray across the table between them and plunged into her report. "I'm not saying this means a thing, mind, only someway—well, here goes:

"You had sent for Joyce Terry, they tell me, but were called out this morning before she got here. So I asked her some questions. She left last night because Mrs. Nordhoff told her she might. That's all she could say when I blew

343

344 Helen Joan Hultman

her up for walking out on us. Incidentally, I tried to call her myself last night at the place where she lives, but she wasn't in. I didn't go into that with her.

"You remember that Joyce spoke of a vague impression that she passed someone as she turned into the fitting rooms just before she discovered the body. This morning she tells me that she is sure that it was a woman, but all the description she can give of her is that she was pulling on a pair of new-looking light buckskin gloves.

"The third detail may be sheer coincidence, but the sequence is good. I told you last night about the woman who had some sort of nervous collapse in the rest room at just about the time we were all rushing to room E. Emma said this woman mumbled something that sounded like 'Ross—Ross. . . .' Well, our own Mr. Galway, general manager as ever was, calmly tells me this morning that a man he happened to know was waiting in the foyer of the French Room when he hurried through on this emergency call. Mr. Galway suggested that perhaps this chap might have observed something to the point. His name? I asked . . . Ross Ingram, if you please—just like that!"

Jessica Brooke did not pause to look pleased with herself, though Bratton would not have been surprised if she had. However, her next words indicated her sense of successful accomplishment.

"But wait until you hear my grand climax, Inspector. A little extra salesgirl in the bargain basement brought this package up to me almost as soon as the store opened this morning. I had posted a notice, you know, about reporting anything that might be connected with what happened yesterday afternoon."

The store detective drew out of her desk drawer a parcel wrapped in the familiar brown and tan striped paper that marked everything that went out of Line and Hollis's.

"I opened it, but I assure you, Inspector, that I was professionally careful about touching what I found inside. I folded it up again so that the package looks now just as it did when it was brought in to me. There was no cord; the ends were twisted together just as you see them now,"

As Jessica Brooke spoke she pressed back the wrapping paper. It was a much larger sheet than the size of its contents would have indicated and she had to make a number of revolutions before what it concealed was disclosed. Bratton stared down at what he saw and swore to himself.

Crusted heavily with blood, the inner surface of the paper likewise smeared, there, unmistakably, was the weapon that had killed Vivian Thayre.

A pair of scissors.

"Another job for the finger print photographer," grunted the inspector and said no more. If he thought Jessica Brooke had been too casual in reporting so vital a discovery, he showed remarkable self-control.

Neither detective had to tell the other how the scissors had been used. The long slender blades folded together had been plunged into the victim exactly as a dagger would have been thrust, and the glossy black enameled handles had been held together by determined, relentless fingers.

"Scissors like these are the standard service pattern in use throughout the store. There's at least one pair on every wrapper's counter," remarked Jessica Brooke after a moment, as if warning Bratton not to consider the case closed.

"You think it's an inside job, then?"

"Not necessarily. The store has no monopoly on that style of scissors."

The inspector nodded as if he rated her an A on that and asked, "Couldn't the scissors here be checked up?"

"In a way, yes, but supplies like these are always getting borrowed from one department to another or mislaid or lost or carried off."

"I see. . . . We'll give it a work-out anyway, and till that's done, we'll say nothing at all about this." Bratton indicated the scissors. "See what you can do. You've talked to the girl who turned them in? Did she know what she had found?"

"No, fortunately for us she hadn't opened the bundle. I had her wait, for I thought you might like to hear what she has to say."

"Send her in."

A scrawny child, so young that she must barely have been able to obtain a working permit, answered Miss Brooke's summons. Yet there was an air of shrewd good sense about the girl and she answered the questions put to her without an instant's hesitation.

Her name, she said, was Norma Schmidt. She had charge of the bargain bins of hosiery in the basement. This morning when she had taken off the dust covers she had noticed the edge of what looked like a package sticking out from a stack of Silkisheen irregulars, nudes, sizes 9 and 9½. She had just read the notice on the bulletin that said report anything queer to room 8 in the manager's suite At Once. The girls all knew that was because of the murder—Norma herself hadn't heard a thing about it last night. That's what you got when you were stuck down in the basement alla time, she mourned. But of course she'd read the papers this morning. So when she found the package she'd beat it right away up to the ninth floor. No, she hadn't touched it except on the outside. She kinda thought somebody else had ought to be the one to open it in case it was the murder. Yes, she herself had put the dust covers over her counters the night before. She hadn't noticed no package then. But there was one thing that she could say positively. Just before closing time she had begun to tidy up her stock like always and she distinctly remembered that in that bin of nude 9's there wasn't a sign of a package.

"So it would have been slipped in there after you rearranged your wares and before the dust cover was thrown over the counter?" Bratton asked.

"Yes, uh-huh—"

"Unless it was done after Norma left the department—after hours. Which again points to an inside job," Jessica Brooke remarked.

"Well, all I know is that it sure wasn't there when I straightened up my stock," repeated the girl.

"After you had done that," Bratton went on slowly, "did any last moment shoppers stop at your counter?"

Norma Schmidt meditated with a serious air. "Yes, sir. Just before quittin' time a lady bought her a pair of seamless gun-metal semi-chiffons, size 10. But that was at the opposite end of the counter from where I found the package."

"Did she pass that end?"

"Not when she first come up she didn't. There was a man with her, seems like. He walked on past sorta slow, but this lady, she stopped and ast to see something in gun-metal not too expensive. She took the first thing I showed her and hurried on like she had to catch up with this man, see, though to tell you the honest truth I didn't pay no more attention. The dust covers and five-thirty was all that was on my mind. She might of gone out past that bin of nudes at that."

"I see. It was a cash sale, I suppose."

"Sure, it was."

After Norma had essayed a none too vivid description of this last customer of hers, she was dismissed. At the door she turned unabashed to ask what was in the package that had assumed such evident importance and was politely told that it was too soon to say.

When she had closed the door behind her Bratton nodded briskly to his co-worker. "Miss Brooke, you might see

whether any of the other sales people in the vicinity of
that kid's stocking counter have anything to add to her
story. And that last customer ought to be traced. Maybe an
ad might bring something—like 'Will lady who purchased
hose in Line's basement department kindly call, etc., etc.'"

Nothing had as yet been said about the identification
of the murdered woman, though Bratton saw the instant
he stepped inside Miss Brooke's office that she had one of
the *Bulletin* extra's spread across her desk.

"Now then," he said and tapped a finger on the screaming headlines, "what dirt can you spill about the Thayres?
Any little thing you know . . ."

"She's the lady that bust up the first happy home. She
wasn't anybody socially then, and she's not made the grade
since, though the circumstances of her marriage would
scarcely have held her back. Rupert Thayre has been making so much money lately that it would have been only
a matter of time before his wife would have been recognized—that's the way this town is."

"What became of the first wife?"

Jessica Brooke shook her head, "Dropped out completely as far as society here knows. Think she ought to be
traced?"

"It would be neat if she'd turn out to be the dame with
the gloves. I'm always hoping to get a story book case
instead of another police blotter record." Dan Bratton
laughed at his own weakness. "In the meantime, I'll talk
to the Terry girl next, if you please."

When Joyce Terry appeared, the inspector observed at
once how worried and worn she looked. More than once,
since taking her first statement, he had been conscious
of an impulse to use the traditional bullying methods of
the police with this girl who had discovered the body of
Vivian Thayre, but each time something had veered him
from such a course. Even at this moment his resolution

wavered. Just the same, he questioned her rigidly for the next twenty minutes, concentrating chiefly, as Jessica took note, on three points: the woman who wore buckskin gloves, Mrs. Thayre's missing hand bag, and what Joyce knew about scissors.

Concerning the first, the girl was unable to add any detail to what Jessica Brooke had already been told. The woman might have come from C; it was just as likely that she had been the patron in B or D. Nor could Bratton shake her in her hand bag story. Joyce had noticed her customer's bag and could describe it. The woman had dropped it on the chair beside her hat. Of that Joyce was positive. She was equally insistent that when she had made her shocking discovery she had been conscious of nothing else except the ghastly figure of the murdered woman. Bratton's queries about scissors were much less direct. What he learned, Jessica concluded, when he asked the girl his sudden question about her last occasion to use scissors in the course of that day's work, was that she betrayed not the slightest association with their part in the crime.

Joyce was allowed to go back to her work. It had been suggested to her that in view of her nerve-racking experience of the day before she might prefer not to meet the curious public today, but she had chosen to carry on as usual. The entire fourth floor staff, of course, had the strictest orders not to discuss the distressing affair with anyone.

"Have I missed anyone, Miss Brooke?" Bratton asked before he too left her office. "I'm going in to see Galway now."

"My notes show statements from everyone with the possible exception of the little girl who arranges stock. I doubt that Dottie has anything to say. Anyway, she's not here today. She's off to go to an aunt's funeral. I'll not forget her tomorrow, if you say so."

The general manager of the great store was pleased to grant Detective-Inspector Bratton a prompt audience. The police had been most tactful, so far.

"Who's this bird, Ross Ingram?" Bratton demanded.

"Scarcely more than an acquaintance, Inspector. I first met him in the locker room at my golf club and a couple of times since at minor social affairs. When I recalled seeing him waiting in the foyer, it occurred to me that a casual bystander like that might have observed something that could throw a little light on this horrible business. The reporters—"

"Yes, yes, I know exactly what they're doing, but believe me, Galway, this is the sort of case that demands screaming publicity. But that isn't what's interesting me just now. I want to talk to Ingram. Do you know where I can find him?"

Galway shook his head; he was evidently none too pleased to become sponsor for the man. "I scarcely know him, I tell you. I have no idea where he lives or what his business is. I saw him yesterday as I went through the department, but what became of him afterwards I don't know."

Bratton then returned to the fourth floor to ask a discreet question or two before leaving the building. As near as he could discover the only employees who had observed the waiting Mr. Ingram were a wrapper at the cashier's desk and one of the saleswomen, Miss Ramby, whose stay in booth B had been so brief.

The wrapper remembered quite plainly the way Miss Terry had fidgeted waiting for Mr. Knox to come back and it wasn't much more than five minutes he'd held her up, either. Mr. Knox wasn't the man to impose on anybody.

While the girl talked she snipped off a length of dark brown wrapping cord and Bratton noted that the scissors she used for the operation were blunt and short bladed, the kind his own youngsters cut out paper dolls with. He likewise noted how expertly she handled the large sheets of wrapping paper.

As for the gentleman waiting there on the settee, the wrapper went on, she had noticed him the minute he came in. He'd stood a minute looking down through the rooms where the customers were and then he'd sat down. Yes, alone. . . . . No, he hadn't done anything special—he'd just sorta looked like Greville Laird did in *Her Lordly Lover* was why she'd kept her eye on him, kind of. . . . The only other thing she remembered about him was that she saw him coming back once and sitting down again in the same chair he'd been in.

Questioning the girl closely here, Bratton learned that it was while Joyce Terry was waiting at the desk that the wrapper had seen her romantic looking stranger returning to his place from the farther end of the reception room. He also asked her whether she had seen him leave. She had not.

Bratton next strolled in the direction the girl had indicated and found a certain excitement in the discovery that that end of the reception corridor led him to a recess beyond the bank of elevators, from which a curtained arch led to the stock room and the group of fitting rooms.

"What of it?" he asked himself sternly and went back to single out Grace Ramby for some additional questioning. But he found himself intercepted by the man whom he recognized as Knox, the floor manager.

"Anything new, Inspector?" Knox asked in a respectfully muted voice. He was a thick-shouldered youngish man, his fair hair already going thin. His display of fraternal insignia was a bit blatant, but otherwise Bratton found him inoffensive.

Yet Bratton's reply to the floor man's question came with official shortness. "Not unless you've got it to tell."

Knox shook his head mournfully. "It's terrible business—terrible. But, Inspector, if I could have one minute of your time, there's a possible explanation of the crime that I'd like to put up to you." His voice sank to a still more guarded whisper. "Maybe we'd better not talk here."

He turned and walked across the department to a desk so placed behind a decorative screen that it did not mar the appearance of the salon. Bratton had kept at his heels, though he knew he should not allow a self-important ass like this to waste his time. With a meaning pressure Knox laid a hand adorned with an elaborate lodge ring on the inspector's arm. "Have you considered that that frightful deed was very likely the work of some mentally deranged woman—"

How long Knox continued to expand his brilliantly original theory Bratton never knew, for as he sat down at the desk his eye fell upon something just within one of its pigeonholes—something with a dull brownish smudge on it, a smudge that looked very much as if it had first been a blood stain. It could be plainly seen on an otherwise virgin order blank.

Knox continued to talk; he had evidently not noticed the quick forward jerk which Bratton had not been able to control.

"I get you," the inspector managed to break in. "A very plausible idea—it had already occurred to us. By the way, Knox, whose desk is this?"

"It's the buyer's—Madame Nordhoff's. Now about my idea—why don't you get in touch with the superintendent of the Mental Hospital—"

"Madame Nordhoff's desk, eh? But anybody in the department would find it a real convenience, I suppose. . . . See here, Knox, while I have this chance, let's have the low-down on that girl—Joyce Terry. I've heard what the women say, but I don't know. . . . Her story is that she was detained at the desk when she went to get her salesbook—detained by you." The inspector's smile was apologetic. "Something about a credit slip, wasn't it?"

"In a way, yes. I did have an inquiry about a credit claim, but if she understood me to tell her to wait till I came back she was mistaken. I can't remember saying that. Anyway, it wouldn't have been necessary."

"I see. . . . However, there can be no doubt that she waited. Where were you, by the way?"

If Knox suspected any sinister significance in the detective's inquiry, his polite, head-usher manner was unperturbed. "Why, I went on up to see the credit manager again. At least I started, but a shopper detained me at the elevator and I was still there when I got the first SOS about what had happened."

Again Bratton nodded in confirmation. "Now how about this Terry girl? Is she straight goods?"

"Indeed she is—Joyce is as smart as we get 'em up here. A red-headed temper, maybe. . . . She and the buyer have a run-in ever so often, but I know for a fact that Nordhoff wouldn't dream of letting the girl go."

A message relayed from the cashier's desk interrupted further analysis of the character and temperament of the girl who had reported the crime in room E. As the breathless messenger put it, the policeman was wanted on the phone. It proved to be Headquarters with certain information Bratton had already called in for. Ross Ingram lived at the Peg Top Club. Apparently he had no business address.

The interruption gave Bratton the opportunity to abstract the blood-marked sheet of paper from the pigeonhole of Madame Nordhoff's desk without calling Knox's attention to what he was doing. A chat with the buyer was plainly on the cards, but as both she and Grace Ramby had gone out to lunch the inspector decided to walk around to the Peg Top Club.

Fifteen minutes later Bratton was having speech with the Peg Top's executive secretary. The secretary was sorry; Mr. Ingram was not in. In fact, he believed that Mr. Ingram was out of the city. He called the porter to verify his supposition.

The porter was a black boy whose only name seemed to be Major and whose disposition welcomed the slightest chance to stop whatever he was doing and chat with the interrupter.

"Yessuh, Mistah Ingram he done left yestiddy evenin' kinda in a hurry like to git to the deepo, but he musta ketched his train all right."

"An unexpected trip, you think?"

"Yessuh, seems like. He run in here long about five-thutty and tell me to call him a cab, and he go on up to his room. The taxi it come right away almost, and jes' as I stahts to call up to Mistah Ingram he come down again and hurry out."

"Any baggage?"

"Nossuh, nothin' a-tall but his ovahcoat."

"Then how did you know he was leaving town? Did you hear what he said to the taximan?"

"Nossuh, he go by me so fast I didn't even git to hold the door open for him. All I know about it is he said somethin' about makin' a train when he fust come in."

"What taxi line did you call?"

"The Quicksilver Company, like I always do."

Bratton traced the call immediately. There was no delay in finding the driver who had answered the call from the Peg Top Club. The man remembered the circumstances only too clearly. The fare had hurried out of the building and down the steps, but as he was about to step inside the cab he changed his mind. He had abruptly dismissed the taxi with what its driver considered an inadequate tip and had walked briskly off toward Hamilton Street. Further than that the disgruntled driver had not observed.

Inspector Bratton was well aware that anyone walking toward Hamilton Street was certainly not bound for the railway station.

6

An Engagement is Announced

Meanwhile Jessica Brooke was busy with the lines of investigation turned over to her by Dan Bratton. Every department in the store was visited with a glib story of a service investigation of scissors. The basement departments made the best showing. Not a pair that had ever been issued was missing, though everywhere Jessica encountered a bright hopefulness that at last something was going to be done about sharpening them. Records elsewhere were not so good. Indeed it was practically impossible to check up conclusively on an article so constantly borrowed and so readily mislaid. In only two cases did the store detective hear anything of possible significance.

The head of the millinery, a department that shared the fourth floor with the ready-to-wear, said that only that morning the girl at her wrapping desk had been complaining that she could not find her scissors. Moreover, she was almost certain that they had been just where they belonged the afternoon before. At least, she couldn't remember not having them. . . .

The other complaint came from the book department. There the head was quite positive that their scissors had disappeared some time during the preceding afternoon. They had only the one pair in the department and they were rarely used at that. Yesterday afternoon the girl on

duty at the wrapping desk at the books distinctly recalled
having used them to cut open a fresh ball of cord. That
had been some time before three o'clock. Within an hour
after that a customer had stopped to ask if she might borrow a pair of scissors for a minute. The girl had promptly
handed them to her and, watching in idle curiosity, had
seen the woman stoop and clip off a tag of leather from the
sole of her shoe—that thin layer that scuffs off raggedly
shortly after shoes have ceased to be new. As far as the girl
could be sure, this woman had laid the scissors back upon
the desk and had walked off. Moreover, she could describe
the borrower in some detail. . . .

Jessica Brooke felt quite satisfied with herself after that
interview.

Naturally Jessica listened with particular care to the
reports from the various ready-to-wear departments, but
there everyone was delightfully vague about scissors. The
girl at the wrapping desk, the same one who had been so
charmed with the presence of Ross Ingram, had been on
the trail of a mislaid pair when she first went on duty that
morning, but they had turned up after a while. Madame
Nordhoff had heard her fussing around and had told her
she thought she had seen a pair lying on one of the little
ornamental tables that were scattered through the department. Sure enough, there they were. . . . As sure as the
wrapper knew, she might have laid them down there herself the evening before. There'd been all that awful excitement in the French Room yesterday. To all of which Jessica
Brooke agreed sympathetically.

Nor did the store detective neglect their own notions
and small wares department where scissors were sold.
Picking out a pair similar to those hideous scissors that
had come to light in the bin of bargain stockings, Jessica
asked the girls whether they had sold any like that the day
before. The third salesgirl questioned recalled that she had

sold a customer scissors of that size. The girl had inquired
as she waited for her change whether the ready-to-wear
dresses were on the third or fourth floor. That had been
early yesterday afternoon. Again Jessica Brooke added a
costume description to her collection.

She next set out to learn something more about the
woman who had collapsed in the rest room. She had carried a package that looked like a book . . . and a woman
who had used scissors at the book service desk. Emma's
description and the girl's did not disagree too violently,
except for the gloves. Emma had spoken of light-colored
gloves, but the girl in the books was quite positive that
the woman who had cut the tag of leather from her shoe
had worn dull grey ones. However, the customer who had
stopped at the notions wore no gloves at all. The salesgirl
had described a ring.

Back to the book department Jessica Brooke hastened.
No one on the floor could remember having waited on
such a woman as Emma and their own wrapper had both
described. It had been a quiet afternoon in the books, the
head explained. Just a few of the regulars browsing around
. . . and people at the circulating library shelves. Just as
Jessica was about to abandon the field the assistant buyer
remembered that she had stepped up to such a woman who
was looking over a table of reprints. The woman had said
she wasn't stopping just then to purchase anything and the
clerk had gone back to the discussion she was having with
one of their habituées. Yes, the woman had carried a package, but it was a bit too box-like to be a book. Judging
that the assistant ought to know, Jessica hurried on more
hopefully. She went directly to the stationery counter. A
book-shaped package might be a box of letter paper.

Jessica Brooke's guess was right. Moreover, the very first
clerk she questioned was the one who had real information
for her. The clerk remembered the lady who had bought a

box of stationery because she seemed so relieved to match the sample which she had produced. It was paper like this, explained the girl, displaying a box she drew from a shelf. It was rather nice paper, though not particularly expensive. Unfortunately the purchase was not charged. That hope blocked, Jessica looked so downcast that the clerk of her own sympathy threw out a life line by saying that the sample to be matched had been a regular letter, addressed and everything, and while of course she hadn't deliberately read the address she couldn't help seeing it and she remembered some of it. "Some of it" was very fragmentary indeed . . . . the name Emily and Sagamore Avenue.

Feeling that she could certainly command some slight flicker of interest from Dan Bratton's blue eyes when he heard what her routine investigations had discovered, Jessica Brooke returned to her office. There she found a report waiting for her which she examined with interest. It was a statement of Mrs.

Rupert Thayre's charge account. It was evident that she did not shop extensively at Line's. Only one item had been reported to the credit office the day before, but the detective found that arresting. It was a fairly expensive, fitted traveling case. The other items on the statement had been bought much earlier in the month and at the same time. Struck by the absence of any ready-to-wear charges, Jessica promptly called the bookkeeping offices and learned that the latest purchase made in that department dated back nearly two years. That would account for no one there recognizing her, she thought.

She next sent for the salesman from whom Mrs. Thayre had purchased the traveling case. A neat, middle-aged man answered her summons. He stated that his customer had appeared about half past eleven the morning before. He had shown her perhaps a half dozen bags of the sort she intimated she wanted. She had made up her mind without much difficulty and given the name and address of her account and then had added another name and address for delivery. She had asked him several times as to the exact time the parcel would appear at this address and he had assured her that by noon the next day it would surely have arrived. The address? Ah, yes, just one moment. . . . Mr. Arthur Lyle consulted his salesbook. "Miss Vivian Agnew, Green's Mill, Ohio. . . ."

Upon request Lyle also described Mrs. Thayre's appearance, which, tallied with the one frightful glimpse Miss Brooke herself had had the day before in the fitting room. She asked him what sort of bag or purse she had carried. Something dark colored that went with her dress, Lyle was pret-ty sure. He was positive it had a strap because he remembered seeing her run the strap through her fingers. She had on light gloves and the dark strap stood out ever so distinctly. And speaking of curious things to remember, little Mr. Lyle had noticed something that fairly startled him, once when she opened her bag to get at her handkerchief. He wouldn't want to say for sure that it was, mind you, only it certainly looked enough like it. The trigger or something must have caught in the lace of her handkerchief, but she slipped it right off quick as a wink and he let on that he hadn't seen a thing. Yes, he'd be willing to swear that the lady had a little revolver or pistol in her hand bag.

After Lyle had gone, Jessica sat for a moment or two in some indecision and then sent for Joyce Terry. The girl slipped in, looking pale and frightened, a noon extra rolled tightly in one hand.

"Sit down, Joyce, and do try to relax. Nobody's going to arrest you for the murder, you know." The store detective had spoken jokingly, but to her distress the girl began to sob wildly.

For a moment the older woman let her weep without comment. Then she filled a paper cup at the water cooler and insisted that she take a long breath and drink the water slowly. "Now, Joyce," she said, "I know you're terribly shaken over this affair—you had a nasty shock and no mistake, but suppose you stop emoting over it and help me do a little plain thinking. I want you to tell me the whole story as far as you were in on it. Try not to leave out a single thing. I mean any tiny little thing that left any sort of impression on you. Begin at the very beginning. . . ."

When Joyce had once more told her story, Jessica Brook put three or four quiet questions to her. "You say Knox detained you at the desk. What about?"

"Why, he wanted to verify a credit slip and he dashed off about that and didn't come back and didn't come back—"

"Oh, so he wasn't there while you were waiting? And you can't remember anything more about the woman who was leaving the fitting rooms when you returned—the one that was putting on light gloves?"

"No, honestly I can't, Miss Brooke. Not really, that is. I'm tormented with a feeling that I'm going to remember something else."

"Heaven grant you do! And come running to me the instant it clicks." It would scarcely be cricket, she decided regretfully, to suggest to the girl that perhaps the woman had been carrying a flat parcel, like a book or box of stationery. "Well," she went on, "what do you remember about the missing hand bag?"

"You mean what I told Inspector Bratton? It was dark green—brocaded silk, I think, and it looked awfully full. I remember noticing that when she opened
it to put her gloves in it—"

"What sort of gloves, Joyce?"

"They were some kind of washable leather, not white but quite light in color. And they looked brand new. But, Miss Brooke, maybe there was something in that bag that whoever killed her wanted. It did look so full, and she handled it as if it were heavy."

Jessica Brooke thought of what Arthur Lyle had seen in the green bag and regarded Joyce Terry thoughtfully. She was more and more convinced that there was something troubling the girl that had not yet come to the surface. Her fingers picked incessantly at the newspaper clamped between them. As Jessica well knew, it was the issue proclaiming to the city the identity of the murdered woman. She turned to that in the hope of still further steadying the shaken girl.

"Now that we know it was Rupert Thayre's wife who was killed," she began, "does anything that she did or said while you were waiting on her mean anything more than it did?"

Once more Joyce Terry collapsed into hysterical sobs.

"Look here, girl. This nonsense has got to stop. What is it that you are not telling me?" She gripped the girl's slight shoulders not at all gently and at last forced fear-filled eyes to look into hers.

"I—I don't know anything about her—about the poor woman who was killed," she gulped at last, "but I don't understand this—and it frightens me so . . ."

A shaking finger pointed out the picture of Rupert Thayre that balanced his wife's. Paula and her colleagues had lost no time. It was an unusually clear reproduction to find in newsprint.

Alertly Jessica Brooke's eyes watched a look of decision stiffen Joyce Terry's face. "If it wasn't for his name beneath, I'd swear that was a picture of Phil Leonard, the man I'm engaged to."

7

The Jade Bracelet

When Inspector Bratton left the Peg Top Club, he walked off in the same direction that the taxi driver had said Ingram had taken. At the first street intersection he stopped and watched the traffic swing by till the signal light winked. It was only a few seconds but it was long enough for him to see a huge inter-city bus lurch by, gaudily placarded with its destination, a sprawling city two hundred miles to the north.

His flashing idea might be a dud. . . . However, he made a speedy return to Headquarters and did a little long-distance telephoning. Likewise he turned over the grisly weapon and the blood-stained sheet of paper he had found in the buyer's desk to the experts who were best fitted to decide what they had to tell.

The inspector was then ready to give a little time to the people waiting for him. Although less than a half dozen hours had elapsed since the screaming announcement that the murdered woman was Mrs. Rupert Thayre, the authorities were counting on reports from casual sources that might account for her time after she had left her home the morning before until her appearance on the floor of the French Room. But from this first harvest Bratton reaped nothing of value. Various specialty shops reported that

Mrs. Thayre had been in and out, but in every instance she had been unaccompanied.

The most promising item that turned up came from the Mermaid's Pool—Baths and Beauty Treatments. A discreet call from the manager of this retreat brought the information that at two on the preceding day Mrs. Thayre had had an appointment for a manicure. She had appeared on time and remained a half hour. The girl who had served her reported that she had been unusually silent during the operation. But, and here the manager's smooth tones became oracular, another patron, a woman whom they were serving for the first time, had asked the girl who was working on her a number of questions about Mrs. Thayre and when Mrs. Thayre left this second woman had followed her out. All of which was so interesting in its possibilities that Bratton asked to have the second operator mentioned sent over to Headquarters at once.

While he was waiting for the girl from the Mermaid's Pool, Bratton accomplished a bit of sleight-of-hand and had Paula Pringle detached from the omnivorous mob of reporters to whom he had promised a statement in time for the final editions. The gypsy imp slipped in jauntily.

"I got the goods on you at last, Paula," Bratton laughed, "but I'll tell the world I thought for a while that you were the mysterious unknown woman in the case, the way you called up Thayre and put him wise about the body." It was true; one of the men from the detective division had spent several intensive hours tracing the mysterious telephone call that had summoned Rupert Thayre to the mortuary.

"Now if you'll be a good girl and not ask papa too many questions," he went on, "I've got a little job for you that may mean a big story—eventually, but not till I say the word. Promise?"

"I'd promise anything and you know it—and you also know that you trust me at your own risk." Just the same,

Dan Bratton and Paula Pringle understood one another very well.

"I want you to dig up some sort of picture of the first Mrs. Thayre and, on the side, any information about her that I might find interesting."

"Ah ha! A suspect, a nice juicy suspect. And my story?"

"When you bring me the picture—no, when you bring me accurate information concerning her present where-abouts, you'll get your story. I mean I'll know then whether or not there's a story for you to get, little one. Now ske-daddle!"

The vigorous gestures of a clerk had announced the arrival of someone, probably the girl from the Mermaid's Pool. So it proved. A sharp-eyed, sharp-chinned young woman presented herself and after some adroit questions which broke down her very palpable nervousness furnished a description of the woman who had revealed curiosity about Mrs. Thayre and who had followed her out of the shop.

"What questions did she ask you about Mrs. Thayre?" Bratton wanted to be exact about that.

"Why, mostly about who she was, see. Just as if she couldn't really believe that it was the lady I said it was."

"What seemed to attract her attention to Mrs. Thayre in the first place?"

"She must have heard someone call her by name. We all knew Mrs. Thayre up there; she's one of our regulars. Any-way, my customer asked me to point out the lady named Thayre."

"I see. . . . Now, are you still sure you haven't any no-tion at all who this woman was that asked the questions?"

"No, sir, I'm sure I wouldn't know. I already told you about the ring on her right little finger with the S cut into the stone."

"Yes, and that's something, of course. Well, in that case, I won't detain you any longer. If the woman should come into your place again, get word to us here right away and—thank you very much."

The wiry little manicurist hurried back to the Mermaid's Pool quite taken, on the whole, with the courtesy of the local police officials. Her previous contacts had been entirely with the traffic force. The boy friend who took her out was always getting bawled out for racing lights.

During the next twenty minutes Dan Bratton managed to clear his desk of the most pressing routine matters, but from the mechanical way in which he worked it was evident that his attention was chiefly on the Thayre case. He shrugged his shoulders at last and reached for his hat, but before he could leave his office his telephone called him back. Rupert Thayre was on the wire.

"I say, Inspector Bratton, Mrs. Thayre's mother, Mrs. Agnew, has just come from her home down state. She's in a rather pitiful condition, naturally—she's practically an invalid at best, but she insists that she wants to see you. To quiet her I had to promise to call you at once, but I think you ought to find it impossible to get around before tomorrow morning. She'd be better able to talk then, you understand."

To this the inspector agreed. The request could stand as if initiating solely from the relatives of the murdered woman. Thayre didn't have to know that the police would have hot-footed it to the mother anyway. . . .

It was the tag end of the afternoon when Inspector Bratton again entered Jessica Brooke's office. He slumped wearily into the chair opposite hers, though there was small trace of fatigue or discouragement in his greeting. "I hope that you appreciate that I come up here for your good news instead of making you report down at my dump."

"I've been trying to get you, Inspector. I've struck a trail that ought to lead to the woman who was in booth C.

Here's the way it looks—" As the store detective plunged into her report the note of pleased excitement in her voice became more noticeable. "A woman on the verge of hysteria in the rest room about twenty minutes of five, just after the crime had been discovered, see. . . . A taxi is called for her, which she does not take. . . . Joyce Terry sees a woman leaving the fitting alcove just before she herself comes upon the body. . . . A person who could be the same woman stopping at the cashier's desk in the book department and using the scissors there—same scissors no longer about. . . . Just before that this same woman who used the scissors in the books bought a box of writing paper in the stationery department matching her purchase by a letter addressed to someone named Emily on Sagamore Avenue, which is the best clue we have to her identity. . . . Emma's woman in the rest room had the parcel that corresponds to the letter paper. . . . It's all of a piece except that the woman who purchased scissors exactly like those that killed Mrs. Thayre doesn't seem to fit in. . . . There's another interesting little contradiction"

"Huh, only one?" Bratton's murmur could scarcely have been called polite.

"The descriptions that Emma, Joyce, and the clerks downstairs give all jibe well enough except for the gloves. The book and stationery woman was wearing darkish gloves and Joyce and Emma both speak of light ones. Mrs. Thayre wore light gloves too, but they disappeared with her bag."

"Maybe the second woman went out of the French Room wearing Mrs. Thayre's gloves," said Bratton quietly.

"Because hers were too badly stained with blood?" Jessica Brooke's usually level tones shook with excitement.

"At any rate, gloves could be easily changed. When we put this dope of yours with what the girl at the beauty shop told me—" Parenthetically Bratton inserted his lately acquired information. Nor did he have to point out that the manicurist's description of her patron did not contradict those that the store detective had collected.

"An S in her ring," mused the woman. "That S couldn't have stood for Sagamore. Maybe the girl can recall a name beginning with S. The clerk in the notions noticed a carved ring."

Bratton shook his head in disparagement. "It's dangerous when witnesses are allowed to be too obliging. They say what you want them to say."

"Of course. 'Very like a whale' stuff. . . ." A comment to which Bratton paid no attention, for reasons.

Instead he turned abruptly to the telephone. "Sagamore Avenue, wasn't it?" He gave Headquarters some succinct directions that set additional machinery in action. "Now then—" he whirled again toward his cooperator. "Did you see any of the paper like that the woman bought? Was it like this?"

He pulled out the envelope which had contained a jade bracelet but no letter.

Jessica nodded doubtfully. "Like enough, but I'll call the girl up with a box from stock."

While they were waiting Bratton gave Jessica details about the envelope and she examined it carefully.

"A man's or woman's writing?" he queried.

"I'd say—a man's," she pronounced. "It's so individual that it oughtn't to be hard to identify. It's not Thayre's by any chance?"

"Don't be silly, young woman. Why should it be?"

"Laugh at me if you want, but I suppose you've had him looked up?"

"Alibi, you mean? Oh, sure . . . sure. Got anything against him?"

But that was all that Jessica Brooke had planned to say to the inspector about Thayre. She had reached a stubborn conclusion to keep silent about the pitiful fear that Joyce had gasped out to her. It must be their secret for at least a day or two. Otherwise, Joyce Terry would have no chance of escaping immediate arrest.

However, before Jessica needed to sidestep the inspector's question the girl from the stationery made a breathless entrance with a grey and white striped box of writing paper tucked under her arm. Much to the salesgirl's disappointment she was thanked politely and expected to withdraw. It was not until the two detectives were again alone that the envelope found in Vivian Thayre's' desk was compared with those in the box. They were identical.

"But does that get us anywhere, I ask you?" Jessica was beginning to feel as dispirited as her question sounded. What she needed was her dinner, as she had enthusiastically overlooked her lunch hour in her triumphant progress from scissors to traveling cases and grey stationery. . . .

"Miss Brooke, you're damn good at unearthing important details, but you're not worth a hoot when it comes to putting two and two together," complained Bratton with unusual brusqueness. "My hunch is that when we find this Emily woman and locate the writer of this letter, we're likely to see a surprising connection."

"Bless the little sunbeam! He doesn't even say *if*; it's *when* with him," she scoffed.

"Have your stationery clerk take a look at this envelope. If the writing's so individual as you say, maybe she can tell whether the Emily-Sagamore Avenue envelope has been addressed by the same hand. This Ingram bird jumped town in a hurry late yesterday afternoon." Bratton's change of topic was rather obvious. "I'm getting sort of curious about finding him—"

"But of course you always get your man." He had that coming to him, thought Jessica, after the frank criticism he had fired at her.

Bratton did no more than toss her a disarming grin and went on as if thinking aloud. "But if—please note the if's, Miss Brooke—this woman who bought the paper should turn out to be the mysterious occupant of booth C, then it would be a wild coincidence if Ingram had written the letter. I've no knowledge yet that Ingram knew Mrs. Thayre. But if this woman should obligingly turn out to be Thayre's first wife—"

"'*Why, then it would be grand . . .*'" quoted Jessica deliberately, an interpolation to which Bratton again could make no comment.

He stuck to his own line of thought. "Of course, it's only logical to assume that a woman did the killing, as a man's chances of getting into those fitting rooms unnoticed would be mighty slim."

"No chance at all," agreed Jessica. "The floor manager is the only man that could wander about unnoticed and Henry Knox would rather die than intrude into the fitting alcove. Anyway, he promptly accounted for himself—some to-do about a credit slip. Level-headed, sensible chap—Henry."

"Still, if it was a woman, she was no weak sister to deliver the blow she did with a weapon like scissors. And another thing—it had to be practically an unpremeditated affair. You couldn't plan ahead to kill someone in such a place. As I see it, no one could possibly have known where the Terry girl was going to park her customer."

"But the woman in C could have heard them talking in the booth next, and when Joyce went away—"

"That Terry girl could have done her in herself. The catch is we haven't got a damn thing on her." Bratton's fingers groped in a pocket for matches; instead he encountered the cool smoothness of the jade bracelet. He drew it forth and slung it across the table to Jessica. "Another one of my hunches," he said. "I've no earthly reason for it, but

I'm inwardly convinced that that trinket's mixed up in the reason for Vivian Thayre's murder."

Jessica Brooke was relieved that the inspector's thoughts had shifted from Joyce Terry. She drew her desk lamp closer to examine the bracelet more carefully. "I can tell you something, Inspector," she said in a moment. "I've seen this bracelet or one exactly like it very recently—in a jeweler's window right around here in Court Street."

"Fair enough. Put on your hat and let's go see about it. If we hurry, we can make it before the place is locked up."

They hurried along the crowded street through the penetrating chill of a murky autumn evening and slipped into Emanuel's just as the proprietor himself was about to draw down his curtains and set his burglar alarm.

Emanuel gave the jade bracelet but a casual glance. "Yes," he said, "the bracelet came from my stock. What's wrong with it?"

"Did you make the sale or one of your clerks?" Which was complimenting Emanuel's place of business, for the shop was so minute that only a pint-sized assistant could have been accommodated.

"It was me that sold it, all right."

"Who to? When?" Bratton demanded.

"I didn't know the gentleman. Last week. Friday, I think it was."

"Did he pay cash or give you a check?"

"Cash. . . . I said I didn't know the party's name."

"Did he take it away with him or have it delivered?"

"Neither, exactly. There was a lady with him—"

"I see. . . ." There was an air of imminent triumph about Detective-Inspector Bratton. "Suppose you describe her. This is police business."

"If you say so. . . ." Emanuel was blandly patient. "But I can tell you exactly who she was—Joe Kendall's daughter. Yeah, it was his girl all right. Her name's Cornelia or Cordelia or something like that. . . ."

8

CONNIE KENDALL

Detective-Inspector Bratton lost no time in presenting himself at the residence of the Kendalls. The house was called Hearthstone Manor and was as showily incongruous as its name. Dan Bratton was not socially sensitive to any marked degree, but he like all the rest of the town knew that Joe Kendall was newly and grossly rich and that he added precisely nothing to the city's cultural background.

A butler who looked as if his employers were almost too much for his rigid sense of the fitness of things admitted him. Bratton took no chances, but flashed his badge and said that if Miss Kendall was in she'd have to see him. The butler registered faint distress at this revelation of official authority and reported that Miss Kendall could give him fifteen minutes before a dinner engagement. Connie Kendall was a good-looker. That was Bratton's immediate opinion. He liked 'em pink and white and gold and slightly cushiony.

With little in the way of preliminary he produced the jade bracelet. "Emanuel says he sold this to a gentleman who gave it to you. How about it?"

The girl gave the bracelet only one glance. The hands that were a size too large for her height did not even pick it up. "Right the first time," she admitted cheerfully, "but what's that to you?"

"What did you do with it after you got it?"

"If you must have the low-down, I changed my mind about wanting it. When I first saw it I was crazy about it and devilled the boy-friend like everything till he came across, and then I decided I'd rather have a pin for my hat, an elephant all brilliants, you know, so that same night I told—"

She stopped at that, and a wary look glinted in the blue eyes that Bratton had been so pleased with. "That's exactly what I've come to find out. Who bought you the bracelet?" Blue eyes had never yet interfered with the inspector's duty.

"Say, look here. . . . I think it's about time you're telling me why you want to know." Connie's voice, not having been completely finished at the Hudson River school that had guaranteed to do something about it, reverted to its native flatness.

"There's no reason in the world why you shouldn't know." Bratton's words came easily as though his only concern was to oblige a young and charming lady. "This bracelet was found in the personal belongings of a murdered woman—"

Connie Kendall let out one terrified squeak. "But you can't think I killed Vivian Thayre, nor that Ross did either," she gibbered, and all the pink except the round spots that had come out of the enameled boxes on her dressing table drained away from her round little cheeks.

Bratton sat forward in his chair. Was the Thayre case going to end with a bang here and now? "You sure are giving me a grand idea that you know something about that murder, I'll say that much, young lady. For instance, just where were you yesterday afternoon at half past four?"

The girl's mad panic had been but momentary. There was now an air of decisive control about her. "That's easy. . . . I was out at the Valley Hunt Club with about a dozen

other people. The Henderson Browns and Teddy Matthews
and Pud and Meg Laycock—need any more names to verify
my alibi? That's what I have to prove, isn't it?" she finished pertly.

"Ross Ingram wasn't there, huh?"

"I don't recall that he was." The Hudson River manner
made an unsuccessful attempt to come to the surface.

"Come now, no foolin'. . . . He was the chap that bought
the bracelet?"

As he said it, it sounded far more like a statement
than a question, and the girl's blonde head dipped in slow
acknowledgment.

Bratton did not betray his satisfaction with the simple
ruse he had employed. "Know Ingram pretty well, do you?"

Again a nod was the only answer.

"When did you last see him?"

"I had lunch with him yesterday at the Pendragon."

"And after that?" snapped Bratton.

"I was dated to play a little golf at the Valley Hunt—
the season's held so late this fall. I thought Ross was going
out, too, but it seemed he had—another engagement, so
a little after two—I think that was about the time we left
the Pendragon—we walked around to the place where I'd
left my car, and that's all."

If this girl was stalling, Bratton was now thinking, he
was a nit-wit. "What was Ingram's other engagement?" he
asked briskly.

"I have no idea."

Bratton allowed a suspicious smile to form slowly. It
seemed to infuriate the daughter of Joe Kendall. "I tell
you, I haven't," she flared. "If you only knew how damn
mad he made me yesterday—I wanted him to come out
to the Club. I couldn't get a thing out of him except that
he had to keep an appointment. I'll bet it was with that
Thayre woman." The blue eyes flashed savage lightnings.

The inspector wasted no more time. "See here, young lady, that's twice of your own accord you've mentioned Mrs. Thayre. Let's have a show down. She was found murdered late yesterday afternoon, as you plainly know. What did Ross Ingram have to do with it?"

"Oh, my poor Ross, what have I done? What have I done?" moaned Connie, wringing her hands with their too rosily tipped nails. "I didn't mean—I'm only jealous. . . ."

"All right, then. Let me tell it. . . ." Bratton regarded the hysterical girl shrewdly. "I figure it that you and Ingram are sweethearts, but Ingram has taken on this other woman, Mrs. Thayre, or else he hasn't quite cut loose from her. Which is it?"

"He told me he'd finished with her—that there wasn't anything to it any more. But he was lying, for instead of exchanging the bracelet for the pin, as he promised to do for me, he must have handed it right over to her. This ends it, I tell you! I'd given him one more chance, and look how he gyps me. Just wait till I see him!"

This outburst gave Bratton another lead, but he was not yet ready to follow it. "What did Ingram have to do with the murder of Vivian Thayre?" he reiterated.

"I don't know—I didn't mean—all I know is he told me he could shut her mouth so she'd leave him alone. But, so help me God, I have no reason to believe or imagine that his appointment yesterday afternoon was with her. Her name was not even mentioned while he and I were together yesterday. I'm jealous and horrid, but I'll hate myself forever if anything I've said is going to get Ross in bad." The fire and vengeance she had so lately breathed were now set aside for tears and contrition.

"He wasn't sitting so pretty before I talked to you, if that will be any comfort to you." Bratton's first impression of Connie Kendall's looks had not undergone any extensive revision and his present sympathy was quite sincere.

"But I need some more help from you. Did you know Mrs. Thayre?"

"She was pointed out to me once. It was down at the races and she was with her husband. I've never met her socially or any other way—never even spoken to her."

"What do you know about her?"

"Nothing. . . . You see, the people who count paid absolutely no attention to her." This was said with so much aplomb that later Jessica Brooke found it difficult to persuade Bratton that the Kendalls for all their money were only on the loosest fringe of local society themselves. Otherwise Connie would never have been permitted the attentions of a man like Ross Ingram.

Deciding that Connie was too young to be an authority on Thayre's earlier marital experience, Bratton picked up his remaining trick. "You've told me when you last saw Ingram. Now what have you heard from him since? Where is he now?"

There was nothing counterfeit about Connie's look of questioning surprise. "Heard from him? Why, nothing. Why should I? And as to where he is now—"

She glanced at a minute watch flashing gaudily on her wrist. "I expect to hear his ring at the door any minute. He's taking me to the Medfield dinner tonight."

Bratton opened his mouth to reply in some detail and then, fortunately, thought twice. After all, just because Ingram had made a hurried disappearance the evening before was no proof that his absence was permanent. This blue-eyed baby-doll was looking for him herself. He'd just stick around and have a few words with Ross Ingram when the gentleman appeared. Even as he so communed with himself, a bell somewhere pealed significantly. Shortly afterward the butler made a silent entrance. "A wire, Miss, just relayed by telephone." He handed a memorandum slip to the girl and withdrew.

She read it, but her face was so carefully guarded that it told Bratton nothing. She looked up at him, straightforward and composed. "I'll give it to you," she said primly, "before you can ask me for it."

From the sturdy hand that Connie had inherited from her Grandma Schneider the inspector took the message. It read:

EXPECTED TO FLY BACK TIME FOR DIN-
NER STOP UNAVOIDABLE BUSINESS COM-
PLICATIONS STOP SORRY DARLING ALL
MY LOVE.

ROSS

"From Chicago, I see. And you didn't know that Ingram had gone out of town?" Bratton asked.

"Look at me. Can't you see I'm all ready to do a little stepping out? I'll have to let Jill Medfield know. . . . But I'm perfectly willing to tell you one little thing that I've just remembered—I called Ross this morning and couldn't get him, but that didn't mean a thing to me then."

"Does it now?" asked Bratton with meaning.

"Nothing more than a business trip. He's always running up to Chicago."

"What's his racket? Bootlegging?"

Connie shrugged her plump shoulders indifferently. "Or playing the market," she amended sweetly. "He never says much about business."

"What hotel did he usually stay at?"

"The Blackstone, I think. . . . I don't know. Now, if you don't mind, I've got to 'phone Jill. She's sure to raise hell—maybe she'll let me bring you instead. How'd you like that?"

Connie went on to the Medfields', volunteering cheerily to let the police know the minute she heard from

Ingram. That would be fine, the inspector assured her, without explaining that any further attempt the man might make to communicate with her would meet with police interference.

9

SORRY ROMANCE

When Jessica Brooke and Bratton had parted company at Emanuel's, Jessica had hurried home to the apartment where she did for herself very tidily. There, as she had arranged, she found Joyce Terry waiting for her. Without referring to the desperate possibility that made their conference necessary, the older woman bustled briskly about her compact quarters and pressed the distraught girl likewise into service. Chops were broiled, coffee set to perking, a salad tossed together, and a delicatessen dessert portioned out upon the best glass plates the Brooke *ménage* could boast. When they had finished their steaming plates of canned soup, Jessica Brooke plunged into the distasteful topic.

"I'm telling you, Joyce. I've made up my mind, if you haven't. If Dan Bratton finds out that Thayre has been playing around with you under another name, it'll not be through anything that I say. But there's every chance that he finds out: that man's no dumb bell."

In spite of the quick flush of gratitude that flooded the girl's delicate face she broke in with an expostulation. "But we're not sure yet—"

"Which brings us to what I started to say: have you made up your mind to tell me the whole story?"

Undiluted misery looked out from Joyce Terry's violet-grey eyes. The deepening of the "dirty finger" with which they had been put in told how racked she was, yet she seemed unable to commit herself to the course that the store detective was urging upon her.

"Good heavens, girl, you don't seem to realize that if I told Bratton what you spilled this noon he could hang a motive on you that would sink a ship. I'm trying to do you a good turn, but you won't even help me to prove that this Phil Leonard isn't—Rupert Thayre."

The deliberate impatience in Jessica Brooke's tone had the effect she desired. Joyce put out an imploring hand. "I'll tell you all about it, honest I will, Miss Brooke."

"Good. . . . Start at the beginning."

"It's only been since last August. It was a pick-up, sort of. . . . I'd been out at Pyramid Park to a band concert—it was during that awfully hot spell. This man was on the same bench where I was sitting and he kept making such intelligent remarks about the music. That's why I was willing to talk to him, I suppose. We sat there talking after the concert was over and he asked me to have something cool to drink, but I wouldn't. Then he asked if he couldn't drive me home—he had his car there. But I wouldn't do that either, though I did let him walk down with me to the trolley station. And when we got there, why, everything was all held up because something had happened to the power and so after a while I thought it was only sense to let him take me home. And he was just perfectly lovely all the way in—he didn't get fresh or anything like that—"

"What sort of car did he drive?"

"I'm afraid I didn't notice particularly, except that it was big and expensive looking, a sedan. Well, he told me his name and everything and said he wasn't in town very often, but he hoped I'd be willing to see him again sometime. I didn't promise. . . . Then the week after that, one night he telephoned and asked for a date, but you know where I live. There's no place to see any company at Mrs.

Fahlmann's, so I told him no. But he must have been hanging around, for pretty soon when I walked from the house up to the little playground park to cool off a little before I went to bed, why, he turned up . . . and we got along just fine. After that, I saw him nearly every week till along about the end of September when he was out of town for a couple of weeks. When he came back, we were just naturally so crazy about each other that the first thing we were engaged."

Joyce dropped her voice as if she had come to the end of the chapter.

"But, Joyce dear, what did you actually know about the man?"

"Only what he said—his name was Philip Leonard and he came from Kansas City and he was a bond salesman. He didn't have any folks."

"Did he write to you between times?" persisted Jessica.

"No. He said it was one of his funny ways—he loathed writing letters. He often sent me night letters, though."

"Did he ever give you addresses when he was going away?"

"Yes . . . but they were always General Delivery," confessed the unhappy girl honestly.

"And large cities, I'll bet," Jessica growled.

Joyce nodded wearily. "Yes, places like Detroit and Chicago and Pittsburgh. Once New York."

"What have you been doing since it got cold? The season for park benches is closed."

"Oh, movies sometimes, and when we want to talk there's a little Kosher restaurant out near Mrs. Fahlmann's, and the long reception room at the public library."

"When did you see him last?" Jessica Brooke probed on relentlessly.

"Last Sunday night over at Kohl's, though last night—"

"Yes?" coaxed Jessica, guessing at what was coming.

"I was supposed to be at the library at eight—that's really why I hated to have to stay at the store so late. But I waited at the library till closing time and Phil didn't come." Joyce pushed her plate aside and began to cry drearily. But only for a minute or two, Then she straightened up, wiped her eyes, and made a determined announcement. "I'm going back there tonight—I'll have to hurry right off. It was silly for me to say what I did to you this morning. Lots of people look alike. Phil will be there, I'm sure of it. . . ."

"Go ahead, Joyce, and if he turns up, give me a ring, but honestly, dear, I don't think there's a chance. And if he doesn't show up, come back here. I'll put you up for the night and see that you get some sleep, too. You look as if you can't stand much more."

As Jessica Brooke washed her dishes and put her kitchenette in order she gravely questioned her judgment in permitting a possible meeting between the deluded girl and the philandering Rupert Thayre to go unwitnessed. On the whole, she felt that she was taking no chance at all. Whatever reason had hindered Thayre from keeping his assignation the night before, granting that he had then been ignorant of what had befallen his wife, the events of the day just past would now make him cautious beyond words.

Jessica knew that she was not playing fair with Bratton, but something had impelled her to try to keep the girl's secret. Once she had proved that Joyce's amorous Phil Leonard and Rupert Thayre were one and the same man— but if Dan Bratton was so sure of Thayre's alibi, what difference how many private lives the man was leading? Yet as she splashed hot water and rinsed out her towels she considered various ways by which she herself could obtain that information. If Joyce heard again from Leonard—but if he were Thayre, the chances were that for many weeks to come he would shun any meeting with the girl who had been the one to come upon the body of his wife. Perhaps she herself could arrange to confront Thayre unexpectedly with Joyce. . . . Busily her active mind considered possible ways and means.

Then her thoughts veered sharply. "What of it?" she demanded of herself. "Why get all steamed up over the fact that Thayre masquerading as Phil Leonard, had made love to a pretty little not too sophisticated shop-girl? What possible connection could that have with the murder of Vivian Thayre?"

Frankly, Jessica Brooke saw two possibilities there. Suppose Thayre was more deeply stirred by the girl than the situation showed on the surface, would his passion have led him to murder his wife? It should not have taken a man like Thayre long to see that Joyce Terry was not the girl to consent to an illicit liaison. Yet the enactment of the crime was such that it would seem wildly impossible for the victim's husband to have been on the spot at the time. . . . Jessica wondered just how careful Bratton had been about that alibi. Then too, if Thayre were guilty, he would have been obliged to act with a certain amount of premeditation, which certainly would not have included the presence of the girl whom he wished to place in his wife's position. Perhaps he had been disguised—no, it was a theory too fantastic, too grotesque to be entertained.

As for the second possibility, that predicated a knowledge on Joyce's part of the identity of the man she called Phil Leonard. Would a girl who refused to become a man's mistress murder his wife to attain her desire? Not likely, Jessica granted. . . . Nor could she bring herself to believe that the girl had known that this woman was the lawful wife of the man she loved. And being ignorant of that, what possible motive could she have for murdering a woman unknown to her? But suppose she had in some way come upon the man she called Phil Leonard and had

unwittingly been pressed into service as an accomplice.
That would account for the great personal distress that
Joyce had shown from the first of the affair. The other
people in the department had been excited and curious;
Joyce had been stricken. True, it was she who had borne
the first ghastly shock.

Jessica Brooke's thoughts continued along these lines,
but she reached no clear-cut conclusions. By the time she
heard Joyce's timid knock, not long after ten o'clock, she
had got no further than her first resolution to bring Thayre
and Joyce face to face and see for herself. . . .

The miserable disappointment in Joyce's eyes made
explanations unnecessary, though the girl attempted something in the way of rambling account.

"He—he didn't come. . . . Of course, our date was for
last night. I'll probably get a wire in the morning. Oh,
Miss Brooke, Phil just couldn't be that other man. Why,
you could tell he was a stranger in town—he never knew
the names of streets or anything like that. . . ."

"How about that first time when he drove you in from
Pyramid Park?"

Joyce did not understand what Jessica meant and said
so innocently.

"Did you have to tell him the way into town that time
and out to your North End address?"

"No-o, not as I remember. . . ."

"And another point, did he ever show up with his car
again?"

"No, never. You see, it wasn't his. It belonged to a
friend—

"His story, of course," Jessica snapped, for she was not
particularly enjoying her role. "A licensee number would
have quickly betrayed him as a local product. But, Joyce,
I'll keep my word. You won't be dragged into this on that
account through anything I let slip, but remember—Dan
Bratton may get wind of it someway, and then. . . ."

10

COOPERATION OF MRS. KINZIG

Detective-Inspector Bratton was early at his desk next morning. There should be certain reports at hand and he wanted a chance to go over them carefully before decisions were necessary and before the people on his appointment list began to present themselves. At eleven he himself must be out at Buckeye Heights to interview Mrs. Agnew, Vivian Thayre's mother.

Chicago in general and the Blackstone in particular had nothing to report about Ross Ingram. He was not registered under that name at any of the likely hotels. In spite of the positive source of Connie Kendall's telegram, Bratton could not forget the Detroit-bound bus that had nearly run him down at the corner just below the Peg Top Club. Being in one city and sending a wire from another was something that could be managed, as Bratton's business had long since taught him. Accordingly he duplicated his instructions and called his confreres in the other city to his assistance. If Ingram had not made himself so scarce he would probably have attracted little attention from Bratton; he had possibilities as a witness—that was all.

He next glanced at the progress that had been made with the Sagamore Avenue assignment. The unknown woman who had been lurking in booth C was, all things considered, the most logical suspect. The woman who Miss

Brooke thought might be she, the one who had been traced
from the stationery department to the books and from the
French Room to the rest room, might be named Emily and
she might live somewhere on Sagamore Avenue. It was not
much to go on, but the inspector could not afford to overlook even a far-fetched possibility. However, the young
woman who had bought scissors at the notions did not fit
in so neatly.

The inspector had assigned Sagamore Avenue to young
McKim. His report, which Bratton was now scanning,
showed that Sagamore Avenue was a fairly long street
and that oddly enough there were only two householders
listed thereon whose christened names were Emily. One
of these was a young wife in St. Martha's with her first
baby, and the other was a hard-bitten elderly widow who
ran a boarding house. There were many furnished rooms
and apartments on the plebeian length of Sagamore Avenue; therefore the report was not yet final. Given as much
detail about "Emily's" personal appearance as Miss Brooke
had accumulated, Bratton was far from being discouraged
about that lead.

Merely as a matter of form, as the inspector had indicated to Line and Hollis's store detective, a statement had
been obtained concerning Rupert Thayre's activities on
the afternoon of his wife's death. Thayre had taken it quite
well. He was cooperating without undue sensitiveness, for
which Bratton was thankful. Without difficulty the officials had collected information covering his entire day.
The morning he had spent at his desk at the City Realty
Investment Company. He had lunched with a prospect in
the Trophy Room at the Anthony Wayne Hotel. Nearly an
hour thereafter he had spent with someone at the offices
of Bellew and Bloch, Brokers. He had then returned to his
own offices but had left at three to meet another prospect
out at the latest subdivision placed on the market by the

City Realty Investment. He had remained on the plat until
the early November darkness fell and then he had driven
back through town and out to Buckeye Heights. Believing
his wife to have gone to her mother's, he had dined alone
and spent the evening at his club.

Bratton studied this report conscientiously, vague dissent possessing him. From three till after five Thayre said
he had been wandering among the vacant lots of a real
estate subdivision. A hole might be punched in that as an
alibi. . . . The inspector made a note to have Becker get
in touch with the prospect with whom Thayre had had
an appointment. Another item continued to tease him.
He must get it by the tail. Ah, so that was it. . . . Milly's
statement and Thayre's had not quite agreed. Thayre said
his wife had told him she might go on to Green's Mill to
see her mother; Milly said her mistress had said nothing
of the sort to her and had even discussed the dinner dessert. Well, the answer to that was that Mrs. Thayre had
been thoughtful about her husband's meals, Bratton told
himself, and tried to forget the detail by wondering why
it had taken Thayre an hour to get from his office to the
mortuary the morning before.

What this sort of speculation would have led to was
postponed for the time, as a clerk now informed Bratton
that the women he had sent for had arrived.

The first to be ushered in was the one who had occupied fitting room A, the woman who had refused to inspect anything except models in green. Even Bratton, who
was no more style conscious than an Airedale, felt that the
jaunty sports outfit in what he would have described as a
raw green was too youthful for her lank figure.

He consulted the notes spread out before him. "I see—
you are Miss Spinner. A school teacher, you told us—"

"I informed you that I am a supervisor of methods."

"I get you—a kind of section boss or drill sergeant—
Well, here's what I wanted to ask you about—I won't need
to detain you but a minute. You spoke of a noise like a
thud. Do you think it was the sound a body might make
in falling?"

"It was much more like—like feet hitting the floor,
though I warn you I shouldn't feel justified in testifying to
that effect." Yankee caution had obviously possessed Miss
Spinner.

"You also heard whoever was in the room next say 'Busy.'
If the occasion arises, do you think you could identify the
voice that spoke?" Bratton demanded briskly.

"I certainly heard that one word very distinctly indeed.
Yes, I believe I could conscientiously—"

"Good. I'll let you know if I need you. That's all. Good
morning."

Miss Spinner would have been only too glad to assist
the police authorities with her keen analytical mind but
their inhospitality left her to do her theorizing on the
French Room murder, as the newspapers had immediately headlined it, with only her pedagogical colleagues for
audience.

There was next waiting for Inspector Bratton's summons a woman with whom he had not yet talked, the customer whom Grace Ramby had taken into B. As the saleswoman had already stated, this patron had stayed only a
few minutes. Grace Ramby knew her customer's name, but
when the police had first tried to get in touch with her
they were told that she had left town. Bratton promptly
satisfied himself that it was in no sense a significant absence—she had driven to her sister's college to attend the
girl's debut in dramatics, it developed—but as he had not
yet heard what she might have to report he was eager to see
this next candidate for inquisition.

According to Bratton's memorandum her name should be Mrs. Wellington Lewis. It was. . . . She was a level-eyed alert young matron, the sort, who no doubt regarded the present occasion as one that demanded her to do her Civic Duty with capitals. Also, it was evident that she had her information neatly marshalled, her fellow customers having already figured in the newspaper accounts.

Yes, she recalled that Miss Ramby had tapped experimentally upon another door before they stepped into booth B. . . . No, she herself had not heard any sort of sound from C during the few seconds that she and her clerk hovered uncertainly in the narrow passage. . . . She had been in the fitting room almost no time at all. The frock she had taken a fancy to was too small and she hadn't a minute to waste. The friends with whom she was motoring to Oldham were waiting for her and they could park on Hamilton Street only fifteen minutes, so she had made a point of hurrying right out of the store. She hadn't even taken time to stop to speak to Madame Nordhoff when she passed her. She wanted her to call her when the Callot replicas came in. . . .

Just where had Mrs. Lewis passed Madame Nordhoff, Bratton inquired.

Near the entrance to the passage. . . . She was hurrying out so bent upon her business that they had almost collided, but Madame Nordhoff had brushed by as if she hadn't noticed.

Inspector Bratton made a careful note and thanked Mrs. Lewis for her clear statement and then asked a final question. Had Miss Ramby already left the fitting alcove?

Mrs. Lewis was not sure; she thought so. . . .

Mrs. Ludlow Wilkinson was next produced. It appeared that she had been made to wait for more minutes than she thought she could spare and she was now more than slightly out of breath and inclined to be edgy.

"I have but one question to ask you this morning, Mrs. Wilkinson. Your report the other afternoon was so exceptionally clear—"

The lady breathed a bit more deeply and relaxed somewhat.

"It's this: how is it that you are so positive that there was no disturbance in the fitting room opposite yours, where Mrs. Thayre's body was found?"

"For no reason, I guess, except that I could hear scraps of what was going on all around me, and I surely would have heard anything unusual right across that narrow passage, wouldn't I? That stands to reason, young man."

Dan Bratton was getting just bald enough to like being called young man.

"For instance, what did you hear?" he asked.

"I heard the girl that was waiting on that poor creature say something about she'd be back in just a minute—she'd left her book at the desk. And I heard someone else say, 'Don't bother to show me unless you have my size in green.' And when I started toward the fitting alcove I heard some woman say, 'Madame Nordhoff is waiting on me herself, thank you. She'll be with me in a minute no doubt.' But that didn't come from the fitting rooms. And all the time the customer in the cubby just next to mine talked on and on—a regular monologue, I assure you—all about Junior's teeth and how she got her husband to eat spinach and how much her doctor's bill was and were her arms too fat for sleeveless dresses and what happened to a friend of hers who got a permanent at a new place in the Arcade. It was quite like spinning the dial on a radio—reception was good. But not a sound did I get from the station across after the clerk said she'd go get her salesbook."

There was no disputing Mrs. Ludlow Wilkinson. Instead, Bratton asked amiably, "How long have you lived in this town?"

"All my life," she assured him.

"What do you know about these Thayres?"

"Nothing at all. That is—I believe I had met the first Mrs. Thayre once or twice. And that's an odd thing, by the way. . . . That woman came into my mind that very afternoon. Why I should think of her I don't know. I could scarcely have claimed acquaintance with her. It was just that we were on the same committee or something like that." Mrs. Wilkinson unfolded a handkerchief that smelled of lilac water and discreetly blew her nose.

"Let's see—that would be how many years ago?" Bratton asked.

"Ten or eleven. It must have been during the campaign the women's clubs put on for more public playgrounds," replied Mrs. Wilkinson, returning the handkerchief to its place in her hand bag.

"I'm going to be very frank with you, Mrs. Wilkinson. You are an intelligent woman; you know something about association of ideas. I've a notion that there was some very real reason why you should have been reminded of the first Mrs. Thayre that afternoon. Do you suppose you could discover what it was?"

Mrs. Wilkinson was both flattered and startled and, for the moment, incapable of speech. Bratton allowed his suggestion to explain itself.

"Do you mean—that maybe I saw Mrs. Thayre—the first one—and didn't actually recognize her?" Mrs. Wilkinson breathed heavily and her voice fell to a conspiratorial whisper.

Dan Bratton had scarcely gone that far himself in his theory of the association of ideas, but he was quite willing to agree.

Then, as Mrs. Wilkinson afterwards analyzed the moment, her native common sense came back and with a snap of her fingers she dismissed the idea. "No. No, I have an excellent memory for faces. If I had seen any woman who made me think of the former Mrs. Thayre, I should have known it—absolutely."

The heavy natural color in her cheeks deepened apoplectically and her eyes blinked with new determination. "I know it's none of my business, Inspector, but then—you've dragged me into this yourself. There's just one thing that I can't feel quite right about, though for all I know I may be doing the poor girl a grave injustice, yet someway or other I think I ought to mention it—"

It was all that Bratton could do to refrain from an impatient reaction that would surely have antagonized the lady who was about to become confidential. "Yes, Mrs. Wilkinson?" he coaxed.

"That girl—the one that waited on me. She was awfully excited about something. I had to tell her three times that I wouldn't consider anything with an uneven hem line."

"You mean—?"

"I don't mean a thing—not a thing, except that if I were the police I'd make it my business to find out what got her so upset." Mrs. Ludlow Wilkinson rose to go. "And there's another thing that I want distinctly understood. I fully appreciate, of course, that when I am in the hands of the authorities there are certain matters that are quite beyond my control, or my husband's, but beyond that I will not go. I have declined to be interviewed!"

On that declaration of probity she made her exit, leaving an amused inspector to bear the sins of an aggressive press. For an instant Bratton considered the sport there might be if he should sic Paula Pringle on to this retiring personality, but the business in hand soon did for this play-boy impulse. He fumbled about among the layers of papers before him and brought to the surface the slip upon which he had sketched the layout of the block of fitting rooms. Frowning, he bent over it. . . . Then, on a fresh sheet from his memorandum pad he made a set of neat queries:

1. Could Miss Spinner in A have heard some-one jumping down into E to do murder or into C after murder had been done?
2. Why was Mrs. Nordhoff so perturbed that she failed to speak to Mrs. Lewis, who was coming from B?
3. Where is the unknown woman in C? Why was she putting on light gloves when J. Terry saw her leaving the dressing rooms? The other clerks report dark gloves. What's the chance she is Thayre's first wife?
4. If the equally unknown woman in D did all the chattering Mrs. L. W. says she did, is she worth investigating?
5. Who took Mrs. Thayre's bag? Why?
6. What woman was Nordhoff waiting on? The Pike girl's statement about shoes points to a lie somewhere. Whose?

It was, somewhat characteristic of Dan Bratton's methods of investigation that after he had thus reduced to writing some of his random reflections he crumpled the paper that bore them and thrust it into his pocket. He seldom gave such notations any further conscious reflection, yet they sometimes bore surprising results.

He had just reminded himself again of his eleven o'clock appointment when a clerk edged in to announce that a swell dame had just blown in who thought she had something to spill about the Thayre woman.

Bratton had a possible margin of ten minutes. The blare of publicity that he had counted on to add to his still meagre store of facts known about that last day of Vivian

Thayre's life had not yet yielded much. Perhaps this would be only another dud, perhaps not. He ordered her in.

An exceedingly decorative lady made her entrance. She cast a practiced eye upon Bratton and smiled lushly.

"I am Mrs. Herman Kinzig," she announced. "My husband has no idea that I've come up here, but it seemed the only decent thing to do, seeing that we practically lunched together the day she was killed. It's not that I know Vivian so awfully well—our husbands had met in a business way. I liked her a lot, though, considering the short time I'd been going places and doing things with her."

"You say you lunched with Mrs. Thayre?" The inspector had to think of eleven o'clock.

"I'll tell you. . . . When I went into Margot's for lunch day before yesterday, there she was all by herself at a table. She saw me and I went across and sat down with her and we ordered together. It was just an accidental meeting, you understand."

"How much time would the luncheon account for, Mrs. Kinzig?"

"It was maybe a quarter of one when I went in and I suppose we were there nearly an hour."

"Did Mrs. Thayre mention her plans for the afternoon?"

Mrs. Kinzig's permanented blondeur made a decisive negation. "Nothing except that she'd seen a dress at Line's that she was crazy to try on. She hated that department at Line's, she said, and never bought anything there, but she was afraid she couldn't resist this dress. That's the only thing she said about plans. . . . You see, she was telling me her troubles."

"Ah-h," Bratton sighed gently. This was the sort of thing he had been praying would break. "What sort of troubles?"

"Well, I mean, she didn't exactly say things in so many words . . . but she'd got a letter that scared her."

Bratton beamed at the enameled lady. This was good stuff. The missing letter that should have been where the jade bracelet was found.

"Mrs. Kinzig, if you can give me exact details of any sort it is your solemn duty to do so." The inspector's voice reverberated with authority.

"It was one of these anonymous letters," Mrs. Kinzig added with a promptness intended to show her complete willingness to cooperate with the forces of law and order. "I tried to tell her that nobody ought ever to pay any attention to stuff like that, but it didn't have much effect on her. It was her guilty conscience, I suppose."

Mrs. Herman Kinzig was pressed to elucidate that remark.

"We-ell, she'd got a crazy idea that Rupert—her husband was running after someone else, and that he knew that she knew, and so she actually thought he might have sent her this letter himself to shut her up, you see. Because of course he knew—"

She stopped suddenly as though cooperation with the authorities was carrying her too far. But the look in Bratton's steady eyes compelled her.

She laughed uncertainly. "You see, Vivian's a person that always had lots of admiring friends herself. And, believe me, it always made her sore when one of 'em tried to drop out of the picture, like—"

"Like Ross Ingram, for instance?"

"Why, Inspector, you know everything, don't you?"

The Kinzig dimples broke through the enameled complexion.

"Not about that anonymous letter, I don't. You'd better tell me everything that was said about it," Again Bratton sounded portentously official.

"Oh, I will—I'll certainly try to! But she didn't mention any names, really she didn't. As near as I could tell from what she said about the letter, it said she was to leave a certain person alone or she'd never be able to wish she had, and I said to Viv that I thought that sounded like a death threat, and she said she was ready to do some killing herself if necessary, and—well, that's all, Inspector." Mrs. Kinzig fingered her vanity case as if she suspected that frankness with the police would lead inevitably to shininess of the nose.

"Did you see this letter?" Bratton asked hopefully.

The blonde head shook emphatically.

"Do you think she had it with her—in her bag, say?"

"No. At least there wasn't a thing said to make me think so."

"You say Mrs. Thayre thought her husband might have written this letter to shield himself. Know who the woman is in his case?"

The little smile on Mrs. Kinzig's carmined lips almost trembled, but not quite. "Oh, Inspector," she murmured, "you make me feel like a sneak. . . . I did tell Vivian there was nothing to it, but I suppose I must tell you that about a month or so ago one night I saw Rupert Thayre having a petting party on a park bench. I couldn't see the girl, but I'm sure it was Rupert."

"But suppose Ingram wrote the letter?"

Mrs. Kinzig's eyes rolled expressively. "He might have, at that, Inspector. Viv was crazy about him and thought she had him just where she wanted him, but I don't know. . . . He was a lot of fun, though."

"There's another thing I'd like to know—where Ross Ingram is this minute."

"That's easy, Inspector. I drove in by Hearthstone Manor this morning—that's the Kendall place, you know—and I saw his car just turning in the drive. To give you the dirt straight, I think Ross is planning to ditch all his girl friends because he thinks he has a chance to annex the Kendall millions."

11

Two Pairs of Feet

Inspector Bratton delayed his run out to the Thayre house only long enough to issue orders that ought to produce the elusive Mr. Ingram, with any sort of luck. Immediately upon dismissing Mrs. Herman Kinzig he had put a telephone call through to Connie Kendall and he had found her curiously willing to assist the police in any way she could. It occurred to Bratton that Connie was getting bravely over her fancy for Ross Ingram. It might take the rest of the day to round up the gentleman. . . . Meanwhile, he'd see what Mrs. Agnew had to tell him.

The trim hedges of the Buckeye Heights house were beringed with the curious and idle, but Bratton approached from the road beyond and entered through Milly's kitchen. With muted tch-tch's the girl was opening box after box of funereal flowers, but one glance at the array of vases told even Bratton that her gift was not floral arrangement.

"See the lovely flowers been sent to the mister a'ready, and the funeral not till tomorrow yet. . . ."

The inspector was not concerned with the floral expressions of sympathy that were being lavished upon Rupert Thayre. He had come to see the man's mother-in-law, Mrs. Agnew.

The interview took place in an upper room furnished as a combined den and office and obviously intended for

Thayre's use. Bratton looked curiously at the woman who met him in the hall and ushered him within. Mrs. Agnew was a dark, grave person and at first her long pale face was washed clean of any emotion.

"There is no need for us to mince matters, Inspector," she began and her voice revealed the same deliberate restraint. "My daughter—my only daughter has been murdered and I anticipate that sooner or later the town will ring with scandal. That is the reason I do not shrink from the consequences of the matter I want to call to your attention. It is something that I believe Vivian never told a soul but me. . . . It happened just before she married Mr. Thayre."

Mrs. Agnew paused and drank half the contents of the glass of medicine that had been in her hand when she met the detective at the head of the stairs.

"You know about the divorce, I imagine," she resumed in her level manner, "so there's no need of going into that. It wasn't what I should have chosen for my girl. . . . Vivian was a pretty girl—popular, you know. She always had lots of beaus, even though we lived in a small place like Green's Mill. But naturally a girl like Vivian wasn't satisfied there and right after she graduated from high school I had to let her go off to Columbus to learn shorthand and typewriting—she gave me no peace. She was engaged to one of the home boys then, though she wasn't eighteen. Clint Avery's got the Buick agency now . . . and there were plenty more she could have had, but the minute she got to the bigger town the home boys never had a chance.

"There was one man in Columbus I still wish she had married, a young doctor. Excuse me, Inspector, I'm afraid I'm just reminiscing. What I want to get to is the way poor Vivian got mixed into Mr. Thayre's divorce. It seems he saw her in an office over in Columbus. It was her first job after she left the Commercial College and she was doing well and going to all the frat dances at State. But Mr. Thayre offered her so much more to work for him that of course she didn't hesitate about taking it. She always sent me money. . . . Then it wasn't very long after she got settled here that his wife began to stir up talk and trouble and all that. Vivian couldn't help it that men always got crazy over her. . . . Anyway, Rupert Thayre surely did the right thing. He never gave the girl any peace after the decree until she married him.

"There was so much talk and all that Vivian came down home during the worst of it, and that's when the thing happened that I have decided you ought to know about now. I wasn't at home, the morning the woman came, but Vivian was so upset about it and cried so, that I soon had the whole story out of her. It seems that Mr. Thayre's wife, who had caused all the trouble and accused Vivian of such terrible things, had followed her down to Green's Mill and threatened her very life."

Mrs. Agnew again paused in her toneless narrative as if she expected Bratton to draw his own conclusions. But Bratton so far was more interested in Vivian Thayre's mother than in the story she was telling him.

His only comment was: "An immediate or a longtime threat?"

For an instant Mrs. Agnew's mournful dark eyes looked blank; then a slow flicker of comprehension appeared in their depths. "Even if Vivian was my very own, I can understand that the other woman probably hated her. I knew what she meant when Vivian told me that there was something—venomous in the way she spoke to her that morning. Sooner or later, she said, God would give her a chance to help punish the woman who had wrecked her happiness—"

"Was it all talk? Did she do anything?"

"She cursed her—Vivian said it was terrible, but no, she didn't lay as much as a finger on her."

"Mrs. Agnew, do you know what became of this woman?"

"No, I do not. I never heard, except that she had gone to New York. That was right after the decree was granted. But mark my words—" Here for the first time the emotion that had been so carefully held in leash flared into the woman's dull, heavy eyes. She rose to her feet and stepped toward Bratton. "Mark my words, it must have been that woman who murdered my daughter!"

She swayed with sudden weakness and sank back into her chair, but the hand that reached for the remainder of the sedative did not tremble. "I've been told not to let anything—anything, even murder—excite me," she murmured in grim explanation.

Bratton did not put much weight upon Mrs. Agnew's statement, for it was based upon so flimsy a premise, though he recognized that the mother's agitation was quite natural. He inquired politely, "Do you think you would recognize the first Mrs. Thayre if you were to see her now?"

"I never laid eyes on her, I'm sorry to say."

The inspector sighed gently and then took the initiative himself. "Now if you are feeling able to and will be so good as to answer just a few questions about some other matters that have come up in the course of our investigations—"

Mrs. Agnew nodded and closed her eyes. Her face looked like a death mask.

"On the day that your daughter met her death we have learned that she purchased a fitted traveling bag, had it charged to her account at Line's, but ordered it sent to Miss Vivian Agnew at Green's Mill. It was so delivered, I suppose? Have you any idea what she meant by that?"

These questions apparently reanimated Mrs. Agnew. She opened her eyes, leaned forward, and gave every appearance of a person who was for the first time putting certain two's and two's together. Then she relaxed and her features set with caution.

"I remember. The bag came yesterday just before I left Green's Mill, but to tell you the truth I never noticed how it was addressed. Anything with the Agnew name on it is always taken in by the girl who does my work and no questions asked. Vivian must have meant it for a present for me."

For the first time since they had been talking tears filled the mother's eyes, but for some reason Bratton was conscious of a quick suspicion of the woman's sincerity.

In a moment she went on speaking. "I never had much to go on when Vivian was a little girl. That was the reason she was so set on being able to earn her own living. Then after she married she had no more worries like that, and she was always awfully good to me, too. . . . And then only last month we got the money my uncle left us—"

"What!" ejaculated Bratton. This was something that might open up an unconsidered motive.

"Just an annuity to me, but seventy-five thousand dollars in Liberty Bonds to Vivian. Uncle Eben always said she looked exactly like his mother. He lived and died an old bachelor. He was one of the queer Underwoods. Cousin Theodoric is going to be another. . . ."

Bratton brushed family traits aside impatiently. "Was this money left outright to her? No strings to it?"

"It was."

"I wonder—did Mrs. Thayre die intestate?"

"Have I had the heart to think of such things yet?" she rebuked him. "Vivian had a pretty good business head, and at the time Uncle Eben's estate was settled I know she went to see a lawyer here in the city about something."

Bratton took leave of Mrs. Agnew with his interest far more centered upon the likely motive that seventy-five thousand dollars might have been for the murder of Vivian Thayre than upon the old threat that a frenzied and heart-broken woman had made at the moment of the crashing of her happiness. He paused in the kitchen long enough to show Milly the grey envelope and ask her to keep a watchful eye for any letters she might come upon written on that sort of paper. Milly's stubby fingers examined the texture of the paper and she agreed to be careful, but her interest was still centered upon the constantly arriving florists' boxes. A grey letter might be thrust among waste paper or between the pages of a book or magazine somewhere, Bratton explained.

As he left the kitchen and walked around the side of the house toward the front he decided that after all the most logical place to expect the missing letter to appear would be in the bag that Vivian Thayre had been carrying at the time she met her death. The bag had disappeared. Had the murderer carried it off? Was it possible that something in her ornamental hand bag had cost Vivian Thayre her life?

Before his speculations had a chance to leap to more fantastic lengths a slight figure catapulted against him and he felt his arm seized chummily. It was Paula Pringle in person.

"Hello, sweetie," she caroled, "I got a peach of a squeegee for you!"

"Is that all?"

"You ungrateful brute! You ought to fall on my neck. The print of Thayre's first wife is plenty swell, but the one crumb of news I scraped up for you maybe isn't so hot. If you're driving me back to town, I'll tell you about it," she bargained.

Bratton's only invitation was the prompt opening of the door of the official flivver and Paula as promptly climbed

in. As soon as they were headed toward town, she began
to talk.

"It's this, old dear: Biddy Muldoon down at our shop,
you know—the one who does the *They Say* column—says
that Mary Whitford Thayre or Mary Thayre Whitford,
whichever way she arranged her name, went out to the
Pacific coast and married again. The only intimate friend
she had here, according to Biddy, is dead now, so it's kind
of hard to check up—"

"You said it, sister!" The inspector's words were emphatic. "New York or California—take your choice. Where's
that print?"

"At your office. And now what does a good, helpful
little girl get?"

"A ride back to town, which you've already asked for."

"Aw, Danny, have a heart. I gotta have a story, honest I
do," wheedled the brown-eyed imp beside him.

"The one I had in mind isn't ready yet. You know I
won't let you down, kid. But you might see what you can
raise with this. . . . Vivian Thayre inherited about seventy-
five grand a few weeks ago."

"Oh, lovely—I get you, Danny. . . . I'm hopping off
right here. Thanks a whole lot."

Bratton sped on to Headquarters, for he wanted a look
at the picture of the first Mrs. Thayre. Besides, there might
be news about Ross Ingram. But there was nothing helpful
waiting among the routine reports he found on his desk.
The promised print he found in a plain manila envelope
under his blotter, just as Paula had said. Bratton looked
long at the face thus disclosed. His first thought was that
the woman must have been older than her husband. There
was a classic serenity about her features, and her dark hair
was parted in the middle, drawn loosely down over her
ears, and coiled low on her neck. In spite of the drooping

lids there was something unhappy, almost inscrutable, in her eyes.

Certainly none of the women whom the inspector had questioned bore the slightest resemblance to Mary Whitford. There remained the woman in booth C. . . . If by the long arm of coincidence she should be the wronged wife, there were those at Line and Hollis's who must be shown the picture at once. He'd take it down now and tell Jessica Brooke. . . .

Unfortunately for Inspector Dan Bratton, as he was about to leave his desk, there came an imperative knock upon his door, though all that entered was a voice. "Come on over!" it boomed.

It was the Commissioner. Promptly as Bratton jumped to follow, his superior was already lolling in a swivel chair that had a doleful squeak and he managed to convey the impression that he had been kept waiting interminably. It appeared that the Chief wished to know just when he might expect an arrest. Nor was there anything particularly polite about the phrasing of his inquiries.

Bratton knew well enough what that meant. If he could not show results within a day or so, the investigation would be handed over to that insufferable young amateur whom the Chief affected and Detective-Inspector Bratton would be sent to round up poolroom proprietors who had not scrapped their slot machines in accordance with the decree of the local Vice Commission. There was nothing to gain by boasting of hot leads that had just come to light. He knew that the Chief considered all his methods too soft.

In due time he left the presence meekly and hurried off to seek the more soothing society of Jessica Brooke. He entered her office as unobtrusively as possible, seeing that everyone on the floor appeared to recognize him at once, which was doubtless what his ego needed after his session on the carpet. He slid into the chair opposite hers and permitted himself a doleful sigh.

The store detective's eyebrows arched into a question which he answered with another exaggerated sigh.

"Behold a cop that can't get results. Look quick, or all you'll see is a poor runt who once thought he was a sort of slick dick, but he's just been—er—deflated."

Jessica Brooke laughed lightly. "Do you mean to tell me that the Big Bow-Wow down there actually worries you chaps?"

"Only look at me—I'm the answer. But, no foolin', we're not getting anywhere very fast, are we?"

"I certainly love the way it's *we* when nothing's right—"

"Aw, now—it will be *we,* too, if I—er—we ever get the damn mess straightened out."

"Keep your despair to yourself just a little longer. You want to talk to some of our girls again, don't you? Maybe that will clear something up. Any choice about who comes first?"

"No, just so Mrs. Nordhoff comes in some time or other. . . . And while I'm busy here suppose you take this"— he produced the photographer's print of Mary Whitford—"and see if anyone who might have seen the woman in C thinks this might be her picture."

Bratton had no chance to check his assistant's reaction to the pictured face, for the first of the clerks whom he was to interview again appeared at the moment he handed over the print. It was Grace Ramby and he had a question he had had in reserve for her for twenty-four hours.

"About this chap whom you noticed waiting out where all those comfortable chairs are . . . did he stay put all the time?"

"I didn't watch him all the time, sir," replied the methodical Miss Ramby, "but once I saw him walking back to his chair, as if he had been strolling around maybe."

"From what direction?" Bratton asked quickly.

"From the far end of the reception corridor."

"When was this?"

"It was after I came out from room B and before I knew anything had happened—I mean before Miss Brooke and Mr. Galway and Madame Nordhoff got to running around."

Edith Pike followed Miss Ramby. Gaunt, homely Ede Pike whom customers asked for more often than for any other member of the department . . . but who was not promoted to the place that Madame Nordhoff had been imported to fill.

Bratton had a direct question ready for Ede Pike.

"Your customer advises me that you were strangely excited during the party the other afternoon. How about it?"

Ede's pale lips narrowed but she hesitated only an instant. "Not excited—just sort of curious."

"More promising still. Curious about—feet?"

"You've said it, Inspector. I told you, didn't I, that I recognized Joyce's shoes going into E—"

"But that you did not observe that she came right out again—as she states."

"Well, the reason I didn't is that I was thinking of something else—you know how you do." Ede rubbed her long nose mercilessly. "I mean I hardly realized at the time what I was thinking, see. Afterwards it came to me that I was wondering whose feet I thought were Joyce's. . . ."

Bratton was inclined to listen with respectful attention, but these convolutions were almost more than he could follow unless she meant. . . .

He voiced his hope. "Do you mean you saw another pair of feet go into booth E?"

"I must have," Ede Pike answered shortly, as if she herself was still puzzled.

"Well?" prompted Bratton.

"Or coming out . . ." she amended. "At any rate, there in the passage between the two fitting rooms."

"But you recognized the feet as Miss Terry's?"

"I didn't say exactly that," she flashed. "I said I recognized the shoes—and that's what I got to thinking about."

The inspector moved impatiently. "See here, if you can explain just what you do mean, for heaven's sake, snap into it."

"I do sound like a half-wit, don't I?" and her sudden smile was quite man-to-man. "I thought it was Joyce going into E because I saw familiar looking shoes, but without my knowing it scarcely I was thinking to myself that there was something not just right about those shoes, if they were Joyce's, see, . . . I've been thinking about it ever since and last night, Inspector, it came to me what was wrong. The shoes were just like Joyce's except that they were at least a size and a half larger. That's why they didn't look just right to me."

Bratton shook his head skeptically. "I'm not so hot about this coincidence stuff, sister."

Ede Pike stretched out a knuckled hand earnestly. "There's nothing wildly impossible about it, Inspector. Joyce always wears inexpensive shoes. She gets them at Hanby's and they sell thousands of pairs of every model they show. It just means that somebody else wears Hanby shoes too."

"Um-m, well—maybe, Miss Pike." Purposely Dan Bratton sounded more grudging than he felt. "That's all for this time. There's a kid called Dottie that I want to see next. Send her along, will you?"

Dottie did not immediately appear and while he waited Bratton made a mental survey of the various women whom he had already examined in the course of his work on the case. The shoes worn by Joyce Terry he had observed carefully the instant Edith Pike had made her first comment about them during his first round of questions. Although he had not checked the point specifically, he could rely safely enough on his memory to be sure that no other woman, whether staff member or customer, had been shod in anything resembling the plain patent leather pump worn by Joyce Terry. The peculiar feature of the small buckle he could distinctly recall. Therefore Miss Millin's customer or the unknown woman in C were his only prospects. Unless . . . unless Ede Pike was going to rather ridiculous lengths to get the Terry girl out of a hole.

The door of the office banged; Dottie Cline popped in and gave the detective a wide-mouthed smile. A sharp-eyed kid like this should have seen whatever there was to see, thought Bratton.

His preliminaries were brief. "Now, Dottie," he went on, "the other afternoon when all this excitement happened you say you were in the stock room?"

Dottie acclaimed that such was her hard luck.

"But you and Miss Terry had left the fitting rooms at approximately the same time."

"Yes, uh-huh, though I didn't exactly see her. She musta been behind me."

"Yes, that's the way it was. Now what I want you to tell me is from what fitting rooms you had collected the dresses that you were carrying back to the stock racks."

"Sure, I will. Why, from the empty ones and the ones where they was through with tryin' on. Lemme see—I can't remember the letters on the doors so good. . . ." Bratton shoved his dog-eared diagram under her nose. "Yes, uh-huh," she went on. "I got it straight now. They was busy here in E and F, and in D Miss Millin handed me a armload, and in C there weren't none—"

"Hold on, kid. Just how do you mean that?"

Patiently Dottie explained that she meant there were no discarded dresses in booth C. Sure, there was a lady in there, a lady who acted kinda nervous. She was all dressed in her outside clo'es. Dottie had assumed that she was about to leave the compartment. No, she hadn't looked particular at the lady and she hadn't noticed her feet at all. All she could be sure of was that she was just putting on her hat when she, Dottie, butted in the way she did. It was a kind of tannish hat, a sport felt.

"So you left the fitting alcove with your load of duds and went back to the stock room. See anyone—or anything the least bit out of the ordinary?"

Dottie shook her wind-blown bob regretfully. "Not a thing. Just customers standin' around and way back in the stock room Madame Nordhoff. I was comin' out again when Miss Terry ast me to go get her quick, and that was the first place I beat it to, you know—but she was back on the floor by that time."

Bratton cast the child a swift, enlightened look. "Was anyone else in the stock room when you went back that second time, searching for Madame Nordhoff?"

"Somebody—Madge Allen, I guess—was back in the 38's, but not another soul. The girls was all busy just then—Poppa Knox was apologizing to some fussy dame about it."

"Where did you see him?" the inspector asked sharply, though his attention wanted to focus on the buyer of the department. It was high time he had a talk with the woman.

But Dottie's answer was so vague that he realized she must have made her complete contribution. He dismissed her and awaited the appearance of the buyer. Whatever Madame Nordhoff might have to say, about one point there was now little doubt in Bratton's mind. The unknown woman in C must have been the distraught creature who had collapsed shortly afterwards in the rest room, the one

Helen Joan Hultman

who had been trailed from the stationery department to the books, where she might have acquired a pair of scissors destined within a short time to wreak the death of Vivian Thayre. But had she passed through the bargain basement almost at closing time and deposited the blood-stained weapon in Norma Schmidt's stocking bin?

The door opened again, but it was Jessica Brooke, not Madame Nordhoff who appeared. "I'm sorry, Inspector, but Mrs. Nordhoff isn't in the store just now. She had to go over to the Anthony Wayne to see a new model the Ninon man's showing. . . . She'll be free the first thing after lunch, she said to tell you."

12

INGRAM'S TEA DATE

Moreover, Jessica Brooke had nothing encouraging to report concerning the print of Mary Whitford with which she had set forth. She had shown it to Emma in the rest room, to Norma Schmidt, to the girls in the books and the stationery, to the clerk at the notions, to Joyce of course—indeed, to the entire French Room staff from its head down.

"To the Dottie kid?" Bratton grunted.

"No, she was with you."

"Have her take a squint at it. And not a flicker, you say, from any of the others?"

"Not a sign. . . . Well, it was a grand idea while it lasted," mourned Jessica and departed to confront Dottie with the picture.

Almost immediately thereafter a little progress hailed the inspector from an unexpected quarter. Miss Brooke's telephone demanded attention. Obligingly Bratton took the call only to learn that Headquarters was paging its wandering member. Somebody over at the post office had unearthed something about the Thayre case and wanted whoever was in charge to drop around.

Within five minutes Bratton was climbing the post office steps in high anticipation of disclosures concerning

letters written on grey stationery. He found the superintendent of mails waiting for him and on the desk before
him lay a bag—a dark green hand bag.

"It's this," said the postal official. "It was picked up
in the package box at Court and Hamilton on the 11:40
collection—just as is. When I saw the cards in it, I called
your shop."

Bratton had not waited to be invited to examine the
bag. His first glance had told him that outwardly it con-
formed to the descriptions collected from the luggage
salesman and Joyce Terry. The contents of the bag left
no doubt, though they did not tell him enough. There
was money and a vanity compact and a card case. The
cards were engraved MRS. RUPERT THAYRE. There was
a handkerchief with an embroidered V. There was a nail
file and a little comb in a leather case, a tiny *flaçon* of
perfume and a clutter of keys. In the folds of the lining
were some ancient tobacco crumbs and one worn looking
aspirin tablet. But it was what was no longer in the bag
that Bratton found most significant There was nothing to
indicate that the bag had ever held a revolver. There were
no gloves. And, aside from the unsullied cards, there was
not a scrap of paper of any sort in the bag. If the letter
that had come in the grey envelope in which he had found
the jade bracelet was to play a role in the mystery of the
death of Vivian Thayre, it was yet to be found.

"Picked up at 11 :40, huh?" The inspector looked at his
watch. "Quick work, that. And the preceding collection
from the same box?"

"At 10:05, Inspector. I called Headquarters at once. . . .
The boys frequently bring in stuff like that. Pickpockets
go through their haul and chuck what they can't use in a
package box. Of course, it's not often that money comes
to light."

"Which means that no pickpocket dumped this bag Into the box. Much obliged. This ought to clear up a couple of little things," and Bratton lost no time in prolonged farewells.

However, he took time enough to walk back to Headquarters. For the moment his speculations were wholly centered upon the bag. Whoever had deposited it in the parcels collection box between a little after ten and twenty minutes to twelve might have slipped out of the huge department store that stood on one of the Hamilton and Court intersections. If so, then there were two possibilities. First, suppose it was the murderer who had thus rid himself of the bag. That would mean that in some way the murderer was associated with the department store. Again, suppose the person who stole the bag was not the murderer. Who could have had the opportunity to take the bag after the deed had been committed? Only two people, as Bratton saw it: Joyce Terry or Mrs. Nordhoff.

But what motive could either have had? Both women had denied knowing the murdered woman, had even denied recognizing her. Dan Bratton had felt an inner conviction of listening to the truth whenever the frightened girl spoke. Of the older woman he was not so sure. Her manner was too suavely controlled. She wouldn't make the world's worst poker player, he decided.

Before these thoughts reminded him that it might be wise to seek the two women at the department store, Bratton found himself entering his office at Headquarters. A man rose from a chair just inside the door.

He was sleekly well-dressed, but his manner betrayed a nervous bravado. "They've been telling me you want to see me," he said, but his eyes shifted before they met Bratton's steady blue gaze.

"If you are Ross Ingram—" the inspector began.

"That's my name," interrupted his caller and offered his cigarette case.

Swiftly Bratton rejected various approaches to the information he devoutly hoped this man had for him. It did not matter just now whether Ingram had reached Headquarters through the activity of his own men or because of the cooperation of Connie Kendall.

"It's about this Thayre case, of course, Ingram—damned peculiar mess. Galway tells me you were up there just about the time the excitement broke." His tone was willfully genial. "I'd like to know—anything you have to tell me."

Again Ingram's eyes shifted but not before Bratton saw them flicker with relief. His answer came promptly and his accent was full-voiced and hearty. "As a matter of fact, Inspector, I was up there, almost on the spot. You see, I had an appointment for tea with a friend of mine and I was meeting her up there in the foyer or whatever they call the entrance to that French shop of Line's—at least, I was supposed to meet her." He stopped and shrugged his shoulders patiently, as if to add, "These ladies—bless their lack of reliability!"

"So the lady did not keep her appointment?"

"No, I waited till long past the time and then—"

"And then you left the store and went around to your rooms at the Peg Top Club, had the hall boy there call you a taxi which you did not use, and left town—but you did not go to Chicago."

Ross Ingram laughed tolerantly. "Been checking up, haven't you, Inspector?"

'That's my job, Ingram, and that's why I must ask you to tell me the name of the lady whom you expected to meet at Line's."

"You've got me now, Inspector, but I'll have to be frank, of course. I didn't know the lady's name. She was a—pick-up, if you must have it," and Ingram allowed one eye-lid to droop significantly.

"Umph, that's just too bad. It puts you in a nasty hole, see. What if you had to establish an alibi? Could you produce the lady?"

"What do you mean—alibi?" Ingram's heavy face stiffened and the hand that held his cigarette permitted ash to dribble untidily.

"We won't say alibi then; I know you were there at the time Mrs. Thayre met her death. What we want to be sure of is—what was your real reason for being up there at that time?"

"Sure, I could produce the lady, all right." Ingram's reply came with more haste than sincerity. "But why drag me in on this?"

"This is the reason, Ingram . . ." and Dan Bratton pulled from his pocket the jade bracelet and swung it lazily to and fro.

Ross Ingram's eyes narrowed angrily and then he pulled himself together in an attempt at suavity. "I don't quite understand you, Inspector—sorry."

"Oh, yes, you do. We happen to know that you bought this bracelet for a Miss Kendall. It was found in Mrs. Thayre's bedroom. You won't be fool enough to deny that you and Vivian Thayre were—pretty good friends, let's say. Well, then—what if the idea gets out that you and Mrs. Thayre had agreed to meet at the entrance to the French Room at Line's. Your desire to break with her in order to have a free hand with Miss Kendall would shape up as a motive. Add to that your precipitate departure from town within an hour after the murder— The department is watching you with interest."

"Framing me, by God! I can explain about the bracelet." Ingram's truculence had been but momentary; he was frankly placating now.

Bratton said nothing weightily, an effective course. Within two minutes Ross Ingram was wetting his lips.

"About the bracelet—it was like this, Inspector. I bought it for Connie—for Miss Kendall, see. The kid had taken a yen for it and then when she got what she wanted, she changed her mind. I agreed to exchange the damn thing for something else she thought she wanted more—you know how women are. Before I had a chance to run into Emanuel's with it, Mrs. Thayre—" He stopped with suspicious abruptness and then went on, too smoothly. "I happened to meet Mrs. Thayre and I was reminded that we'd had a little bet up, which I hadn't paid and—well, the bracelet was just in payment of this little bet, see. And a kind of farewell gift, too." He gave a sentimental sigh and glanced warily at the stony-faced inspector. Then he risked what was plainly intended to be a final statement. "We had been friends—yes, but she was happily married and I had no wish to embarrass her. In short, we had already determined to see no more of one another."

Bratton's eyes glinted like blue ice. "So the bracelet was the symbol of the grand renunciation, was it? That's a great story, Ingram—it sure is! Under those circumstances, then, it must have been rather embarrassing to run into her that afternoon at Line's, especially when you were there to meet another lady, whose name you hadn't bothered to learn."

"I've told you I didn't know Mrs. Thayre was there. I didn't even see her," Ingram reiterated peevishly.

"That's where this unknown girl-friend of yours could do you a mighty kind turn."

"If she wasn't there, and I told you she failed to keep the appointment, how the hell could she prove I was there?"

Bratton did not answer the question, but he scored one for Ross Ingram. It was not necessary to explain the

exact nature of the kind turn that he might ask the unknown lady to perform. "In that case," he went on slowly,
"suppose you tell me how you left the building. Perhaps
someone you passed on your way out can help verify your
movements."

Ingram glared resentfully but did not refuse to reply. "I
went to the nearest elevator and down to the street floor,
as anyone naturally would. I left by the Court Street door
and went on to the club where I live. I was in a hurry because I wanted to make a bus—I had a business appointment in Detroit."

"When did you leave Detroit for Chicago?"

"Yesterday noon. I was held there longer than I expected. I wired Miss Kendall, as you have already informed
yourself. I got out of Chi on the midnight to find myself
wanted by the police when I hit town this morning."

Ingram paused as though he expected sympathy or
commendation. He received neither. The inspector's dour
silence was making him nervous. After an uneasy interval he broke forth resentfully. "It's true that I knew Mrs.
Thayre and that I had the bad luck to be up there at the
store yesterday when some crazy dame did her in, but outside of that what in hell could you have on me?"

Bratton raised one eyebrow a trifle but there was something about the gesture that added nothing to Ingram's
equanimity. "What have we on you? Nothing—I sincerely
hope. But you were there, as you quite cheerfully admit.
Your tea date was for four-thirty, you say?"

Ingram nodded.

"And you reached the French Room at Line's about
four-twenty?"

Another nod.

"And waited—"

"Till after five. Then I—"

"Rather a long wait, I'd say, Ingram. Comfortable chairs and all that up there, no doubt, but you didn't stay put, did you?"

Ingram stared at him, apparently uncomprehending.

"Perhaps this is what we have on you, Ingram. You see, you were observed while you were waiting in the reception corridor. You were seen to return from the general direction of the fitting rooms just shortly before the murder was discovered."

"I swear I never left the divan—" The abrupt pause told its own story. He laughed weakly and made much ado over lighting another cigarette. "Why, yes, I did too, now that you speak of it. It was a bore waiting, and I prowled about a bit hunting a water cooler or drinking fountain."

"Exactly," agreed the inspector pleasantly. "And you found one in the recess just beyond the elevators?"

Ingram's slow nod was plainly apprehensive.

"The other end of that recess happens to lead to the entrance to the fitting rooms." Bratton's explanation sounded very genial. "And, as I believe I mentioned, we have a fine, upstanding little witness who saw you coming from there just after the murder had been committed."

"Good God, Inspector—" Ingram's lips could only shape the words, not sound them.

"So whenever you—er—remember the name of the lady you 'picked up,' I'll be mighty glad to talk to you again." Bratton rose briskly. "Until then, that will be all. Good day."

By the time Ross Ingram reached the street Jeff Gryce, whom Bratton had promptly detailed to follow him, was already on the job, but for the moment Ingram was too dazed to be wary. From the window above the inspector watched him make off down the street.

"If the poor coot wasn't so yellow," he was thinking, "he'd know that if there was a real chance of pinning this thing on him, I'd be there with a jumbo safety. But he couldn't have known just where Mrs. Thayre was trying on her dress—he says he didn't know she was there, but I can take a chance on thinking she was expecting somebody up there at half past four. . . . He might have helped himself to scissors from the cashier's desk, but the little girl there who had her eye on him would have said so if he'd strolled over to her desk. . . . Another thing, he couldn't have got away from the fitting room, if he were the murderer, without blood on him somewhere, if it was only in a pocket where he might have stuck the scissors. But I'll be damned if he's the coldblooded type that could have strolled back nonchalantly after a party like that to lounge there on the divan where Galway saw him—and that's another trick I oughtn't to miss. . . ."

Inspector Bratton shot a glance at his watch and seized his hat. "Good Lord, the Nordhoff!" Once more he left Headquarters bound for Line and Hollis's.

13

Inventory of Suspects

The afternoon was mounting steadily toward its peak when Dan Bratton again appeared on the fourth floor of Line and Hollis's. He made his way first to the cashier's desk and had a few minutes' chat with the girl who folded gowns and wrapped boxes. Her part of the dialogue was marked by much nodding and pointing and one or two vehement negative gestures. After that he strolled along the reception corridor, pausing now and then as if lost in thought. One of these stops was made by a divan that might have been the objective of one of the obliging wrapper's wide-flung gestures. Certainly the inspector shifted the cushions about, more or less absent-mindedly, and even circled the piece of furniture before he moved on, more briskly, to the elevators.

From the fourth floor he mounted to Jessica Brooke's office. He found the room unoccupied. Picking up the telephone he asked to be connected with the department he had just left. "Have someone tell Mrs.—er—Madame Nordhoff that Inspector Bratton is waiting to talk to her. . . . Yes, up in Miss Brooke's office, if she will be so good."

While he waited for the buyer to answer his summons he moved restlessly about Jessica Brooke's restricted quarters, scowling at his thoughts. On Jessica's side of the desk he paused to stare down at the pictured face of Mary

Whitford. He had just time to wonder whether Dottie Cline had had anything enlightening to say about the print when the door opened and Madame Nordhoff entered.

"Quite the queen of the high-hatters," he was thinking as he gave her a careful scrutiny. "Just the sort of dame to give the million dollar touch to a dress joint. . . ."

She seated herself and with an air of detached graciousness waited for him to speak. Her white hair was coiffed high, her complexion so skillfully touched up that even Bratton doubted that her age could account for her silver locks. Her black gown fit her not quite slender figure exquisitely and her dull black kid shoes were long and narrow. Not Hanby's shoes, Bratton admitted ruefully.

"There's a point or two I'd like to discuss with you, Madame Nordhoff," he began urbanely. "We're freer up here, don't you agree? Your girls—curious and excitable, aren't they?"

Her rouge-defined lips smiled slightly but she said nothing.

"Here's one routine question I hadn't asked you: when Miss Terry sent for you did you notice whether the victim's hand bag was still in fitting room E?"

"It was not, Inspector." Madame Nordhoff's speech was rather obviously British, Bratton thought. Certainly there was nothing Middle-West about it.

"Um-m, then that means. . . ." He allowed the conclusion that he was apparently forming to die away, as though he were thinking aloud.

"Don't tell me, Inspector, that you suspect Miss Terry might have purloined it!" There was a shocked note in the clipped syllables.

Bratton hunched an awkward shoulder. "Of course it might also mean that the murderer took it—or else you, yourself. It's only sense to assume that one of you—three can account for it."

Madame Nordhoff lifted the thin line of her eyebrows with quizzical grace. "Am I seriously considered as a suspect, Inspector?" she asked dryly.

"I have always found that the feminine mind leaps lightly to false conclusions," retorted the inspector. "I shouldn't have said that you were one of those who could have taken the bag if I had not considered you much too wise a woman to misunderstand me."

"Thank you, Inspector."

"My case against you would be this:" he continued in the same facetious vein, "you were called to booth B by the stock girl, Dottie Cline. There you found—what Joyce Terry showed you. You sent her off to get Galway and Miss Brooke and remained alone with the body. If the murderer didn't take the green bag and if Joyce didn't, then you did. That's simple logic. Then of course you left the store to go over to the Anthony Wayne Hotel this morning before eleven-thirty."

Madame Nordhoff's laugh was a trifle uncertain and her glance fluttered downward from the inspector's sharp blue eyes to the photograph lying beneath his hand on the desk. "Really, Inspector, my errand was quite legitimate."

"I'm sure it was, Madame Nordhoff. I was just giving you a little exercise in circumstantial evidence," soothed Bratton. "That's the way detectives are, you know."

"Doubtless your circumstances are *a propos,* but your evidence—isn't that lacking?"

"Maybe it is," agreed Bratton, "maybe it is. . . ." But he would have sworn that his mention of half past eleven had not gone unremarked. "By the way, another thing I really meant to ask you—just where were you on the floor when the Dottle kid brought you the S.O.S.?"

"I was speaking with Mrs. Dunn Marlay, one of our patrons. She was interested in a Lanvin model—"

"Which you had just brought out to her from the stock room?"

For an instant Line and Hollis's prize buyer looked distinctly surprised. "Yes," she agreed, "yes, I had just brought it out."

"From where you were standing with this customer could you see any part of the reception foyer?"

"Only the end near the cashier's desk."

"Did you see Miss Terry leave the fitting alcove and return to it?"

The beautifully poised head shook in vague regret. "I'm afraid we have only the poor child's word about that," she murmured.

"Is zat so?" scoffed Bratton inwardly and redoubled his attention. "Then I don't suppose you saw this woman who we suppose was in room C. Miss Terry reports that she ran into such a person."

"Indeed. . . ." Madame Nordhoff's skepticism became more marked.

"It was you, I believe," he continued blandly, consulting a memorandum, "who reported that Mrs. Thayre was apparently looking for someone before she was shown into the fitting rooms."

"Such was my impression, certainly. Whether she saw anyone waiting for her out in the foyer, I could not say."

With one of Miss Brooke's pencils the inspector tapped the pictured face lying before him. "You're sure you didn't see anybody around that afternoon who looked like this?" he asked.

"Quite sure, Inspector," but the inspector was aware that the buyer's gaze was directed to a spot fixed beyond and behind him.

"Only one more item—you've been very patient about your time. Do you have the exclusive use of that desk down there in your department?"

Genuine surprise, but not alarm, flashed into Madame Nordhoff's keen eyes. "The cashier's desk?" she asked softly.

"I think you know which one I mean—the little jigger behind a screen—"

"I almost never use it. I find it a bit too low for my height. Circumstantial evidence again?"

"And you're leaping again, Madame Nordhoff," he laughed.

She rose to go. "Surely, Inspector, with your logical mind it has occurred to you that unless this crime was the deed of an insane person it is almost inconceivable that it could have been committed by an outsider. . . . Terry's customer may have been dead a little longer than we think."

"There would be the question of motive," mused Bratton as steadily as though her insinuation was his own.

"A little investigation would doubtless bring that to light," she murmured smoothly.

With that the interview came to an end. The inspector stepped forward to open the door and as he turned back after closing it he stopped short and stared at himself in a mirror that hung on the opposite wall. A minute later he had seated himself in the chair in which Madame Nordhoff had been sitting. Still he gazed in the mirror, though his head had now to be tilted backward at a sharper angle. He frowned and whistled noiselessly and his eyes dropped to the desk behind which he had been stationed. With that the whistle grew clear and loud though not wholly triumphant.

Once more the door squeaked. Jessica Brooke stepped briskly in. She had not known the inspector was in possession, but the smile with which she welcomed him flattered him soothingly.

"Good work! I was just sending a brain wave after you. I want some information and I don't want to be asked why I want it. Even if you think you see the drift, don't say anything—it may bust the bubble."

"One of these hold-your-breath ideas, is that it?" Jessica asked and installed herself at her own side of the desk.

"Not even that much to it. . . . But first, tell me what Dottie had to say about that picture," he demanded.

"Not the woman she saw in C, she's certain, but she's equally certain that she's seen somebody on the floor recently who makes her think of the photograph. However, Dottie's only a harum-scarum youngster with an embarrassing urge to be agreeable."

"When this store employs people, I suppose they fill out a pretty detailed blank or questionnaire in the modern big business manner," Bratton asked abruptly, no longer interested in Dottle Cline and her temperament.

"We've huge files of such documents," replied Jessica.

"I'd like your docket on both Mrs. Nordhoff and the Terry girl then," he directed briefly.

At the mention of the latter name the store detective gave the police official a quick glance. Her deliberate suppression of the Phil Leonard complication worried her, for Jessica Brooke was a conscientious operative; but she was also persistent enough to want to work out certain plans to her own satisfaction.

"Employees check in and out by time-clock, don't they? Well, I want to know whether Joyce Terry left the building at any time this morning."

"That will be a matter of record. We have a system that is almost fool-proof."

"What's the arrangement governing parcels carried out by employees?" the inspector next wanted to know.

"Now you're coming up my street. I'm always doing business with somebody who's trying to smuggle something out. Any article purchased in the store by an employee is sent to desk number four in the service department and held there until closing time. When the employee claims it there's a special tag on it which identifies it as O.K. to

Daddy Baynes, who is on duty at the exit door which must be used by all employees leaving the store at any time. The same general procedure applies to bundles that anyone brings in from the outside."

"This rigmarole take in everybody?"

"Everybody except executive heads."

"All right. Do you suppose you could rush the dope on the two women? Lord, it's late, isn't it? Almost quitting time. I tell you what—I'm going to stoke up. I haven't had a mouthful since morning. You can catch me at Headquarters in half an hour, say."

But Inspector Bratton was not to dine in peace and quiet atop a stool at Steve's Quick-Lunch. He had ordered his steak and French frieds and spread out a five o'clock final on the counter to read what the public was being told about the Thayre murder. What he found that was news to him diverted his attention so thoroughly that one of Steve's most masterly steaks was devoured mechanically and he forgot to order a second cup of coffee.

The paragraphs were boxed and written in the sprightly style that made a by-line unnecessary. Paula had certainly got down to business with the tip he had handed her, but there was something in her feature story that wasn't told, some faint inuendo. . . . He'd have to have a show-down with Paula.

Uncle Eben Underwood's seventy-five thousand-dollar Liberty Bonds had become Vivian Thayre's only two weeks before her death, the Pringle narrative stated. Had the Beautiful Young Heiress had a Premonition of her End? Or had her romantic early career as Business Woman guided her acumen? Whatever her motive (and this was one of the subheads that had made Bratton restive), she had promptly made her will. Her Entire Estate, Paula capitalized, with the exception of her personal effects, was left to her Bereaved and Broken Husband. The bonds, safely boxed, reposed in the safety vaults of the Somers National Bank, but their erstwhile owner lay stark in death before they could add their drop to the rich cup of pleasure from which she had always sought to drink.

"I'll say the kid's in training for the tabloids," grunted Bratton and reached for his check. "The little devil! She's dancing up and down about something or I'm a flatty. . . ."

Her triumph was verbal rather than terpsichorean, for he found Miss Pringle entertaining the desk-sergeant and switch-board man when he strode into Headquarters ten minutes later.

"There you are, Dannie darlin'," she chirruped. "The Big Boss here told me there was no chance paging you. Seen my stuff?"

"And how! March right in here, young lady. . . . Now tell me what they wouldn't let you print." He plopped himself into his protesting chair.

"So the Heavy Thinker's wheeled into action, eh what?" scoffed Paula swinging her trim but mud splashed heels against the laden desk upon which she perched.

"Now, kid, no foolin'. You've got hold of something that worries me. Out with it."

"My story tells All, honest it does. Vivian inherits the bonds, slaps them into safety-deposit, and makes her will. Why she didn't make whoopee instead with the seventy-five thou' is more than I know—it would have been her line. And she and Rupert must have been hitting it off better than her hectic interest in Ross Ingram might have led a young and innocent sob sister to suppose. Uncle Eben's bonds came from her side of the house—you might have expected her to leave the money to her own relatives. Maybe they'll try to bust the will," Paula speculated hopefully.

"How are chances that Thayre has been doing some stepping out of his own?" asked Bratton.

"If he has, he's been careful. No, Danny, it looks more as if he's been getting all his thrills out of playing the market. There have been times in the last few years when seventy-five thousand bucks would have looked like mighty small change to Rupert, though lately—"

Bratton's blue eyes narrowed. "Yeah?"

"The bereaved and—er—broken husband," Paula quoted dreamily, "might have regarded even half that much money with more respect."

"Thanks a lot, Paula. You're not so dumb. What can you spill about Ingram?"

"Am I going to get another story?" she bargained.

"Anything you dig up is yours."

"But that squeegee—"

"Oh, that—" and the inspector smiled airily, "—that hasn't jelled yet. Come on—tell papa all about Ross Ingram."

"Feature me being Betty Fairfax to a policeman! Ross makes a profession of being boy friend to ladies of leisure, but his big business—you know very well he's agent or something for our very best Detroit and Toledo bootleggers."

"How deep was he in with Mrs. Thayre?"

"Not to the extent of being kept from a try at Joe Kendall's money by way of Connie, who ought to know he'd be a mistake if she ever hopes to make Junior League."

"Any other women?" insisted Bratton.

"Heaps of has-beens. Us girls go goofy over Ross," smirked Paula.

At that point a caller was announced whose arrival meant Paula's dismissal. It was Jessica Brooke with the dossiers the inspector had asked for.

"Run along, little one," he counseled Paula. "If you can produce the original of that picture, I'll pin a leather medal on you myself."

Line and Hollis's store detective reported briefly and mechanically. She too had had a full day, yet in spite of her fatigue there was more to come, she hoped, during the course of the evening.

"Joyce checked in at eight-forty-five this morning and out at five-forty tonight. She spent her noon hour in the store—didn't even go out of the building for lunch. That's that, I hope."

"It is," and the inspector nodded with satisfaction.

"And here's a copy of the two application blanks, plus the correspondence in connection with Mrs. N's. She was an imported expert, you see. And also a summary of their records since they've been with the store. I think that ought to cover everything."

"It ought . . . and thank you very much, Miss Brooke."

The inspector plunged into a study of the documents that the store operative had brought in. For a quarter of an hour not even the telephone interrupted him. Then he lifted the receiver himself.

When the subordinates he summoned appeared he gave a series of detailed orders. Foster was to verify these statements about the Terry girl. That would mean that he would have to run over to the little Indiana town from which she had come. Morning would do for that. . . . Getty must take the ten-twenty to Chicago. The personnel people at Field's would help him check up on this Nordhoff data and if he found he had to go on from there, why, he was to use his head and go. . . . Where the hell was Gryce? Still tailing Ingram, huh. . . . McKim—this to a neatly moustached stripling—was to turn in every detail that could be rounded up concerning the financial status of the City Realty Investment Company and its treasurer, Rupert Thayre. "And in the morning," Bratton concluded, "there will probably be a trip to the Somers National for you to make. A little better form than you showed on the Sagamore Avenue assignment wouldn't hurt, either."

Foster, Getty, and McKim saluted and left, but before the door quite closed behind them another of Bratton's detail entered. It was Red Becker and he looked as if his report would quite settle the case.

"I've turned up something dashed queer on the Thayre alibi, Chief. Everything clicked okay till I got as far as this guy he was to meet out at his subdivision, see. Thayre went out all right—got there a little after three. That is, his car was parked alongside the plat office from then on till after five. But his prospect never showed up. It was a man named Neinheimer and he tells me that he 'phoned Thayre himself that he couldn't keep the appointment. And listen, that ain't all. This same party that can testify about Thayre's car says they saw him thumbing a ride back to town and no longer after he'd parked his car than it would take to walk across the plat to the street car loop."

"Good work, Becker," and Becker knew that his chief meant what he said. "You've only cut out another job for yourself, though. Find out who picked him up, where he went, and how he got back to the plat—if he did—or who drove the car back to town at five. Your witness reliable?"

"Nothing else but. He's a retired preacher who's fixed over that old farmhouse that sits across from the City Realty outfit. It's the only occupied house within sight, and it seems this old bird was puttering around covering up his roses or winter wheat or what have you. Then he streaks off across the lots to get him a basketful of some special kind of dirt he wanted, and that's how he come to see Thayre getting a lift back to town."

When Becker had gone, Detective-Inspector Dan Bratton likewise put on his hat and went home. He walked the mile and a half that lay between Headquarters and the

Bratton bungalow, but it was not because he was especially susceptible to the beauties of the crisp November starlight. He was pondering upon the vagaries of a case that was dividing his attack among a half dozen candidates for guilt in the murder of Vivian Thayre. There were Joyce and the unknown woman in C. Their chances had been obvious from the beginning. Maybe Ross Ingram was not so likely . . . neither could he be completely discarded. The day's events were forcing him to consider Mrs. Nordhoff more seriously and now Paula and Becker had swung the spotlight around on to Thayre himself. And there was the stubborn possibility of the first wife. . . . Nor was Bratton forgetting what he had seen in the mirror.

14
Another Grey Envelope

If Bratton had counted on a quiet evening at home during which he would think some of these matters through to a finish, that mental exercise had to be postponed, for the voice of the telephone again spoke. It was a long-distance call relayed from Headquarters.

"Say, Chief, this is Gryce," came the youngster's husky whisper. "I'm talking from Green's Mill. . . . Yeah, followed Ingram down here. Say, what do you know? He goes to the Agnew house and gets a bag. . . . Yeah, that's all and it looks like he's fixing to come back to town by the dinky that'll be pulling out in two-three minutes. . . . Sure, he's still got the bag. I'm on the job all right, but I thought maybe you might want to meet the train. . . ."

So, a half hour later, Bratton met the local that puffed in from Green's Mill and points east. The passengers that stepped off were not many. Among the first was Ross Ingram, natty and debonair, but empty-handed. Bratton, stationed in the shadow of the gateman's shelter, frowned ominously till the sight of a cautiously emerging Gryce revived him. For Gryce was carrying a new and very lady-like looking traveling case.

His attention again centered on Ingram, Bratton was aware that his man was hailing a taxi. A show of authority and the starter was repeating to him the address he had heard, the Peg Top Club. That looked as though Ingram was going home. He signaled Gryce, already at his heels, and the two boarded a second taxi and started after the first.

"What's the meaning of this?" snapped Bratton and glared at the bag dangling between Gryce's knees.

"He left it, Chief—left it stuck under his seat. I waited till I saw he was through the gates and then I lifted it, see."

Bratton grunted, but whether in censure or praise his subordinate could not tell. "Let's have your report, quick, before this boat makes the Peg Top. Looks as if Ingram wasn't faking his destination."

"You must have knocked him cold, Chief, for all he does for a good two hours is ramble around like he's sleep walking. I bet you I could have marched along with him arm and arm and he wouldn't have minded. He walked out Ninth as far as Madriver Drive and then just round and round that block till I got dizzy myself, but he didn't speak to a soul or go in anywhere. Then he gets him a cab and streaks out to Buckeye Heights—yeah, to the Thayre dump itself, but when he saw a uniform parked there he must have changed his mind. At any rate, he swings back to town again and down to the depot where he buys him a return trip to Green's Mill. So do I. It was the shoppers' special and full enough that it was no trouble dodging him. He was still acting all in, at that.

"When we got to Green's Mill he went straight to a hash joint and fed himself chile and pie. That perked him up enough so that he got chatty with the bozo behind the counter. I was spooning soup myself by that time but not making so much noise I couldn't hear what was said. All about how Mrs. Agnew's daughter up in the big burg had gone and got herself murdered and how the old lady had gone right off to her rich son-in-law's . . . but nothing was dropped that we didn't already know.

"As soon as he'd polished his plate he beat it out again and around to a side street to a neat looking place set back in a big yard. He went to the back door and knocked and somebody let him in. I did the best I could but for all I could see Ingram was just handing this hired girl a hot line. She nodded her head once or twice and went out of the kitchen. When she came back she was carrying this bag, see, but all she did was hand it over to Ingram. He came right out with it and went back to the station to wait for the up train. I about froze loafing outside on the platform and listening to the baggage chap boast about his brother-in-law who used to go with the Agnew girl before he went to work at Line's. Just the same I managed to check up by him that it was the Agnew house where the bag had been called for. And all the time Ingram sitting inside the waiting-room . . . the only time I took my eye off him was when I called you. We sat in the smoker coming into town and all he did was read a newspaper. Then he walked off the train without the bag."

"You didn't see him open it, I gather. . . . Well, then, what chance did he have for examining it without your being any the wiser?" demanded Bratton.

"Not a chance, unless he did it while I was in the telephone booth, and the train was whistling then."

The taxicab drew up across the street from the Peg Top Club in time for the detectives to watch their man pay off his driver and enter the building.

"What I'm going to do next depends entirely upon what I find inside this bag," and Bratton did a bit of tinkering with the lock. It snapped open without difficulty.

There had been a time, earlier that day, when Bratton might have bet that Vivian Thayre's missing green hand bag was as likely to pop out of the traveling case she had purchased as to appear in a parcels post collection box. He could still hope, no more rationally, that the case might contain the letter that should have been in the grey envelope.

At first sight it contained nothing except its fittings. Bratton's examination was thorough, but when the last screw top had been replaced and every pocket in the lining inspected he had to admit that his first glance had indeed told him as much as the bag had to tell.

"Wait here," he directed Gryce, "and hold the cab in case— I'm going in to talk to that bird." The inspector slipped out of the taxi and into the Peg Top Club leaving a disillusioned underling behind him. He was good enough to do all the foot work, he communed with himself, but he wasn't invited in on show-downs. He'd bet that guy Ingram would take the chief for a Federal dick. . . .

Bratton's former acquaintance, the leather-brown Major, was on duty in the hall and he managed to inform the inspector that Mr. Ingram had just gone up to his suite, number 32 on the third floor. Bratton followed on the next upward trip of the elevator. Ingram's return to his apartments must have been leisurely and unsuspecting, for Bratton caught up with him just as he was closing his door.

"Thought I'd tag along and bring you this, Ingram," he explained, thrusting forward the traveling case. As an introductory speech it was more than adequate. The man started nervously and let his hat and top coat slide to the floor. His yellowish skin glistened with sudden perspiration.

Bratton surveyed him with complacence. "Will you talk here, or would you like a ride down to my shop? I could put you up for the night, you know."

Ross Ingram understood the implications of the inspector's words. He motioned vaguely toward a chair and sat down himself in a manner verging on collapse.

"I happen to know just where you have been and what you have done since our last little get-together," Bratton informed him, "and now—I want to know just what it all means. And, believe me, Ingram, I intend to find out."

Of that, apparently, Ingram had not the slightest doubt. "My God, Inspector," he groaned, "who wants to get mixed up in a murder! I don't . . . all I did was try to keep myself out of it. It's a damned frame-up." A shiver of fear shook him.

"Don't say that again—you're putting ideas in my head, big boy. What did you go after this bag for?"

"To keep out of this damned mess—if I could!"

"What did you find in it that would turn that trick for you?"

"Not a thing—not a line! I swear it, Inspector."

That sounded like letters, thought Bratton joyfully. He still clung to the hope of a grey letter. Ingram was probably lying; it would scarcely be safe to assume otherwise. He could be searched in any case.

"See here, Ingram, just how did you happen to know that Mrs. Thayre had bought a traveling case at Line's and had it delivered to the hick town where she lived before she was married?"

Ross Ingram gulped miserably and batted his eyes. He saw where he had put himself. "Why—why—" he stuttered and swallowed again.

"You're mixed up in murder, Ingram, and mixed good and plenty. Let me have it straight." There was that in Bratton's voice that convinced his wretched hearer.

"You'll not believe me, Inspector," he began to mumble, "but I'm going to tell you the truth. It was Vivian I had the date with. She 'phoned me that morning and said for me to meet her at Line's at half past four. She knew I was through with her, see, but, all right, I agreed to take her to tea. I sat there and waited and waited but, believe it or not, Inspector, I never laid eyes on her. Now here's where it's going to sound phony . . . but would I tell you this if I didn't have to? It was after four-thirty and I was getting fed up. Suddenly a woman sailed by on her way to the elevator. She slowed up just long enough to whisper something and on she went. What she said, Inspector, was that if I knew what was good for me I'd get out—quick while the getting was good."

The inspector's amazed expression was sufficient interruption. "Who was the woman?" he demanded.

"I tell you—I don't know." Ingram tried to light a cigarette but gave it up and continued. "I didn't see her coming toward me and she was off again before I could get a good look at her. From the back she was—uh—not so very tall and rather heavy-set. No spring chicken, I'd say."

"Then what?" Bratton's question was unnaturally polite.

"Naturally, I didn't know what to make of such an extraordinary thing. I felt like a fish out of water up there anyway, so in a little while I left. That's all."

"The hell it is. I'm an old-timer, Ingram. What about that little stroll you took along the corridor toward the fitting rooms? And when you finally left the store what made you race out of the place? Didn't know we were on to that, did you? . . . And we know plenty more, too. . . . Why should the babblings of an unknown woman give you the guilty knowledge that murder had been done? You say she was tall and slender and wore a brown hat?"

"Yes—no, no! I didn't say that at all. I don't know what she looked like. I didn't know her, I tell you—never saw her before in my life."

Bratton said nothing, well content. Ingram stirred and his hunted eyes swept his comfortable quarters restlessly.

Bratton let him sweat for a little longer before he again spoke.

"This has all been very interesting, Ingram, even thrilling, but I have yet to be told your reason for going down to Green's Mill after an empty bag."

"It was empty," Ingram repeated weakly.

"Suppose it was. Just what had you expected to find in it?" urged the inspector with suspicious amiability.

"She said she had something to show me," admitted Ingram, "but she didn't say what it was."

"You mean Mrs. Thayre? Um-m . . . and I presume she likewise informed you that she was going to buy a bag and have it sent down to Green's Mill."

"Y-yes, she did. . . ." Then he recanted and his lax jaw set with curious stubbornness, but that went unnoticed. Dan Bratton's blue eye had caught sight of something more interesting, so interesting indeed that he could not resist his desire for immediate investigation.

He rose briskly. "It's just too bad, Ingram, but there's nothing else to do. You'll have to go back with me to Headquarters. May not keep you long, though. That just depends—"

When he had escorted his virtual prisoner down to the waiting cab and turned him over with a few terse directions to Jeff Gryce, he made an eager return to Ingram's rooms. "Search warrant or no search warrant," he informed his more disciplined self, "I've got to have a look at what's torn up in that scrap basket."

He scooped up a handful of ragged grey bits and painstakingly assembled them on the blotter under Ingram's reading lamp, but as he worked his enthusiasm waned perceptibly. They were scraps of grey-striped writing paper, it is true, and the writing thereon was exactly like that on the envelope he had found in Vivian Thayre's bedroom, but again what he succeeded in piecing together was no more than an envelope. It was addressed to Ross Ingram, but the letter that should have been in it had not been similarly discarded.

He thrust his official scruples aside far enough to satisfy himself that the drawers of the table-desk contained no other letters bearing that handwriting. He noted also with increasing disappointment that the only stationery supplies with which Ingram was equipped were the buff bond sheets bearing the letter head of the Peg Top Club. His persistent hunch that Ingram had written the grey letter had gone to pot.

However, he sealed the grey scraps into one of the buff envelopes and thrust it grimly into his pocket. They might be worth something after all. As for Ingram's suite, it would have to be fine-combed later. Just now it was up to him to get back to Headquarters.

Gryce was waiting for him, ready to report that not a thing had been found on Ingram. On the chance, Bratton himself took a look at what had been turned out of his pockets. There was indeed nothing that could have been placed in the traveling case by Vivian Thayre while she was examining it preparatory to purchase.

Armed now with a hastily made out warrant, the inspector accompanied Gryce and Ingram back to the latter's rooms. As the search went on, if the glowering Ross noted that his rather extensive wardrobe was being inspected as if for stains of one sort or another, he made no sign. Neither did he gain much comfort from the lack of interest the two detectives exhibited in a certain loose-leaf notebook that contained tell-tale memoranda concerning business deals that could have been traced across the border. . . . No further correspondence committed to grey stationery came to light.

Bratton bade Ross Ingram good-night with mock courtesy. "We'll be seeing you, old dear. Sorry to renig on that
half-way invitation of mine to have you spend the night
down the street, but I'm still hard- boiled cop enough to
blurt right out like this that I'm keeping Gryce on the
job."

15
Lovers' Meeting

If Dan Bratton had spent that evening at home telling bed-time stories to the junior Brattons, as he had planned, Jessica Brooke would have been spared an ignominious half hour the next day. Likewise she might not have felt the incentive to restore herself to favor in the eyes of the inspector and consequently one of the longest steps towards the solution of the French Room murder might not have been so promptly taken. Jessica tried to tell the inspector that she had called him that evening but when she realized that it was only a child who was answering the telephone she had kept her news to herself. The Bratton youngsters knew that papa's messages were always important, but someway the domestic system had slipped a cog. The maternal Bratton, engaged in attempting to incarcerate a lately acquired terrier in the garage at the moment that the telephone bell rang, was doubtless the villain of the piece, but that simple fact did not save Jessica Brooke from the blue wrath of the inspector's eyes.

Jessica had worked on the case all day, faithfully executing Bratton's assignments, but she was conscious of the undercurrent of her own interests.

Was Phil Leonard Rupert Thayre? Was Thayre Leonard? How could she discover the truth for herself and the heart-sick girl who in all likelihood had been duped? If she could prove that there were two separate and distinct individuals involved, then Joyce would have nothing to worry about. But if Leonard should be demonstrated to be a rash alias for Thayre, then what? It was absurd to feel that Joyce Terry was thereby jeopardized. Dan Bratton was not the sort of police official to press a case against an innocent participant in order to clear his docket of a stubborn problem. Yet there remained something about the situation that chilled Jessica. Suppose Thayre himself had a more sinister connection with the taking off of his wife than anyone had yet suspected. . . . Nonsense, Jessica reminded herself, there was not a shred of evidence to support such a fantastic theory. Yet all day the fear tormented her.

First, she must establish, if it existed, an identity between Joyce's Phil Leonard and Rupert Thayre. She solved that problem with characteristic directness. When she had delivered to Bratton the statements he had asked for concerning Joyce and Madame Nordhoff, she left Headquarters and went home to her apartment. There, according to her instructions, she found Joyce waiting for her. She prescribed a hot bath and a nap for the still distraught girl and as soon as the sound of running water prevailed she proceeded to establish telephonic communication with Rupert Thayre.

This was not easy to achieve, but tactful persistence edged with a faint threat of authority finally brought results. Thayre was informed that he might learn of an interesting fact in connection with the murder of his wife if he would call at such and such an address at eight o'clock. Afterwards he was free to use his own judgment about getting in touch with the authorities, but before—well, Mr. Thayre might find it embarrassing. At this point Jessica let a little laugh tinkle icily. She hoped she was giving the impression of a polite lady blackmailer.

It was an insane trick, Jessica groaned to herself more than once during the interim of waiting, but if Thayre should show up she would have evidence of more than a possible identity between the two men. It would certainly look as though he had cause to worry guiltily about something. And if he did not appear it would be simple routine for her to discover whether he had reported his mysterious message to the police.

At ten minutes of eight Jessica remembered that she must leave a message for the laundryman with the janitor. Joyce wouldn't mind answering the telephone, she asked as she whisked out of the apartment. She went no further away than the one across the hall, which was unrented. Jessica knew how to get in. She slipped inside the door and waited with it ajar.

At three minutes after eight the entrance door one flight below clanged open and shut and masculine steps ascended the concrete stairs. Jessica could not see the man's face as he stood jabbing the bell beside her number, but it could be no other than Thayre.

Then everything happened very quickly. The door swung wide and the light within rayed off about Joyce's dark curls. There was a strangled cry.

"Phil—darling!" As helpfully as though she had been coached Joyce flung her arms about the neck of the astonished man. Jessica, ready to cut off any attempt at retreat, also heard what sounded like an abortive "Joy—" before she shepherded the pair within her own precincts and stood confronting them, her back to the door.

So that was that. Rupert Thayre was Joyce's Phil Leonard. For Joyce's sake, Jessica Brooke would now have been only too glad to permit the situation its obvious explanation. Kind-hearted Miss Brooke had found the girl's errant sweetheart for her. . . . But both Thayre and Jessica had to face another matter and Jessica wished mightily that she could drop Joyce out of the window for the time being.

She plunged blindly ahead. "Mr. Thayre, it was I who sent for you. I hope your alibi for day before yesterday from four to five, let us say, can be more satisfactorily established than the one you might present for last Sunday evening." At random Jessica Brooke referred to the last meeting between Joyce and the man she called Leonard.

Joyce's arms slipped from the man's shoulders and he backed awkwardly against a little table, blinking with surprise. The nonplussed expression in his slightly puffy eyes, strangely enough, assured the detective. This man might possibly be a criminal, but he was not a formidably astute one.

He managed at last a feeble "What the devil—" Then he cast a sidelong glance at Joyce, now cringing against the wall of the little living-room, lips trembling and violet eyes wide. "I—I guess you've got me right," he muttered thickly. "What's the answer?"

"That's for you to say," returned Jessica Brooke, trying to think what lady blackmailers would do in moments like these. "You'll agree that it's a nasty complication in the light of the murder of your wife. How would you propose to account for its happening while Mrs. Thayre was—her customer?"

That brought a choked and tortured cry from Joyce that was to haunt Jessica Brooke long afterwards, but she had chosen her line of attack.

"But she—I can prove—" Thayre's hoarse words rumbled into stricken silence.

"I can quite understand that you will find no difficulty in proving that your wife's death fits in rather conveniently with your engagement under another name to this child whom you have made your cat's paw."

"That's a lie," roared Thayre suddenly. His stunned manner left him. "Whatever your game is, woman, I don't have to talk to you. I'm going to talk to the police."

Whether it was Joyce's gasping sobs or the jaunty "Oh, I should think twice about that, if I were you" that Jessica managed in order to cover her fervent prayer that he would fail to observe that her telephone was just behind him, for the moment Thayre made no move to carry out his threat. He, too, was in need of time out to think.

"Money's the answer, I suppose," he said at last. "Well, how much?"

Jessica deserved that. The role she had embarked upon had been eminently successful, but she found the fact disgusting. She flung her head back and stared him down. "Be careful, Mr. Thayre. I should tell you that in a sense I represent the police."

"The hell you do! Then I am dished." His shoulders slumped and he began to twist his watch chain, the first sign of twitching nerves he had evinced.

"Do they have to—to know about Phil and me?" moaned Joyce. The other two had almost forgotten her presence.

Then Jessica Brooke muffed her role, thus proving to Dan Bratton's later annoyance that she was far from being a hard-boiled woman cop. "If you can assure me that your relations with this girl had nothing to do, directly or indirectly, with the death of your wife, I see no reason why the wretched business should be made public."

"I can swear to that." Thayre's answer was solemn. Then he went on more wordily. "I know nothing that accounts for that insane attack upon my wife. It has never occurred to me to suspect Miss Terry. My conduct with her has been unpardonable—I admit that, but to drag it all up now would only be more brutally unfair to her. I've been responsible for enough. She'd never live it down."

Jessica Brooke's lip curled. She noted that Thayre was
unable to meet either Joyce's regard or her own as he made
his plea, yet her sympathy for the girl prevailed. Why
should she insist that Joyce's sorry romance be served to a
sensation-greedy public as a mere garnish to a sufficiently
thrilling and mysterious murder?

"I shall keep Joyce's secret," she said shortly.

Ten minutes later Rupert Thayre left the detective's
apartment, his thoughts confused and foreboding. Whew,
that had been a jam. . . . What an ass he had been to walk
into a trap like that! Let the police investigate Vivian's
murder from now till kingdom come, they couldn't tie him
up with that, thank God! He must arrange about offering
a reward. It would look better. . . . It was preposterous
to think that he might be suspected. Surely they couldn't
seriously consider it . . . but if they should, then he wasn't
out of the woods yet. How in the name of heaven had that
woman hit on that four to five o'clock business? He'd be
sunk without a trace if that had to be explained.

Thus Rupert Thayre's thoughts milled through a sleep-
less night, but it was not until the events of the morning
to come harried him further that he determined upon his
surprising course of action. When Thayre withdrew from
the apartment Jessica Brooke had first to deal with Joyce.
For a few minutes she was afraid she would be obliged to
call in a doctor to cope with the girl's rising hysteria, but
her own measures were at last effective. Rational explanations of what she had said to Thayre were useless; when
Joyce should have regained her self-control they could be
advanced. Till then Joyce must continue to think her a
heartless monster, though one dealing in alcohol rubs,
bromides, and glasses of hot milk. By the time the girl
sank into a heavy sleep Jessica was beginning to regret the
course to which she had committed herself. It was then
she rang up the inspector's house and was told that papa
wasn't at home.

Not that Jessica Brooke intended betraying Joyce and her Phil Leonard. She meant exactly what she had said about that. Only she wondered whether Thayre had noticed that her promise, if such it could be called, had not been a blanket one. The impulse that led her to the telephone was to put to the inspector a judicious injury about Thayre's whereabouts at the time of the murder. Her second reference to this point ought to register with the obtusest of detectives, and there was nothing like that wrong with Dan Bratton. Common sense told Jessica that the chance that Thayre had actually been anywhere about the fourth floor of Line and Hollis's on that terrible afternoon was exceedingly remote, but Bratton ought to be made to think a little about the victim's husband before giving him a clean bill of health.

After all, she decided, her interest in Thayre's alibi could wait till morning. The inspector would undoubtedly look in at the store bright and early! She wondered whether he might not commission her to attend the funeral, which, she recalled, was set for half past ten.

Inspector Bratton, however, did not appear at the department store as early the next morning as his colleague there had anticipated. Events at Headquarters were moving too briskly. When Bratton came in McKim and Foster were waiting with the first results of their assignments. The latter had done routine on Joyce Terry but had learned concerning her life since she had come to the city to work at Line's nothing more suspicious than Mrs. Fahlmann's certainty that she went out to meet a fella sometimes and that the last two nights she had not spent under her landlady's roof. As Bratton knew with whom the girl had stayed the first of these nights he was not particularly excited about the second. Dutifully warning Foster that there was small chance of anything coming of it, he sent him off to the Indiana town just across the border where Joyce Terry had spent her childhood.

The inspector was not so certain of the unimportance of what McKim had to tell. The youngster had done a good night's work. All the boys on the squad had their moments of snickering at Dudley McKim, for he aspired to be a detective in the grand manner, but he had occasional luck. McKim called it a justification of his methods. . . . Boiled down, McKim's report informed Bratton that the City Realty Investment Company, like many other real estate organizations, found its ambitious expansion program a heavy burden in these days of a dead market and high annexation taxes to meet. Yet its treasurer's prosperity constantly increased. He played the market with uncanny foresight, though he had had several narrow squeaks. He did no business with any of the established brokers of the city but through a one-horse office that had been mixed up in more than one shady deal. Thayre never seemed at a loss for collateral, though he was apparently playing straight with the City Realty outfit.

At this point Bratton interrupted McKim. He crossed to the safe and withdrew the huge manila envelope in which reposed most of the exhibits already collected in his investigation of the Thayre murder. He extracted the green brocaded bag which the postal authorities had turned over to him the day before. Opening it he produced a circlet of silver chain that held three or four keys. Indicating one he said:

"Mac, take that and beat it up to the Somers National. It'll be nine by the time you get there. That's the key to Mrs. Thayre's safety-deposit box. Explain yourself to the old boy in charge and get a look at what's in her box. Maybe there'll be seventy-five grand in Liberties in it and maybe there won't. That's all I want to know . . . no, it's not! Find out when the box was opened last and by whom. Find out whether Thayre ever uses it. Then you can look up his off-color broker."

Before he left Dudley McKim had one more item to report. He was rather tiresome in his insistence that he himself considered it wholly coincidental. He had managed to inspect the Meade Building offices of the City Realty Investment Company and he had observed that one or two of the desks were equipped with scissors like those the men on the case had already examined. One pair was shinily new. Moreover McKim had found a sales check and merchandise envelope in the nearest scrap basket. The check bore the date of the murder and the imprint of Line's notion section.

That surprising detail ought to be checked at once, if only to prove coincidence, but the offices of the City Realty Investment Company were closed for the day because of the Thayre funeral. Bratton made a note of the matter and answered his telephone.

Otis Galway from Line's wanted to tell the inspector that a woman had at last appeared in answer to the advertisement which he had instructed their operative to insert concerning their basement hosiery department. As Miss Brooke had not come in yet, what did Inspector Bratton want done? Galway was directed to send the woman down to Headquarters at once. "Send somebody along with her. She may think she's in for trouble and try to bolt."

Within ten minutes Norma Schmidt's buyer of gunmetal semi-chiffons was answering Inspector Bratton's questions. Any upspringing of hope he might have permitted himself in the interim promptly withered, Mrs. Alec Higby had transferred at Court and Hamilton on her way home from work that night. She washed out, she explained. She had run in the store by the basement entrance, because she had to get her a pair of stockings before she could go to lodge that night and pay her dues, and right out again just in time to catch her car. She lived out by the Flats and only one trolley out of three went the whole way out.

There had been no man with her—she'd thank the inspector to know she wasn't that kind of a fool. She hadn't even seen a man.

That was all from Mrs. Alec Higby and it was the only response the personal in the *Bulletin* brought forth.

Ban Bratton snatched the interval before the next outside interruption for a thoughtful reexamination of the various technical reports already on his desk. The photographs of the body slumped in room E, the enlargements of the confused mass of fingerprints—these of no value at all—the transcript of the proceedings of the purely formal inquest, the findings of the medical examiner, the coroner's final report, an analysis of the blood incrusted upon the scissors—all were gone over. However fascinating the by-paths of investigation in this affair were proving to be, he peremptorily reminded himself that he must not forget that it dealt primarily with a woman who had been stabbed to death in a department store fitting room hemmed in by scores of people. It could not be a premeditated crime, he'd be jiggered if it could . . . and how a man could get by with it— Abruptly the inspector's thoughts circled to Getty in Chicago. He might expect a wire or long-distance by noon.

Dan Bratton pawed about on his cluttered desk without finding what he was looking for. That owl-eyed chap in the lab was damned slow. He'd sent the blood-stained order blank he had found in Mrs. Nordhoff's desk right along for his report, but he was sure taking his time.

Once more Bratton spread out the scraps of paper salvaged in the Peg Top Club envelope. There was plenty of room to theorize, for the pieces of grey paper told him nothing conclusively. The postmark on the torn envelope bore a date three days previous to that of the murder and as in the case of the one that he had found first it too had been mailed in town. The same hand had clearly addressed both.

His opportunity for deduction was cut short. His clerk mumbled a name that was a preposterous mouthful of something. Not even a policeman could be expected to get a name like Schwankenzuber the first time. But when Bratton saw the smooth plump cheeks and the black bonnet and the full calico skirts and heard the high flat voice he knew the name belonged to Milly. He felt a quiver of excitement.

Milly set out to explain in her own way that she didn't want to get in late for the missus' funeral—it was 'way out at the cemetery chapel, but oncet she was all cleaned up and before her feet give out on her she figured she'd brang it up herself.

Properly encouraged Milly produced from a pocket in her voluminous skirt a tidy little packet wrapped in newspaper and tied with quantities of string. In spite of her thrifty protests Bratton cut the much knotted cord and tore off the covering until a folded bit of heavy waxed paper gay with a baker's advertisement was revealed.

"I wrapped it in that there bread paper because it was sopping wet. It was stuck down in one of them good vases. The mister's mother-in-law, she'd threw the flowers away but hadn't outened the water. It wonders me it hadn't fell out on her oncet. When the boxes of flowers kept coming yet I was now obliged to take down even them good vases. That's how come I found it still. It's grey paper, ain't?"

Milly was quite right. She had brought him the remains of a grey letter sheet. What if it was the one the inspector had been searching for? The sodden mass would hardly survive the first examining touch; the lines written upon it were already blurred beyond casual recognition and in great gaps obliterated. However, he thanked the girl punctiliously and bade her good-morning.

16

A Quarter after Four

Thanks to Milly Schwankenzuber's zeal in committing her find to an air-tight wrapper instead of spreading it out immediately to dry, the letter was still too wet to handle. Bratton turned on the steam and spread out the pulpy lump on his radiator. It had to dry out before he dared attempt to read it.

At that point young McKim darted in again. He tried to assume the dilettante pose of the fictional crime solvers he so admired, but his news was fatal to such a detached attitude.

"There are no Liberty bonds in her box—not even a fifty. The box was last called for a week ago today by Thayre himself. The manager of the vault says this is the first year she'd rented one from them, but he thinks he remembers her saying that she'd let her husband take care of the other key, as she'd be sure to lose hers sooner or later. There was nothing else in the box except a half dozen old love letters signed 'Hal'—and darned hot, I'd call 'em—and a mess of out-of-date jewelry."

Bratton had come to a quick decision. "Let Thayre's broker go for the time. Maybe Gryce can take care of this end. I want you to go to the funeral. You're better dressed for that than I am. Keep an eye on Thayre and, for that matter, anybody else that calls for it. After I've heard from

Becker it may be that I'll be sticking around myself. If you see me, that will mean Thayre's going to be asked to step down here. If not, call in for further instructions."

Regretfully the inspector again decided that the grey paper still cooking on his radiator was too wet to do him any good. He wandered out front to make inquiries of the lieutenant at the switchboard concerning calls from Chicago and barely managed to sidestep the tardy arrival of the Commissioner. If that political figurehead would only let him mind his own business in his own way for a day or two longer there was a chance he might find out some of the answers.

He put on his coat and hat and was halfway down the drafty wooden stairs that led to the street when he met Red Becker coming upward two jumps at a time. "Got something more, Chief. Want to stop now?"

"If it's that good, yes," and the inspector turned back to his office. He had intended stepping up to Line's. Miss Brooke was probably attending the Thayre funeral—he rather hoped so. He could see her the first thing after lunch.

"I've been out at the plat having another little visit with my friend the rose garden husband," Becker proceeded to relate. "What that little bright-eyes don't see ain't worth seeing, I'm telling you. He didn't know the name of the chap who picked up Thayre Tuesday afternoon but he could describe him and his rattle-trap car and tell me that the guy made several trips a day in and out of that end of town. So I went across to the pike and hung around a while and sure enough before long an outfit like he described comes banging along. I stopped him and went for a ride too and—well, it was the fellow that picked Thayre up all right.

"He said the gent gave him a couple of good smokes and hopped off his bus at the corner of Court and Hamilton at a quarter after four. What do you know about that for a lucky break! He knows it was that time because he was on his way out to a candy factory where his daughter works and he looked at the clock in the Somers Tower to see if he was going to make it to the shop by the girl's quitting time."

The corner of Court and Hamilton at a quarter after four.

Red Becker construed the inspector's silence unfavorably. "What became of Thayre after that, I fell down on— sorry. Except that Barnaby Warde—that's my preacher friend—says that when he went out a little after five to shut up his chickens Thayre was backing his car out of the drive, leaving for town. He is sure it was Thayre in the car."

"I think," said Inspector Bratton and looked at his watch calculatingly, "that a little chat with Thayre is now in order. He'll be at the funeral just now— Mac's there too. You get out to his house and if he comes back there afterwards that will mean that you are to bring him down here. Nice and easy, Red. No rough stuff. Tell him I've got hold of something he ought to know about, see. . . . If he doesn't show up at home you'll know I've already got to him."

Bratton climbed into a waiting automobile and in the face of the first snow of the season made his way out to Sylvan Acres, the city's burying ground. He had none too much time, and when he was held up at an outlying grade crossing by a dilatory freight he was not surprised to find even the morbidly curious leaving the cemetery by the time he turned in at the gates. The others were already homeward bound.

No matter, his directions to Becker had been explicit enough. The drive back to Headquarters would give him a chance to organize his approach with Thayre. He'd been doing so much leg work on the case that it was high time he went into the silence. The facts needed sorting out.

The snow-sticky pavements, however, were not conducive
to the kind of meditation the mass of conflicting data
demanded.

Whatever plans he might have formed to deal with
Rupert Thayre he would have been obliged to scrap, because the latter took the lead into his own hand.

Bratton had no sooner reentered his own quarters and
snatched a wire from Getty which informed him crypti-
cally that he was using his head and taking the Overland
out of Chicago than Dudley McKim made a needlessly
surreptitious entrance through the door that led to the
inspection room beyond.

"He's out there, Chief, and coming right in to see you.
But listen, it's his own idea—absolutely! I mean, after
everything was over out at Sylvan Acres he put his mother-
in-law into somebody else's car and drove back to town
alone in his. I tagged along. He came the long way around
through the parks and in by the new boulevard, not driving very fast, as though he was thinking or making up his
mind about something. Then he parked across the street
and came right up here."

With the words the door from the outer office opened
and Rupert Thayre was shown in; McKim loitered expectantly but his superior issued a crisp order. Let Dudley's
sharp eyes and slender fingers see what they could make of
the wad of greyish paper.

Thayre made of the inspector's gruff nod of greeting an
invitation to be seated. He lowered himself into the chair
facing Bratton's like a man grown suddenly old.

"Inspector," he said, "I have come up here to make a
statement to you which I do not find easy to make. It has
nothing whatever to do with the death of my wife, but
it involves such a startling coincidence that I—I prefer
that you should learn of it through me. I consider myself
an intelligent person. I mean by that that I have suffi-

cient confidence in the integrity of the police department, particularly in you, Inspector Bratton, to believe that my disclosure will not be broadcast. It—it concerns a very personal matter."

Thayre paused. Bratton wondered whether he had rehearsed the speech. "Since this resolution of yours," he replied gravely, "is a result of the distressing affair which it is my sworn duty to solve if I can, I must hear what you have to say before I can commit myself about my attitude toward it. In any case, I can promise you a minimum of newspaper publicity."

He waited for his visitor to continue. What the chap needed was a drink, he thought, noting his twitching eyelids and restless hands. Undoubtedly his urge was fear, or he never would have rounded up here immediately after his wife's funeral. It was ghastly. . . .

"Inspector," Thayre began again, leaning forward to steady his shaking hands by clutching the edge of Bratton's desk, "I'm no saint—few of us are. I've never pretended to be. It's this way—I've been seeing a lot of a girl here in town these last few months. She didn't know my real name—I don't think she knew it. It is the girl—" his voice was a hoarse mutter—"the girl who found my poor wife."

Bratton's jaw clamped and his eyes narrowed. So this was the loose end he hadn't caught up with yet. He should have ridden the girl from the start.

"Thayre," he barked, "are you accusing the Terry girl—"

"My God, no!" and Thayre buried his head in his hands.

"That fact alone could convict her—and you too, as an accomplice." Bratton rose to his feet and faced the craven man. He had determined to work fast.

"No, Inspector—no! I came to you of my own free will. All I want is to help— The murderer of my wife must be found, but Joyce—not that child—I swear she had no idea—"

"*Had* no idea, is that it? But she's found out and you're beating somebody to it, huh? Now, Thayre, suppose you pull yourself together and let me get this business straight. You had an appointment to meet a Mr. Neinheimer out at your sub-division at three o'clock or thereabouts on Tuesday, the afternoon of your wife's death. He 'phoned you that he couldn't make it, but you went out there anyway."

"I—I never got his message," faltered Thayre.

"That's odd. Neinheimer says he talked to you himself. However, there'll be somebody in your office who can settle that. You went out to the plat, I say, left your car in a conspicuous position, walked across lots to the pike, and rode back into town with an accommodating chap who as accommodatingly has told us all about it. He dropped you at the corner of Court and Hamilton Streets at a quarter after four. At a quarter after four," Bratton repeated with deliberate emphasis.

"Now, Mr. Thayre, you yourself admitted a few minutes ago that you were an intelligent man. Therefore you see that it would have been very easy indeed for you to have walked into Line's store—you were at its very entrance—and up to the department where you knew Mrs. Thayre would be. She had discussed her plans with you at breakfast that morning. I have not been idle, you see; we have collected other equally interesting and embarrassing information. We might, for instance, be able to prove that you had already made your plans with the Terry girl. . . ."

Months afterward, when justice had had her last word with the criminal, Dan Bratton was to confess to Jessica Brooke that he would have considered it his duty to break any of his men who had tried to pull off a scene like that. "I smashed every rule of my own game," he cheerfully admitted, "but as I handed out that hair-brained theory to him and realized that he wasn't even attempting to tell me where he actually had been, I began to sort things out in my mind in a fashion that carried me a long way ahead in the case. Mind you, I hadn't yet got hold of Thayre's stenographer and I was only guessing about the bonds. The scissors in his office too—fool's luck! I've not had much of it."

The interview that so backhandedly clarified Bratton's problem had one more surprise for him. After his sketchy implication that the murder could have been committed jointly by Thayre and Joyce Terry he reminded the man that a double motive existed in his case. Under his wife's will he inherited her property, so recently augmented by her uncle's legacy. "With the market the way it's been this fall," the inspector hinted, "many a man has taken dangerous chances to save his investments."

Thayre huddled limply in his chair but said nothing. The bold move his night of anxiety had led him to make had turned out to be a boomerang. He had only one card left to play, but it might in some measure help to establish his good faith with this blue-eyed devil who had so enmeshed him. His fingers fumbled with a bulkiness in the pocket of his top coat. He tugged at it until he had extracted a thickish package.

"Here," he said, "this is probably what you think you have on me. I took them from my wife's safety-deposit box a week ago, but, Inspector, neither you nor anybody else—now!—can prove that I took them without her knowledge and permission. I didn't have to kill her to get hold of seventy-five thousand dollars—much less to keep her from knowing that the bonds were no longer in her box."

The compact bundle fell heavily on the desk between them. Bratton's eyes glinted but he waited a long minute before he spoke. His question had nothing to do with Eben Underwood's Liberty Bonds.

"Mr. Thayre, did your wife or you possess a gun—a revolver?"

With some effort Thayre focused his attention. "Why, yes—yes, there is such a thing about the house. Just an ordinary .32."

"Your wife, I presume, knew where it was?"

He nodded, his face still blank.

"Where can it be found—now?"

"We always kept it in the upper right drawer of the desk in the corner room at the back on the second floor."

That would be in the room in which he had talked with Mrs. Agnew, Bratton thought as he picked up his telephone. He must get in touch with Becker. He found him more expeditiously than usual. Within a surprisingly short space of time Red Becker was calling back that there was no gun to be found in Thayre's desk.

"I thought not," replied Bratton calmly. "Hurry along down here. You'll have to carry on from this end."

If Thayre gathered what that meant he gave no sign. It was the inspector's next question that pulled him up tautly. "Where's the first Mrs. Thayre?"

The look in the man's blood-shot eyes went a long way toward confirming Dan Bratton's present suspicions. "I—I don't know." His stiff lips could scarcely form the words.

"Have you seen or heard from her since the decree was granted?"

"No. She went out of my life completely. She wouldn't listen to a settlement—made no claims for alimony—nothing."

"Thayre," and Bratton came from behind his desk to stand over the man as though he would pull the truth out of him, "have you any reason to believe, or even suspect, that your wife Vivian was ever in communication with her?"

Again there was that strange flicker of comprehension in Rupert Thayre's eyes. "If she had," he answered, "I would never have been told of it. From the day I married Vivian she never mentioned Mary's name."

"In these years between have you ever known where she was?"

"No. It was a closed chapter." The man's voice was now more vigorous, and more grim, than at any time during the scene.

"Are you sure, Mr. Thayre, that you would recognize Mary Whitford if you were to see her again?" The inspector tossed off his question casually but he was alert to catch its effect.

"Do you think a man forgets?" Nothing that Thayre had yet said to Bratton sounded more sincere than this reply.

Once more the irrepressible Dudley McKim opened the door at the rear of Bratton's room. One eye-brow was cocked triumphantly, but he dodged out of sight again before his chief could speak. It was merely his story-book manner of announcing developments in the latest assignment Bratton had made him. It brought results.

Bratton opened the outer door and sent a well understood signal towards Becker's red head. He had that moment returned from Buckeye Heights.

"Sorry, Thayre," said the inspector with official precision, "to leave you in this uncertain position, but until you are willing to make a straightforward statement about your movements between four-fifteen and five, I intend to follow out my idea about what occurred—and I don't expect to be long on my way."

Thayre left Headquarters groggily, and like one who locks the stable door on second thought went to seek counsel of his lawyer. Bratton, meanwhile, was giving young Dudley McKim his complete and respectful attention as the two of them bent over the fragmentary evidence offered by the grey letter.

17

AFTERNOON OF A DETECTIVE-INSPECTOR

Detective-Inspector Bratton pushed McKim's magnifying glass aside. He felt let down and he didn't mind letting that young squirt know it. The sequence of words that McKim had deciphered from the water-soaked paper was so broken that nothing conclusive could be learned from it. The letter had evidently borne no heading though there was trace of a signature. The soft grey paper combined with an unusually pale ink had not withstood the prolonged wetting it had been subjected to. Bratton took another disgusted look.

"*. . . my man . . . kill you both. . . . He cannot . . . ask him!*"

Those were the only words that could still be read. The first two phrases, McKim wished to point out, appeared to occur in the middle of sentences, the third was the beginning of another, and the last the end of one.

"What of it?" grunted Bratton, but his third inspection of the place where the writer's name had been signed prolonged itself significantly. The writing was a hopeless bluish smudge, but a vindictive pen had dug so deep that three slightly sloping horizontal scratches in the paper were still discernible. Two lay almost parallel; the third was further to the right. The inspector stared down at what he saw, for the moment oblivious to his subordinate's insistent comments.

"It's my opinion, Chief, that the letter was really written by a woman. I don't mean just because of the phrasing. It's the character of the writing itself. Of course I'm judging from the two envelopes you brought in as well. At first glance it looks far more like a man's than a woman's writing, but lots of smart sophisticated women affect a bold type like this. There are those ads for Blenheim cigarettes, for instance—"

"Dry up, Mac, for the love of Mike!" Bratton's glass was hovering over the pasted together shreds he had found in Ingram's waste paper basket. "If you're so darned smart take a look at this E—East Quincy Street, see—the Peg Top address. You see those strong cross bars and the way the t's are crossed in street. They've made marks in the paper just like the scratches that are all that's left of this signature." His finger tapped the obliterated name.

"You're right, boy," and Bratton thumped the astonished Dudley between the shoulders. "The letter was written by a woman, and her name's Emily or mine's mud! She wrote this threatening note to Vivian Thayre. Vivian decides to talk it over with Ingram—he's the man in the case, that's clear. But she must have been worried enough to pack a gun— Emily sure was on her trail. And that's the woman you failed to find on Sagamore Avenue. Well, what you must do now is pick up Gryce somewhere. He's on Ingram. I guess I've got to make that boy talk."

The remainder of that day was not long enough for all that Inspector Bratton tried to squeeze into it. Until Ingram should be brought in there was much apparently unrelated detail to check up. No matter how the present wind was blowing every line of investigation that had suggested itself must be pushed to its period.

Therefore specimens of Ross Ingram's writing were collected from the Peg Top Club and expertly compared with that on the two envelopes and the damp mass that Milly had rescued. If they were forgeries, Ingram was not their author.

Another chore concerned Joyce Terry and her Hanby shoes. As she had not been able to report for duty that morning—Miss Brooke certified her on the verge of a break-down—the inspector had to make a trip out to the store detective's apartment himself in order to annex the shoes. He had to refuse pointblank to let Miss Brooke go, though he gave her a half promise not to question Joyce for the time being. That was after the bad half hour Jessica Brooke lived through trying to explain her motives to the inspector for not reporting the Phil Leonard angle at once.

Bratton learned that Joyce had worn the shoes every day since the afternoon she had walked so blithely back to booth E. There was small chance, therefore, that any traces of blood still remained on their soles. If there had been spots on the uppers, no sign remained. But Bratton's examination for such details was only incidental. He carried the buckled pumps back to Line and Hollis's and sent for the girl in the books who so obligingly had handed a pair of scissors to a chance customer. When the girl entered Miss Brooke's office, where Bratton held forth alone for the time, it did not take her long to tell the inspector that the woman who had cut a bit of leather from her shoes had been wearing a pair just like these. Only they were newer, the girl qualified.

The clerk at the stationery counter was likewise called away from her work for a few minutes. She looked at the samples of handwriting the inspector showed her, but she refused to commit herself. She really couldn't be sure that any of these were like the writing on the paper she

had matched for the lady who had bought the box of grey
letter paper.

It took brisk work to catch up with the girls from the
City Realty offices. The one Bratton particularly wanted,
Thayre's stenographer, was at last paged at a matinee.
There was a shrewd assurance about her answers and the
inspector gathered that she was none too pleased with the
salary scale at the City Realty Investment Company. She
had put Mr. Neinheimer's appointment down on her boss's
engagement calendar herself and when he called in right
after lunch that day she remembered switching the call to
Mr. Thayre's 'phone. All she had heard of the conversation
was: "You can't? That's too bad. Some other time then . . ."

The scissors she had bought herself during her lunch
hour with money from the petty cash. No, she hadn't lost a
pair. One of the salesmen had broken them trying to open
a bottle of ginger ale. Seeing that she had to trim down
every blue prospect card she filed a pair of good sharp scissors was coming to her. The inspector thoughtfully noted
the gaudy carnelian ring she wore on her forefinger . . .

Likewise Bratton ticked off the obscure broker on
Canal Street whose connivance Thayre found so profitable.
His name, oddly enough, was Herman Kinzig. It would be
his duty to report certain facts concerning Kinzig's oper-
ations to the Chamber of Commerce, but that could come
later. Just now his own show held the boards.

He was on his way back to face Ross Ingram, he hoped,
and to pick up anything that might have come in from
Getty. Decidedly it was no moment for Miss Connie Kendall to interfere with a police officer in the performance
of his duty, but interfere she did, with results that were to
justify her impulsive conduct before the end of the Thayre
case.

It was now late in the afternoon and the murky twilight
was rapidly closing in. As he turned out of Canal Street a

smooth glittering coupé blocked his passage and a plump hand gave an imperative tap on the glass of the car door. Then the hand flung the door open and Inspector Bratton was told to get inside. Connie couched her order in polite finishing-school words, but her agitation was so evident that the inspector obeyed.

"Of all the luck, Inspector," gasped Connie and he could tell then that something had given her a jolt. "I was just on my way in to see you. It's an outrage—but so exciting! I called you right up but they said you weren't in. I couldn't stand it—I just had to do something, so I jumped in my car and came on in. I knew you'd listen to me."

"I'll listen just so long as it takes you to draw up at Headquarters, Miss Kendall. I'm afraid I haven't much time just now."—If this spoiled kid thought she could coax him into letting Ross Ingram out of a tight hole—well, she'd soon learn that her dimples were not equal to that.

For answer she jerked something from the cuff of her coat and let it drop on the inspector's knee. Then the coupe lurched forward through the traffic and swerved around the next turn. Putting her own business first, Connie had willfully swung into a one-way street that led away from Headquarters. But the route they were taking was now a matter of indifference to Bratton, for he held in his hand another grey letter-sheet.

It was crumpled and mud-stained and the speed of the car made the words leap crazily, but by stooping to her dash-board light he made out the words. They were written in the bold hand he had already spent so much time examining, but the message was unsigned.

"He's mine, but your silence must help to save him. If they get him for this, it will mean death for both of us."

"To think that I would ever get a death threat!" Connie was saying. "It's just too thrilling for words, but I'd rather not be taking any, thank you." Again the coupé skidded in the treacherous slush, but to death in that form she was superbly inattentive.

"Let me hear how you got this," Bratton ordered, restraining his instinctive gesture toward the brake.

"I was at home and practically alone when it happened." She began her recital with nervous haste. "We've a long sun-room along one side of our place and I was out there with Trix—that's the new Scottie I'm training. I'd romped with her until I'd got all steamed up. Just as I had my hand on the catch of one of the windows Trix let out a growl. I turned to look at her and crash! something smashed through the glass and hit poor Trixie. It was a stone almost as big as your fist wrapped up in that grey paper. I'll admit I hardly looked at it at first—I was more concerned about Trix. She got a nasty bruise. But when I smoothed the paper out and read what was written on it, believe me, little Connie was scared stiff for a minute. Then I snapped into a little action. I should have gone right out through the window, but I backed in through the house and let myself out by a side door. By that time there wasn't a sign of anyone, except for the footprints."

"Footprints?" echoed the inspector somewhat woodenly.

"Yes, a whole mess of them under the shrubbery where the snow hadn't melted. Whoever threw that stone had been standing there watching me—it makes my blood run cold! And across the lawn there were little heel marks. The ground was so soggy they dug right in. I made Parsons bring a flash light and we traced them as far as the drive. That's gravel and from there on we couldn't tell. Then instead of hunting around any more—I wish now I had; she couldn't have been far away—I came in and tried to

call you, and then I ran on in to town. I felt safer. It's no
fun having your life threatened."

"Nonsense, Miss Kendall, you're in no danger," but
Inspector Bratton was determining how far he would have
to share with her what the grey letter had told him. "People that go about making melodramatic threats never do
anything. I'll take care of it, though. The man on the beat
out there will keep his eye peeled, or somebody else will be
getting a fright. By the way, what makes you think it was
a woman? I notice you said 'she.'"

"Because the letter sounded exactly like a woman worried sick over a man. But why she should think I—"

"Look here, Miss Kendall, I wish you'd answer this one
question without throwing a fit. Can you tell me the name
of any other woman who is in love with Ross Ingram?"

Connie passed a truck, clearing it by a millimeter. The
inspector did not recognize that as her reaction to his ill-
starred phrase, "any other woman." When she was through
with a man, she was through! "No ghost threw that letter
in at me," she replied a moment later, "so it couldn't have
been written by Mrs. Thayre. As for other women, nothing
would surprise me though the line he could hand a girl
never sounded like it. Now I'll ask you one: If this is all
melodramatic nonsense and I'm not to worry and so on,
why bring in Ross Ingram?"

Bratton calmly ignored the girl's alert thrust. "Whoever wrote the letter," he said as if to give the impression
that he was merely thinking aloud and had not heard her
question about Ingram, "infers that she is equally involved
in something with the man she prizes so highly. 'Death to
us both' doesn't mean to you and her, but to him and her. I
wonder . . . well, it's about time, young lady. If you hadn't
delivered me pretty soon the least I'd have done would
have been to tie a ticket on your wheel."

Bratton stepped out of the coupé which had at last been brought around to Headquarters. "Don't worry about the crazy letter. It's not worth it."

"You're keeping it, I notice. And to show how much that keeping silence stuff means to me, I'll tell you something else. I used to get lots of notes from Ross, written on paper just like that."

The coupé shot off. Inspector Dan Bratton climbed the wooden stairs that led from the street to the official precincts. Connie Kendall's farewell speech lapped in neatly with certain conclusions that were shaping themselves in his mind. One troublesome detail in particular might now be checked off, though it did not mean at all what the girl thought it meant.

18

THE WOMAN IN C

Inspector Bratton clumped on to the top of the long flight. His resentment toward Connie's highhanded interference with his time returned. "A regular Joe Kendall trick," he muttered. "She could have left the letter and a statement and gone on. Now it's too late for me to go back to Line's. Wonder if Gryce and. Mac have got Ingram in yet. I could do with some food before I begin on that baby."

But Jeff Gryce, McKim, and Ingram were not waiting for Bratton, nor were there any reports. Red Becker called in to say that Thayre had gone to his club after escorting Mrs. Agnew to the Green's Mill train. He was told to stay on the job until the man holed in for the night. There were no messages from Getty, but Bratton found a scribbled memo on his blotter that must have been left there by someone from the municipal laboratory. Just what was wrong with the blood tests, the inspector couldn't make out, but as the chemist had now gone home his troubles would have to wait till tomorrow.

Expecting momentarily to confront Ingram, Dan Bratton forgot about his dinner in the luxury of a few minutes for uninterrupted thought concerning the Thayre problem. As facts now stood, he supposed he might as well cross three of his possible suspects off the list. Perhaps a fourth. . . . That would leave just the one to concentrate on tomorrow. He settled himself in his creaking chair and began to peel the tinfoil from what he considered a really good cigar.

Jessica Brooke's day had come to an end at last, too. The store detective at Line and Hollis's was tired in body and disgruntled in spirit. It had not been pleasant, facing Dan Bratton's cold blue gaze. The shrug of his shoulders that said, "Just like a woman," was what she minded most. Her suppression of Joyce's relation with Thayre had been quixotic, she was now almost ready to admit. She might have known that a man as human as Dan Bratton would not have arrested the poor girl merely because of that surprising situation alone. What Bratton was making of her hunch about Thayre's alibi he was obviously not telling her. Punishing her, was he?

The raw wet wind that had followed the earlier attempt at snow made the wait for her street car intolerable, but when she had at last worked herself aboard, the thick atmosphere within the car was equally disagreeable. Jessica Brooke was very much the poor working woman that evening.

This would be the end, she tormented herself, wedged narrowly between a broad expanse of moth-ballish overcoat and a steamy window. She'd be the inspector's idea of a flat tire after this. There would be no more friendly tips about rounding up the big-time shop-lifters, and as for her chance of heading the new bureau the Commissioner had hinted about, she could no longer hope for a boost from Dan Bratton.

The street car jerked along, stopping optimistically at every crossing to squeeze on a few more passengers. Jessica mopped a spot on the misty window and peered out into the growing darkness. Goodness, no further than Madriver Drive after all this time. These Ninth Street cars were the world's worst. She rubbed her peep hole again and stared out unbelievingly, her peevish complaints forgotten. Then she resolutely wormed her way back through the crowded car, ready to leave it at the next stop.

She splashed unheeding through the slush and when she had gained the sidewalk reversed her direction until she had returned to the corner of Madriver and Ninth. There she paused to look again. It was there, an apartment house, its entrance arched with its name—the Sagamore.

"It's a chance—just a chance," she could hear herself say, "even if there should be an Emily Somebody living here."

She missed it the first time, but her second, more deliberate perusal found it—a card bearing the name "Miss Emily Scott."

She was so excited that she almost started up the stairs without equipping herself with the number of Miss Scott's apartment. It was 35, which designated the third-floor front. But her repeated knocks on the door of 35 brought no answer. That was just as well, no doubt, for Jessica needed an interval to regain her breath and plan a campaign.

Before she had completely accomplished the latter, ascending steps sent the detective half way up the next flight. The steps tap-tapped like a woman's and they paused at a third-floor door. There was the click of a key. Someone had entered 35.

"Now!" Jessica Brooke challenged herself. "It's only a chance, but it won't hurt to try. I've got to get a look at her."

Marshalling all the descriptions that had been accumulated of the woman in booth C, Jessica rapped hesitantly upon the door. It was opened almost immediately by a woman still wearing her coat and hat. The hat was a brown sport felt. That was the first detail Jessica noticed. That the woman was tall and slender and dark-eyed she saw next. Her pale face was drawn with an emotion just under control and she was breathing shallowly. That might be climbing two flights of stairs, thought Jessica, and picked up a cue.

"I'm afraid I'm all mixed up," she explained in a thin, timid voice. "I'm hunting for a cousin of my husband's. We knew she'd been sick, but we hadn't heard that she lived in the Sycamore until today."

"This is the Sagamore. I'm sorry, but that must be the mistake you've made."

The door was swinging shut.

"You don't say! Sagamore for Sycamore—that's the way I am. Her name is Rollins—Mrs. Callie Rollins. Maybe you know her—oh, you have a telephone. Would you mind— could I just call up my husband and tell him where to pick me up? It's real nasty out tonight."

The door of apartment 35 closed, but Jessica Brooke and the woman who corresponded to the scattered descriptions of the unknown occupant of the fitting room next to the one where the body of Vivian Thayre had been found were both on the same side of the panel.

The woman made an indifferent gesture toward her telephone and Jessica called the number that might betray her purpose. But the sequence of digits that made up Bratton's number meant nothing to the dark-eyed woman.

It was while Jessica was waiting, none too sure that she would hear the inspector's crisp response, that she noted the mud on Miss Emily Scott's shoes—great gobs of it. Melting snow on city pavements would scarcely account for their condition. If Bratton had not been so displeased with Jessica that afternoon she would have observed something else about the shoes that would have heightened her excitement still more.

"Oh, Dan, is that you?" She had to carry it through like that. "This is Jessie. Come and get me right away, won't you, dear? I'm waiting at the Sagamore Apartments, way out on Ninth Street. At the Sagamore, Dan—are you sure you understand? Right away . . ."

Jessica replaced the receiver upon its hook. She felt weak. She stole a glance at the slender figure still standing near the door. If Dan Bratton hadn't understood—if this woman had . . .

It was too much to expect to be invited to wait in 35. She must post herself down in the lobby, for the inspector would need some quick explanations. If the woman should attempt to leave by the front entrance, she'd have to follow; but if there was a back way. Was she crowding her luck? Twittering her thanks, Jessica withdrew from apartment 35.

The next fifteen minutes were the longest she had passed for many a day. At last an unobtrusive car slid to a stop at the curb and Bratton hurried across the sidewalk. When he saw who stepped forward to greet him his eyes twinkled forgivingly.

"Cheers! You don't mean—"

"Oh, I think so. I felt sure enough to call you. The name on the directory board is Emily Scott."

"It would be," said Bratton thinking of the signature he had tried to recall to legibility on Milly's water-soaked find. "Any reason why we shouldn't go right up?"

"You want me, Inspector?" Jessica Brooke was humble.

"I need you. There ought to be a witness." Thus was Jessica restored to favor.

Going up the two flights to 35 she imparted another impression her first encounter had left with her. "She had her hat on, so I couldn't be sure, but I had a feeling for a minute that she looked like that picture—the first Mrs. Thayre."

After Bratton's authoritative knock it was so long before the door opened that Jessica grew panicky. At last it swung inward. The nudge Jessica gave the inspector was meant to tell him that with her hat off the woman still reminded her of the picture of Mary Whitford.

The succeeding interview was in Bratton's hands. "You are Emily Scott?" he inquired. "I am Detective-Inspector Bratton from Headquarters and I have been wanting to talk to you ever since last Tuesday afternoon."

"I have been at home all the while," she replied and gave Jessica an inscrutable look.

"Until late this afternoon, you mean." The inspector's glance flickered downward and came to rest not on mud-stained heels but on beaded brown satin slippers. "Tuesday's shopping expedition made seclusion necessary, no doubt."

She stared at him but cannily said nothing. Bratton made a new attack.

"Last Tuesday afternoon you were at Line and Hollis's in their French Room at the time that a woman was killed—murdered. If you do not choose to speak of your own accord, I shall arrest you as a material witness."

She raised her eyebrows skeptically and Bratton frowned. He was thinking of the print that Paula had unearthed for him.

"You are quite mistaken," she murmured, "quite. I have nothing to say. Do you mind if I sit down?" She sank into a chair and Jessica noticed that her hands gripped its arms spasmodically.

At that Bratton shifted his position in order to face her squarely. The move brought into range the room beyond the one they had entered. It was a bedroom and he could see a muddy pair of shoes that had been kicked aside and left just under the bed. They were patent leather pumps with a distinctive little buckle. They were newer shoes than Joyce's and longer, but they were the same Hanby model.

"That's right," agreed Bratton heavily. "Anything that you would say might be used against you."

Her slender fingers tightened their hold upon the chair arms, but still she said nothing.

"Circumstantial evidence is tricky stuff—who ought to know that better than I?" Inspector Bratton smiled at his own parenthesis. "But when instance after instance involves the same person I'm wise enough to take it for what it's worth. Suppose I tell you some of the circumstances I have against you—you'll see why I mean business."

There was no response from the drooping dark head. All sorts of impossible possibilities tore through Jessica Brooke's mind. Suppose this—this murderer had already outwitted them by swallowing a dose of poison . . . sensational ideas like that.

Bratton's quiet reasonable tone continued. He sounded as if he had her where he wanted her, Jessica thought.

"You were seen, you know, any number of times. You procured your weapon in the book department and followed your victim into the French Room, even as far as the fitting booth next the one she had entered. You could tell when the clerk left her and you slipped in then and accomplished your revenge. You were seen coming out of booth E." The inspector's voice deepened and fell and his eyes once more grazed the muddy patent leather shoes lying under the bed.

"You were seen leaving the fitting alcove, as well, and in the rest room. You did not make use of the taxi you had called. That was because you had decided to leave by way of the basement, passing the stocking counter there—"

"But she couldn't have had the scissors in the rest room. Emma would have seen them." Jessica's interruption was a silent one. The inspector had slipped there. What was he saying now?

"Your own gloves were doubtless badly stained by that time. That is the reason you had to make use of your victim's lighter ones."

Emily Scott, if that was her name, was listening now, and relaxing curiously. Both Bratton and Jessica noted that. Once a little half-smile moved her lips. Suddenly she spoke.

"You are quite mistaken—really. I was not there."

"And I know you were there." There was a deadly insistence about the inspector. "Furthermore, there is the evidence of the letters you wrote, those letters on grey paper like Ross Ingram used."

At this reference Jessica Brooke was ready to go off the deep end. The inspector's last words affected Emily Scott even more noticeably. He went on: "You went to some pains to match the paper exactly that afternoon, doubtless because you had other letters to write. One you delivered by hand this afternoon."

That sunk Jessica completely.

"However, your warning to Ingram on Tuesday was ill-advised. Too bad—"

She smothered a tortured scream, goaded beyond endurance. Springing to her feet she flung out her arms and turned as if flight was the only way out. But Bratton's bulk near her entrance door and. Jessica's swift movement toward the passage leading backward through the flat was the answer to that.

"Very well, I did it—I did it! But not Ross—oh, you must believe that. It wasn't Ross." She sank back into her chair, her hands framing her pale and ravaged face. It was then that Jessica observed that she was wearing a ring set with a dull carved stone.

Bratton was thinking—thinking of the letter that this woman had thrown in to Connie Kendall scarcely two hours ago. Silence about Ross Ingram. . . . Well and good; he knew now how to get what he wanted from her.

"My dear," he resumed in a calm fatherly manner that his years were hardly equal to, "I happen to know that Ross Ingram did not kill Mrs. Thayre. Don't give that another thought. Just tell me your story."

Jessica was thinking what dreadful business detecting was. . . . Deceiving the poor creature like that and Dan Bratton saying it as if he meant it. Emily Scott, too, was patently suspicious yet pitifully eager to believe.

"Ross safe? Yes, yes, of course he is. I know he is—*I know it!* I did it myself." She shook in a long slow shudder.

"Tell me," repeated Bratton softly.

"He is mine—he always comes back to me, but I have had to stand so much and she—she had everything! When I saw her there I thought I would tell her—tell her about Ross and me. I was good enough for him once but with easy money—yet he had always come back to me. So I followed her in."

Incoherent and rambling as the woman's words were, her listeners hung upon them, convinced of imminent revelation.

"I stood up on the little stand—where they measure skirts, you know, and looked over the edge once, just to be sure." Her voice broke and her eyes shifted. "Then I jumped down"—Bratton checked off the thudding noise Miss Spinner had heard—"and went in. She didn't turn—she never saw me. . . . Then I threw the knife out of the window and—and—yes, I did pick up her gloves. I couldn't let mine be seen, could I? But Ross didn't do it. . . ."

"He was there," the inspector reminded her.

The woman's voice rose to a harsh wail. "When I saw him sitting there—*sitting* there instead of—" She controlled herself with a noticeable effort. "I merely spoke to him and hurried on."

"He knew you?"

Her smile was proud. "Ross would know me."

"He had come to meet her, you see." Bratton wished afterwards that he had left that unsaid.

"I saved him from her," she said dully.

Inspector Bratton's manner became warmly genial. "I surely appreciate your statement, Miss Scott. I'm only sorry you didn't make it sooner, but, believe me, it was worth waiting for. The weapon—a knife, I think you said—you threw out the window." He laughed gently. "That settles it, then; I can't arrest you for the murder. There's no window in the fitting alcove, for one thing. For another, whoever killed Mrs. Thayre didn't use a knife."

"But Ross—" The involuntary cry was poignant.

"I told you once not to worry about Ingram."

"But I did it—there must have been blood all over the dress," she moaned.

A knock rat-a-tatted on the door of 35. The inspector jerked his head and Jessica moved to answer it. A policeman in uniform stood in the hall.

"Inspector Bratton here?" he asked. "Sergeant Gryce is waiting below, sir." The policeman was now talking over Jessica's shoulder. "He says will you step down at once. It's urgent."

Inspector Bratton shrugged patiently. "You carry on here," he directed Jessica. "I'll be right back, but in case I shouldn't, just stick around—all night, if necessary."

"You're not going to arrest—"

"Certainly not, Miss Brooke. Knives—!"

"But you didn't even ask her if she was Mary Whitford . . ."

"Seriously, Miss Brooke, do you still think that question necessary?"

19

In the Thayre Garage

"Ingram's been pinched," blurted Jeff Gryce.

Such a turn of events had confused the sergeant. He had been detailed to watch Ingram and he had done a good job, so he was willing to admit, though nothing suspicious had occurred until the middle of the afternoon. Then Gryce recognized that his man was trying to give him, or someone else, the slip. Gryce had tagged along. Ingram had gone to a bowling alley out in Spidertown. Then without even his—Gryce's getting wise to it, the raid had been pulled. Sure, that was what he was trying to tell the inspector. Ingram had been arrested by the enforcement squad. Somebody in the Tovky gang had split.

By that time McKim had caught up to him and he was on the job while Gryce was reporting, but if the inspector wanted to give Ingram the works he'd have to fix things with the deputy marshal.

Bratton considered the situation. It was now a matter of indifference to him what befell Ingram, though it might be wise to see that his release on bail should not be too speedily accomplished. He knew now, and from the woman herself, all that he had hoped to squeeze out of Ingram.

Let this interruption stand, he concluded. It was working to his advantage. He dismissed Gryce and climbed into the car in which he had made his hasty trip in response to

Jessica Brooke's cryptic telephone message. Dan Bratton chuckled to himself. That had been a slick trick of hers, one after his own taste. But for the time she could be left to think that some imperative duty had indeed called him regretfully away from the woman in the Sagamore Apartments. It must have been Apts. instead of Ave. that the girl at the stationery counter had seen.

The inspector's car scudded onward, in and out of traffic tangles. Yes, Miss Brooke could look after that end satisfactorily. What he himself was going to do now was to analyze all his case notes. Emily Scott's ridiculous statement indicated that that was now essential. There was something that little Mrs. Lewis had said—or was it the girl who wrapped the boxes? Mrs. Nordhoff might know . . . or the Cline kid. He should have asked Miss Brooke whether Joyce Terry was still staying at her apartment or at Mrs. Fahlmann's.

Once again concentrated thought on Inspector Bratton's part met with interference. He had just spread out the miscellaneous jottings he had made in connection with the French Room murder when the long overdue report from Getty came in. It was a long-distance call from Denver. The connection was not good and the inspector alternately listened and roared, "Say that again! I can't hear you." When at last he banged the receiver back to place he mopped his perspiring face and regarded the notes he had scribbled, half in chagrin and half in triumphant excitement. "Maybe I'm cockeyed . . . maybe I'm cockeyed," he murmured, "but she never would have carried on like that if she hadn't seen him—or thought she saw him."

He stared at the jumbled scrawls that represented his summary of Getty's precise report. "Nordhoff . . . two years in Chicago . . . husband died in 1924 . . . a child . . . no resources . . . specialty shop in San Francisco . . .

started in 1921 . . . bankruptcy . . . the kid in Denver . . . a widow from the East . . ."

Bratton shook his head and sighed. It could be—it could be, he was forced to admit. Only in that case Emily Scott would never have staged the show she had. Once more he pawed through the documents in the case and brought to the surface Mrs. Ludlow Wilkinson's emphatic denial that she had seen anyone resembling the first Mrs. Thayre. Hold on—what was this about that old girl's saying she had overheard a customer say that Madame Nordhoff was looking after her herself? And Dottie had said that she had seen the buyer back in the stock room. Maybe Knox would remember that. . . .

Abruptly Bratton jumped from his chair. There was one point he might as well settle right away. He could telephone—no, it wouldn't take long to drive out, but he'd have to step on it or she'd be tucked in for the night. He used the telephone, however, long enough to ascertain that the girl he wanted was not at Mrs. Fahlmann's.

Joyce Terry, bathrobed and frightened, admitted him into Miss Brooke's apartment.

"That's all right, child," he attempted to remove the startled look from her eyes. "I just popped in to ask a question that only you can answer. You told me the other afternoon—Tuesday, you know—that Mrs. Thayre had tried on two or three dresses. I want you to tell me just what those dresses looked like—not that it will mean much to a mere man," and he laughed cheerfully.

Joyce looked soberly up at him, her hands deep in the pockets of her blanket robe. "There was a powder blue model with a bolero. I believe that was the one she asked to see. It had been in the window, I know. But the bolero wasn't becoming, we both agreed. And a beige chiffon velvet. That's the one she bought. And a dark green crêpe satin, an Anjou number. I brought that out because I could tell she wore green on account of her bag—the one that disappeared, you know."

The inspector nodded comprehendingly. Not yet had he divulged what he suspected about the bag. "What would become of those dresses, Miss Terry?"

"Why, I carried the beige velvet out with me to the desk when I went for my book, and Dottie would—" She caught her breath and the violet eyes grew almost black.

Bratton gave a quick nod. "You are remembering that when you came back to booth E. there were no dresses there, except the one that Mrs. Thayre had worn. Isn't that true? What size were they, Miss Terry, and how would you describe them? In fashion words of one syllable, please. . . ."

Five minutes later he left, saying in farewell, "If I were you, I'd not come back to the store till Monday. Everything will be—quieter by that time. Meanwhile you know how to get me."

At the nearest public telephone booth Bratton stopped to make two calls. Two were necessary because there was no answer when he tried Knox's number. Otis Galway was the more logical person to talk to and after a time Galway answered pettishly, a doubled five spades having been interrupted by the inspector's insistence.

"Of course, Inspector," snapped Galway. "The watchman will let you in at the Court Street entrance. You're your own best authority—he'll let you alone."

By the time Inspector Bratton had rummaged about in the remotest depths of Line and Hollis's fourth floor stock rooms and had subjected a green gown to a minute examination he was whistling cheerily to himself. Let the Commissioner thump on his door—he could take his own part now! He hung the green dress back exactly where he had found it and bade the watchman good night.

On his way back to Headquarters he stopped at an all-night stand for a cup of coffee. He rated that, he considered, for there had been no dinner bell in his crowded day. Yet Red Becker's private opinion remained that if he had caught the inspector the first time he called some of the kudos might have been his. At that, it was only a ten-minute delay.

"That you, Chief?" Red squawked when he finally got him on the wire. "Thayre's croaked. . . . Yeah, Thayre. I'd say carbon monoxide. Come on out."

Once more Inspector Bratton started his engine. Once more he made the run out to Buckeye Heights. Carbon monoxide . . . was this accident or suicide? He thought of his last interview with Rupert Thayre. Had he pushed the man too hard? He thought, with a definite sense of relief, of Joyce Terry. . . .

It was now long after midnight. The weather had fulfilled its earlier promise of winter. There was no more snow, but the wind had not died down. Out in the more open district of the Heights the slush had thickened into ice. Consequently the roads were nearly deserted and the fresh excitement at the Thayre house had not yet attracted much attention.

As the inspector stopped his car Becker moved forward into the path of the lights. "Back in the garage, Chief. The pulmotor crew's there and a doctor named Morris," he explained. "But it ain't going to do any good."

The two detectives advanced along the drive that curved to the garage. It was part of the house structure forming an ell with the main portion of the basement. The stairs that led from the back hall of the house to the cellar paused half way down at a door which opened into the garage. As Bratton stepped through the wide swung doors from the driveway and before his eyes swept the stooping figures at work over something on the cement floor, he saw at this inner door the cowering form of Milly Schwankenzuber.

Red Becker continued to jerk out his story. "I did just like you said—hung on to Thayre. While he ate his dinner at the club I was in the kitchen chinning with the chef. Then he went upstairs to a little side room and sat there by himself, reading the newspapers. He'd eaten alone, too, with his back to the rest of the dining-room. Nobody came near him and he didn't talk to anybody. He didn't make any telephone calls. I was in and out all evening—it was blamed cold outside and the door man got wise to what I was doing. I was beginning to think that maybe he was going to sleep there and I might as well call it a day when he come out. It wasn't quite ten-thirty. You can't wonder that the poor devil didn't want to go home. By the time he'd got his car out of the club parking space I'd managed to raise a taxi myself and was all set to follow. He drove straight out here, only he stopped once, just a block down and a man got out—

"Yeah, a man. That's what I said. Where he picked him up, don't ask me. I'm telling you, Chief, the only damn place he could have would be there where his car was parked. I was rounding up my taxi then. Well, Thayre drove right up the drive and into the garage here and I heard the doors slam shut and saw a light flash on. I got out of my cab and told the boy to wait on the corner below and then I slipped up the drive just to be sure, like you said, Chief, that Thayre was signing off. I could tell that there was still a light in the garage but I couldn't see in—you can look for yourself what kind of glass he's got in the doors. Then in a minute or two the light went off and I turned back to the street, but my taxi was gone. I could just see its tail light about four blocks down the road. Some guy must have looked like a bigger tip than I did. . . ."

There was a cessation of the feverish activity on the cement floor of the garage. The young doctor let his stethoscope dangle hopelessly. He looked at the head of the life-saving squad, who nodded his tousled head in affirmation.

"Guess we'll have to notify the coroner after all." He addressed the inspector, whom he recognized and whose appearance he had at once associated with the recent sensation about the dead man's wife.

The young physician swung on his heel. "The man is dead," he pronounced. At the words Milly, huddled on the bottom step of the half flight, began to sniffle.

"All right, Jerry. I'll take charge." Bratton stepped forward into action. "Have one of your boys call the coroner. You stand by till he comes," he directed Dr. Morris.

For an interval there was nothing to do but wait. The inspector allowed the others to establish themselves more comfortably in Milly's kitchen but Becker he detained in the garage.

"Listen, Red," he commanded. "I haven't heard everything yet. How did you know this had happened?" His gesture indicated the still figure on the floor.

"That's why I called you, Chief. It struck me so darn queer. My taxi was gone, see. I don't know how long I fooled around figuring some way to get back to town without walking. They don't seem to have drugstores out here and I kind of hated to knock up a private residence to get at a phone. Believe it or not, every house around was dark. I walked as far as the corner of Hillside and Mayberry thinking I'd run into the man on the beat, but before he crossed there I thought of it."

Becker paused there as if he considered it the proper place for an exclamatory interruption, but none occurred. He ventured to light a cigarette.

"It came to me—just like that!" Red snapped his match in two for simile. "The light in the garage had gone out but none had come on in the house. Not a flicker, see. I don't know why, but it got to worrying me and I beat it back here. Everything was nice and quiet. I pussyfooted around and the more I thought about it the queerer I thought that business of the lights was. The second time I snooped around the garage I began to get excited. I was pretty sure I could feel it—the engine, I mean. There was a vibration inside that I felt more than I heard. So I gave the garage door a shove and by heck, Chief, it wasn't locked at all! The engine was racing all right and Thayre was slumped over the wheel.

"For all I knew there wasn't a soul in the house, but I took a chance and banged away till some girl come down. She had a fit while I telephoned. I guess she thinks I had something to do with her boss passing out. That's the way things stand up to now, Chief."

Inspector Bratton gave his assistant a level look and stepped over to what the *Bulletin* would be calling in its forthcoming editions the death car. He opened the door to the right and began a leisurely examination, Becker at his shoulder. He supplemented the lighting of the garage with the ceiling and dashlights of the car and his own flashlight.

"Give this a look, Red," he said in a moment and pointed at the floor of the car. The carpet showed damp spots more noticeably toward the right of the driver's seat than about the clutch and accelerator.

"Feel 'em, Red," Bratton further commanded. "Still wet, aren't they, though those to the left are nearly dried out. Yes, Thayre had a passenger all right, and he'd stood around in the wet longer than Thayre had. He only walked through the slush from the club to his car. I wonder . . . just how long he waited to be picked up by Rupert Thayre.

That's your job, I guess, Red. Find out if anyone in this neighborhood rode home with Thayre and trace your taxi driver. I should think you'd like to know who had the nerve to swipe a cab from under your nose. And if I were you, I'd start right now."

That was the reason Inspector Bratton continued his search of the automobile unobserved. He examined every mar and scratch he could detect on the interior finish with a suspicious eye. He removed the cushions and he ransacked the side pockets. It was perhaps as good a way as any to occupy the time until the coroner should arrive.

Thayre's heavy outer coat which he must have been wearing had been removed, and when hope had been abandoned it had been thrown over his body. Swiftly Bratton knelt and ran his hand through its pockets. With one exception what he found did not interest him to the point of removal. From a left-hand pocket he drew forth a yard of stringy scarf. A woman's scarf. It was violet-blue in color and at one end, encircled by a cross-stitched wreath, there was an embroidered initial. The letter was J. When Dan Bratton saw that he frowned uncertainly and then thrust the scarf quickly out of sight in his own pocket.

A sound at the inner door disturbed him. It was Milly, swathed in yards of grey flannel wrapper, her feet encased in knitted bedroom slippers. "Ain't it awful," she began conversationally. It was evident that Milly now regarded Bratton as an old friend. "I knowed there was something wrong. I couldn't fall back to sleep again and then that pounding on the door yet . . ."

Her bulging eyes lighted on the covered form and involuntarily she backed a step or two up the flight out of range. Bratton obligingly followed. The boys in the kitchen could not hear what she might say, though maybe it would not matter if they did.

"My week's up Sat'day night and I wasn't quittin' on the mister till then, but I didn't like it so well staying here all alone oncet. Poor Mis' Agnew went home this afternoon still."

"But you expected Mr. Thayre to return tonight, didn't you?"

Milly's neat head, still in its transparent white hoodlike cap, nodded vigorously. "Yes, Mister, and I kep' listening for his car. Oncet, just before he come, seems like I heard a step down in the drive but it didn't wonder me none—I wasn't what you'd say, scairt. And anyways, in a minute I heard the mister's car, so I turned over and dropped right off."

"Did you notice that Mr. Thayre didn't come into the house?" Bratton asked.

Milly shook her head. "No, after I heard the garage door go to, I didn't worry no more."

"That's right, Milly, keep your head." Bratton had no desire to alarm the girl further. "You can go back to bed before long. I'll leave somebody on duty down here."

The coroner's brakes could now be heard in the driveway. Inspector Bratton turned to greet the county officer, debating just how to say what he wanted to say. "He must have dropped off to sleep in his car. Another carbon monoxide case, doc. In case you decide that something else might have knocked him out first, you'd better tip me off before you broadcast your report. The man's the Thayre whose wife was murdered at Line's. . . ."

20
In Search of a Motive

There was not much left of the night when Dan Bratton at last returned to his home. His slumber though brief was sound and he particularly enjoyed his breakfast. Over his bacon and eggs he chatted amiably of this and that, picking up from his wife odd items of information concerning face lifting, eyebrow plucking, and dental plates, and. the consequent effect upon feminine facial contours.

He gave the Brooke apartment an early ring, hoping to forestall the arrival of the morning papers. He remembered too late that Jessica Brooke herself was probably still playing guardian angel to Emily Scott, and so had to speak to Joyce. Rather awkwardly he avoided the situation by hinting that there was some news in the papers that would distress her and then he hurried on to say that she wasn't to let herself be alarmed by anything she might read in later editions. "Don't talk and keep away from the store—that's my advice to you," he concluded.

The morning papers announced the tragic death of Rupert Thayre with the more or less evident implication that it had been suicide. Its bearing upon the murder of his wife came in for some speculation, though the tendency, Bratton noted with satisfaction, was to ascribe Thayre's act as a natural result of the harrowing week he had passed.

So far so good, thought the inspector and held a brief telephone talk with the coroner. "Let me know," he ended, "as soon as you are sure."

The next person heard from was Jessica Brooke, faintly plaintive but insistent that she really must get into the store that morning.

"Sure, that's all right," replied the inspector. "Get a taxi and bring friend Emily down to me. I'm going to let her tell her story to the reporters this morning."

"Not the one that you know isn't true!" gasped Jessica.

"Sure—why not?" But the satisfied gleam in his blue eyes did not travel successfully over telephone wire.

Bratton strode into Headquarters calling for Becker, who was already waiting for him. "I got the bird that drove me out to Buckeye Heights all right. That was a cinch, Chief, because I hadn't paid him off yet. He doped it out that since I was following a car I was connected with the police and so he found me before I found him, see. But that's all it amounts to, because it was like I thought, a couple that had to make a train in a hurry paid him pretty heavy to let them grab the bus. He said he knew he could find me today and collect—can you tie that!"

"What about the man who left Thayre's car?" demanded Becker's superior.

"Yeah, I asked him about that—this smart-aleck taxi bozo—and he said he saw him turn in at a house with a high roof. Well, that agreed with what I'd seen myself, so this morning I went out, but the folks that live there have gone to California for the winter—left the first of the month. Was I downhearted? Not so's you'd notice it! I roamed around enjoying the beauties of sunrise on the Heights till I found that from the backyard of this place with the high roof I'd just naturally drifted across an alley that led to the Thayre garage. Take it or leave it, Chief. . . . Now what?"

What Inspector Bratton made of Red Becker's report he did not say. Briefly he outlined his next moves. McKim was to go to this address—the inspector scribbled something on his scratch pad—but on no account was anyone there to suspect he was from the police. It would be a good time to try out one of his stagey disguises. The woman who had been concealed in fitting room C was to be brought in and the reporters summoned. They would keep her busy for the next few hours, but nobody connected with Headquarters was to question her story or interfere in any way. Of course she wasn't to be let go.

Again the inspector had a session at the telephone. It was the painstaking young chemist from the municipal laboratory. Bratton listened to his detailed dilemma. Then he smiled beneficently at the black mouth-piece. "If that's all that's holding you up, I can sure help you out. . . . Yeah, found some more last night. I'll be sending it down. . . ."

Bratton then hurried up the street to Line and Hollis's, where he demanded speech with Dottie Cline. Dottie, he was informed, had not reported for work that morning.

"Why not?" he demanded. "Where does she live?"

Otis Galway undertook to answer these questions. The girl's address was merely a matter of record, but what Bratton learned about Dottie's absence whipped his zeal immeasurably. They had had to let Dottie go, Galway explained. The red ticket had been in her pay envelope the night before. She could have worked up to Saturday night—in fact, it would have been only decent for her to do so, but what else could you expect from cheap help like that? She was a cheeky little piece and the head of her department hadn't been satisfied, so they had told her she was through— The department head hired and fired then, Bratton wanted to know. Practically, yes. Such a recommendation okayed by the floor manager was always passed

by the personnel. Of course only underlings were treated
so summarily.

Dottie's absence forced a change of plan upon Bratton.
He would have to make a run out to the child's obscure
address, for there was no telephone listed. She must be persuaded to return to the fourth-floor department at some
moment during the day. Lacking Dottie, he was forthwith
obliged to take Jessica Brooke, that moment arrived, into
his confidence regarding the green dress. He might have
saved himself this trouble last night—his present step was
unnecessarily theatrical, he admitted. In masculine weakness he consulted Joyce's description and gave Miss Brooke
specific instructions concerning the Anjou model.

Inspector Bratton made his way from the executive
offices down to the fourth floor. He wanted a word with
Madame Nordhoff before he left the store. The floor man
was the first person he encountered and Bratton loitered
in his vicinity while he waited for the buyer to appear.
An advance showing of imported models was advertised
for that morning and the head of the department found it
inconvenient to be interrupted even by the police. Knox
was occupied too, urbanely directing the surge of feminine
traffic toward the special offering of the day. What a place
for a man to work, thought Dan Bratton, forgetting that
at the moment he was earning his living in the self-same
place, and more terribly.

At last Madame Nordhoff swished forward, her eyebrows
sharp lines of displeasure. "If you could possibly wait until my luncheon hour, I could give you more time—"

"Unfortunately, no. But I shan't detain you long. Last
Tuesday afternoon you reported that you observed the customer with whom Miss Terry was engaged, but that you
had not noticed the woman who we now believe followed
her into the fitting alcove and concealed herself in booth

C. . . . That's as I have it. Pardon me for repeating. I'm not forgetting how busy you are. But the point is this—I'm speaking confidentially, of course." Bratton lowered his voice appropriately so that a dowager whom Knox was bowing into the French Room could not overhear. "We've found this woman—yes, not a doubt of it. It may be that before the day is over it will be advisable for you to take a look at her. You may recognize her, you know. You'll do that? Thank you very much, Madame Nordhoff. . . . And by the way, one other item—"

His voice rose a notch as the floor manager hurried forward to greet a fresh influx from the elevators.

"Can you tell me what became of the two dresses that Mrs. Thayre did not buy?"

Inspector Bratton clenched the hands that were thrust so nonchalantly into the pockets of his sack coat until he was conscious of the blunt tips of his fingernails. He might be ruining his whole case that minute, but his eyes rested calmly on the woman's face. She was truly superb, he thought, as he heard her reply.

"Terry was showing her a blue model, I remember. I sold that myself the next day to the second woman in the stock company. And the green Anjou—wait, I'll send Leona for that."

A leggy youngster, Dottie's co-worker, was dispatched. She returned within two minutes. "It ain't there—not nowhere," she reported. As Inspector Bratton had already observed the store detective crossing the floor of the department headed toward the elevators and carrying a Boston bag, he was neither surprised at this report nor disappointed in its purpose. Miss Brooke had obeyed her instructions. The cautious young chemist would soon have the green gown.

He waved Leona aside and laid a warning hand upon the buyer's black silk arm. His voice assumed its most

official tones. "Madame Nordhoff, do not concern yourself about that green dress. And you are not to say one syllable about it to anyone—to anyone. Do you understand?
These are police orders."

Bratton gave the floor manager a brotherly salute as he
hurried toward a down car. Judging by the throngs of shoppers eddying about, he concluded that the murder in the
French Room had not fulfilled Knox's gloomy forebodings.

On his way to find Dottie Cline the inspector made
but one stop. That was at the Somers National Bank where
once more an explanation was made of the necessity of
opening Mrs. Thayre's safety-deposit box. The seventy-five
thousand dollars in unregistered bonds were scratched off
the list, but there might be something interesting in the
bundle of old letters. Bratton gathered them together and
hurried on in search of the little picker-up.

Dottie was at home and genuinely glad to welcome the
inspector. So were so many members of her family that
confidential interchange was gravely handicapped. At last
the Cline parlor was cleared.

"Well, Dottie, I hear you've lost your job. How come?"

"Much I care. I'm going down to Randolph's today and
get me a better one. Old Nordhoff was too cranky to suit
me."

"Anything special cause the blow-up?" probed Bratton.

Dottie gave her head a pert toss. "Aw, she was always
pickin' on me, but she sure got good and sore when I
said that picture Miss Brooke had made me think of her.
It didn't much—just sorta, but after I saw it was gettin'
her goat I wouldn't of backed down for nothing. And Mr.
Knox—he does anything she says, so it wasn't any good for
me to honey him up. Stayin' out today served 'em right,"
she finished darkly.

"I'm sorry about that, Dottie. You could have helped me
if you had been there this morning, but never mind about

that now. I'll tell you what I wish you would do, though. After you've seen about your new job at Randolph's, and I rather imagine you'll walk off with it too, go back to Line's and report to Miss Brooke. She may have something for you to do—to help me, I mean."

Bratton felt that he could rely upon Dottie's voluble promises. With a final scattering of chewing gum sticks among the lesser Clines the inspector made off again. Next on his schedule was a trip to Green's Mill. Jeff Gryce was to accompany him. He wanted Jeff to drive him down for two reasons. One was that with the car in his subordinate's charge he himself might manage a look at the letters from the bank en route. In the second place Jeff was the logical person to look up the man at the Green's Mill station while Bratton would be talking to Mrs. Agnew.

He had to wait for Gryce only a few minutes but long enough to discover that the first of the noon editions was already on the streets. He snatched at one to see what the reporters had made of Emily Scott. His head thrust between outspread pages, he was unaware of Paula Pringle's approach until he heard her voice.

"A hot yarn, isn't it, old dear? But you needn't think I'm going to drop that gorgeous lead about the first Mrs. Thayre just because a bootlegger's common-law wife crowds into the picture and kills off her better-dressed rival."

"Better let the public enjoy that story to the full before you spring something else," Bratton mumbled.

"Atta boy! I knew there'd be something else to spring. And it will be my story—you promised."

"See here, Paula, I'm not trying to sidetrack you, but if you'll forget about that picture for twenty-four hours, I'll slip you something else, and it's a hot tip, believe me. Thayre wasn't alone in his machine last night. There must have been a woman with him. Look—this was found in the car." He pulled out the violet-blue scarf and displayed its initialed end.

Bratton paid no attention to Paula's subdued whoop, for he caught sight of the approaching Gryce. "Sorry we're not going your way," he called back as his car started off. Later he might explain his tactics to Paula. That would depend, however, on their success.

On the way to Green's Mill Inspector Bratton failed to make much of the packet of letters that had been treasured by Vivian Thayre. That was partly because he had instructed Gryce to make the trip at the maximum speed. He must be back in town again by four o'clock if possible. Also, he could not be sure of the identity of the writer of the letters. Some small-town Romeo, it was evident, though the place headings differed widely.

Arrived in Green's Mill, Bratton outlined Jeff Gryce's share in the expedition and himself followed his subordinate's directions to reach the Agnew house. By this time Mrs. Agnew would have been informed of Thayre's death, but the inspector thought it unlikely that she would make another journey to the city until the day set for the funeral of her son-in-law. If she could withstand a second shock of this nature, it occurred to him, she was scarcely the invalid she was reputed to be.

However, Mrs. Agnew's prostration was apparently genuine. A neighbor was in charge of the household and she was fussily uncertain about admitting Bratton to Mrs. Agnew's room. "Just two or three questions," he urged without revealing his identity. "It's a matter of life or death, or I wouldn't insist." Certainly the outcome of his business would mean life or death to someone. . . .

Mrs. Agnew was flat on her back, her face a putty-colored masque, but her manner composed. Bratton showed her the letters and asked her to tell him what she could of their author. She did so briefly, indifferently.

"He was always a quiet boy," she concluded. "If he was that set after Vivian he shouldn't have been so meeching about it. That was no way to get anywhere with a girl like her. He left town when she began going with Clint Avery and I knew he was writing to her, but I never paid much attention. I suppose, because I knew Vivian wasn't interested."

Mrs. Agnew's weakness precluded further insistence, yet Bratton risked a question on another topic. "Mrs. Agnew," and his eyes looked soberly into hers, "I think you know something about that traveling bag. Won't you tell me?"

An emotion which the man could not analyze drifted across her gaunt features but in her own time she spoke. "No one man could ever hold a woman like my daughter. Whenever she used her old name, I learned to know . . . that that mood was upon her. Not that it matters now. . . ."

Bratton thought of what Joyce had reported that Vivian Thayre had said so lightly about one of the ten commandments and agreed, silently, that it no longer mattered.

As he was withdrawing from the chamber the woman raised herself from the pillow to ask hoarsely:

"But I told you—it was that woman who did it. Have you found her yet?"

"I think I have, Mrs. Agnew." Bratton paused and gave his watch a glance. "I shall know within the next few hours, I hope. But whether I shall have your daughter's murderer rounded up so soon I am not so certain."

What Gryce had picked up from the man at the railway station lessened Bratton's uncertainty but made necessary an even speedier return run from Green's Mill. If the coroner's findings and the delayed experiments in the city laboratory bore the inspector out, he must seek Otis Galway at once.

21
THE FIRST MRS. THAYRE

Upon his return to town the first move that Bratton made was to get in touch with Jessica Brooke. He gave her a string of directions and she assured him that everything would be in readiness when he appeared. Since Madame Nordhoff was expecting a summons there ought to be no difficulty.

While the inspector was waiting for the coroner he ran through some mail that had come in on the noon delivery. At the first letter he gasped and reread, pop-eyed. It purported to be from Rupert Thayre's lawyer and was merely a terse covering statement for an enclosure. His client, the lawyer wrote, had sworn to the enclosed before a notary and had directed that in the event of his death it be sent to Inspector Bratton. As said statement had been made out only the afternoon before and as the present writer had been shocked and distressed beyond words upon reading the news of his client's demise less than twenty-four hours later, he hastened to carry out instructions. It was his opinion that his client had deliberately contemplated suicide.

With shaking fingers Bratton tore open the enclosure. If what he was about to read should prove him all wrong about the murderer of the Thayres . . .

"I make this statement in order to safeguard an innocent and unsuspecting girl," he read.

"On the afternoon of Tuesday, November 7, I went out to the real-estate subdivision in which I am interested. I was aware that no client awaited me, but I wanted to be alone— to think. But I could not think calmly about Joyce. I knew myself well enough to understand that my interest in her would not last long, but that that fact would not restrain me from creating unhappiness for her.

"I walked across the plat that afternoon, trying to determine a course of action. As I came to the road a friendly driver misinterpreted my actions and slowed down. Desire and opportunity were too much for me. I jumped in his car and came in to town. I think I intended going directly to Joyce and begging her to go away with me, but thank God, I didn't. No less than three acquaintances spoke to me as I crossed the street toward the store where I knew Joyce was employed. Discretion cleared my hot head and I swung off in the other direction and eventually took a taxi back to the plat and my own car.

"When I learned what had happened to my wife, I saw at once all the ugly possibilities. My newly formed resolution of the afternoon before had to hold. . . . I had already kept myself from meeting Joyce that evening.

"I could say, in all honesty, that my wife and I played fair enough with one another . . ."

As abruptly as that it ended. The document had been written out by hand and the signature was properly attested and sealed. Bratton read it through again, then folded it, and slipped it into the manila envelope that already held so much miscellaneous evidence. He frowned slightly and withdrew the letter and placed it finally in one of his own inner pockets.

"If things break the way I think they're going to break," he murmured, "it will never have to be used. At any rate it doesn't spoil my case."

What the coroner had to tell Bratton was not at all conclusive. Careful examination had revealed no blow, bruise, nor scratch upon Thayre's body. An autopsy had been performed and carbon monoxide gas as the cause of death confirmed. A quantity of alcohol was present in the stomach. "He'd just had a pretty stiff drink of fourth-rate hooch, I'd say, but I doubt that a man like Thayre could have been knocked cold by one snifter," said the coroner.

Also, the young chemist from the testing laboratory was at last ready to commit himself. The inspector listened to him at length, his satisfaction mounting steadily as he noted each specific, technical detail. He joined the research worker in regret that the blood stains found on the order blank in Mrs. Nordhoff's desk were not more extensive. Analysis would have been easier. Likewise, he agreed that the spots on the green dress really clinched the matter.

"If it hadn't been for the additional samples on the dress, I doubt that I could have been sure about it," explained the chemist. "What the scissors carried was all I had to go on, you understand, and when I noticed the discrepancy in the tests for the stains on the paper, I couldn't check back convincingly. I certainly gave three cheers when that dress came floating in this morning. The topic is one I want to do some independent research on, and an actual case like this is a god-send."

"Yes, yes," said the inspector returning to the point of the problem that concerned him. "I take it that you are ready to give expert testimony on two points. First, that

the blood stains on the paper are at least twelve hours
fresher than those found at the scene of the crime or
on the green dress. Second, that while the blood on the
paper is undeniably human, yet you have observed a
certain difference—in other words, its source was from
another person."

"That's rights Inspector," agreed the chemist, "though
as I said, I'd like the chance at further research before I'd
set up as an authority on that last point."

A pessimistic report from Becker and a mildly exultant
one from McKim were next acknowledged and the two
men ordered to proceed to Line and Hollis's. Bratton then
turned to a white-faced and weary Emily Scott still sitting
under a matron's eye. When he had told her what he intended to do she agreed apathetically and made ready to
accompany him to the department store.

Before the car arrived which they were to use Bratton
seized his chance to slip across the street and into a flo-
rist's shop. When he emerged a gay red carnation was thrust
through his button hole. It is true that as he stood at the
counter making his choice he thought of violets and Joyce
Terry, of Jessica Brooke and a rose and orchid corsage,
even of his wife's favorite chocolates, but lastly of his son's
imminent tonsillotomy, which is doubtless the reason he
symbolized his triumph by a solitary plebeian carnation.

At Line and Hollis's Inspector Bratton escorted Emily
Scott to Miss Brooke's office where he left her in the store
detective's charge. He then knocked confidently upon the
general manager's door.

"Mr. Galway," he announced with deliberate portent,
"I have come to straighten out the affair in booth E.
Before I leave I expect to make an arrest."

Galway murmured a nervous something and caressed
his chin, thus calling the detective's attention to a jagged
shaving nick.

"I must request your presence," the inspector continued, "but I desire no interruptions unless I ask for them,
no matter what turn events may take."

There came a tap at the door, prearranged with Jessica
Brooke. "That will be Mrs. Nordhoff," said Bratton.

It was. Both men rose as she entered and the inspector
turned with some formality to Galway. "Mr. Galway," said
he, "I should state that Madame Nordhoff is a former res-
ident of this city. She was the first Mrs. Thayre, the Mary
Whitford whom I have been so interested to find."

As if anticipating the detective's words, Madame Nordhoff's face had gone grey. But she held her head high and
her eyes did not waver. "Well?" she challenged.

"Sit down, Mrs. Nordhoff," bade the inspector. "That
is really her name," he explained to the general manager.
"Mrs. Whitford was married to Oscar Nordhoff in 1922 in
San Francisco. However, that fact is of no particular moment this afternoon. What I intend to do now is to state
my case against Mrs. Nordhoff."

Bratton swung his gaze from Mrs. Nordhoff to Galway
and back again. She had regained her poise but Otis Galway looked shocked and miserable. "Tuesday afternoon,"
he resumed methodically, "Mrs. Thayre entered what you
call your French Room. Mrs. Nordhoff saw her and recognized her at once. I suspect that this was not the first time
she had observed the woman who had broken her home
and set her adrift almost ten years earlier, though there
was no reason for Vivian Thayre to associate the Madame
Nordhoff whom you see now with the frantic woman who
upon one occasion threatened her life. She saw her suc-
cessor, as I say, still young, lovely to look at, a woman
beloved. Would it be unlikely that long repressed hatred
again shook her? She saw Mrs. Thayre follow the salesgirl
into the fitting alcove. She left her own customer to fume
untended and slipped off by herself into the depths of the

stock room—in an attempt to pull herself together, shall
we say?"

Bratton's slight pause enabled him to note the glint of
interest that could now be detected in Mrs. Nordhoff's
eyes. He went on with more inner certainty, although his
manner had shown no lack of assurance from the first.

"One of the first facts I noted"—the inspector directed this comment solely to Galway—"was the position of
the fitting alcove in relation to the stock room and the
reception corridor. You are familiar with the arrangement.
Anyone can gain quick and unobtrusive access to the block
of fitting rooms from the stock room and, we must not
forget, from the reception corridor as well. You remember also what weapon was used. That offered a nice point
in deduction, though your Miss Brooke should have full
credit for assembling the facts. I submit this as not an utter impossibility:

"The scissors used must have come from this department. In fact, the girl at the wrapping desk thinks she
mislaid hers some time on Tuesday. She found them later,
Wednesday morning. It was Mrs. Nordhoff who pointed
out to her that a pair was lying on a small table nearby.
There was a pair there, but not the same type that this girl
had been using. What did she care whether she was cutting
twine with the same pair of scissors she had employed the
day before? The scissors she retrieved on Wednesday morning happen to be remarkably like a pair that completely
vanished from the millinery section that same Tuesday."

There were times when Dan Bratton questioned his
choice of occupation. He could see himself as a trial lawyer, haranguing a jury. He was rather fancying himself that
moment.

"Be that as it may, Vivian Thayre was killed by a powerful thrust of a pair of scissors. A Mrs. Wellington Lewis,
a patron of the store personally known to Mrs. Nordhoff,

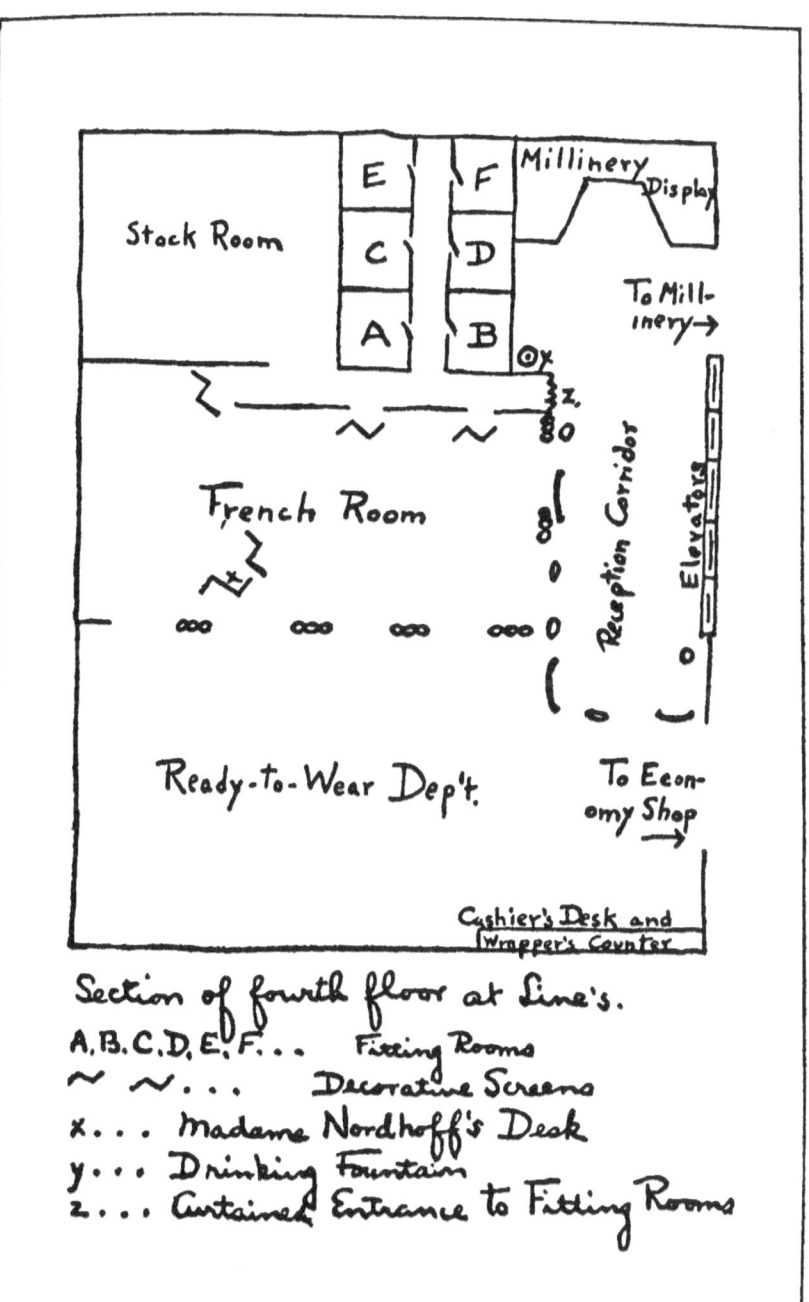

Section of fourth floor at Line's.

A. B. C. D. E. F. . . .   Fitting Rooms
~ ~ . . .   Decorative Screens
x . . . madame Nordhoff's Desk
y . . . Drinking Fountain
z . . . Curtained Entrance to Fitting Rooms

can testify to the buyer's extremely perturbed state. She passed Mrs. Nordhoff near the entrance to the fitting alcove during the time in question. To be exact, this was immediately after Miss Terry had withdrawn from E and therefore just before the attack upon Mrs. Thayre. I must also point out that a Mrs. Dunn Marlay, who was Mrs. Nordhoff's customer at the time, can offer evidence about the length of time she was left to herself during Mrs. Nordhoff's ministrations.

"Now, Mr. Galway, you will recall Miss Terry's story of the finding of the body. She sent immediately for Mrs. Nordhoff, who commissioned herself to remain alone at the door of room E while the girl was dispatched for help—for your aid, among others'. The consequent excitement was great, of course, but in time it was noted that Mrs. Thayre's bag had disappeared. With it went the easiest proof of the victim's identity. The reason for that move is clear, I think. Although Mrs. Nordhoff had every reason to believe that the stress of her life since her divorce from Rupert Thayre had worked irremediable changes in her personal appearance, yet there remained the constant chance that some former acquaintance might recognize her. She was always seeing women whom she had known in the old days—indeed one was present that afternoon. Perhaps you have forgotten Mrs. Ludlow Wilkinson—"

Bratton addressed Madame Nordhoff politely, but her only response was a slight flexing of one hand.

"I'm sure she will be interested to learn that the reason she was so strongly put in mind of the first Mrs. Thayre was that she had actually seen her. But I was saying, Galway, that Mrs. Nordhoff removed Mrs. Thayre's bag in order to delay identification and thus avert as long as possible the inevitable connection of past scandal with present motive for crime. We learned who the woman was the next day, but the green hand bag did not come to light until after the photograph of the first Mrs. Thayre entered the case. Then the bag appeared with suspicious promptness. Its contents were intact with one, possibly two exceptions. Whether Mrs. Thayre's gloves were inside the bag or lying near it, they were gone. However, I know what became of them. But I do not know what became of the small pistol which Mrs. Thayre was carrying in her bag, although I am quite sure I understand why she was so armed."

Madame Nordhoff moved slightly as Bratton spoke of the vanished weapon and then relaxed again into immobility. Once more the inspector thought of her possibilities as a poker player.

"I should like to mention next," he went on smoothly, "a most enlightening fact that I discovered on Wednesday morning. I reasoned, and correctly, it transpires, that the escaping murderer must have been marked by blood in some way. Our search was careful. The men were busy all night but nothing was found. However, the next morning I came upon unmistakable blood stains as if fingers had been drawn across a sheet of paper, though prints were not formed. This incriminating paper I found in a pigeon-hole of Madame Nordhoff's desk. The longer I considered the circumstances under which this clue came to light the more certain I felt of its value. I turned the matter over to technical experts for verification. Hunches don't go in court, you know.

"Before the end of the next day I had discovered something else. Mrs. Nordhoff was afraid of the picture of Mary Whitford that I was circulating. She was expecting me to accost her as the first Mrs. Thayre. Her involuntary glance into a mirror to reassure herself of her changed appearance betrayed her to me. Yet even that advance in my case did not shake my hunch. Naturally I looked up Mrs. Nordhoff's record and antecedents and so learned the truth concerning her identity."

Bratton paused weightily. He had indulged his secret weakness for oratory beyond reason, but he must permit himself a final sentence. "Mr. Galway, it is not Mrs. Nordhoff, whom I intend to arrest."

None of the tenseness melted from the woman's erect figure and her eyes were wary. When she spoke it was as if to herself. "Very likely it's a trap. . . . I should refuse to speak without advice of counsel, but I can hurt myself no more than you have done already. I can see my position . . . and the diabolical maneuvering that has placed me there. I could have killed Vivian Thayre—I can see that. You have even made me remember the way I once cursed the girl who had robbed me of everything. So I suppose no one will believe me when I say—I did not kill her."

"You must have misunderstood me." Dan Bratton's voice was gentle. "I do not believe you killed Vivian Thayre. I wish—Galway and I both wish that you would tell us your story."

"But you have it all—so nearly the way it happened, as far as I know." She paused again and then her tones became firmer. "No one will understand why I consented to come back to this town. Believe me, it was only because the past was so dead in my heart that I considered it. When I left after my divorce I planned to go into business in New York. I had a little capital, money of my own, but I soon felt that there might be a greater opportunity in Hollywood or some coast resort place. It worked out that eventually I opened a lingerie shop in San Francisco.

"Not long after that I met Mr. Nordhoff. After our marriage he became my business partner as well, but his judgment—in short, after a series of unfortunate deals the business failed. My husband became ill. We had been married a little over two years when he died. There was a child, Mr. Nordhoff's son by a former wife. The boy became my only reason for living—is still that. . . . I had to earn our living and my only experience lay in the sort of work I've been doing here. I have had to go where the jobs were. The boy went with me of course. The last winter I was in Chicago he was very ill and the doctors said he must be taken west to live. But I could find no opening there that would pay for the care he needed. The firm I had been with in Chicago recommended me for this place and for my son's sake I was forced to come. Richard is better now— he's enrolled in an outdoor school near Denver, but I must stay here in order that there will be money.

"That's why I am here—not to haunt the scene of my first marriage. And I had changed so—aged, if you will. My hair's gone white; but sometimes I think there has been a still more radical transformation in my personality. I have been through a great deal since that first discovery of a man's unfaithfulness. I assure you, I rarely feel like the woman who was Rupert Thayre's wife."

For a moment she relapsed into revery. Then with a slight smile of apology she continued. "It is true that I saw Vivian Thayre come in and that I recognized her, but I assure you that I went on about my business. I had not the slightest knowledge of what had occurred until I went to Joyce Terry in response to her message. Then when I saw what I saw I felt that everything that I had lived through before was closing in on me—I couldn't stand being involved again in horrible publicity. It was just a moment of blind panic—surely you understand! While Joyce was gone I was mad enough to snatch up the green bag—I knew her name would be in it. I tucked it up under my arm. You may recall that I was wearing a gown with a rather extreme cape collar. As soon as Miss Brooke came down I found an opportunity to slip the bag into my personal locker. Two days later when I was asked if I recognized my own picture I had another of those sick moments of panic. If I should be recognized as the former Mrs. Thayre then having the green bag in my possession would be fatal. So I disposed of it, though before the day was over the inspector knew what I had done and was torturing me about it."

Bratton raised a deprecating hand but did not interrupt.

"There were no gloves in the bag, Inspector, but the pistol—I kept that for myself . . . in case the situation should get beyond my control." There was a quiet resolution about these last words that revealed the scars of past suffering.

"But you took one or two other precautions as well. Joyce Terry, for instance, and Dottie." Bratton ticked off the names. "You would have sacrificed Joyce to save yourself. That fact was so evident to me that it aroused my suspicion. Or perhaps you knew that Miss Terry was much in the company of a man named Phil Leonard?"

The inspector made the reference at random, but he did not miss the quick questioning look Mrs. Nordhoff gave him. Whether he had told her something which she had only guessed, not known, or whether she meant to remind him that here was an item best left undiscussed, Bratton afterward tried to make out, but long after the Thayre case had become ancient history he remained uncertain.

He went on to speak of Dottie. "I was not much surprised when I heard that she had been fired. Her testimony could tell against you. She saw you within that dangerous radius Tuesday afternoon and, too, she was beginning to chatter about the picture. Odd, isn't it, that someone who had never known you when you looked like that ten-years-old photograph should be the one to catch the fleeting likeness that can be seen only after one realizes that the present Madame Nordhoff was once Mrs. Rupert Thayre. . . ."

Bratton stirred abruptly. "But I am forgetting—what you have been saying has been extremely interesting to me. I have only one more question. Where were you last night between ten and twelve?"

She looked at him in some dismay. "I must have been in my room. I live at the Women's League. I know I was in bed by ten-thirty."

"You room alone?"

"I share a small suite, two bedrooms and a sitting room, and I have the inner room. You might speak to Miss Philbank. My room mate is a lawyer and understands the importance of alibis." Mrs. Nordhoff had replied with remote dignity.

The inspector laughed. "That will be all right, Mrs. Nordhoff. Now I mustn't keep the others waiting, so this will be all for the present. My advice is that you knock off for the day, and I'm sure that Mr. Galway will agree."

Otis Galway was beyond speech. As Mrs. Nordhoff left the room another feminine figure entered, but the manager's troubled gaze clung hypnotically upon the inspector's face.

22

INCREASING NERVOUSNESS OF OTIS GALWAY

"Miss Scott," said Bratton ceremoniously, "may I present Mr. Galway, the general manager of the store? There is one feature of your experience last Tuesday afternoon that I am particularly eager to have him understand."

When the three were seated he added, "Miss Scott's presence in booth C is the chief reason that I cannot force a case against Mrs. Nordhoff, as I think you will agree. Unfortunately Miss Scott is in a highly nervous condition, but she tells me that she is now willing to answer any questions that I may put to her. By way of preliminary I am going to tell you that Miss Scott, as she prefers to be called, could be legally addressed as Mrs. Ross Ingram, for she is his common-law wife. She became jealous of Ingram's relations with the late Mrs. Thayre. Is it not true, Miss Scott, that you sent a threatening letter to Mrs. Thayre?"

"Yes," she managed the syllable faintly.

"There was one factor about the letter—or letters, for traces of at least three entered the case—that complicated my problem needlessly. The explanation was, I found, quite simple. Miss, Scott affected a certain kind of grey stationery for no other reason than that at one time Ingram himself had used it. Some women are like that," and Bratton nodded in Galway's direction to indicate that they too could reveal the foibles of enamored women.

"At last I made certain that the letters had been written by Emily Scott. Another thing—it must have been the threatening tone of the one received by Mrs. Thayre the morning of the day she was killed that moved her to carry the gun that was kept in her husband's desk drawer.

"Now, Miss Scott," the inspector resumed his questions, "had you ever met Mrs. Thayre? . . . You had doubtless seen pictures of her in the papers? . . . You had picked up the current gossip?"

A shake or nod of the woman's head answered sufficiently.

"So when she was pointed out to you in the beauty shop you obeyed a primitive kind of impulse and followed her. Miss Brooke will tell you, Galway," Bratton addressed the, manager quite pointedly, "if you are interested, what we learned for ourselves concerning Miss Scott's activities in your store. The matter of the scissors in the book department, for instance. She made use of them to trim from her shoe sole a tag of leather. Please note that the shoes were fairly new. Subsequently these scissors could not be found. They haven't been found yet, in fact. My suspicion is that somebody down there absent-mindedly used them for a book mark. . . . Miss Scott, did you or didn't you stop at the notion counter and buy a pair of scissors?"

"I did not. After I bought the letter paper I caught sight of Mrs. Thayre again and followed her up to the French Room. I told you that all I wanted to do was to speak to her." This longer speech told Bratton that any tendency toward hysteria was for the time safely under the surface.

"Who could that have been?" he mused. "Thayre's stenographer, perhaps. Well, no matter. No need to be distracted by that detail now. . . . To go on—you followed Mrs. Thayre upstairs and eventually into the fitting alcove where you concealed yourself in booth C. Is that quite clear, Mr. Galway?"

Galway nodded mechanically and fumbled for a cigarette which he did not light.

"Miss Scott, let me remind you that you promised to answer my questions truthfully. You heard Miss Terry leave her customer?"

"Yes."

"What next did you hear?"

"It sounded like a man's step and then I heard—" Her face twisted dreadfully as if she were again experiencing what she had felt that afternoon. "I heard a horrible soft impact—oh, I can't describe it, but I knew—I knew something terrible had happened. How I did it I don't know— nor why—but quick as a flash I put my hands on the top of the side partition and raised myself till my eyes were level with it. I could see over."

"What did you see?" demanded Bratton.

"I saw her—like that—what had happened to her, you know . . ."

"But you saw something else?" persisted the inspector.

"Yes . . ." Her reply was almost a sob. "I saw someone leaving the little room—oh, not to tell who it was—just the trousered leg and back of one shoe and the flutter of something green as he stepped out into the passage. All I could be sure of was that it was a man." She shuddered and fell silent.

"Then what did you do?"

"I dropped to my feet and then—I couldn't believe that it had happened. I looked out into the passage but there was no one there. I took a couple of steps and pushed in the door of the next booth. It was true—what I had seen—and heard. I could scarcely, make it seem real even then. I—I touched her. I got blood on my gloves. When

I saw that, then that terrible nightmarish feeling left me.
I pulled off my gloves and stuffed them in my purse and
picked up—hers."

"About that time, Galway, your Miss Pike made certain
observations about feet shod in Hamby's best. . . . As you
hurried away from the French Room to whom did you
speak?" Bratton's question called forth a look of appeal
from Emily Scott but she answered.

"Ross—Mr. Ingram," she said so low that Galway heard
her with difficulty. "I thought—oh, you know what I
thought." Her voice rose with unexpected shrillness. "You
say I am wrong—that he didn't do it, but he told me himself he hated the very sight of her."

"No, Ingram did not kill Mrs. Thayre." The inspector
spoke decisively. "You don't think so, either, do you, Galway?"

"I—I don't—know," replied Galway, his lips stiff.

"Just on general principles, let's say," resumed Bratton, "you warned Ingram—told him to get out while the
getting was good. The mere fact that he was still hanging
around ought to indicate to you as strongly as anything
could that he had no idea what was up. Later he sensed
that something had gone wrong and his innate discretion
did the rest. I can understand that, can't you, Galway?"

Otis Galway looked helplessly at the detective and
mopped his forehead.

"There's just one more question I'd like to ask you,
Miss Scott, and then you may go. I mean—go home, you
understand," and the inspector gave her a quick sympathetic smile. "Where were you last night between ten and
twelve?"

"Why don't you ask Miss Brooke that question, Inspector?" she countered dryly. "I hardly think she took me
sleepwalking."

"Pardon me. My error." Bratton's grin was broad. "I'm not going to badger you about Miss Kendall. You might let that stand in my favor. The bit of melodrama you tried with her was really quite fortunate for me. Eventually it ruled you out as a principal in the murder of Mrs. Thayre." Bratton rose as a signal that she was now free to go.

In silence she moved to the door and then she turned. "Ross?" she asked, her voice scarcely more than a whisper.

"In a little—business difficulty at the moment, I understand, but I have no doubt that he has powerful friends who will soon arrange matters. I shouldn't worry . . . and, Miss Scott, for whatever it may be worth, let me tell you that throughout this affair we could get not one word out of Ross Ingram about you. It was not he who betrayed you to us, but yourself."

Emily Scott's eyes filled with tears. "Thank you—oh, thank you," she murmured and left the room.

"There's a woman, Galway," Bratton enlarged, "who's so crazy about her man that she's in danger of going off her nut. Everything she did had uncontrolled jealousy behind it, except that wild yarn she tried to hand me about killing Mrs. Thayre herself, and there her motive was simply another phase of the same thing. She was afraid the man she saw might be Ingram—"

At that point Galway tried to say something but the inspector continued blandly. "It's true that Ingram wouldn't crack a thing about her although he finally admitted that a woman, a complete stranger he insisted she was, had warned him to leave. But I doubt that his motive was loyalty to Emily Scott. My guess is that he's plain scared of her—she cramps his style."

There came a knock at the door just as Bratton stole a second look at his watch, and the floor man from the French Room entered. Knox ignored the inspector's presence. With a troubled frown he addressed the manager.

"Galway, couldn't this matter wait till after five-thirty? This has been an unusually busy Saturday afternoon and we're one short down there."

Before Galway could reply Inspector Bratton spoke. "Just one minute, Mr. Knox, and then my business will be finished. We've been interviewing some of the women who are mixed up in the Thayre case and there's one more who is waiting to come in. If you don't mind waiting—you needn't leave; there's nothing secret about the situation. You've seen the papers, haven't you? The Scott woman's story is straightening out a lot of things."

He waved Knox to a seat near Galway and crossed to the door. Behind the woman who entered when he opened it he could see Jessica Brooke, who was making no effort to conceal her excitement. McKim, Gryce, and Becker were also waiting, as ordered.

Bratton closed the door and addressed the woman, whose *grande dame* manner was a visible prop. "Mrs. Dunn Marlay, I believe?" he asked. She bowed and accepted the chair offered her.

"I shan't detain you long, Mrs. Marlay, but we—the officials of the store and I—" his gesture included the two men—"hope that you will be able to clear up a small matter for us. It is connected with the sad business that occurred last Tuesday afternoon. You were in the French Room at the time, I understand. Madame Nordhoff was waiting on you?"

Mrs. Marlay bowed.

"From time to time she left you in order to bring out for your inspection other dresses or what not; wouldn't that be so?"

"Yes, of course—"

Before the chill note of protest in her tone could deepen Bratton went on. "Mrs. Marlay, is it not true that at one such time while you were waiting seemingly unattended someone asked you if you were being served?"

"Yes-s, I recall—"

"You recall that you said, 'Thank you . . . Madame Nordhoff is waiting on me herself.' Now, Mrs. Marlay, do you recall to whom you said those words?"

Mrs. Marlay's fine eyes looked into Bratton's and then wavered between Galway and Knox. "Really, I have no idea of the individual's name," she said with frigid distinctness, "but I'm quite sure that I recognize the person there as the one." Mrs. Dunn Marlay was much too refined to point. The merest tilt of her head sufficed to indicate Knox.

"Just one more question, if you please. Do you remember what the gentleman carried over one arm?" Bratton was tensed and ready to spring, but his query caused no outbreak.

Mrs. Marlay bit her thin, unpenciled lips in her effort to concentrate. "Dresses, I think—yes, one was green. I meant to suggest the color to my daughter-in-law, but it slipped my mind."

Inspector Bratton flung wide the door leading to the outer offices. The three waiting detectives were plainly visible, if that was of interest to any of the party in the manager's room. "Thank you, Mrs. Marlay, thank you very much indeed. That will be all. Good afternoon!" He stood graciously aside as she made her exit.

As though his duties could no longer be neglected, Henry Knox rose to follow, but when he saw the phalanx without he hesitated. Bratton shut the door.

"Well, Knox," he said quietly, "you realize we've got you."

Henry Knox turned and resumed his seat, his lips twitching ever so slightly. "Got me for what, if I may ask?"

"On a double count," snapped the inspector. "For the murder of Vivian Thayre last Tuesday afternoon and of Rupert Thayre last night."

Galway half rose in protesting unbelief, but Knox only shook his head in deprecation. "That will have to be proved, you know," he murmured.

"All right, I've got a case. First, as to motive: You were born and brought up in Green's Mill. You like more than one of the young fellows there were devoted to Vivian Agnew, though as far as the town knew she paid you scant attention. However, there was some secret encouragement on her part which you misconstrued into something more serious. In fact, you considered yourself engaged to her. But Vivian was the typical small-town flirt and soon let you know where you got off. You left town and for a time bombarded her with what I should call impassioned letters. They were more than love letters but they meant little to Vivian Agnew. As you know, she too soon left Green's Mill and went on to a scene where her charms had a wider scope.

"How have I learned these facts? From the letters themselves which Mrs. Thayer for some unknown reason preserved and from Mrs. Agnew. I wonder, Knox, that you didn't remove Mrs. Agnew. Perhaps she would have been the next to go? The letters, you understand, are going to tell heavily against you when they are offered in evidence, for they reveal so much of your peculiar psychology. I shan't take time just now, Galway, to read you a sample, but any correspondence course psychoanalyst could interpret them.

"Within a year or so after Vivian Agnew's marriage to Thayre you too had come to this town, but I rather imagine that young Mrs. Thayre made it plain that she did not care to continue the old-home-town friendship. That rankled, didn't it? For there was the suggestion that the department store clerk was not as socially welcome as the bootlegger, for instance. That may be only a guess on my part, but I'm not guessing when I say that you must have been the reason that Mrs. Thayre so very rarely came into your section of the store.

"Now, as to means and opportunity: You must have been surprised when you saw her enter your department the other afternoon. You are welcome to take what comfort you can from the obvious fact that the first murder could not have been a premeditated one. I have been convinced of that from the beginning, but the second one—

"As I say, when you saw Mrs. Thayre come into the French Room on Tuesday something slipped a cog. I wonder . . . she may have refused to speak to you—even to recognize you. When Miss Terry came up to the wrapper's desk after her salesbook you heard her say that she'd just sold her customer in E. Of course you had already noted which one of the girls was taking care of Mrs. Thayre. In fact, you had turned her over to Joyce Terry yourself. You told Miss Terry to wait—that you'd be right back as soon as you had seen the credit manager, and while both girls at the desk were surveying the frock which Mrs. Thayre had purchased you slid the scissors from the counter and hurried down the corridor toward the elevators. Certainly it looked as though you were on your way up to the credit office.

"But there is that curtained entrance that leads almost directly to the fitting alcove and it was through that door that you went. What if you were seen, weren't you the only man, not even excepting Galway here, who could have passed comparatively unnoticed through any section of Madame Nordhoff's department? You were so familiar a figure that no one would pay any attention to you.

"You drove home the blow that killed the woman who had so consistently flouted you. Then, when this long-repressed emotion had been released, you began to think. Circumstances chanced to be in your favor, it is true, but for the rest of that day you acted with canny wisdom. You held in your hand a horrible looking weapon. In all probability there was blood upon your person—upon your right coat sleeve, for instance. You snatched at the dresses that Mrs. Thayre had tried on but discarded and threw them over your arm in such a way that the scissors were completely concealed. You withdrew from the fitting closet as silently as you had entered it. But you were seen. . . ."

Bratton paused a moment there. Time enough later on for the man to realize that though he had been seen he had not been recognized. He must break him down first, if he could. Blast the man, he sat there in smug pride.

"When you left the fitting alcove it looked to anyone who might have been noticing—apparently no one was—as though you were emerging from the stock room. You spoke to Mrs. Marlay, quite as your office demanded. Fortunately for us, she remembered about the dresses. Then you retreated into the stock room and back to a section very irregularly visited by any of the sales people. There you rid yourself of the dresses and the weapon. You saw that one was unmarked, so that presented no problem. But the other one, the green, had been thrown directly over your hand that held the scissors and was badly stained."

Without taking his eye from Knox the inspector once more flung open the door. "Send her in," he roared.

Dottie Cline appeared, a very much dressed-up Dottie, for a free Saturday afternoon was no time for the duller effects of working uniforms.

"You remember the blue bolero dress?" Bratton demanded. "Where did you pick it up that Tuesday afternoon? Late it would be, just before Miss Terry called you."

"Well, after Miss Terry called me, I didn't do any more pickin' up a-tall," explained Dottie, "and seein' that I had just hung that there blue back where it belonged before Miss Terry called me, I remember, plain as anything. It was layin' right inside the stock room door, all wadded up on the floor. If Nordhoff hadda found it, wouldn't I of got it. . . ."

Dottie was dismissed as summarily as she had been called in. Bratton continued. "It was I, Knox, who had the pleasure of finding the green dress. I grant that our department should have turned it up immediately. The place was searched thoroughly enough, but women's clothes are the devil. . . . Of course if you had left the scissors with the dress, the chances are we would have seen them both, but you removed the scissors very shortly after the excitement broke. You had unlimited opportunity to move about unnoticed. You had access to wrapping material. But the blood-stained green dress would have made too conspicuous a bundle. So you let it hang when you went in to the stock room to remove the scissors. My theory is that you had parked them temporarily merely by hanging them over the hook upon which you had hung the dress. The folds of material in the garment absorbed some of the blood with which the scissors were still wet. The stains on the dress very soon showed only in dark, blackish blotches because of its color. Call that another alibi for my boys not noticing anything on their first round if you want to.

"You removed all traces of finger prints from the scissors and wrapped them, using one of the large sheets of paper stocked at the wrapper's desk. The package could have gone in your coat pocket until you were ready to place it elsewhere. We were running all over the building that night and some of the store men, Galway and you and old Baynes and others, stuck around to act as guides, one might say. That's the way the parcel came to turn up the next morning in a basement stocking bin which had not contained it at five-thirty the evening before.

"Now, Knox, I am going to tell you where you made your mistake. Not when you killed Thayre—long before that. . . . It was when you yourself led me to discover the ridiculously incriminating evidence against Mrs. Nordhoff. That was the next morning, you recall. You deliberately took me over to her desk, where you had placed the bloodstained paper. Only a blind man could have missed seeing it, but you gave no sign of observing it. You were full of your theory of an escaped maniac. Of course you weren't the only one to hand me that line. The others who suggested it had their own good reasons for attempting to divert my attention.

"In your case I began by wondering what you had to conceal and then I considered your admirable strategical position. But, Knox, you should have known more about the chemistry of the blood. The stains on the paper did not agree with the traces of blood on the scissors and dress. I suspect when we examine you we shall find a sizable cut or scratch on your body which furnished your false clue.

"Yes, I soon saw that you had the means and the moment, but the motive caused me more trouble. Only a woman, it seemed at first, could have gained access to the fitting alcove; only a man, it was equally obvious, could have delivered the powerful blow that killed Vivian Thayre.

"I'm not boasting that I was so sure of you . . . though since Thursday I have felt positive that someone connected with the store was guilty. That narrowed it to two people. The other one had what I considered an adequate motive. Frankly, in your case I was still up a tree about motive, though I held the right cards in my hand all the time. The letters in Mrs. Thayre's safety-deposit box for one thing, and one of your admiring in-laws in Green's Mill . . . but it was not until we found the woman who had hidden herself in booth C that I picked up the lead that brought me to you. Her story bore every earmark of being told to shield a man; therefore she must have grave reasons to believe that a man was involved.

"That kept me plugging away—that and one other remark she let slip, something about a dress. I myself had seen only Mrs. Thayre's street clothes in booth E and I knew I could rely on Miss Brooke's word that nothing had been touched after she came on the scene. I concluded that something irregular had happened to the dresses that Mrs. Thayre must have tried on and last night I found the green dress. I let it hang where I found it, for I didn't want to alarm—well, it was not impossible that Mrs. Nordhoff had removed the dresses. As for you, the longer the dress hung there undiscovered the safer you were; there was really no need to risk its removal. It would be found eventually, but the burden of explanation would be on the head of the department. This morning I satisfied myself that she had no guilty reactions about green dresses. It had to be you—motive or no motive.

"In the meantime Thayre had been murdered. Yes, my friend, I suspected murder immediately, though it was so subtly done that you may well wonder how I intend to prove it. By the way, what alibi are you offering for the time between ten and twelve last night?"

"I don't have to answer that," Knox replied coolly. Galway stared at the man as though he had uttered something unbelievable.

"You certainly don't," agreed Bratton, "and you're going to need a slick lawyer to tell you what to say when the time comes that you have no choice about answering it." The inspector made no further reference to his own attempt to call the man by telephone during the course of the evening in question. Again he strode to the office door.

"McKim!" he called. "Inside a minute."

Dudley McKim made as smart an entrance as though he had clicked his heels and saluted his superior officer.

"What did you find?" demanded Bratton.

"This, sir," and McKim extended a modest looking pocket flask.

"What's in it?"

"Gin, sir, laced with what the chemist tells me is a particularly vicious sort of knock-out drops."

"We know where we found that flask, Knox, and so do you. You offered Thayre a drink last night after he had picked you up, and by the time he had turned into his garage he was already so far gone that he didn't know that you had slunk in after him, to turn the lights out and the engine on."

For the first time Henry Knox showed signs of breaking, but his emotion was only momentary. He remained impassive even after Bratton said, "Well, boys, I guess we're ready to start . . ." but when he saw the inspector step toward him, handcuffs in hand, he gave a strangled, animal-like screech and gained the door in one leap.

He got no further. Red Becker was waiting and eager to function. And that was the beginning of the end for Henry Knox.

23
Justifiable Grievance of Jessica Brooke

During the course of the trial and conviction of Henry Knox for the murder of the Thayres there was more than one individual among those who crowded the court room as mere lookers-on or played a more important part as sworn witnesses who felt that her own share in the unravelling of the mystery had been of paramount though unacknowledged value. Mrs. Ludlow Wilkinson, for instance. . . . Whenever other activities palled she had only to revert to Inspector Bratton's hint that she had seen the first Mrs. Thayre somewhere on that memorable Tuesday afternoon to launch into an exhaustive defense of her own infallible memory for faces.

There was Mrs. Dunn Marlay whose premonition that she would be subpoenaed as a witness was so well borne out. Her lady-like resentment gave way in time to a pleasant sense of superiority, fostered by the rampant envy of her youngest daughter. "My mother—can you feature it, my dear? Sitting in on the Thayre trial . . . and her hard-boiled chee-ild—what ever happens to me? I've hitch-hiked from here to Palm Beach on a bet and not had the ghost of an adventure. All my life's been like that. . . ."

The prosecution had some difficulty with Milly Schwankenzuber. "Us Dunkards don't hold for lawin'," she protested, but the attorney at last won her confidence. In fact

he secured from her a chance item that cleared away one of
the remaining tags from the case. Mrs. Thayre was going
to spend the coming week-end in Cincinnati with an old
friend, she had told Milly, but Mr. Thayre was to think
she had gone to her mother's. Though this did not have
to be offered in evidence, Bratton satisfied himself that it
was Ingram she had planned to meet. Ingram in time even
went so far as to acknowledge that she had some letters of
his that worried him and he had agreed on the proposed
jaunt only if she would turn them over to him. Hence his
hurried search of her possessions in Green's Mill. As no
letters of that sort were ever found, Bratton concluded
that Vivian Thayre had resorted to this device to strength-
en her weakening hold on Ingram.

Naturally an affair like that in the French Room became a kind of date-line at Line and Hollis's. Knox's exit
was dramatic enough, but on top of that came Madame
Nordhoff's resignation. She was going to take over similar work in Omaha. . . . Good old Ede Pike received her
long-delayed promotion and announced that there was to
be no madame business about it, either. That same week
there came the cable from Mr. Hollis instructing that a
special bonus be paid to every employee who had assisted
in any way in the downfall of the man Knox. From Norma
Schmidt in the basement to Emma in the rest room, from
Jessica Brooke to Dottie Cline, it was felt that the old man
was a grand old man indeed.

Dottie Cline could have had her job back but she
spurned it, though she did accept the bonus. No matter
how much others preened themselves on the extent to
which their observation had hastened the denouement of
the Thayre murder, Dottie wasted very little time culti-
vating her sense of importance. Let the detective-inspector owe her as much as he wished—he attempted a pretty
speech at one time—it had all worked out perfectly swell

for Dottie. At Randolph's where she got another job as easy as anything she met Jerk O'Connor, who drove one of the delivery trucks and who dated her the very first Saturday night after she started in at the new place. . . .

The satisfied look in Detective-Inspector Bratton's blue eyes remained during the course of the trial. It deepened into positive peace when Mrs. Agnew stated from the witness stand that her son-in-law had known that Knox had been one of his wife's discarded suitors and that Thayre had also known that the man was employed at Line's. Consequently the prosecution made the most of this as the fear motive that had led Knox to attack Thayre. What had passed between the two men during the drive from Thayre's club to Buckeye Heights on the Friday night was never learned, for Knox admitted nothing beyond the fact that he had accosted Thayre that evening to claim a memento of the dead woman whom he too had loved, a sentimental touch from which Knox's lawyer wrung the ultimate tear. . . .

Paula Pringle and her friends had their own suspicions about the ramifications of the case. The usefulness of seventy-five thousand dollars' worth of Liberty Bonds became apparent when the shot-to-pieces condition of Thayre's investments was revealed after his death. The mystery of the violet-blue scarf marked with a J remained a mystery to the public, though Bratton explained to Joyce that he had been forced to use it to give Knox the idea that there was no suspicion of a man in connection with Thayre's death. The reason for Emily Scott's hysteric confession made startling headlines, but neither she nor Ingram could protest effectively. As effectively as the Kendall money. . . . There was a sudden silence concerning Connie and Ingram, and therefore the scandal that could have been made of his affair with Vivian Thayre, had the grey letters and the jade bracelet been played up in Knox's trial, had no opportunity to develop. They had served their purpose in leading Bratton to Ingram and hence to Emily Scott, but they concerned Henry Knox not at all.

Nor did Paula ever wheedle out of the inspector anything about the first Mrs. Thayre. "I told you you'd have your story when you produced the woman. Can't you understand that I had the crazy idea for a while that maybe the first wife killed the second, but now that Knox is waiting in the death house, you'll agree that my hunch was all wet."

Of all the people who had been involved in the Thayre case none was so personally aggrieved as Jessica Brooke. "I made my mistakes and all that," she fumed to her intimates, "but I put in some good licks for Dan Bratton and I don't mind saying so—and then what happens? The afternoon when he's staging the big showdown scene with Knox what does he do but relegate me to the outer office where I'm allowed to do nothing but round up the actors. Of course getting Knox up there he left to me and I know he never suspected a thing from my message. But it was only coming to me to sit in on the grand finale. Instead it was Otis Galway . . ."

Certainly it was Otis Galway who was forced to go for a complete change to French Lick after everything was over. "It was the most grueling experience of my life," he upbraided Inspector Bratton. "I can't see yet why it was necessary. I was not involved in any way and Knox—it was hideous seeing the net close over him like that. I had always liked the chap, you know—he didn't play a bad game of bridge. But the worst was the devilish way you almost made me feel that you were going to hang the whole business on me. That's what got me down. . . ."

Dan Bratton laughed good-naturedly. "I'll admit it, Galway. Once or twice I did have qualms that you were going to yelp out a protest or a confession or something equally uncalled for. But here's my emanation, if it will cheer you up any. I was trying my case out on you, see. I hadn't had a chance to test much of it, though I was betting my neck that it was all going to hang together. I could see that I was convincing you all right, and your presence helped to convince the others, particularly the two women, that I was more interested in you than in them. Even Knox felt a sense of security when he saw you."

The inspector accepted one of the manager's cigars and laughed again. "It was a great case, Galway, but, believe me, it's the last time I ever want to have to run down murder in a department store. I'm not that kind of ladies' man. . . ."

About the Author

Helen Joan Hultman (1891-1985) was a Dayton, Ohio, native who graduated from Denison University and went on to teach English at Stivers High School in Dayton for thirty-five years. Her first mystery, *Find the Woman,* received the Doubleday-Doran prize for best mystery story sent in during the summer of 1928, and it was published in 1929. She wrote it while teaching full-time, and noted that when it was published, "They were loosening up old Victorian standards." She wrote five more mysteries by the early 1950s, one of which was reprinted under a second title. Most of these were set in anonymous southwestern Ohio locations: Windward Hill was patterned after the pinnacles of Calvary Cemetery (near Carillon Park), while Line & Hollis was modeled after Rike's Department Store formerly in downtown Dayton.

In a 1946 newspaper column, Helen discussed her writing: "Many persons ask about my side line, those murder stories to which I am addicted. Whenever anyone asks me how I do it, or even bluntly, why, I never know what to say. I don't know any sensible answer, except that it's fun and positively my favorite occupation. . . .

"How do I get my ideas? The backwash of all sorts of trifles goes into it but they're almost unrecognizable when they get into a story. . . . Settings often get me started."

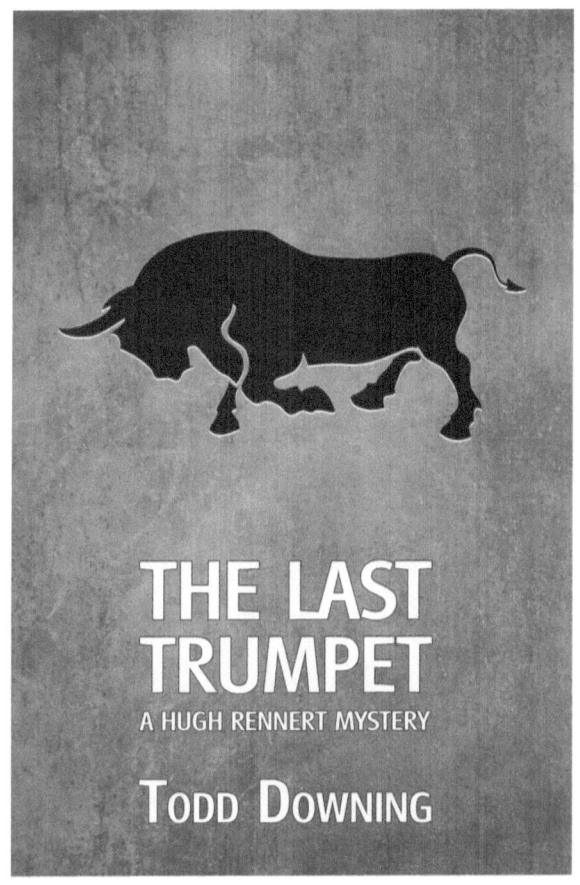